e-males.allen jarvis

allen.jarvis@iname.com was born in Luton
and now lives in Crouch End.

GW01044147

e-males.allen jarvis

PAN BOOKS

First published 1999 by Pan Books
an imprint of Macmillan Publishers Ltd
25 Eccleston Place, London SW1W 9NF
Basingstoke and Oxford
Associated companies throughout the world
www.macmillan.co.uk

ISBN 0 330 37387 0

Copyright © Allen Jarvis 1999

The right of Allen Jarvis to be identified as the
author of this work has been asserted by him in accordance
with the Copyright, Designs and Patents Act 1988.

All rights reserved. No part of this publication may be
reproduced, stored in or introduced into a retrieval system, or
transmitted, in any form, or by any means (electronic, mechanical,
photocopying, recording or otherwise) without the prior written
permission of the publisher. Any person who does any unauthorized
act in relation to this publication may be liable to criminal
prosecution and civil claims for damages.

1 3 5 7 9 8 6 4 2

A CIP catalogue record for this book is available from
the British Library.

Typeset by SetSystems Ltd, Saffron Walden, Essex
Printed and bound in Great Britain by
Mackays of Chatham plc, Chatham, Kent

This book is sold subject to the condition that it shall not,
by way of trade or otherwise, be lent, re-sold, hired out,
or otherwise circulated without the publisher's prior consent
in any form of binding or cover other than that in which
it is published and without a similar condition including this
condition being imposed on the subsequent purchaser.

for Sue

ACKNOWLEDGEMENTS

Thanks to my agent Mic Cheetham, her son Oliver, and my editor Peter Lavery for making this the reality you see before you. Thanks also to Peter Hook for his kind comments about said book. Many, many thanks to all the boys and girls who've contributed, in part, to this novel. You know who you are and I have thoroughly enjoyed the research. I am forever indebted to your friendship. Special thanks to Mum, Dad, Sarah and Davy, for all the reasons in the world, and heartfelt thanks always to both Sue and Row for their support during *e-males*. Finally, personal recognition of that 'Soviet' moment and the inspiration it duly, sadly, spawned.

'Love warps the mind a little from the right.'

Smugglers and Poachers, George Crabbe (1754–1832)

The only other passenger in first class looks a right homme: all fopped hair and pouting pretty features. He is unaware of the potential threat close by. The only other passenger in first class is just lolling in his seat, flicking through a *GQ* and he's wearing this obnoxious orange-and-grey check shirt, and his sole item of luggage is a square black bag emblazoned with the logo EIGHTBALL RECORDS, NEW YORK. The only other passenger in first class might well be a dead man, should any wrong move, displaced sigh or tainted gaze prompt me to inflict the full brunt of my unhinged frustration and anger upon him.

I'm just sitting staring, staring at the only other passenger in first class, burning my steely-grey eyes into his face, scanning for some simple signal to attack, scarcely conscious of the blurred panorama spinning past, of the black clouds, the crows and the petrels slung low in the murderous sky, or of the wind-drubbed sheep dispersed haphazardly throughout opulent lowlands. Nothing really matters any more. My whole being, my entire persona – this mishmash of thoughts, sentiments and remembrances that have melded to form the haecceity that is Damian Henry Shaw – are now all of trivial

1

consequence. I am twenty-four years old, I will be twenty-five in a little over one month from today, yet my future is now nothing more than a wreathing trek toward hell and damnation – because, just yesterday, Jo told me she couldn't love me any more.

I hadn't been in touch with Stuart Wallace in the four months since his transfer to our Scottish office, yet he was still pleased to see me when I arrived, unannounced, on his doorstep late yesterday evening. Out-takes from an impromptu Edinburgh stopover; chatting up the barmaids in the Burnt Post (me the big clubby blonde, Wallace the scrawny unblonde); singing along to eighties pop songs in l'Attaché; slow-dancing with this French thing in Mercado; caning Moët with vodka chasers in the City Café; deep-fried Cadbury's creme eggs from the local kebabby, which tasted as bad as they looked; this row with Dougie, Stuart's indecorous brother, on the sorrowful state of Scottish football; a leisurely breakfast at Montpelier's; a lift to the station, and a hollow promise to return soon. Stuart Wallace was pleased to see me – but Jo told me she couldn't love me any more.

I am trying to read, struggling to occupy my mindscape, but I simply cannot concentrate, can't even be bothered to tally the blondes and the unblondes in the magazines spread out before me, and my attention keeps returning time and time again to the haunted face of this thing on the cover of *Mixmag* and the ominous caption 'Are Drugs Driving You Mad?'. And, although I'm heartened to discover that this thing is in fact a model, that she's not just some clubber netted out on the town, her image still persists in tormenting me. Newcastle station finally authenticates our defection to England and, as we traverse the Tyne, I find myself focusing on this bridge stretched away to the right, and I'm attempting to visualize Michael Caine in *Get Carter*, or some scene in that gangster flick starring Sting and Melanie Griffiths. We're delayed at Darlington by ten minutes – running early, the driver says. England is flat, joyless, downcast, the rain finally managing a piteous drizzle against the window.

This mangy traveller-type, facial piercings and crap tattoos, a token dog in attendance, lurches his way through our carriage and breaks our tranquillity by informing us that he 'fucking hates' first-class passengers, that we're a 'disgrace to our nation' and that we'll be 'first against the wall come the great revolution'. After a half-thought I decide to let the mangy traveller-type's niggling outburst go unchecked, snug (or is that smug?) in my transcendent knowledge that, if I did deem to unleash my wrath, this crusty would find himself praying to Hawkwind or the Spiral Tribe or whatever-higher-spirit he so chooses to follow, praying that he'd not chosen this carriage, on this Edinburgh to London Inter-City on this wretched Sunday, to vent any drunken grievances he might possess on the obvious failings of the British class system or the misplaced distribution of this country's wealth. Besides, I concur with his gripe to a lesser degree; I'm in first class only because I possessed the prescience and intellect to fork out a few extra pounds for a Sunday saver supplement. I'm simply a standard-class traveller with brains.

Doncaster looms, along with eight unsightly chimneys, great phalluses fucking a cold sky. Grantham coughs up a trainspotter staring at me through dark, bottomless eyes; his mouth hangs open as I slide soundlessly past, and this unnerves me. Dour weather introduces Peterborough; the overspill satellite of Stevenage is dead and forsaken, a rain-sodden spectre of a new town. We pass through Cuffley, vapid and unexciting, and I manage an inward smile at myself, grasping the notion that I'll doubtless be living in some equivalent dire suburban netherworld by the time I reach my early thirties.

Somewhere beyond Crews' Hill, a tractor cuts a swathe through a field in the driving rain. I slip some dance compilation into my Walkman and manage an ironic sigh as this thing croons brazenly through my earphones, singing something about me being free to do what I want to do, and this pivotal phrase – *You're free* – just iterates endlessly in a loop like some rapt avowal of purpose, pied-pipering me into absently chanting the line, and prompts the orange-and-grey-checked homme to look in my direction, throw an obliging glance and maybe giggle a bit at my actions, and so I'm at him, ablaze from my seat, facing up, demanding if this homme wants to know, but he just shrinks back in his corner, bleats about not looking for trouble, and so I slap him – hard but just the once –

4

broad on his left cheek, but he maybe blubbers slightly, burns crimson, reburies his head in his *GQ*, and my alogical act doesn't even exact any retaliation from him, any scant symbol of defiance.

Jo told me she couldn't love me any more; she's set me free to do what I want to do.

We're hurtling through Palmers Green, then Finsbury Park, three tower blocks to our left, a dilapidated high-rise to our right, then past the University of North London, Polytechnic as was; then through a blackened tunnel, then the Telecom tower is ascending in the distance, then another tunnel, then finally King's Cross Station where I catch a black cab home.

'Sorry, mate, I've only got a Scottish tenner,' I say, handing the cab driver – Irish but with only a slight hint of an accent – my fare.

'That's okay, son. They're perfectly legal down here,' he replies, taking my money.

I wave away the change and hiss, 'Not if I had my way,' as the cabby attempts a U-turn against the traffic, to take him back towards Highgate.

There's no one home. I drop my overnight bag in the hallway, then stop to study the Anna Nicole Smith calendar adorning the back of our kitchen door. Anna's coy pose sort of reminds me of Jo, and I'm just warming to that notion when I unexpectedly sense something amiss here, something way off the mark, then it strikes me that I'm looking at the month of March, and so I quickly revise said calendar to display April's shot – an unpolished one this, displaying Anna naked, lying flat on a beach, white sand and halation blurring the accentuated contours of her womanly form.

Disillusioned, I bid a retreat to my bedroom, stick some Paul Oakenfold at full volume on my stereo, do a line of coke to hone my senses, then quickly change into this navy Lacoste polo shirt I borrowed from Jo's father quite some time ago. I then check the answering machine for any calls, but calls-recorded reads at zero, so I scour the living room, the fridge, the notice-board for any messages of deliverance proclaiming, 'Dame – Ring Joanna'. But, alas, I find no such messages, just this newly pinned snap of Hooky from New Order added to my collection of similar band cuttings, among images of Russ Meyer prodigies and of the spectacular Anna Nicole Smith, this new picture probably having been cut from some music magazine or other and across which Thom has Tippexed the bathetic platitude, 'Your hero.'

Unsatisfied, I make as if to phone Jo, but only dial her first four numbers (0141) before deciding that I'm being stupid, that I must give her space to think, to find unqualified absolution in her heart. It's seven-fifty p.m. and I was due to meet Thom and Benny nearly an hour ago. I still need to dig out the address of that party we're supposed to be meeting Kelly at later, down in Kentish Town. And I'm wondering if Kelly will be wearing her kinky boots tonight.

*

I find Thom propping up the bar in the King's Head, his cheeks sunken, eyes drawn, his sharp features further emaciated by a hard weekend's clubbing.

'You're late,' is all he can manage.

I order us two pints of Kronenbourg, then Thom slowly raises an index finger towards the far corner of the pub where I catch Benny settled down before his precious Treasure Quest. I add a third pint to our order.

'Congratulations,' Thom muses, stares past me through the huge front window-panes.

'Not exactly,' I have to tell him, after a pause.

'No?' he asks.

'No.'

'What happened to you last night, then?'

'Stopped at this geezer I used to work with's gaff, out Edinburgh way. I turned up at Jo's right in the middle of some family get-together. Her mother let me in, but Jo just asked me to leave.'

'Just like that?' Thom asks, seems genuinely surprised, straightens himself in his seat and catches my gaze.

'Yeah. Just . . . like . . . that,' I reply, spacing out the words as if I'm accentuating their meaning. But these words have no significance and no merit. They're little more than a cumulus of phonemes aligned in such an order that I may correspond and articulate with my fellow man in such hackneyed and banal situations as this, even when there is simply nothing that can or, indeed, should be said. Whether I deem to drawl these words, or stammer them – maybe burr or trill them, intone or inflect – it all boils down to the self-same thing. Tommy Cooper may've made his mark with such a catchphrase, but the only thing now of any consequence to me is that Jo told me she couldn't love me any more, just . . . like . . . that.

'Look, I'm, er, really sorry, mate. I—' Thom is starting to say.

I stop to draw breath, then sigh, on auto-pilot. 'It's okay, it was my own stupid fault.'

'Can't believe it,' Thom says and looks away through the window once again. 'Thought you and Joanna were gonna last for ever – thought that you of all people would find a way through this.'

'Bit like you and Lisa, eh?' I mutter, half-joke.

'Yeah, erm . . .' Thom falters for words, we lock eyes again and for an agonizing moment I'm near tempted to headbutt the miserable fuck, crush his nose to a bloodied pulp, knock him clear from his bar-perch, then methodically set about his squirming form with my size-ten Timberlands, helping to appease myself somehow, wreaking vengeance for all the heartache he's engineered . . . but then, bizarrely, I just find myself shrugging my shoulders and blurting, once again, in poor parody, 'Just like that.' Thom sniggers, we both down great gulps of Kronenbourg, and the situation diffuses. There are only five things in the pub tonight and they are all unblonde and all unworthy of an appearance – no matter how brief – in any Russ Meyer movie.

'Beth phoned yesterday,' Thom mentions after a while.

8

'Oh?'

'Yeah, four times – phoned early and was chatty, but I think she was getting annoyed 'cos she was quite offhand later on.'

I can only sigh. 'Bollocks.'

Thom suggests we join Benny, our man whispering sweet nothings to the gaming machine, totally engrossed in his trivia frenzy, so we make for that corner of the pub, and I stop en route to meliorate the output of the jukebox but, to my dismay, New Order's *Technique* actually has a track-listing for a George Michael record labelled next to it (of all the cheek), though, to my exorbitant relief, after trekking through the CDs, first left and then right, I do eventually track down a copy of *Republic*, which has another misplaced album sleeve flagging it (a Depeche Mode cover I think, though can't be certain), and for one pound I elect the tracks 'Special', 'Regret' and 'Ruined In A Day'. The lyrics to 'Special' sort of remind me of Jo; the titles of the other two are apt tributes to such a significant weekend. Maybe I should've also selected 'Liar' but you only get three tracks for a pound and, besides, I doubt we'll stay here long enough to even hear my first bout of selections get aired so somebody else will just have to benefit from my impeccable choice in popular music.

'Dame!' Benny acknowledges without turning to face me.

'Benny,' I respond and nod at the back of his ruffled red barnet.

'Right,' Benny starts. 'See if you can get this one,

allen jarvis

boys. I need the second least popular answer . . . right, who smokes the least – twenty Austrians? nineteen Romanians? twenty-two Belgians, or twenty-one Micks?'

'It's gotta be the Irish,' Thom says.

'What has?' Benny asks.

'Who smoke the most,' Thom replies.

'Yeah, but I can only move two places – I need the third least, the second most.'

'Try the Austrians,' I offer.

Benny slaps the machine a split-second before his time runs out. 'Bollocks,' he sighs. 'One move. Good try, Dame. They smoke the most.' Benny's illumined box icon takes one pace forward to land on a death's head, prompting the machine to cough up the message, GAME OVER.

'So, who smokes the least?' Thom asks, confused.

'Fuck knows,' Benny answers.

'So, why didn't you want the right answer?'

'Because there were death's heads if I stepped one, three or four places.'

Thom looks from Benny to me, to Benny once again, sighs, then says, 'I don't get it.'

'That's 'cos you're a thick cunt,' I tell him gently.

'Anyone for tequila?' Benny asks, still shaking his head at Thom's trite observation.

Thom and I look to one another, both answer, 'No.'

Benny disregards our responses, gets a round in anyway, and proposes a toast: 'To friendship!'

'I don't need this,' Thom moans as Benny and I sink analeptic shots. 'It's been a rough weekend.'

'Yeah, you look a little run-down,' Benny says. 'What time did you stay till last night?'

'Went the distance – stuck it out till after seven, didn't I?' Thom raises his glass towards me and explains. 'All went to Bagley's, Dame. Jay was there, and Five.'

'Yeah, and Mike too,' Benny adds.

'They'd all phoned the gaff yesterday afternoon, looking for you,' Thom continues. 'I'd told them you were otherwise engaged.'

'Any good?' I ask the pair.

'The best,' Benny tells me. 'Excellent tunes and Mike had some wicked gear, courtesy of his brother.'

'Charged us tens for the bloody things, though,' Thom moans. 'We could all do with a new bloody supplier.'

'Or just get 'em at Mike's knockdown prices,' Benny mentions.

'Yeah,' Thom and I agree, both nod our heads in unison.

'I ain't complaining, though,' Benny sniggers. 'I was at Natalie's by five then kept her awake till ten. She wasn't complaining either.'

'I dunno,' Thom says. 'The exuberance of a new romance, eh?' He then raises his glass towards me. 'That'll be you again in a few weeks' time, you'll see.'

Benny just looks at me quizzically and, as he opens his mouth, I warn him with, 'Do not say anything.'

'What? You broke up with Beth?'

'Not Beth, no – broke up with Jo.'

Benny looks confused. 'Thought that was over a month back, Dame,' he says and scratches his temple.

'Yeah, well, I went up to see her yesterday – thought I could smooth things over, but she wasn't having any of it.'

'Well, at least you've got Beth,' Benny tells me and slaps my arm. He then stops to think, 'Oh, you have still got Beth haven't you?'

'Yeah,' I tell him sullenly. 'She's there if I want her.'

'Nice one,' Benny replies, looks really smug, and I sense something appalling in the offing. 'You should just forget about Joanna, Dame,' he says, his words puncturing me as if in slow motion. 'Stick with Beth, mate – she's lovely. Joanna's all in the past now.'

I stand here rocked by Benny's words, by the way he's so utterly misjudged my emotions, and whilst I'm floundering for an effective riposte, for some simple phrase to dull the pain I'm suddenly feeling within, Thom winks at me and asks, 'What's the score with you and Kelly, Dame?'

Side-tracked by his assuasive intrusion, I murmur, 'Oh, er, just good friends.'

'She bringing a mate along?' he asks, keeps the conversation rolling.

'Yeah . . . er, another Aussie, Nina,' I reply, still slightly dazed.

Thom grins. 'Set me up with her, will you, Dame?'

'Nah, she's bound to prefer me,' Benny jokes, and as the final syllable trips from my supposed friend's tongue

I discover my mindscape awash with all manner of landmine thoughts – totally anti-personnel.

Once at the party, I spot Kelly through the kitchen windows, out in the back garden, as Thom attempts to coerce sixteen cans of Kronenbourg into an already bloated fridge-freezer. Kelly would not look out of sorts auditioning for a Russ Meyer movie: she's long and slender and top-heavy in front. I met her in The End two months back – Thom and I were down there following up some half-arsed lead with two Italian things who'd simultaneously pinched our backsides in Leicester Square the previous night, and who we both secretly knew were highly unlikely to show. Thom had been seriously incoherent, was gurning for England, his face contorted like a Gotham City villain, yet once the club petered out we still somehow persuaded Kelly and her mate Rebecca onto Bar Italia for freshly ground coffees and groundless chit-chat, and from there onto Hyde Park where we spent four delicious hours soaking up the chill air, smoking ourselves stupid, and putting the universe to rights. Thom fucked Rebecca that very afternoon – *only* that afternoon of course, as he always does before sauntering back to his pathetic thing, Lisa – but Kelly and I saw each other for another two weeks until she binned me for being too, in her words, 'unstable'. To this day Kelly thinks I'm a dentist. She told me I was only her seventh lover, but women generally lie about such matters.

13

'Hi, Damian, how are you?' Kelly says, grinning at the sight of me, air-kissing my left cheek.

'Fine, sweetheart. Just fine,' I lie.

'Damian, this is Nina,' she tells me and introduces this unblonde – not that good-looking, yet somehow fuckable all the same.

'I've seen you before, Damian,' Nina says to me, shaking my hand. Her cheeks are rosy, her teeth slightly bucked.

'Yeah?' – I quasi-panic, not recognizing her – 'Er, where?'

'Oh, only out by the front door five minutes ago,' she says. 'I was just coming down the stairs. I thought it must be you – Kelly told me to keep an eye out.'

'Oh, yeah? And what exactly did Kelly tell you to keep an eye out for?' I ask, glare at Kelly.

'Three good-looking lads,' Nina states flatly.

'Yeah, with one of them looking like some kinda Nazi,' Kelly adds and laughs.

I fix Kelly with a look of mock annoyance and roll down my bottom lip. 'Moi?' I enquire.

'Oh, Damian,' she says, 'you know I love you really. It's just . . . oh, with your blond hair and those piercing eyes of yours, you look so fierce sometimes.'

I inherit my iridium eyes, greyed the colour of steel, from my father – just about the only thing of any interest that splenetic bastard's handed on to me. As for my hair colouring, I have my mother to thank. It's remained the one length all over since Thom and I got close crops for a holiday in Ibiza some two years back. Thom's hair's long since returned in its full resplendent glory, but I've just kept getting mine 'tidied up' every couple of weeks or so. Jo said she preferred me with short hair.

'Come on, let's catch up with the boys,' I am saying, mockingly disgruntled. 'Besides, it's kinda chilly out here.'

Kelly is not wearing her knee-length boots tonight – just a pair of heavy black Caterpillars. Jo wasn't wearing her kinky boots either when she told me she couldn't love me any more. Nor was she wearing her hooped earrings. I should've read the signs.

'Hi, Thom. Hi, Benny,' Kelly says, again smiles broadly, as we step from the patio into the lounge. She has beautiful teeth, this truly ravishing smile.

'Good to see you again,' Thom says, and kisses Kelly's right cheek.

Benny and Nina remain silent, both smile awkwardly.

'So, how's Rebecca?' Thom asks Kelly. 'She miss me?'

'Oh, she's back home in Victoria now,' Kelly answers, attempts to light a cigarette – Silk Cut Ultras if I remember rightly – her lighter misfiring. 'She had to cut short her trip because her mother died.'

'Oh, I *am* sorry,' Thom says, attempts to feign genuine concern.

Thom, Benny and I all top the six-foot mark: Thom the tallest at six-two, an inch taller than me, but I'm of a much broader build. Kelly is a good five-ten – an inch shorter than Jo – whilst Nina is only five-six, maybe five-seven. The last time I'd seen Kelly was in the 'O' bar on a night when I kept caning (even by my immoderate standards) coke in the toilets – on a night when I just knew we had to split because Jo was due down that coming weekend (Kelly had developed this annoying habit of turning up at our flat totally unannounced, at the oddest of times), on a night when Kelly, thankfully, had enforced the break, telling me that I was not in complete control of my emotions, that I was blowing hot and cold on her too frequently for her own liking. Kelly used to babble on in French when I fucked her – this made me laugh.

Kelly and Nina are driving Thom and me home in Kelly's boss's Volvo after the party was cut obtusely short by the host, another Aussie or Kiwi or whatever, when it came to light that their video had been pilfered during the course of festivities. Kelly is a nanny, Nina is currently unemployed, the girls share a flat in Clapham. We left Benny back in Kentish Town, where he was catching a tube to meet his new woman, this Natalie, at her flat down Vauxhall way. I didn't exchange a single syllable with that primordial slime after his retarded outburst against Jo in the King's Head, just returned all his insipid remarks with perfunctory 'hmmms', slight shifts of the shoulder.

'For fuck's sake, Kelly, keep your eyes on your driving!' I am screaming as we hurtle up Junction Road, the car lurching left to right.

'Don't swear at me,' she retorts, actually turns to face me as she continues to drive.

'Jesus, let me outta here, Dame,' Thom jokes. 'This thing's one hell of a fucking mad driver.'

'Do you two have to swear?' Nina asks and peers to catch my reflection in the rear-view mirror.

'Yeah, you tell 'em, Nina,' Kelly says. 'Aussie men would never speak like that in the company of such delicate women as ourselves.'

'Aussie men are all sexist pigs,' Thom states.

'Yeah, drinking and fighting, eh, Brucie?' I mock in this coarse Antipodean accent.

'Okay, maybe so,' Kelly says, laughs. 'But it's nice to be treated like a lady sometimes, you guys.'

'Yeah, thought you English men were supposed to be real gentlemen?' Nina adds.

Thom and I just look at each other blankly.

Kelly parks – badly – outside our flat on the Broadway, Muswell Hill. The girls want to carry on drinking down the road, but I'm tired, I'm beginning to get irritated by their abhorrent accents and all I really want to do is get home and check the answering machine, but I don't really want to leave Thom alone with both Kelly and Nina, and I am just slightly in need of a drink after neglecting to pick up my Kronenbourg upon leaving the party. So I eventually, begrudgingly, after lots of coaxing and ego-massaging from Kelly, agree to tag along and we head for Ritchie's, where Thom and I vegetate on stools at the bar and watch Sky Sports and I tally six blondes and thirteen unblondes in our immediate vicinity, and Kelly and Nina proceed to get horribly drunk on a cocktail of Kronenbourg and draught cider, and this thing, Julie, this unblonde hairdresser with pretensions to be a drum-and-bass DJ, who Mike fucked in our bathroom after Gerry's birthday piss-up last Christmas, tells me I look miserable and asks me if I'm okay and I tell her that I'm fine, that life simply couldn't be bettered, and I fix her with my widest of grins, but I'm miserable inside and the alcohol is only serving to make me morose. On the way back to the flat, Kelly also tells me I look miserable, but then she is very drunk.

Kelly is lying on my futon and she's telling me that I want to fuck Nina.

'Sweetheart, I do not want . . . to . . . fuck . . . Nina,' I repeat to her. I am splayed across the armchair in the far corner of my room, keeping my distance from Kelly. This Talking Heads compilation CD is playing on the stereo. I wanted some New Order, but we had to have Kelly's choice as it reminds her of her brother Kelvin, back home in Australia – a justification I can relate to, as New Order would've principally reminded me of my azoic brother, lost in the bleak malady that forms sub-urbia. Thom is in his room, asleep or maybe re-reading porno-mags or listening to another dysfunctional mantra from his blessed George Michael collection, and Nina is watching *Brookside* on video in the lounge. I had wanted to commandeer the video in order to watch some Russ Meyer, to ogle his bra-busting starlets, but the damned girls objected – as is always the case.

'But you've hardly spoken to me all night, Damian,' Kelly whines.

'That does not mean I want to fuck Nina,' I snap at

her, then light up another joint in the eerie green half-light emanating from the display on my stereo. The Talking Heads are singing about buildings on fire.

'Grrrrrr.' Kelly actually growls at me.

'Fuck you,' I whisper after a while, then stop the CD player and slip on my Walkman to give Wagner's classic 'Ride of the Valkyries' one brief airing then sit, disconsolate, in the dark, before finally powering my PC into life when I'm positive that Kelly's fallen asleep. I then realign the phone connections and hook into the Internet to bring down my bookmark for this Anna Nicole Smith links page, but no new links have been added since the weekend, and I've already exhaustively cogitated over every picture reachable via this site. So, bored, I elect to bring up my Photoshop instead, and double-click this picture I've scanned: a snapshot of our holidays last year, all the boys on an Easter jolly down Tenerife way, Playa las Americas, and we're lined up to order outside Lineker's Bar, stood before this huge billboard which reads, THANKS FOR YOUR VISIT, SEE YOU SOON, and there's me, back left, wearing Jo's dad's navy Lacoste, a pair of Oakley's on me forehead, one arm slung behind Mike's shoulder, who in turn leans into Benny and Thom and Weatherface, then there's Five, Jay, Matt, Tyler, Gerry squatting before us, each of us tanned, festive, archetypally male, MDMA and testosterone fuelled. I study this fashioned memory for a moment too long, then, on a notional whim, encircle Benny's head with my cursor, stretching his image first left, then right, then quashing his features down before deciding to slap a black nothingness across the bitmap where his face once stood. I then resave the image, liquidating Benny's sickening visage.

On the answering machine, when we finally returned home tonight, there were three messages: one from Lisa, one from Thom's old rich sow of a mother (well, she does actually own this flat) and just one for me – from Beth, not Jo.

'Got off with this wee lassie last night,' Carl Smith is telling us. 'She had a minge like a mouse's ear.' I'm lunching in the staff restaurant with Carl and Nicholas Spencer-Jones who are both my age and straight, and with three members of 'The Family', the company's hommes: the aged Russell Bishop who actually goes both ways and would love to fuck both Jo and myself and keeps reminding me so; the promiscuous James Comley, nicknamed the 'Sperminator'; and the ugly confused homme, Richard Moore, who we suspect only turned after a near lifetime of failures with women. It's just past midday, I arrived into work at a quarter to ten – late, but still a good forty-five minutes earlier than Carl and, sadly, with mere months gone past, he's now well in the lead for the Latecomer of the Year Award as contested amongst the low-lifes on our project.

'A minge like a mouse's ear,' Richard repeats to himself. 'That's so gross and disrespectful, Carl.'

'Yeah, but just picture it, though,' Nicholas says. 'Small . . . Warm . . . Furry.'

'Tight an' all,' Carl says.

Everyone laughs except Richard.

'So, how does this explain your late arrival today, Mr Smith?' Russell asks – rather formally I think, but Carl does report directly to Russell, so I guess it's only fair he should explain himself, especially after our project manager, Hubert Dodd, called a ten o'clock meeting this morning at which Carl's absence would've been carefully noted.

'Condom split – took the bitch for a morning-after pill,' Carl answers.

'That's okay: perfectly acceptable excuse,' Russell says, continues with his salad.

'Bitch? Bitch? How can you say that, Carl?' Richard shrieks.

'Yeah, s'pose you're right, Rich,' Smith smirks. 'She was a good lassie – a top GHS.'

'Er, GHS?' I have to ask.

'Good . . . Hard . . . Shag,' Carl says, spacing out his words.

'Oh, of course,' I mutter, then ask, 'So, what did everyone else do this weekend?'

'Or rather . . . who did they do?' James Comley quips.

'Me and Ally went to Wales,' Nicholas says. 'To stay on her grandfather's farm.'

'Me and Ally, me and Ally,' James mimics in a high-pitched squeal.

'Yes, I'm worried about you, Nicky-babes,' Russell says. 'You're far too young to be settling down.'

'Yeah, especially with someone from work,' I tell the table.

'Oi, you're a fine one to talk,' Spencer-Jones retorts, and I'm wondering to whom he's referring, me having only slept with the one girl from our office – Tasha Doran, Jack Howe's secretary – but that was only some meretricious one-night stand just before Jo and I got together and well before I really started associating with Nicholas.

'Allison's a lovely girl,' Russell says, seems concerned. 'But she'll have you living in the suburbs before you know it. She'll have you organizing Neighbourhood Watch meetings.'

'Attending gymkhanas,' James cracks. 'And holidaying in the Lake District.'

'Make you watch your alcohol intake,' I mention.

'Yeah, she'll come between you and your motor,' Carl blurts through a mouthful of food.

Nicholas appears shocked. 'My MX5?'

'Yeah, and you should never let a woman come between you and your motor. A car says a lot about a man – it's a status thing.'

'But Russell drives an MX5 as well, and he's twice my age—'

Russell interjects. 'Not quite twice, dear boy.'

' – and he's gay.'

'Bi,' Russell states.

' – so, what does that say about MX5 drivers?'

'I drive an Escort Bonus,' James tells us.

'And, amigos, I've got a mini,' Moore offers.

Everyone looks at me, I sip from my bottle of Evian, then say, 'I take the Northern Line . . . I can't see the point of a car in London.'

'Yeah, well I had a TR6,' Carl continues, 'until some bastard nicked it. But at least that was a real man's car – a pussy magnet. No woman ever came between me and that car.'

'How do you know it wasn't a woman who nicked it?'

'I just do.'

'Er, how?'

'I just do.'

'Yeah, but . . . how?'

'Because it was nicked by some thieving wee mechanical from Tottenham.'

'Mechanical?' James asks.

'Yeah, you know . . . mechanical digger – nigger.'

There's a brief pause before Richard tuts, asks Carl, 'So how do you know it wasn't stolen by some thieving *female* mechanical from Tottenham?'

Carl pauses – all eyes on him – thinks, then blabs, 'Aw, just fuck up, right? . . . Just fuck up, Rich.'

'Oh, chaaaarrming,' Moore retorts.

The Blonde from Financial Services – Pamela Ward – is seated at a table on the far side of the restaurant and I'm wondering whether she's trying to figure out who I actually am, because I've been sending her e-mails from a redundant user id under the alias of 'Connor Ferguson', this contractor who used to work on our project. I finally described myself in my last message, detailing where I sat in the restaurant each day – though, of course, she's under the sweet tenderfoot impression she's actually looking out for a Connor. The Blonde replied saying she preferred to date younger men, but I didn't take this as a convincing rebuff and intend to work further on her, even though she's said that she doesn't drink to excess or take drugs and she's never even heard of New Order and even though she thinks Anna Nicole Smith is an 'old tart' and she doesn't earn that much money – some 19K per annum less than me, according to my source in Payroll – and doesn't have that nice a face. She does however resemble the perfect Meyer woman: she has shoulder-length straight blonde hair, has these huge collagen lips and a fantastic body – tallish with a showy bust and bantam waist – and she is only eighteen years old and she looks as though she would prove to be a really filthy fuck, should I finally get to lay my hands on her.

'So, what's *your* excuse for being so late, Mr Shaw?' Russell asks me. 'More morning-after pills, or another train down from Glasgow . . . perhaps even a mixture of both?'

'Er, yeah,' I reply sullenly, 'the train.' This morning Kelly and Nina treated me to a fried breakfast down the Oval Platter in Crouch End, Kelly's driving none the better for a good night's sleep, nor untempered by the heaving onslaught of the rush-hour traffic along Park Road. This, after Lisa had woken the entire flat by dropping off two crates of Kronenbourg (a gift from a client company, supposedly) on her way through to customer offices in Friern Barnet. Such a pity she found our Antipodean friends comatosed in the living room – still, maybe she'll suspect Thom was up to no good, even though he wasn't, but I can always wish. Their pitiful excuse for a relationship disgusts me. Beth phoned me an hour and a half ago to arrange a possible date for Wednesday, which I unwittingly agreed to, though I can't for the life of me think why. I've just spent most of today moping, simply going through the motions, smiling when expected to smile, laughing when requisitioned to laugh, waiting on that one redeeming phone call from Jo . . . which, sadly, is yet to come.

'Good weekend, then . . . was it?' James is asking me.

'What?'

'Scotland, dear boy,' Bishop says. 'Frolicking with the scrumptious Joanna.'

'Er, yeah, I guess. Actually, I made my way over to Edinburgh on Saturday and had a night out with Stuart Wallace.'

'Stu? How is he?' Nicholas asks.

'Stuart's fine,' I tell him.

'That's good,' the Bishop says. 'But . . . has he come out of the closet yet?'

'Stuart?' Richard interjects. 'He was as straight as they come . . . surely?'

Russell winks. 'Oh, you never can tell, dear boy.'

'I argued a bit with Jo, though,' I mindlessly mutter aloud. 'Things are a little fragile between us right now.' I wince and instantly regret such an arrant confession – as congenial a bunch as the Lunchboys undoubtedly are, they're still little more than work colleagues, not true friends, and I regard it as unethical to share such confidences with their ilk.

But the Bishop appeases me with, 'Oh, we are sorry, Damian.'

'Just give her a wee slap next time she's down. That'll sort her,' Carl thrums, looks away, uninterested. 'I know how to treat our Scottish lassies – just fuck her up with a good slap.' Carl is Scots also, from Aberdeen I think – at least that's the team he supports.

'Carl!' Richard exclaims. 'Will you please keep your crude mouth shut whilst I'm eating my dinner. You're putting me right off my food.'

'Fuck up, faggot,' Carl snarls back, annoyed.

Richard tuts again.

'Russeeeellll,' someone asks after a while. 'Have you actually been in love with both a man and a woman?'

'Oh, of course.'

'More men or more women?'

'More women probably – less stigma attached.'

'Yeah, but who makes for better lovers?'

'Oh, men . . . Definitely!'

'I'll second that,' the Sperminator says.

'But you've never had a woman to compare with,' I have to tell James.

Richard places his cutlery neatly across his plate. 'You breeders just don't know what you're missing out on.'

'And how would you know, dear boy?' Russell asks him.

'Yeah, how would you know? . . . Virgin!' Smith sneers.

'Look, I'm not sitting here tittle-tattling about my sex life with the likes of you lot, thank you very much,' Richard says hurriedly.

'Or, indeed, lack of sex life,' James adds.

Carl smirks.

On our way back through the restaurant I stare at the Blonde as I pass by her table, hoping to catch her eye, but she fails to look up from her food, so I turn to Carl and ask him earnestly, 'Just how tall was this thing you fucked last night?'

I'm catching a District Line tube, westbound from Blackfriars, to Putney, where Beth lives, owns a flat, and I'm sitting next to this anonymous unblonde who I didn't give a second look to when I got on, but now I'm bored, I've nothing to read, and I've left me Walkman and me New Order tapes in the office, so I keep staring down at this thing's long naked legs, at her weird shoes, long straps snaking round her ankles, keep staring down at her knees, her short skirt and I sense myself getting an erection, and I visualize my hand reaching out to touch her left knee and I toy with the idea of knocking my right leg into her left leg, but as I do this she shifts position and both her legs veer to the right, away from my attentions, so instead I stare at this skinheaded geezer directly opposite and try to figure out if he's looking at me or at the unblonde or is maybe asleep, because I cannot see his eyes through his Oakley sunglasses, and he's wearing this dirty white T-shirt which is too small for him, too tight, and the print on it shows this Union Jack which, I swear, is luminous, and wording underneath which reads ON HER MAJESTY'S SERVICE but I don't think it's a reference to any film or book but is maybe the name of some football firm though I can't remember to which team they're affiliated, and he's got two bloated sportsbags at his feet and what seems to be heat rash on both his arms and I wonder where he's been to pick up any sun whatsoever because, at present, the weather is none too clever in London. The skinhead alights at Victoria, the unblonde remains on the tube until after my stop, but I turn to catch her face before I get off and her face is ordinary and unoriginal and I can see why I didn't give her a second look when I first sat down.

Beth is pleased to see me and attempts to hug me as I enter her flat, but I brush past her and ask what's for dinner and she answers this by telling me I can eat whatever I decide to cook. We order out for pizza. There's a photo of Elizabeth Hurley in *Cosmopolitan*, and Beth asks me if I want to cut it out as a keepsake. I ask her why and she tells me that people have told her that she looks like this actress, but I tell her I cannot see any similarity. Beth is not my type: short (five-six?), older than me (twenty-eight), slim bordering on skinny, with no hips or any tits to speak of (B-cup) and is unblonde. But, in her inordinate favour, she does own a car (BMW Compact) and a flat (two-bedroomed – the second bedroom vacant, awaiting her sister's return from a work-stint in Kuwait) and does earn some 8K a year more than me. I met Beth some two months ago at a party in Clapham thrown by Martin Murphy from work – Beth used to live with a friend of a friend of Martin's flatmate's brother, or was it his sister? We didn't actually start sleeping with one another until after that fated day with Jo, nearly a month ago – the incident which split Jo and me apart and left my life in the dissonance I now find myself.

I'm sitting, watching *Brookside*, Beth snuggled up to one side of me and I'm wondering if Jo has maybe phoned me today. The thought insists on reverberating throughout my mindscape – the answering machine will definitely be on because Thom's at Lisa's – so I tell Beth I've got to phone home as I'm expecting an important call from my mother but the only call registered is from Jay, who sounds slumberously stoned and wants to know if there's anything going down on Saturday night, so Beth tells me I can phone my mother direct if I so wish but I tell her the call really wasn't that important. I decide it's far too much hassle to initiate a split with Beth tonight, so I retire to the sanctuary of her bed early – well before Beth – and I pretend I'm asleep when she joins me so we don't end up having sex, and in the morning Beth tells me I kept muttering in my sleep something along the lines of, 'Don't you think I've got a beautiful body?' which I immediately recognize as a quote from Russ Meyer's *Vixen*. I do not think I will see Beth again.

'No, I wanna be Bexy. Why has Dame gotta be Bexy?' Thom is whining.

''Cos Dame looks more psychotic than you. Dame's got those piercing eyes,' Matt tells him.

'I'm not psychotic,' I retort.

'You look fierce,' Matt says.

'I ain't,' I repeat.

It's late and I'm in Café Pelican with eight of the boys. We're all fairly drunk, having spent the entire evening necking ale in Soho, followed by a quick meal in China Town, where Gerry and Weatherface refused to order any food, proclaiming that eating interfered with their drinking, and Tyler spent the entire duration of our stay, moaning, 'This is . . . shit!' every five minutes or so, and Jay insisted on spouting some garbage on how he thought the word Schwarzenegger (as in Arnie – *The Terminator*) could be used as a newfangled racist insult because schwartzer's a word some people use for blacks, and 'negger' could be seen as a bastardization of negro or nigger. I can readily trace a common thread identifying me with all the boys: from a healthy group of nine, five of us are wearing single-breasted navy suits, me included; three of us sport uniform hooped socks from Hackett, me included; four of us brandish woollen ties (all in creditable dark tie / dark shirt combinations), me included; seven of us are dressed in choice shirts with cutaway collars (even Tyler, who spends his working days on a building site – now that is class), me included; all of us are dressed up like the dog's bollocks, again me included. I fit in with these people, feel ultimately at ease in their presence. Jo always chastised me by saying I thought more of my friends than I ever could of her. I do so love my friends – they've always been of principal importance to me, but, since Jo told me she couldn't love me any more, they're now all I have left.

Matt is sipping his coffee. 'You look like a homme, Thom. You can be Simon, Bexy's right-hand man, he looked like a homme – all that neatly coiffured hair.'

'I ain't a homme,' Thom moans.

'You look like a homme,' Gerry offers.

Jay leans in, closer to the table, demands, 'What the fuck are you geezers on about?'

'Yeah,' Five says, also leans closer, spilling his cappuccino across his tie as he does so. 'What in God's name are you lot ranting on about?'

'*The Firm*,' Matt, Thom and I chorus.

Mike, now confused, sweeping that stupid blond fringe from his eyes: 'Yeah, but I mean . . . where's Tom Cruise in all this?'

Matt clarifies our situation. 'No, not the film – the TV drama about football hooligans.'

'Anyone got any drugs?' Tyler interjects, actually pronounces this word: der-rug-zah! 'I'm fucked. I need a bit of a pick-me-up.'

31

'I've got a little coke,' Thom tells him.

Tyler smiles. 'Nice one.'

'But you can't have any. I've only got a little left, and I want to save it to get me out of bed in the morning.'

'You're a git, Thom,' Tyler snarls.

'I've got some speed back at my gaff,' Jay mentions.

Tyler gives him a hard stare.

'Oh, right, not much use there, is it,' Jay admits. 'Sorry.'

'I've got a few Es,' Mike announces.

'What sort?'

'Stars,' Mike says.

'Weren't those the really weak ones?'

'Were they, bollocks,' Mike complains. 'You just try shutting your eyes and seeing if you can still walk in a straight line on one.'

'Your brother still dealing, then?' I ask Mike.

He stalls for a second. 'Er, nah. He just, um, does some DJ-ing now and then – spends most of his time editing some fucking dance fanzine or something.'

'Oh, man,' Five says, 'you Ealing boys are just so-o-o damned tren-dee.'

'Oi, I was born in Ealing,' Thom complains.

'West London's better than the North, boys,' Mike tells us. 'It's all hommes and nigger-lovers up your way, ain't it?'

'Yeah, and don't forget the Greeks and Micks,' Gerry adds.

Matt raises his hands. 'Hey, hey, enough of the interracial bantering, guys. We're getting away from the discussion in hand, away from the real burning issue of the day.'

'Which is?' Tyler asks.

Matt blows out his cheeks, bristles a tad, then says, 'Which character does each of us – seated here in this fine establishment tonight – match up with in *The Firm*?'

'Er, what's *The Firm* actually involve, then?' Jay asks.

'Well,' Matt says, 'it's a drama about hooligans, right? There's three separate firms, and they all get their top boys to battle it out to see who's gonna lead an all-England firm in Europe against the Dutch.'

'So, which firms?' Weatherface asks, his first words in ages, attempting to sound like he's genuinely interested or something.

'Er, I dunno. It's not important. They're not named,' Matt says, annoyed. 'But, for the record, Gary Oldman runs this firm called the ICC, which is s'posed to be based on West Ham's travelling firm—'

Thom butts in. 'Leeds are one of the others.'

'Nah, not Leeds,' I tell him. 'Gary Oldman's lot fight them in Birmingham.'

Thom looks stumped. 'Do they? Hmmm, maybe you're right.'

'I dunno . . . Northern accents all sound the same to me.'

'Oi,' Gerry and Five retort together; Gerry's from Accrington or Macclesfield or some other Mancunian satellite, whilst Five's a scouser from the Wirral – a posh scouser with a civilized accent. The rest of us hail from the Home Counties or from London itself. We came together at university, the majority of us all stranded together in the same flat, our very first times away from the apron-strings of immediate families. Funnily enough, Weatherface was the first introduction I made – he's now the only one I'd rather not associate with. Mind, Thom's also excelled himself in those stakes of late. Him and Benny, of course. Benny may as well forget I ever regarded him as a friend. I've now all but erased his perfidious spectre from my memory. There are no blondes or unblondes in Pelican at this time of night, no things whatsoever.

Jay again. 'Er, have I actually seen this film, *The Firm*?'

'We all sat round at ours watching it a couple of months back,' I remind him. 'That night after Madame Jo-Jo's.'

'After we'd hooked up with that hen night from Chorley,' Mike adds.

'Fook . . . me . . .'arder!' Thom groans, mimicking the hen he secured that night, mooting a ripple of laughter from the assembled boys.

'Oh, right, I think I remember,' Jay says, his flat palm brushing back and forth across his shaven head like some preening ape. He then asks innocently, 'Was there any porn in it?'

'No,' I sigh, exasperated.

'Guys! Guys! Does . . . it . . . really . . . matter?' Matt moans. 'We were just trying to figure out which one's of us would match up with which characters – that's all.'

'Okay, boss, down to business,' Mike says heartily, then asks, 'Right, how many in each firm?'

'Just the top boys – ten,' Thom says.

'Okay, Thom, name them,' Matt quips.

Thom looks to the ceiling as if he's reading the names off a list inscribed high above our heads. 'Well, actually there's eleven in the main firm, 'cos they include an under-five – that's someone who's under the age of sixteen, for the uninitiated . . . Right, there's Gary Oldman as Bexy, the leader.'

'We've decided that one. Dame is Bexy,' Matt says.

'Why has Dame gotta be Bexy?' Thom moans again, still looks skyward. 'Bexy's got a moustache. No one here's got a moustache.'

'I had a goatee once,' I muse.

'Yeah, but that only lasted a month at the most,' Gerry says, accuses.

'Hey, nearly two months – then Jo made me shave it off.' I feel myself cringe openly at the mere mention of her illustrious name. Thankfully, everyone's oblivious to my plight and the incident passes without anyone attempting to replicate Benny's retarded observations from the weekend.

'Look!' Matt demands. 'Dame is Bexy, end of story.'

'Yeah, Dame's the best organizer, anyway,' Mike adds. 'So it's only fair he should be leader.'

'Organizer, my arse,' Thom says under his breath.

'Who organized this tonight?' I half-ask, half-tell him.

Thom turns his head slowly towards me, opens his

mouth to speak, then closes his mouth, turns away from me and moans, sullenly, 'Yeah, only 'cos you're a lazy fucker who spends his whole day on the phone when you should be working.'

'Nice work if you can get it,' someone utters.

'Right, moving on,' Matt says briskly, 'the number two in their firm – Simon, Bexy's right-hand man – that goes to Thom.'

Gerry laughs.

'Bollocks,' Thom moans.

I put my hand to the back of Thom's now slightly bowed head. 'Cool out, guy,' I rasp in this crude Jamaican dread, imitating a line Gary Oldman throws at some point in the film. Only Thom and Matt offer smiles, the others not seeing the joke.

'That's well out of order, Bexy,' Thom barks back, adopting a thick East End patter. Weatherface maybe smirks, thinking there's a gag there somewhere; Matt and I both look to one another – po-faced.

Then Matt, turning back to face Thom, pipes up, 'Nah, you've got the wrong bloke, mate. You're Simon. That line was said by the actor who plays the big Irish bloke in *Coronation Street*' – Matt turns to me, clicks his fingers, racks his brain – 'Oh, c'mon, Dame, what was his name in *The Firm*? Remind me, eh?'

'Trigger,' I say flatly.

'Yeah, that's it, guy – Trigger. Who's gonna play him, then?'

Thom just sits, ashen-faced, like he's sulking.

'What's he like?' Tyler asks. No one else seems in the slightest bit interested.

'He's a big bastard,' Thom murmurs, looking down into his coffee cup.

'It has to be Five then, guys,' Matt snaps heartily, slapping his hands together.

'Hey, hold on! Hey!' Five starts. 'What about Gerry – he's a lot bigger than me.'

'Taller not bigger,' Gerry tells him. Gerry is by far the tallest of us boys, standing a good six-four, maybe six-five, in his stockinged feet.

'Oh, c'mon fellas,' Five moans, raising his arms aloft like he's surrendering or something. 'I was big once, but that was years ago. God, you lot can be such bastards at times.'

'Yeah. S'pose we'll have to stop calling you Five-Bellies soon. You're getting far too thin these days, honey-child,' Tyler says.

'You used to have a gut Orson Welles would've been proud of,' Thom jokes.

'Pity he didn't have the brain to match,' I add.

'Dame,' Five starts, stabs a finger at me, 'you're so fucking sharp you could cut mozzarella.'

I pull this stupid face at Five. He sticks his tongue out in return.

'Right, then, if it's not to be Five-Bellies, then how about Three-Bellies?' Mike asks, motioning to each of us in turn.

'No, look' – Five pursues his point, knocks the table

with his hands held together like he's practising karate –
'I went to see the official belly-master at work last week.'

'The belly-master – who's that?' Weatherface asks,
rather dumbly I think.

Five looks a touch annoyed, probably because it's
Weatherface who's had the cheek to interrupt him. 'Er,
this guy – Bob Stafford – but that's not important. We
were all measuring our bellies in the pub last week, and
Bob – who's one huge lump of a bastard – said I
officially had zero bellies.' Five looks full of himself, as if
this Bob's opinion is going to make one jot of difference
to any of us.

'You'll be telling us you've got a six-pack next,' I
mention.

'More like half an egg-cup,' Thom sighs.

'Bollocks,' Gerry starts. 'Look, we've all got at least
one extra belly 'cos we all drink so much.'

'Speak for yourself. I work out,' Mike offers, pats his
stomach. 'Erm, sometimes.'

'And I shag around,' Jay says.

'You wish,' Gerry aims at Jay.

I look to Matt, raise my eyebrows and ask, 'Well,
what do you reckon? Five's now got zero bellies, so he
says.' I look from Matt to Gerry to Tyler, all lined up
facing me. 'So, votes, please, boys, on changing Five's
nickname from here on in to . . . "Zer-o-o-o"?'

'Oi, you can't call me zero,' Five is moaning. 'What
if anyone hears you call me that? I don't want it for a
nickname. It implies that I'm a nothing, I'm worthless,
a real zero.'

Tyler ribs him. 'Better than your real name any day
. . . Colin!'

'That,' Five begins, 'is . . . well . . . out-of-order,
Bexy.' It's a crap impersonation, but we all snigger
nonetheless. There are five mobile phones face-down on
the table, one of them being mine, yet another generic
link I readily share with the boys.

'So, what about me? Who can I be?' Jay queries.

'They got any blacks in *The Firm*?' Tyler asks, turning
his head from Matt to me to Matt again.

'Er, what about that Benny from *Grange Hill*?' Gerry
asks. 'Jay can be him – they're both quite short, anyway.'

'Nah, he's a half-caste. Jay's far too black,' I say to
Gerry, realize that I'm actually pointing at Jay like he's
an inanimate object or something.

'Okay then, what about the flash bloke off that
Channel 4 comedy – the one about the Peckham bar-
ber,' Gerry offers in response. 'He might not shave his
head like Jay does, but his hair's bloody close all the
same.'

'Yeah,' Matt says, 'Jay can be that git who was
in *Desmond's*, the bloke who's always ducking and div-
ing, a-wheelin' and a-dealin'. A real ladies' man, right,
Jay?'

'Sounds good to me – what's he called in *The Firm*?'
Jay asks expectantly.

'Snowy,' Thom says through his teeth.

Jay's face drops. He shrugs his shoulders and sighs,
'Snowy? A good name for a black man . . . I don't
think.'

'So, who's gonna play Benny from *Grange Hill*?' Matt asks the table.

'Guess it'll just have to be Jinxy John,' Thom admits.

'Yeah, but he only tags along when Toolboy shows his face. Hey, where is Toolboy tonight, Dame?'

'Couldn't get hold of him. He wasn't answering his mobile or his e-mail.' I pause then add, 'And I haven't got Jinxy's phone number.' John's an old schoolmate of Toolboy's, out west, from Boston Manor. He didn't go to university with us, but he's always around whenever Toolboy puts in an appearance.

'Oh, well, Jinxy's Benny, then. What, with being black, he's the only viable choice, guys,' Matt says.

'Hold on a mo,' Five interjects. 'Where's our Benny tonight?'

'Saw him last Sunday,' I tell everyone. 'He's seeing his new woman tonight.'

'Sad cunt,' someone says, then tuts. The simple truth is Benny did e-mail me, at home *and* at work, to ask if there was anything going down this week. I could have ignored his query, maintained that it'd been lost in deepest cyberspace, but I mailed him back to say I wasn't sure, that we'd just have to wait and see if anyone else wanted to do anything. In that case, he mailed to say he'd probably spend some time with Natalie, so he may just be with her as we speak. Benny must have some sort of death wish – he dared to insult my memory of Jo.

'I'm fucked,' Tyler says, sounds exhausted. 'If no one's gonna ply me with some stimulating pharmaceuticals, then I'm afraid I'm gonna have to call it a night, children.'

'Homme,' Thom calls him.

Tyler rises slowly to his feet, steadying himself on the table. 'Look, I'm fucked, and I've got to get all the way back to Plaistow. Besides, I've got to feed Brooking. He'll be starving by now.'

Thom whistles. 'You and that bloody cat of yours.'

'Look, I'm tired and I'm probably gonna fall asleep on the tube and end up in bloody Dagenham or some-where, then have to catch a cab back into Plaistow, and you know I can't really afford it, so how's about just letting me get away in peace, huh? Come on, I'll even let you tell me just which *Firm* geezer I can be, so you don't go ahead and decide behind my back.'

'Okay, Tyler – you're Dominic,' Matt tells him.

'Yeah? Er, why Dominic?'

'Because . . .' Thom says, 'he was a homme or at least looked like one.'

'I'm no fag,' Tyler says, insulted.

'Well, you're wimping out early on us,' Gerry says.

'Fuck it, I'm too tired to argue.' Tyler raises his hands in defeat. 'Okay, I'm Dominic. I am a homosexual. You can all gang-bang my cute butt next time we meet up.' He skirts the table, arms still held aloft. 'Catch you later, honey-children.'

'Love to Brooking,' we all coo after him.

'Yeah, er . . . I'm gonna have to be making a move too,' Mike announces, a touch sheepishly.

'Big girl's blouse,' Jay says into his coffee.

'So . . . who can I be, before I leave?' This question appears to be aimed solely at me.

Gerry airs his opinion. 'Ah, fuck this. This is bollocks. Who gives a fuck, anyway?'

'Well, er, guess I'll be chipping, then,' Mike says.

'Erm, anyone for another coffee?' Weatherface asks. No one answers. Mike leaves.

'So,' Five sighs, 'who's up for a really late one, boys? . . . Dame?'

The thought of a late finish does tempt me: another night on the prowl for Meyer women. I need a fix, need to gawp at some big clubby blondes with their pouty lips and skimpy clothes, their firm bodies and Lipizzaner legs – but I still answer Five with a penitent, 'Nah.'

'Thom?' Five asks.

'Nah, no club for me tonight. I'm wrecked. Think I'll make a move as well.' Thom turns to me. 'Share a cab home, Dame?'

'If you're paying,' I say.

'Toss for it?'

'A coin, you mean?'

'What else?' Thom winks.

'Okay, go on then,' I say.

'Matt? Five? Catch a cab back up north?' Thom asks.

Matt looks to Five, as Thom and I rise to our feet, me gulping down the cold remnants of my coffee, leaving a bitter aftertaste in my mouth which, oddly enough, somehow reminds of Benny.

*

'We have got to win some money,' Thom is telling us. 'Not too much – just enough – a nice win at the bookies or the dogs. We could all always do with a little extra money; there's so much to do in London. We should all be living it up a little more, be out every night of the week while we're still young.'

I look to Matt who in turn looks to Five. The taxi draws to a blunt halt at traffic lights. For a basic salary, Thom actually earns some 5K per annum more than me; he inadvertently let his last month's payslip disappear down the side of our sofa. I discovered it during one of my irregular cleaning stints, and obviously felt duty-bound to read it. Mind, I have the option of overtime in my profession, unlike Thom, so if I do ever feel threatened by his advantage I can always strive to make amends.

'The first money I win,' Thom continues. 'The first money I win, I'm gonna buy all the boys some tarts. Get them round our flat – we've got the nicest pad. Loads of them, loads of tarts. Not your King's Cross rubbish – proper agency call-girls. And we'll get all the boys round and get the girls to perform a strip for us – you know, get them to come in one by one and intro-duce themselves. They could say stuff like "Hi, I'm Cindy and I'm a 36D and I just love giving deep-throat," you know, that kind of thing. Then, after they've all stripped, we'd get them to perform lesbian sex scenes for us. What do you think, boys – cool idea or what?'

Matt looks at Thom as if he's mad, just screws up his nose.

'Yeah, superb idea, Thom,' Five says sarcastically.

I'm trying to figure out just how Thom can suddenly seem so intoxicated.

'I wouldn't fuck them, though,' Thom says. 'No, don't get me wrong. I wouldn't fuck those hookers. I am not paying for it, no fucking way.' Expanding each point with his lily-white hands, he perseveres, 'But I'd bathe one of them – I'd like that. In a deep hot bath foaming with bubbles. I'd pick the one with the biggest lungs and slowly wash her big soppy tits for her. Of course we'd have to video it as well.'

'Of course,' I concede, sensing that the taxi driver is actually giggling at our expense, as Thom's voice is raised louder and louder.

'We'd have to video it,' Thom repeats, ''cos then we could get the video out another time when we're all round ours – say when Jay's around – 'cos you know what Jay's like where porn's concerned, don't you, eh? Jay is the iron filing to the magnet of porn' – even I have to laugh at this line – 'because we won't have invited Jay along. We'd have had the tarts round with Jay a noticeable absentee . . . And we'll stick this new porn on and Jay'll be sitting there, right in front of the telly, and he'll see all these beautiful sorts come in and it'll slowly dawn on him that he's looking at a video of our flat, and then the birds'll do a strip for all of us. God, can you just picture his face, boys? Eh? Eh? Can you just picture his face, boys? It'd be worth it just to see his little black bemused face.' Thom slaps me on the arm, perhaps a little too hard.

'Yes, Thom,' we all say, feign interest. 'We can just picture his face.'

Thom is hollering down the corridor, 'Dame, the Manchurian Candidate's on the phone.'

I'm lying spread-eagled on my futon and I'm listening to this CD of *The Vikings* film score, the soundtrack which used to announce New Order's arrival on stage. 'The Manchurian Candidate' is Thom's dumb idea of a joke, though this joke started to wear near anorexic many moons ago – the eponymous film character was called Ray-mond Shaw and, as far as I can remember, was always referred to as such throughout both the film and Richard Condon's novel. My brother's name is simply Ray, and that's exactly how my parents had him christened – 'mond'-less.

I stumble into the lounge, bid a brusque 'Hello' to Lisa, then pick up the phone and drag it into the hallway, carefully closing the door behind me, over the cable.

'Alright, Ray?' I mumble into the phone.

'You took your time,' my brother says.

'Yeah, sorry. Thom and his woman are listening to George fucking Michael again.'

'You should tell 'em to stick on some New Order.'

'Too right,' I agree.

'Still sounds noisy though.'

'Yeah, it is a touch.' I put my hand over the mouthpiece and shout for Thom to turn his crap music down.

He maybe shouts 'Fuck you' back, then the sound drops several notches.

'That better?' I ask Ray.

'It'll do,' he says, pauses. 'Look, Damian, I've got some news . . .'

This sounds ominous and I find myself swamped with trepidation, like I'm teetering on the brink of some inconceivable catastrophe.

'Go on,' I manage, as a Siberian wind thunders past.

'It's your father.' Cough. 'I mean, our father . . . he's gonna be a dad again.'

After a pause I ask, 'Is that it?'

'Whaddayamean, "Is that it?" Isn't that bad enough? Imagine how Mum's gonna feel when she finds out.'

'Can't be as bad as last time – when he finally left her,' I tell my brother.

'Yeah, well, I s'pose not. But *I* certainly don't want to be the one to tell her.'

Confused for an instant, I ask, 'This is with Gillian again, yeah?'

'Yes, why?'

'Thought he might've moved on from her by now. I mean, I never thought he'd actually leave mother.'

Ray sighs. 'Yeah, well, I guess once we were both grown up, he could afford to turn his back on Mum. With Gillian, he's got a two-year-old to look after . . . that, at least, should keep them together.'

'How is mother?' I ask after a while.

'Same as ever – still wrapped up in the church.'

'Too bad,' I say.

Thom – in his new Chelsea away top – piles past me, out of the lounge, makes a beeline for the bathroom, nearly tripping over me on his way. The lounge door slams hard behind him, ricochets, and starts to swing slowly open again, so I shout to Lisa and catch sight of her arm, dripping in heavy silver jewellery (this stirs something age-old inside me. What? – I don't know) as she reaches to pull the door shut. George Michael is carolling something about wanting your sex.

'So, when's the baby due?' I ask.

'Six months. I bumped into the old man in the Sportsman a couple of nights back.'

'Was he drunk?'

'No.'

'No?' I ask.

'Nah, it was early. He was well on his way, though.'

'Figures.'

'Yeah.'

'So-o-o . . .' I start. 'Have you had any success on the baby front yet?'

'Nah.' Ray sighs. 'I've been on shift-work, been working nights. Haven't really had much time to think about it.'

'To think about it?'

'Well, you know, we've been arguing a bit. We haven't actually been doing it.'

I wince at my brother's confession. 'Oh, er, right.'

'How's Joanna?' he asks.

'Okay, I s'pose.'

'Whaddayamean, "I s'pose"?'

'I mean, I don't really know. We've broken up.'

'What? You and Joanna? Broken up? Nah!' Chuckle. 'Oh, you're . . . you are kidding, right, Damian?'

'No, we've broken up,' I tell him. 'I went up there the Saturday before last and, er, we've finished.'

'Oh, I'm so sorry. How do you feel?' Ray says – doesn't really ask – so I don't bother to answer. 'So, what did you *do*, Damian?'

'What do you mean, *what did I do*?!'

'Well, proper couples don't break up without a reason. Okay, then, what did *she* do?'

'Nothing. She did nothing,' I mutter. She told me she couldn't love me any more.

After a pause Ray sort of tells me in a serious voice, 'Mum's worried about you. She wants you to find a nice girl to settle down with.'

'A nice girl to settle down with?' I laugh. 'Mother won't be happy till I marry a Catholic virgin.'

Ray chuckles. 'Yeah.'

'Like you did,' I add, snigger.

'Hey, Sharon isn't a Catholic,' he retorts. Then, in the pregnant silence that hovers between us, I'm sure that we're both thinking the self-same thing – that when Sharon hitched up with Ray she most certainly wasn't a virgin either. This morning, I received an e-mail from Benny, telling me his change of address. He's moved into his new woman's flat, down in Vauxhall. And in the regular mail I got a postcard from Jo's cousin, Slinky, all the way from Singapore, which closed with the line: *Hope you're still taking good care of Joanna.*

Ray is asking me something that I don't quite catch. I just mutter, 'I'm seeing someone else now, anyway.'

'Already? Yeah, who?' he asks excitedly.

'Oh, just this thing called Beth.' I should maybe elaborate here a little, but I cannot think of a single element of worth to say about her.

'Oh, don't tell me, Damian. Blonde, yeah? No, maybe not blonde 'cos you were involved with that other big thing for a while – that gorgeous raven-haired bird – that one you were with at university. Oh, you know the one.'

'Yes, I know the one,' I murmur acerbically.

'The one Mum liked.'

'Yes, I know the one,' I repeat.

'She started seeing whatshisface after you, didn't she?'

'Yeah,' I admit sullenly. 'Look, I thought we were talking about my *new* partner?'

'Ah, right, so we were. So, this new one's got to be at least five-ten, yeah?'

'Nah, she's short – you'd like her,' I say, thinking: you can take her off my hands.

'What's short?'

I offer, 'Five-six?' I'm wondering just how heavy my brother is nowadays: he's let himself go since he got married, literally piling on the pounds, the stones, in recent years. This afternoon, I swapped all the keys from my navy leather key-ring (which once boasted the white cross of St Andrew until it faded) onto this Day-glo red plastic key-ring which Matt picked up for me in some topless bar in New York when he was last there on business. Jo had bought me the previous key-ring adorned with the Scottish flag; I refuse to accept the notion that we're completely finished, but perhaps it's best to make some small gesture towards living my life without her?

Ray sighs and says, 'Look, I better be going, I guess.'

I repeat his phrase. 'Yeah, better be going.'

'I'm dropping in on Mum tomorrow. I said I'd go round for lunch. Do you want me to give her a message for you?'

'Yeah, um . . .' My turn to sigh. 'Just tell her that I'm thinking about her, and that I'll visit her soon.'

'And Dad? Any message, in case I bump into him again . . . in a pub somewhere?'

'Yeah, you can just stab him in the throat for me,' I say, deadpan.

Ray laughs nervously, pauses, then probably realizes I'm being deadly serious, that my encouragement to commit patricide is quite kosher. He just stammers, 'Like I said, better be going.'

'Yeah, take care,' I tell him.

'Oh, just one more thing,' he says.

'Yes?' I ask.

'At which gig did New Order give "1963" its first airing?'

'Reading Uni, 30 June 1987,' I return quickly. 'It was a Tuesday.'

'And where did it come in the set?'

'Fifth,' I lie after a calculated pause.

'Sixth!' Ray retorts gleefully. ' "All Day Long" was fifth. Foxed you that time, bruv.'

'Ah, but which slowy did they encore with?' I ask without thinking, then wish I hadn't, not wanting to catch my brother out, though the buzzword 'slowy' should really prompt him.

There's an electric pause where I'm just willing Ray to speak, but then he answers, quite deliberately, 'That would've been . . . "Lonesome . . . Tonight".'

'Correct,' I tell him, and the line goes dead, just fizzles down my ear – my good deed for the day now passed, my brother's self-esteem raised one tiny minim.

I turn to make my way back to my room, suddenly sensing the urge to blast out 'Ride of the Valkyries' from my stereo – an attempt to raise my own self-esteem that extra minim – but it's then that the phone rings again.

It's Mike. 'Listen, Dame, I've got a proposal to put to you. I think I've unearthed a perfect opportunity to make a little extra money for the boys . . .'

The majority of my closest friends are here, all straight from work, all suited and booted, with the exception of Tyler who sports his statutory plaster-encrusted building-site finery. We've commandeered a corner of the Doggett's, my work's local overlooking the Thames, and I'm sat staring through the huge windows, staring out across the bridge at St Paul's Cathedral as this train rolls sluggishly into Blackfriars station, and as Mike lolls back in the chair beside me and closes his presentation with, '. . . and that, boys and girl' – Mike shoots a playful glance at Jay; Jay pulls a sneery face in return – 'is . . . it!'

The silence is ear-shattering. The boys greet Mike's words with a montage of stony, poker faces, no one daring to give too much away.

Then Gerry leans forward to pick up his bitter, slowly brings the drink to his mouth, takes a long cool slurp on the ale and, with a froth moustache atop his upper lip, sighs and prods Mike with, 'Ten thousand, you say?'

Mike nods his head and looks deadly serious, 'Yes, boss, ten thousand of the things.'

Benny lets out a low-pitched whistle.

'And we'll shift most of them through your brother?' Five asks apprehensively. 'Doubling our money, right?'

'We can definitely shift most of them straight away. I promise you that much,' Mike answers. 'And you'll probably double your money. My brother usually sells on in bulk, at anything from seven to nine notes.'

Matt enters the debate with, 'But, what if we're left with, like, hundreds each?'

Tyler and Weatherface nod in unison and shuffle their chairs ever closer to the table.

'You won't be. I'll sort it,' Mike says, sounds convincing.

'Hey, I want a few to myself,' Benny interjects. 'I'll easily knock 'em out at fifteens where I work. You know what it's like in advertising – so many parties to attend.

There's this bloke who charges twenties whenever he gets some in, and people just lap them up. The wankers at our place like to think they're trendy fuckers, but half of 'em have got their heads shoved up their arses. They just like to keep "in" with people – they couldn't score with an *A-Z* of London crack houses.'

This is the scam. This is Mike's intuitive little way of making extra money for the boys. Ten thousand Ecstasy tablets, all at bucketshop prices – four notes apiece. We buy them wholesale, we sell them on at substantial profits. Nothing could be simpler. Only we need the cash up-front – a cool forty grand. And Mike thought it appropriate we should get a consortium together, do the thing professionally, get our closest friends in on the act, so as to have ten shareholders stumping up an affordable four thousand each. Jo always maintained I thought more of my friends than I did of her, but this is just the kind of once-in-a-lifetime business opportunity that friends put one another's way.

I do love my friends and seven of them – Tyler, Matt, Mike, Jay, Gerry, Five and Weatherface – are mustered here tonight. Benny's here also – he's still regarded as a friend by Mike. I didn't think it necessary to air any grievances against him just yet; I'll bide my time and see him sorted at a later, more suitable date. Toolboy really ought to be taking tenth spot, but that would've meant involving Jinxy John, and neither Mike nor I wanted that, so Toolboy's been blackballed, which is a genuine shame as we've been close for a long time. Thom's another absentee, but Mike fully understands my reasons for seeing him relegated. How can Thom be trusted after such recent pitfalls? The tenth share is to be taken by Mike's brother who, unfortunately and for reasons still unexplained, couldn't make this most momentous of meetings tonight. As I said, nothing could be simpler.

'So, you're sure we can get rid of most of 'em via your brother?' Five is asking Mike this for the second time.

'Yeah, through my brother's people – the small-time dealers he offloads his gear on,' Mike explains. There are five mobile phones set down on the table. I unthinkingly left mine at Beth's. This is an atrocious mistake on my behalf, as the five phone-users now share a common nexus to which I am not presently a party.

Five's all at sea, muddle-headed. 'But why is your brother just putting up *some* of the cash? Why isn't he taking all the glory for himself?'

Mike sighs. 'I had this chance meeting with my brother's "man" down Ealing Broadway last week. We had a few beers together, got a bit pissed, and he made me this offer. This is *my* deal, not my brother's.'

'So, he's not annoyed by any of this?' someone asks.

'My brother? Nah. He's gone all legit now anyway.'

Matt now, troubled: 'Legit? I thought you said he was DJ-ing or something? He's hardly trying to tear himself away from the scene is he?'

'Oh, he still does the DJ-ing, but he's got himself a proper career now.' Mike pauses for words. 'He's got himself on an accountancy course. He's not strictly into dealing.'

'You sure?'

''Course, I'm sure.' Mike's now slightly flustered. 'Hey, look, I said he'd provide us with the contacts to shift all the gear, so what's the problem?'

'There's no problem,' Matt tells him flatly, but still looks unconvinced.

Personally, I'm slightly perplexed by Mike's brother's half-arsed involvement, letting Mike steal the adulation – but Mike and I go back a long way. Mike's a good friend and I trust him. Up at the bar some geezer in tartan trousers with a frog tattoo on his right forearm and a T-shirt which bawls FIGHTING MAD IRISH is arguing with this thing in a pair of lime-coloured jeans. The thing in the lime-coloured jeans is the only blonde, indeed the only thing, in the pub, and has these barrage-balloon breasts of Meyer-esque proportions and, for those two inestimable reasons, I am very nearly tempted to wander over and break up their argument, to rescue this fair damsel in distress, wreak some venomous damage on this geezer, but instead I find myself just staring at her, trying to fix her with this look that Jo so fervently idolized – my head tilted slightly forward, my brow furrowed, trying to look serious with my mouth pursed like I'm about to blow her a kiss. But when this blonde finally catches on to my attentions she just looks back to Mr Frog-tattoo once again, seems wholly unimpressed, and audibly, quite coldly, informs this geezer. 'Look, I want my money. If you can't get it from him, then just go for his mother.'

'Hard bitch,' someone behind me – Jay? – mutters.

Mike returns my attention back to the deliberation in hand. 'Come on, are you all in or what? It's only 4K each. If you haven't got it handy, I know you can all get hold of it on credit.'

'Look, I don't mean to spoil the fun, but you know I'll never be able to raise that kind of capital,' Tyler says apologetically.

'That's the beauty of the thing,' Mike says. 'Like I said earlier, I've stalled for some time. The payment's not due for three months.'

'I'll never get the money together,' Tyler just bleats. 'I'm only doing casual labouring. I'm skint most of the time.'

'Cut down on your lifestyle, geezer. Put in some extra hours on the site. You said they'd asked you to do some overtime – so do some,' Jay tells him, and Five and Gerry make noises in agreement.

I sense that Mike may have broken the deadlock. We had Jay pencilled in as a certainty from day one, but Mike may be close to convincing Five and Gerry too.

'Ah, I'm knackered just working weekdays. The weekends too would kill me,' Tyler grumbles, wipes something from the lens of his glasses – this cool pair with a heavy black frame that look really sixties-ish, like Ronnie Kray used to wear.

'It'll be worth it, though, Tyler. You'll be letting us down otherwise,' Benny tells him, and it appears we may just have another convert in our midst. Such a pity it has to be Benny.

'Yeah, maybe. But why us? Why choose *us* to pump

up the cash?' Tyler asks the table, his gaze purposely skirting Mike and me – the intended recipients of his query.

I mollify the throng with, 'Look, boys, Mike couldn't raise forty grand on his own, so he contacted me to discuss the proposition. I mulled it over, and in turn got each of you here tonight to bring this whole project that one step closer to reality. I think Mike's been good to us, letting us in on his scam. And none of you would be here if we didn't trust you.'

Remarkably, I'm actually looking at Benny as I deliver this last line.

'Well, why not Thom? Why isn't he here?' Matt asks.

Mike, amongst others, shoots him a knowing look.

'Oh, right, sorry, Dame. I forgot,' Matt apologizes, blushes, then audibly whispers, 'But you're no fucking saint now, are you?'

'Matt, shoosh now,' Mike hisses at him then reaches to light a cigarette with cool aplomb.

'Well, what about Marky Mullen? We're still thick with him,' Matt adds.

'Oh, be reasonable,' I complain. 'Marky doesn't live in London, and he's just so-o-o fucking unreliable anyway.'

Matt can only nod in agreement. 'True, true.'

I stop to stare out of the window, into the still night air, stare down as this huge Gothic thing makes her way across Blackfriars Bridge. I've never fucked a proper bona-fide Goth, with all that gloomy make-up, frilly black lace and beetroot-purple hair. I suspect I never will – nothing could indeed be further from what is generally perceived as my type.

Jay bangs his pint glass down on the table. 'So, what sort of Es? Not some ketamine shit, I hope. Or some caffeine.'

'Oh, I dunno. I enjoy a dose of ketamine once in a while,' Five mentions.

Mike tokes hard on his cigarette. 'Look, we can get all sorts – doves, playboys, stars, dolphins, buffaloes, swallows, whatever you want. I reckon we should just go with doves though.' Mike pauses, scratches the side of his nose. 'I mean, the man's got these little red things – dinosaurs – that he says contain nearly 200mg of MDMA, but if you want to shift 'em for higher prices at work, or whatever, then I suggest we go with the doves. People know where they stand with a dove. People trust doves.'

There's an uncomfortable silence then I announce, 'I have to agree with Mike.'

'Me, too – I agree with Mike and Dame,' Weather-face blurts, his first words in an age. All faces turn to study him, perched on the far end of the table. 'And I'm, er, more than happy to stick in four grand. It's just the chance I need to make a bit of money.'

The boys are stunned into oblivion – even *I'm* taken aback by the unmitigated enthusiasm as portrayed by our resident weak link. If Weatherface is willing to join the affray, then there's no way the others will back down, no way that anyone will be prepared to play second fiddle to Weatherface. Mike and I are possibly the only two people here who've still time for him, and we both regard him with a quasi-disdain. He's a virtual outcast since he got a mortgage with that Heather thing. Weatherface and Mike do meet for lunch every three weeks or so – they work in adjacent buildings near Tower Hill, Mike hitting the heady heights of finance on a wage identical to mine, but Weatherface just slumming it with some disjointed publishing firm – so I'm privately hoping that if Weatherface does ever decide to marry Heather, the great Lord forbid, it'll be Mike who gets lumbered to stand in as best man.

Gerry coughs, leans back, places his hands behind his head and crosses his long gangling legs. 'You'd better count me in as well, then.'

In immediate response Benny exclaims, 'Me too. I'm up for it.'

Five looks to Matt. Matt just raises his eyebrows. 'Rachel will kill me if she ever finds out,' Five says, pauses. 'But you can add my name to the shareholders' rollcall.'

Mike lets out a small cheer, Gerry claps his hands.

'Me too, guys,' Matt concedes. 'Jenny would kill me as well, but – hey! – that's peer pressure for you.'

All eyes fall on Tyler. 'Oh, honey-children, you've got me banged to rights here.' Tyler stands, raises his pint glass as a prompt to a toast.

Gerry plays dumb. 'So, er, does that mean you're in or not?'

''Course I'm in,' Tyler snaps.

'You sure you can afford it?' Five asks, goading Tyler.

'Yes, I'll do the overtime. Now, are you all gonna join me in a toast, or what?'

Collectively we push our chairs back, stand to raise our glasses, all of us except for Jay, who remains seated, his head bowed, a fine layer of stubble adorning his scalp, like he's not been bothered to shave his hair off for a week or so.

'Hey, what's eating you, boss?' Mike asks.

Five appears worried. 'Yeah, Jay, surely you're in – ain't you, mate?'

Jay raises his head, whispers, 'I might be. You haven't really bothered to ask.'

'Oh, c'mon, guy,' Matt complains. 'We just assumed.'

'You shouldn't assume,' Jay half moans.

'Okay, I'll ask you nicely,' I tell him. 'Jay, will you please come and play with the big boys?'

Jay springs to his feet and smiles. 'Geezers, as if I'd let any of you down.'

Gerry and Tyler slap Jay on the back. Someone calls for Mike to propose a toast.

'Nah, nah, I can't do it,' Mike whines.

''Course you can,' we all tell him.

'Nah, c'mon, Dame – you do it, eh?' Mike urges me. 'Oh, but one thing first . . .'

'What's that?' I ask.

Mike delves into his suit pocket, then pulls his arm back slowly, presenting the group with his clenched fist. Then he spins said fist purposely, uncurling his fingers like a flowering bloom as he does so, to reveal, once fully opened, a small colligation of pills upon his plateau-ed palm. 'We all have to take a sample,' he informs us. 'Lovely white doves, courtesy of yours truly.'

'Oh, do we have to?' Weatherface is the first to complain. 'I've got an early start in the morning.'

'Yes, you have to. We've all got to do it,' Mike proclaims, so we pick a pill apiece then each place it quite purposely on the ends of our tongues, showing for all to see.

'Right then,' I announce, talking thickly with my tongue still out. I then hold my pint glass aloft. 'Right then,' I blubber again. 'Gentlemen, I propose a toast . . . to the everlasting pursuit of oversized Meyer women and, most importantly . . . to friendship.'

'To friendship,' the boys all chorus, wolfing down their pills. Then there's havoc as we each cross arms, chinking one another's glasses, swapping pleasantries and pulling silly faces until there's just Benny and Five purposefully tapping their pint glasses together, then I'm busy downing the remnants of my Kronenbourg as Benny signals to me and says, 'Dame, c'mon, Dame – I don't think you and me got to clink glasses. To friendship, eh, Dame? To friendship . . .'

We're in my favourite Chinese restaurant – Honey-moons on Park Road – me, Tyler, Mike and Beth. It's Sunday evening and we're the only ones left from my birthday contingent. I was twenty-five just yesterday. We kicked off the celebrations in the Polar Bear at midday

Saturday, and all ended up wasted at Freedom close on seven this morning. There's no higher feeling than dancing en masse with your mates, all grouped together in uniformity, the only words of wisdom spoken being 'This one's a fucking tune!' whenever an acknowledged track comes to the fore. No higher feeling, perhaps, than actually rucking alongside your mates but, though the place was overrun with equally sized mobs of lads, most a lot younger than us, real scally material, everyone was just too merry and in touch with one another for anything major to ever go off.

Jay and Thom both pulled, Thom claiming that the thing he brought home let him scrawl Ws on both her bottom-cheeks, so that when he bent her over it spelt out the word WOW. Mike was in such a state of euphoria that he headed off to Trade as the rest of us all wobbled, jelly-legged, back to our beds. The only real absentees of note – apart from Jo of course – were Five and Rachel, who are away travelling in Goa for two weeks. Marky Mullen was due down, but he failed to show, as is usually – sorry, always – the case.

I ended up doing seven Es – mostly doves, three of them presents, from Mike, Toolboy and Matt's woman, Jenny. Consequently, I've been a bit of a mess today – grinding me teeth, sucking on my gums, and making attempts to keep chewing my tongue. I'm not really sure as to why I invited Beth along, though to her credit she did buy me this ketchup-red polo shirt courtesy of Thomas Burberry, criss-crossed with these fine blue lines, one inch square, and though Toolboy did point out I now resembled Spiderman – thus prompting an endless cavalcade of gags all night – it's still a classical style timelessly indicative of the English Lad since I was first a young geezer, so it came gratefully received nevertheless. Instead of a card, Jinxy John gave me this photo of Anna Nicole Smith cut from one of the week's tabloids. Jo hasn't yet sent me a card – maybe one will arrive in the post tomorrow?

I've promised to pay for Tyler's meal, as he's missed his Sunday overtime to attend my birthday. I don't want him biting into his savings: to start falling short of his four-grand target just yet. We've ordered the 'Executive Banquet' for four, and have just finished picking at the starters' platter (most of which is actually rubbed into the tablecloth), when Tyler prompts Mike with the question, 'What's your favourite word, honey-child?'

Mike feigns a look of shock, puts his hand to his mouth, slaps his lips, then says in this weird, exhausted voice, 'You know, I really can't remember.'

'But you said it a couple of months back – when we were all at that do down in Holborn,' Tyler says, appears really concerned. 'Remember, Dame? You were there.'

'On Toolboy's birthday? Yeah, I remember the night but not the word.' Jo was with us – she'd painted her fingernails in alternate royal blues and vehement greens for some unearthly reason. I wonder what she's doing right now?

Mike ponders. 'God, what was it now?'

'Something normal sounding,' Tyler says, readjusts his glasses.

'Something short and insignificant,' I chime.

'Nah, sorry. It's escaped me,' Mike admits, shrugs his shoulders, flicks his blond fringe. There are no blonde things in Honeymoons tonight, and none of the unblondes present appear that tall, Beth included. However, one of the unblondes, this Greek-looking girl sat with her boyfriend by the windows, is wearing a pair of Jo-style hooped earrings – two pairs in fact – and this serves to arouse a little something inside me and sets me wondering: would I actually deem to sleep with someone solely on the brittle basis of their jewellery conforming with Jo's?

'What's your favourite word, sugar?' Beth asks me.

'Enough,' I say without hesitation and reach for my wineglass.

'Enough of this conversation – or enough is, like, your favourite word?' Tyler asks.

'Enough is my favourite word,' I say. 'I remember it from a spelling test when I was seven. This teacher read out the word "enough" and I just froze, couldn't figure out how to spell it. My mind went blank.'

'So, how did you spell it?' Mike asks.

'First of all – i-n-u-f-f' – Tyler laughs, Beth smirks – 'But, I knew that was wrong and ended up with e-n-u-f-f. Got thirty-nine out of forty in that test.'

'I always thought "voluptuous" would be your favourite word,' Mike tells me, and chuckles.

'Nah, I had "buxom" down as a strong contender,' Tyler adds.

I think for a moment. 'I quite like "buxotic". It's an old Russ Meyer word.'

Beth screws up her face like a walnut. 'So, what's your favourite word, then, Tyler?' she asks.

'Remember, Tyler, that honey-child is – technically – two words,' Mike says.

Tyler answers with, 'Bun.'

'Bun?'

'Yeah . . . bun.'

'You sure?'

'Yeah, it's one of those weird words that doesn't look right on paper – like it's not a proper word or something.'

Beth giggles, then excuses herself from the table.

'Congratulations, Dame. That's a fantastic woman you've found there,' Tyler tells me and leans forward to pat my shoulder. 'She looks like that actress, you know – that Elizabeth Hurley. Her surname isn't Hurley, is it? Hey, bet you've no regrets about the break-up with Joanna now, eh?'

I'm submersed by this deluge of cosmic murk. As if in slowed-down motion, I find myself exaggeratedly tapping my pocket, like I've lost or misplaced something of importance, and although I'm secure in the knowledge that ten crisp twenties are tucked safely away there, I'm muttering in this faraway voice, 'Er, Mike, I think you're gonna have to pay for Tyler's meal. I've left my wallet back at the flat. Beth'll pay for me.'

'Sure, Dame, no worries,' I think Mike tells me, as

Beth seats herself back at the table, and as the waitress arrives with our second course – the soup.

'I've just remembered my favourite word,' Beth announces.

'Yeah?'

'Yeah . . . piping-hot-chicken-and-sweetcorn-soup.'

The boys are laughing, but I'm just sitting here, smouldering, enraged by an avalanche of contempt, glaring at my latest adversary, this hateful subhuman, this Tyler character, and then I'm thinking to myself that no true friend of Damian Henry Shaw's would ever – *ever* – consider 'Bun' as his favourite word.

We're in the Rose and Crown and I'm already half-cut. Most of the Lunchboys are here – it's Martin Murphy's last day at work and the ales are flowing. I thought it best to show my face for the sake of office etiquette, before heading off to do something far more interesting with my friends. Whereas I love my friends, the Lunch-boys are strictly acquaintances – people I must simply appease to get me through the drudgery of a working day.

We've already had the stripogram and the scene where the girlfriend storms out in disgust, and I'll admit Martin's woman had every conceivable right to be annoyed, as the stripogram was a fucking moose with this really matted pubic hair. And though Martin was none too impressed by our choice, he still did his best to partake in proceedings, as we'd all chipped in good money to acquire her unenviable talents. Dino Denton booked her, and claims he 'slipped her a length' upstairs before unleashing her on poor Martin. But Dino – who works on the third floor (I'm on the fourth) – is a compulsive liar and I don't ever believe a word he says.

I'm talking to Rod Ellis and to Alasdair Marshall, who is giddy drunk and who asks me if I'm still seeing my new woman. I tell him that I am, and show him this black-and-white snap of Beth I keep tucked inside my gold travel-card – this picture that Beth tucked inside my gold travel-card, because she so wants me to carry a picture of her (heaven knows why as I've never carried a picture of Jo with me, and I actually love her).

Alasdair's eyes are glazed and he's slurring his words. 'You seeing her tonight, Damian? Is she the reason you're gonna leave so early?'

'Nah, I'm off to a party in Brixton – a friend of a friend,' I answer.

'Think I might be able to keep her company then?' Alasdair asks, studying the picture, struggling to focus his vision.

I think about this, but have to tell him, 'You're a married man.'

Alasdair shows the picture to Rod, who nods a seal of approval, smiles and says, 'Nice-looking woman you've got there, Damian.' Alasdair is thirty years old, Rod's past forty. I do not work with them directly. I first met them in the bookies on Blackfriars Road.

'So, what about your Scottish bit then, Damian?' Alasdair asks, inebriated. 'You still seeing her as well?'

I say, 'No, it's finished.'

'But you were telling me how much you loved her last time we spoke. What's wrong with you, eh?' he asks, somewhat aggressively.

I reiterate, saying it's all over. This takes its time to register with Alasdair.

'So, what's wrong with you?' he asks again.

'The distance,' I say. 'Scotland to England – it wasn't working.'

'But you still love her, don't you,' Alasdair tells me. 'What's wrong with you, Damian?'

'Leave him, Al,' Rod says and puts his hand to Alasdair's shoulder. I cannot look Alasdair in the eye – I can sense that he's somehow disappointed with me. A misted red rage gains momentum from the depths of my skull, and I'm visualizing myself head-butting this Alasdair cunt in slow motion, gloating as he near crumbles in my wake.

'Come on, Damian. I'll buy you a pint, son.' Rod steers me towards the bar. 'Ignore Mr Marshall, he's just a little drunk – he's been having a rough time of it at home lately.'

I catch sight of the gruesome Allison Coyle with Nicholas Spencer-Jones, arm-in-arm together, stood across the far side of the pub. Allison smiles at me, Nicholas raises his hand and waves, the blind anger within me unhurriedly subsides. There is nothing wrong with me.

'It's okay,' I tell Rod. 'Al doesn't bother me.' I neck the pint from Rod as Alasdair stumbles into Jack Howe, our Senior Manager, knocking Jack's pint clean out of his hand. Someone (the Bishop?) tells Alasdair he ought to go home, that he's had more than enough to drink. Despondent, he leaves. I say my farewells to Martin Murphy, wish him all the best for the future, then bid adieux to James Comley, Carl Smith, Graham Watson and Gregor Daley before heading out into the night. I flag down a black cab whilst en route to Waterloo Station, determining it to be a faster, more direct option than the Northern Line and, once finally in Muswell Hill, I change quickly whilst watching the optimal sketch in my Anna Nicole Smith Playmate video, this simple scene where Anna's prancing around her home town, dressed in this blue flowery dress and a pair of brown cowboy boots and wearing these huge hooped earrings and, for some weird reason, she really reminds me of Jo in this skit, though Jo never owned such a dress or boots. I then catch a minicab from Queens Avenue all the way back south to Brixton.

I'm late.

I'm in the Prince of Wales with Five, Matt, Thom and a collection of Five's workmates, none of whom he introduces to me. We're all watching the television set high in the far corner of the pub, all nonchalantly sipping at our pints, all of us wearing Ralph Lauren polo shirts.

'I thought Gerry was due here,' I say after a while.

'You cut your knuckle, Dame?' Matt quizzes me.

'Yeah. Smacked fuck out of some geezer from work,'

I tell him quite brightly, thinking about Alasdair Marshall. 'So, what about Gerry?'

'Er, he's staying home,' Five tells me, regards me with a modicum of concern. 'Said he ain't gonna be showing tonight.'

'Yeah, Andrea phoned him today,' Matt hums. 'He's not up for socializing. Andrea's finally sorted some op to get rid of his tattoo.'

'Tattoo?' I ask. 'That one on her tit?'

'Yeah,' Matt chuckles. 'That one on her tit.' Andrea has the word 'Gerry,' traced from Gerry's very own signature, inscribed in inch-high lettering across the uppermost contour of her right breast; she'd had it done as a surprise present for Gerry's twenty-first birthday.

'But Gerry and Andrea broke up over – what? – two, three years back?'

'Time she got rid of the tattoo, then,' Thom notes.

'Prove to Gerry it really is over,' someone says.

'Don't know how he's gonna get over this one,' Five comments and sips at his pint. 'I mean, how do you cope when the one true love of your life has your name surgically removed from her tit?'

'Hmmm, I thought *I* was fucked up,' I reveal to the boys.

'Yeah, thought *I* was fucked up, too,' I think Thom says, and I look across at him but his face is expressionless, virginal like an untouched canvas. He's still watching the television, and I'm wondering what the hell he could possibly be fucked up about, wondering if this comment was solely aired for my benefit, somehow sniping at me me for a past indiscretion like it's really affected his life or something (I very much doubt this). There's this real Meyer woman stood by the front windows, just up from us, looks a touch like Babette Bardot in *Common-Law Cabin* – blonde, broad, Valkyrian – but she's with six other geezers so I just fantasize about her from a distance and hope that I'll find a woman of similar physical magnitudes at Five's mates' party.

The party is within walking distance from the pub – just off Brixton Hill. Five introduces me to his workmates once we reach our destination, but only after I've cajoled him for being such an ignorant homme. I forget all his workmates' names in an instant. I am drinking Kronenbourg and K Cider and I've taken some acid – a strawberry, courtesy of Matt – and I'm dancing to Duran Duran and to Spandau Ballet and then someone (Five?) puts on The Jam and the lounge erupts in a mass of threshing bodies, so someone else puts on some Soft Cell instead and I stop dancing.

I always like to remain drinking whilst doing acid – you can still retain that trippy sensation, the ale doesn't appear to take much of an edge off it. Totally unlike E, of course – lager and pills don't make good travelling companions. The last time I scored acid off Matt was two years back at some Return To The Source bollocks – a time when I was candy-flipping, intermixing my acid and Es, when I spent the rest of the night convinced that Frankenstein was chasing me round the club. I didn't deem to tell anyone, just spent the whole night on the move, never stopping in one place for any great length of time, fearing that Frankenstein might somehow make up the distance between us – strangely enough, he was always on the opposite side of the club to me, never came any closer. It's a much safer bet to score gear off Mike or his trendy little brother; they're usually laced with the finest narcotics.

I'm profoundly strung out by the fact there's a lot of geezers at this party wearing make-up, dressed in what appear to be blouses, and I begin to look at Five in a new light (I've never suspected him of homosexual tendencies before) until Matt points out that this is, in fact, an eighties theme party and they're supposed to be New Romantics, which relaxes my tension immensely and makes me feel a hell of a lot happier with the whole affair. Five lets me into a secret, tells me he's heard from Benny; tells me that Natalie, Benny's woman, has been receiving anonymous death-threats; tells me that Benny's stumped by the whole affair, is worried for Natalie's safety; that the calls can only be traced to public phone-boxes in central London. I feign astonishment at the news, and Five fails to register the beads of perspiration gaining momentum on my forehead. I attempt to talk to the only really tall thing at the party but she waves me away, telling me she has a boyfriend and I tell her that this does not matter to me as I am gay anyway and I am Thom's lover and I only wanted to speak to her because I thought she was another geezer in drag. I then commandeer this shortish girl, but purely because she's wearing these huge kinky boots like Jo used to wear, but I drop this conversation flat when I come to my senses realizing that she'd be far shorter, near pigmy size, if she had not invested in the big block heels making her height that much more creditable and engaging. Acid or no acid, I should endeavour to uphold my standards. Matt keeps blabbering on about the E deal, about how excited he is at the prospect of all that money, and eventually Five has to tell him to shut up, to keep his voice down in case Thom, or anyone else for that matter, starts to cotton on.

I am sitting on the stairs talking to this petite half-caste thing – her hair tied in little bunches, Icelandic Björk style, a line of red freckles staining her flattened nose. I am in love with her and her crooked smile, and I think that maybe she loves me too. I am drinking Kronenbourg and K Cider and I've taken some acid – a strawberry, courtesy of Matt. This thing has a Hawk or an Eagle or something tattooed on her right arm. She is telling me that I am really out of it, that my eyes are on stalks, tells me that she still really likes my eyes because they're 'penetrating'. I cannot close my hands properly, cannot grip tightly; my arms tingle with electric shocks. Thom is motioning at me from the kitchen and I shout to see what he wants and he shouts back at me, telling me that everyone's heading north in a minicab, so I say to him, stroppily, 'But I wanna go down Turnmills, wanna stay out la-a-a-te . . . Oh, wait a minute, then,

Mr Spoil-sport,' and I say to this beautiful half-caste creature, Tonya, 'I have to leave. Come home with me, please.'

She tells me, 'No,' sweetly, and then says, 'Sorry,' and just smiles at me.

'I must at least have your phone number then,' I say to her.

She is shaking her head and is giggling. I begin giggling too.

'What?' I purr. 'What . . . is . . . it? What's so-o-o funny, sweetheart?'

'Nothing,' she tells me, her words beautifully mashed and warped. 'It's just, well, you . . . you're mental.'

'So? Your number then?' I ask in hope.

She leans close and pecks me on my left cheek and whispers, 'Maybe not, eh, Thom? . . . It was so nice meeting you, though. Enjoy your life.'

We are both giggling, I don't know why. I am wondering if I actually told her that my name is Thom, and then a death-knell sounds deep within me and I'm thinking of that miserable cunt, Alasdair Marshall, by now lying battered and bruised on some sickbed, and I am wondering: what is wrong with me?

The Lunchboys again. I'm the only one at our table who's not wearing a shirt with an eyesore of a top pocket; these boys dress so blue-collar, really need some fashion tips, should be educated to buy their shirts with removable collar stays, mother-of-pearl buttons, double cuffs, two-piece collars and yolks, invaluable garments courtesy of Thomas Pink. Steve Kerr, our new graduate trainee, is asking us, 'The Edge in Soho – is that, um, gay or something?'

'On Soho Square?' Richard Moore answers. 'God, yes. One hundred per cent, amigo. Why? When were you there? Or rather, why were you there?'

'Oh, only on Saturday. Didn't know what I was doing really – had a nose full of Bolivian marching powder and—'

I interrupt him. 'That is no justification, Steve.'

'Yeah, s'pose not.' Steve shrugs his shoulders. 'I was actually wondering why there were only three or four women in there.'

'And most of them probably weren't women,' James Comley winks, taps the side of his nose. 'If you catch my drift.'

'Well, one of them was my girlfriend,' Steve says.

James looks aghast. 'You're . . . shagging . . . a . . . a transvestite?'

'No, I went with Vanessa,' Steve starts. 'You know, my girlfriend – the nurse.'

'The older one?' I ask.

Steve nods an affirmative. When Kerr first joined our project team I genuinely perceived him as a bit of a gift-horse, that he'd be good for fresh introductions to some nubile young things – he does seem to live a fairly hectic social life away from the office – but, alas, Kerr has this unaccountable penchant for the much older woman.

Steve looks flustered. 'Yeah, oldish – she's only thirty-three, I think – but as for this transvestite . . .' Pause. 'Oh, er, right. You're kidding, yeah? Oh, man, you guys really kill me sometimes.' Steve is so-o-o slow on the uptake – God knows how he even remembers to come to work most mornings. Actually, I'm surprised he isn't doing any better in the Latecomer Awards, though I'm sure he'll pick up when he's settled into the general company ambience. A week ago he told me that his all-time favourite song was Level 42's 'Love Games' – bit of a sad choice in my opinion, but apparently it reminds him of his first true love, so I should excuse him for that reason alone. My all-time favourite song is probably 'Dreams Never End' by New Order because: (1) New Order are my all-time favourite band, (2) Hooky sings it, he's my idol, and (3) it prompts my mindscape to remember sunnier times with my brother, of this gig they did supporting Bronski Beat at the Academy years ago, when I was just fifteen and I still looked up to Ray, and New Order had just played 'Ceremony' and we were right down the front, crushed in the heaving mêlée, shirts off, sopped in sweat, both exhausted, screaming for them to follow with a slowy, but New Order just upped the ante, launched into 'Dreams Never End'. Such joyous memories, I thought I was going to die.

'So, where did you go on Saturday, Richard?' Dino Denton from the third floor is asking. 'Seeing as how you appear to have missed your chance with Steve on the cruise in Clapham . . . Up the Anvil again, was it?'

'Oh, heavens, no. No, no, no, no, no. I'm more of a fluffy bunny type of queen – I leave all that axle grease

and armour-plating lark to the monkey-wrench brigade.'
Richard motions at his fellow 'family' members – James
Comley and Russell Bishop – both sat at the head of our
table.

The Bishop blows Richard a kiss and winks. The
Sperminator just blows out his cheeks.

'Changing the subject—' Russell starts.

'Please do,' Dino tells him.

'Changing the subject, did any of you boys know I've
just had three twenty-year-olds move into one of my
flats in Balham?'

'Er, male or female?' I ask.

'Females, dear boy. All lovely virginal female students.
They're far too young for me – well, not too young for
me but probably too young to be interested in me. I'll
e-mail you all with their address this afternoon. I'm
assuming that they'll be having a flat-warming party
which you can all be invited to – for a small introduction
fee, of course.'

'Oh, of course,' James whines.

'Russell, you do not want three twenty-year-old student girls living in your flat,' I tell him.

'Why ever not?' he asks. 'Less trouble than three
young males, surely?'

'No way, Bish,' Ashwin Patel from Credit Risk says.
'They'll have their boyfriends round every night anyway,
so you'll end up with three girls and three fellas.'

'Really? Do you all think I've made a mistake, Ashy-
babes?' Bishop asks.

'Yeah – definitely.'

'Girls'll trash your flat.'

'Or, if they don't, their boyfriends will.'

'Parties every night . . .'

'Smoking pot all the time – burning holes in your carpet.'

'Probably sell off your washing machine.'

'Use their feminine wiles to avoid paying the rent.'

'Well, I never,' Russell exclaims and puts his hands to his cheeks. His mouth agape, he almost resembles Munch's 'The Scream' for a split second.

'Have you set up that video camera yet, Russell?' Ashwin asks directly. 'So that you can capture any footage – should their boyfriends really decide to pop round?'

'Yes, yes. Do you see that red light, girlies?' James mimics Russell's camp tones and points at the ceiling, his hand to Dino's shoulder. 'That's not a camera – don't be fooled. That's actually a highly sensitive infra-red burglar alarm.'

'Or, how about installing one-way mirrors in the wardrobes? So you can get to watch them at it?' Dino asks.

'Hmmm. I actually quite like the idea of two-way mirrors for everything – so we can get to watch each other at it!' Russell tells us.

'Er, I think you'll find that's called a window,' I say, deadpan.

'What's the decor of this place like, Russell?' Richard Moore asks.

'Oh, it's gotta be rubber ceilings.' Dino.

'And a black leather hallway.' Me.

'No, it just has to be mirrored ceilings and floors.' James.

'Actually.' Russell. 'It's a teeny bit like your place, Jamie-babes – I've installed sluice holes in the corridor, so that I can wash away the blood more easily.'

'Ugh, Russell, that's gross. Adios, amigos. I'm off to do loads of drugs in the toilets,' Richard squeals, collecting up his things.

'Yeah, think I might just have to join you there, Richard,' I am saying. 'Er, I mean . . . in "leaving", not as in "doing loads of drugs in the toilets".' Late last night I was trying to ascertain what might happen if I were to – and I hope I'm not tempting fate here – die. I mean, who would actually . . . tell . . . Jo? Indeed, would she even be concerned? Thom's tried to reach me at Jo's parents in the past, so he has the number. Would he think to phone her? Would she attend the funeral, show grief? What would she think of Beth? In the aftermath, when I'm extinct and earthbound, which one of my 'closest' friends might espouse the episode as a ruse to 'comfort' Jo, act as her emotional parawalker? Or, possibly, even Beth?

I'm sitting with Benny in the Burger King in Euston station.

'What did you do to your finger?' I ask him, motion to a thick wad of bandaging.

'Oh, that?' Benny says, offers his hand up to the light

and studies it. 'I was getting some money out of me wallet the other day, and I accidentally sliced it open on a razor-blade. I keep the blade there for when I'm chopping up coke.'

I wince, sort of tut. 'Filthy habit.'

'Yeah, isn't it just?' Benny says, still studies his finger, the puffed-up bandage.

'So,' I start, 'what's so urgent that I have to meet you here first thing in the morning?'

'Nothing really,' Benny says. 'It's just that I wanted to talk to you without the rest of the boys around. I hope you don't mind.'

''Course not,' I lie heartily. 'Why here though?'

Benny points past me. 'Oh, I'm on a course over that way, just down Gray's Inn Road.'

'Anything interesting?' I ask as I slurp my tea.

'Nah. Interpersonal skills.'

'Yawn,' I say with hesitation.

'Yeah, yawn,' Benny concurs. 'And I've already shot me bolt, making enemies of everyone there. Too many hillbillies from outside London – fucking provincial morons.'

'What, you?' I simper. 'Surely not, Benjamin, sweetheart?'

'Yeah,' Benny chuckles. 'We had to go round the room on the first day and introduce ourselves. You know, talk about our hobbies and stuff.'

'And?' I prompt him.

'Well, what the fuck do I put down for hobbies?'

'I dunno. Drinking? Clubbing? Fucking?'

'Exactly,' Benny tells me, and raises one eyebrow.

'Surely you didn't say that?' I ask as I shift in my seat.

'No, not exactly . . . but close,' Benny says, raises his coffee to his lips, blows on the hot liquid and takes a deliberated sip from the cup. 'When it came to me I said I didn't have any hobbies. I said hobbies were for people who didn't have a life.'

'Well, they are,' I say flatly.

'I mean,' Benny continues, 'if you go out every night of the bloody week, then where the hell do you fit any hobbies in?'

'And evening classes?' I offer.

'Yeah,' Benny smarts. 'God only invented evening classes so that life's misfits could get out of the house for an hour every other Tuesday.'

'And, am I to believe that the rest of the people took offence at this radical theory?'

'Yeah . . . funny isn't it? I mean, I could slip into their boring introverted lifestyles so fucking easily, and none of them could ever live life up the way we do, yet they all treat me as if I'm some kind of leper now.'

'Maybe you *are* a leper,' I say quite candidly without even the slimmest whisker of mordancy registering anywhere in my voice.

'Only as leprous as you, Dame,' Benny returns, sidesteps my subtle stab at an insult.

'I really don't think so,' I return smilingly then take another great gulp of styrofoam tea. I can very nearly sympathize with Benny's position in this instance, can align myself to his social viewpoint, but my enemy's enemy has to be seen as my friend, no matter how genetically inferior they may be, so I have to respect the views of Benny's course-mates on this one, even though I curiously find myself at loggerheads with my own internal conscience. I prompt Benny for the conversation soundbite I've been patiently hankering for with, 'Surely you didn't ask me here just to talk about some poncey course?'

'No, you're right.' Benny sighs into his coffee cup.

'Well?' I query him.

'Look, Dame, I hate to spring this on you, but, er . . .' Benny wavers, stops. 'I think I might, er . . . I might have to drop out of the scam.'

'Drop out of the scam,' I repeat, sort of ask.

'Yeah,' he confides. 'Drop out of the scam.'

I'm sidetracked for a second, studying this filthy old tramp at the next table, scrutinizing his thrown-together garments, his T-shirt which reads HASCHISCHIN HEDONIST, trying to figure out what pedestrian thoughts might be punctuating the old boy's mindscape.

'Is it because of the money?' I eventually ask, almost brightly.

'No, nothing like that, Dame – I can borrow some from Natalie, if needs be. No, it's just . . .'

'Just what, Benny?'

'It's just . . . oh, you'll think I'm being stupid, or paranoid. Most probably both.'

'And?' I sigh.

Benny slides an envelope across the table between us.

'What's this?' I ask him.

'You'd better open it,' he says, sips from his coffee cup. 'Natalie received it in the post.'

I'm careful to appear confused, furrow my brow slightly and study the computer-generated address, holding the envelope up to the half-light. I then gingerly withdraw a single sheet of A4 paper and unfold it to reveal this crude photocopy of Benny, a picture of him drunk, sunbathing topless, sticking two fingers up at the camera. 'What's this supposed to be?'

Benny sighs. 'I'm not sure, but I think someone's trying to stir up trouble.'

'Trouble?' I ask.

'Yes, trouble.'

'Who?'

'I dunno.'

'Thom?' I offer.

'Eh?'

'Thom?' I repeat.

'Er, no,' Benny says, regards me like I've caught a strain of variant Creutzfeldt-Jakob or something. 'Thom's the last person I'd suspect, Dame – oh, after you of course. No, I think it's one of the others.'

'One of the others,' I repeat half-heartedly.

These two ugly things – fat secretarial types fresh from commuter-land – clip-clop past in their chunky heels, and I hear one of them comment, 'I've only done coke the one time – at our office party last year when the director dragged me off into the toilets.'

'Yeah, one of the others,' Benny repeats, then whispers, 'The other boys in on the scam. It can't be Thom – he doesn't know anything about our little scam.'

'What makes you think it's to do with the scam?' I ask him, study his reddish hair, think that he's maybe started to go a little grey around the temples, or is this just the light?

'No one suspected a thing though,' the first secretarial type continues. 'Everyone thought we were in there having a shag!'

The second secretarial type cat-cackles out loud, bringing all eyes to attention on the pair.

'Someone stick a dick in her gob,' Benny moans to himself and takes one final sip of his coffee, gurgling it as he does so.

Benny and I bought our first suits together – for interviews – in our third year at university, both opting for charcoal double-breasted numbers from Top Man. We actually considered such items admissible at the time, neither of us previously being used to wearing anything more than snugfit 501 jeans, band-name T-shirts (mine all New Order, of course) and un-brand-name rollnecks. I've embraced progress since those distal times, come on in leaps and bounds – now only deeming to consider single-breasted numbers in navy, charcoal or black, always Jermyn Street. Suits that require braces, not belts. Benny appears to have relapsed however, still preferring the ungamely double-breast, but now in bottle greens and the wateriest greys, suits with zip flies. He even chooses to wear DM boots to the office, unsuitable attire which only serves to make his cheap trousers hang even sorrier. This is an apt indication of the measureless chasm now existing between us.

Benny is still talking. 'Well, this photo was definitely taken at uni – out by the lakes, when we used to hang out there in the summer term – so one of the boys must've taken it.'

'Hmmm. I s'pose you could be right.' I purse my lips, look like I'm thinking hard on the subject in hand.

'I reckon someone's just trying to wind me up by getting at Natalie, trying to stir up trouble. They're hoping to get me to drop out of the scam, isolating me from the rest of the boys.'

'Who would do such a thing?' I ask.

'I dunno, Dame,' Benny says, shrugs his shoulders. 'I really don't know. I've already told Five about this hassle with Natalie – she's been getting phone calls as well. I reckon one of the boys has just got cold feet and doesn't want in any more. Whoever it is thinks he can get me to drop out first, thus clearing the way for him to step down too. I just can't think of any other explanation. I mean, I haven't done anything to upset anyone, have I?'

'Haven't you?' I ask Benny in tender flowery tones, but deliver him a stone-cold look packed with the ongoing momentum of a renegade juggernaut, to which – typically – he appears oblivious.

'Nah, not me. Who could I have possibly hurt?' he reflects innocently.

'Well, Benny,' I start calmly, 'maybe you *should* drop out and save yourself any further hassle.'

'Yeah, I have been giving it some thought,' he sighs. 'I mean, if you can't trust your mates, then who *can* you trust? And there's a lot at stake here, with all those Es and that.' Benny draws a Marlboro from a packet in his top pocket and stops to consider the two fat secretarial types still clacking away at a table somewhere behind me.

'So-o-o, do you think you'll drop out, then?' I ask him pointedly.

'Someone is gonna end up marrying one of those two some day,' Benny mentions bemusedly, then stops to focus on lighting his cigarette.

'Benny?' I prompt him.

'Oh, what?' he says, snapping back to reality. 'Yeah, but . . . then again.' Benny pauses, stares down at his trouser leg, then licks at the corner of his napkin and wipes something from his thigh.

'Then again . . . what?' I ask, put my hands together, interlocking my fingers, wait in anticipation for Benny's certain reply.

'Oh, nothing. It's probably not one of the boys, anyway. Whoever it is can just go to hell,' Benny sighs, looks up at me. 'I still want in on the scam.'

'But . . . eh?' I ask, rock back in my seat, flabbergasted.

'But nothing, Dame,' Benny tells me, pats my hand. 'No one's gonna isolate me from my mates and this E deal. Fuck the git who's trying to muddy the waters.'

'But, Benny . . .' I'm crying.

'But, nothing,' he returns reassuringly. 'Talking to

you has helped put my mind at ease. Thanks, Dame. You're a real mate, you know that?'

'But . . .' is all I can manage again, as one of the fat secretarial types heehaws hysterically in the blindspot past my left shoulder.

My mother phones. 'So,' she says, 'your brother tells me you've got a new lady-friend in your life. Is that right, Damian?'

'Yes, mother. Elizabeth . . . er, Beth for short.'

'So, is this it, then?' my mother asks.

I'm nearly taken aback by such a bizarre intrusion. 'Um, no, I don't know.' Pause. 'It's early days yet.' Pause. 'We get on okay, though.'

'Good. That's good,' my mother says. 'Is she a sensible girl, Damian?'

More inane questioning. 'Er, yeah, I guess so.'

'Good, good. I was going to light a candle for both you and Joanna when I heard that you'd split up, but there's really no need now that you've found yourself another nice girl so quickly.'

'How is the church, mother?' I ask, rather abruptly, steering the conversation away from the unpalatable subject at hand.

'The church is fine. Father O'Shaughnessy is ill at present, so we have a temporary priest in for the time being – Father Anthony.' She pronounces the 'th' in Anthony as you would the 'th' in anthem. 'He's a nice young man, but he's a bit too modern for my tastes. He has some funny ideas about religion, but he's a pleasant young man all the same.'

'Um, yeah. Nice.' I'm trying to remember just how old my mother is – is she fifty this year or next? She seems to have aged so much of late, she may as well be in her eighties. I start humming Wagner's 'Ride of the Valkyries' somewhere in the back of my mindscape. This month's picture in my Anna Nicole Smith calendar features Anna lying fully naked on her front, draped in this huge black feather boa, in the middle of a godforsaken salt-flat somewhere, and she's dripping in heavy jewellery, her nails a luxurious tomato-red, her bare rump in ample evidence, sinfully tasty. I cannot quite fathom what she might be saying to me in said shot, but I think if I'd have been there in the flesh she would perhaps be making ready to crawl her way towards me, her gaze unblinking, actually thriving on my confusion as to her proximate motives – i.e. is she going to let me fuck her or isn't she?

'To tell you the truth, Damian,' my mother is saying. 'I'm a bit concerned about your uncle Noel.'

'Yeah? What's he been up to now?' My uncle Noel is an alcoholic (we think) and is three-times divorced and has a son Leon – so called because his name spells Noel backwards. Under normal circumstances I'd probably be quite endeared to my uncle, as he is what most may regard as a bit of a 'character', but, as is my reality, I simply cannot bring myself to stomach the barbarous way he insists on taking advantage of my propitious mother. In many respects he very near rivals my father in those particular stakes. Some may revere these pair as scamps, scallywags or just loveable rogues, but to me they represent nothing of a higher living order than toxicant scum.

'Well, Noel's living in a hostel, somewhere out near Bedford, and just last week he walked into his room – he has to share a room with three others – he walked into his room to find this young man, younger than you I think, injecting drugs straight into his eyeball with a syringe.'

'Ugh, that's gross.'

After a pause, my mother sighs and says, 'I suppose you come across that kind of thing all the time, what with living in London.'

'Um, not really,' I say – throw my head back and mouth the word 'What?!' at the ceiling.

'Well, anyway, I'm thinking of asking Noel to stop here with me for a while – just until he gets himself straightened out.'

'Noel can look after himself,' I state inflexibly, knowing full well that Noel would never leave once he got his foot in the door, and that it'd be down to me or Ray or perhaps even my father (though I doubt it), to set him going on his way once again.

'But the house is so empty since your father left and, besides, Noel should be back home near his family.'

'Famil-ies,' I mutter.

'What was that, Damian?'

'Nothing. Noel can look after himself.'

'But he's my brother. If I can't help him, who *can* I help?'

'Noel can look after himself,' I tell her one final time.

After a while my mother says, 'I hear your father and Gillian are expecting another child.'

'Er, yeah,' I say and wonder who's told her. Why hadn't she mentioned this earlier?

'Do you ever see your half-sister?' my mother is asking.

'Um, no. I've only met her the once, and that was over a year ago.'

'Cassie, isn't it? She'd be nearly two now, wouldn't she?'

'Yeah, I s'pose.'

'And Gillian . . .' my mother begins. 'How old is she?' She says this in a voice which implies she already knows Gillian's age, but that it's slipped her mindscape for an instant.

'Gillian? Oh, um, early thirties I think.' Gillian was in the year below me at school – she's twenty-three, maybe twenty-four.

'Oh,' is all my mother says, and something in her tone suggests I'm lying.

'Look, I'm going to have to rush now. I'm due round Beth's, er, I mean Elizabeth's, in an hour or so.'

'Okay, son. Will I be seeing you home soon?'

'Er, I'm busy for the next few weekends,' I say. 'So, er, maybe I'll pop up one night midweek.'

I sense the dejection in the wooden silence that skulks

between us, and I'm staring at Thom's car keys sitting atop the television when my mother finally says, 'Okay, then. God bless you, son.'

I respond with a hearty, 'Yeah, bye-bye,' then whisper, 'I love you,' once I hear the line crackle dead.

And I'm still staring at Thom's car keys.

'I don't believe you sometimes, Dame,' Thom quibbles and slams back in his seat, his arms folded taut. We're sat upstairs in the middle bar of Turnmills, at The Gallery: me and Thom and Lisa and Beth. This was a last-gasp junket inaugurated after Thom and Lisa and I had demolished twelve cans of Kronenbourg and two grams of coke back at the flat, then had decided to venture out to unearth some momentous action. Try as I might, I couldn't get hold of Jay or Matt or Five, all of whom had answering machines switched on and mobiles powered off, so instead I'd opted to phone Beth to avoid playing the surrogate gooseberry with Thom and his keeper. The blonde on the door was good enough to let Beth slip in with us in the members' queue – Beth has never been to Turnmills before (she's never been anywhere), nor even heard of it.

'Go on then,' I tease Thom before taking a deliberated sip of water. 'Name one good George Michael track.'

Thom leans forward, then throws himself back in his chair once again. 'Right,' he starts: ' "Freedom" . . . "Fast Love" . . . "Faith".'

'Lots of Fs', I mention, then joke glibly, ' "Fist-fucking", per chance?'

' "I Want Your Sex",' Lisa adds.

'I bet you do,' I snicker and raise an eyebrow.

'All classics,' Thom quips.

'Never heard of them,' I lie, then re-raise my bottle to my lips.

'Damian, be reasonable,' Beth sighs to my right, as she toys with her bottle of Hooch.

'Dame always could be quite irrational,' Lisa quips. 'Especially during our time back at uni.' Lisa then winks theatrically in my direction and, sensing myself blush crimson, I just bluster back into the debate with, 'George Michael is crap. You can say what you will about Andrew Ridgley, but Wham made far superior tunes.'

'Bollocks,' Thom moans. 'Wham were good, but George is God.'

' "Club Tropicana",' I assert, recounting off one finger. ' "Wake me up before you go go" . . . "White Christmas".' I count off a second then a third finger. 'Brilliant pop tunes.'

'Nah, nah, I have to disagree,' Thom says, shaking his head. There are four young things – three blonde, one unblonde, all four dressed in black – sat two tables away from us, none of whom looks a day over sixteen although it's possibly just the onset of ecstasy that's hazing my immediate vision and bestowing the world with that greener, fresher outlook and, though I cannot quite ascertain any of their heights, one of the blondes looks tall or at least has a very elongated back, but then she might just possess stumpy dwarf legs, cancelling out her obvious advantage. Either way, I suddenly wish Beth was not here, as I want to head over to their table to join them, bathe in their uncharted dialogue. Nevertheless, I opt to continue my current point. 'Paul . . . Weller,' I declare.

'Oi! I like Paul Weller,' Lisa starts, snaps her fingers at me.

'Yeah, I know . . . I remember,' I concede, and unwittingly catch her eye. 'But . . . Paul Weller is crap.'

Lisa snaps her fingers again. 'Stop . . . right . . . there, Dame.'

'Alright, maybe not crap, as such, but The Jam were infinitely better. They even had, like, four number ones or something.'

'A Town Called Malice, ooh-yeah,' Thom semi-sings.

'So, Dame,' Lisa starts, snatches her breath as Thom continues to croon, badly. 'Shut up, Thom,' she smarts. Thom shuts up. 'So, Dame, you're saying that The Jam are better than Paul Weller just because they sold more singles?'

'Erm, yeah,' I accede without thinking.

'So, what you're saying is . . .' Lisa stalls dramatically, 'that the Spice Girls are better than New Order?'

'Er, no.'

'By your definition – Dame – the Spice Girls are better than New Order.'

'No.'

'Yes, they are. The Spice Girls are better than New Order simply because they sell more records.'

'No,' I splutter. 'That wasn't what I said.'

'Well, what were you trying to say, then?'

'Just that Paul Weller is crap,' I return quickly, strangle a quick chortle from Thom and Beth in a nugatory attempt to give myself breathing space, thinking time. 'And, erm, you know, to say that you shouldn't break a winning team no matter how bizarre the combination?' I actually lock eyes with Lisa once again, time-honoured barricades of self-preservation slowly corroding, as Beth reaches to take a solacing grip on my hand. Beth probably thinks I've said something dead romantic and abstruse – I hope Lisa's mindscape isn't administering similar syllabi.

'Bit like New Order, eh?' Thom queries me.

'Exactly,' I return to him. 'New Order? – metaphysical. The constituent parts of New Order? – pap. The Other Two had a few quirky tunes, Monaco show promise, but sound too much like Oasis in places, and as for Electronic—'

'Yes,' Lisa apes me: 'And as for Electronic . . .'

'And, as for Electronic,' I continue, tranquil, 'Electronic made one seminal album close on six years ago.'

'Yeah, don't I just remember?' Lisa soughs. 'You played that bloody thing to death in our first year at uni.'

'Hush, Lisa,' I contend respectfully, and raise my hand as if to placate her. 'But their second album was

94

probably the singularly worst record I've ever bought in my entire life.'

'Never thought I'd ever hear you say that about Bernard Sumner, Dame,' Thom comments.

'So, this winning combination stuff . . .' Lisa starts, pointedly. 'You wouldn't have anyone in mind though, would you, Dame? For your winning combination, that is.'

There's this redoubtable silence where Lisa and I glower across the tabletop like two case-hardened pugilists sizing up for one final death-match where victory delivers all and defeat can bring only indignity and opprobrium, but then Thom relieves the pressure, splicing the air with an unhurried, 'Dame's just talking bollocks, anyway.'

'Alright, then,' I pipe up. 'Take Sting.'

'I wish you would,' Lisa quips.

'Hey, I like Sting,' Beth moans.

'Look, as I was saying . . . take Sting.'

'Don't tell us,' Lisa interjects. 'Sting – crap. The Police – brilliant.'

'Exactly,' I tell the table, and we all laugh.

We demolish another round of waters and Beth has another Hooch, then we make our way down the stairs and through the throng to take up a spot by the furthest bar, sited at the back of the first dancefloor. The furthest dancefloor isn't open tonight; I've only ever seen it in use when Oakenfold's been DJ-ing here. Beth is finally persuaded onto the mineral water, and I tell her she's a good girl for doing so.

'I should be able to drink a little more,' she complains.

'Not if we ain't going home for another six hours,' I tell her. 'I don't want you falling asleep at three.'

We don't talk much, the four of us trance-dancing in a line, squaring up to the overhead laser. Two boys squat by us, against the back wall, use a pencil torch to aid their deliberated skinning up, illuminating the pair for all to see.

'Bit obvious,' Thom mouths, motioning towards them.

I sigh, mouth back, 'Too dark to skin up otherwise.'

The sixteen-year-old things I spied earlier are now dancing just a short distance before us. One of them – the one with the elongated back – is indeed really tall, has such substantial tits but has a fat arse to match, with staunch thighs hovering beneath her like huge cold cartoon hams, yet oddly these only serve to fortify the erection I already sense cloying with blood down below. The sixteen-year-old has blonde hair scraped tightly from her face, looks really clubby, is apparelled head to toe in handsome black garb: tight lycra top, a pair of ballooning satin shorts and regulation kinky boots. I just catch myself murmuring, 'The . . . tits . . . on . . . that.' But she's too young, pure jail-bait. I catch her eye through the smoke and smile. I think I would like to fuck her tonight – I'm galvanized by the simple sight of her. I am rapidly growing tired of Beth proffered up as some object of desire. The jail-bait looks past me to

Beth, but Beth is looking up at the laser-lights. I would kill to embark on a sexual marathon with this jail-bait tonight. I catch her eye again and this time she smiles – openly. Or at least I think she does – it is dark in here and my senses are slightly nonplussed. Then again, everyone smiles at everyone else in here; it's a good atmosphere, a happy place to be. I find myself wishing that Beth would crawl under a rock and die.

Beth digs me in the ribs, shouts in my ear, 'Are you alright, sugar? You look miles away.'

I'm smiling to myself. 'I'm fine – just fine, sweetheart,' I mouth.

Dancing my way slowly through the crowd, I play at catching the jail-bait's eye once again, but she's too engrossed in her friends and the lights to notice me any more. I remove my Lacoste top and tuck it in the back of my jeans, probably looking like some prized cockerel (or is that just cock?) on heat, all chest-thrusting and swagger, pumping at the hot air with my groin. I'm daydreaming, visualizing this blonde nonchalantly making her way over to me, her telling me she's aware that I'm with someone tonight, but stopping to take my phone number to call me later in the week. I return to the fold and cadge a cigarette off Thom – the jail-bait is smoking heavily and I want her to see that I can smoke too, that I'm not some whinging retard who might take offence at her nicotine addiction. Lisa's moved off, right to the centre of the dancefloor, where the overhead laser dips and slices her at neck-height like some huge luminous guillotine. Even Beth is swaying to the clunk-ing groove that envelopes us. The Gallery is beginning to take off.

'See that thing at the bar,' Thom shouts close by, right into my ear, and points out this petite unblonde, not three metres away, wearing a T-shirt which says BITCH ON HEAT. 'She's got great lips – just like an ex, that Beverley Larsson. Ohmygod, did you see her smile just then? Perfect blowjob mouth.'

'Yeah, and her mate's got a bit of height on her,' I'm shouting back above the din of something I recognize off Trade's second compilation. 'Beth,' I holler, tugging the back of her shirt to gain her attention. 'Be a good girl and trot along to find someone your own height to play with – me and Thom want to chat those two up.'

Beth laughs, mouths something at me which I can't quite decipher.

I head for the men's toilets, up the stairs by the club's entrance. Both the cubicles are locked so I wash my hands and study my face in the mirror set high above the basins – I appear pasty, my eyes bloodshot and underlined by heavy dark shadows. My chest is glittering with damp sweat. In the back of my jeans I have tucked this navy Lacoste polo shirt I borrowed from Jo's father some time ago, and, down in the cloakroom there's my heavy black leather jacket which Jo bought me two Christmases back (well, went halves on with me, as it cost close on four hundred notes). Jo used to love The Gallery, our nights spent cavorting to a hard-house diet. This big shaven-headed geezer joins me, stands wiping perspiration baubles from his extended forehead. He's dressed in nothing more than a pair of cut-off jean-shorts and huge purple DMs and he appears to have more hair sprouting throughout his back, curled thick like wirewool, than he does across his proud chest.

'You're here on the wrong night,' I rib him.

'What?' he asks, catching my reflection in the mirror.

'Trade's tomorrow,' I tell his image.

'Ooh, bollocks to that,' he giggles and blows my mirrored self a kiss. 'I fucking hate poofs.' And with that he squeezes my side then disappears back toward the noise.

This huge mean-looking black geezer vacates the left toilet cubicle. I enter it quickly and, after locking the door behind me, retrieve a wrap of coke from my back pocket and hastily devour what I consider to be three lines' worth. I've already taken a little acid, just this half strawberry I had left over from that eighties' theme party, but as yet it's having no effect on me. A half tab should do the trick, though – it was fairly lethal gear from what (little) I can remember of the night in Brixton. I then stand and toy with this huge red disk of a pill I've been saving for months in an open condom wrapper tucked neatly in my wallet. Another strawberry, funnily enough. But this time ketamine – the ultimate in stupid fucked-up cartoon highs. And I really want to get fucked up tonight.

I am with Thom and Beth again – they are talking at me but I cannot decipher what they are saying above the musical blitz. Thom points past me towards the bar, and I turn to catch sight of Jay engulfed in an entourage of geeky-looking geezers. He is laughing, and is cloaked by an oversized Burberry check shirt.

'He picked up your message on his answering machine,' Thom shouts. 'Brought his workmates down here for a laugh. Had to borrow one of their shirts.'

'Looks like he's wearing a fucking tent,' I think I am telling him. I stare at Jay for an age, trying to concentrate on his features, but I decide against going over and saying anything – I'm slightly wired: the ketamine and the acid are starting to kick in. Anything I say now will doubtless emanate under the guise of inane gibberish.

Beth buys me another water, which I don't really want, and I spill most of it on the floor as this top tune called 'Schoneberg' swoons in and I escape back towards the centre of the dancefloor, shrouded inside a veil of dry ice. I lose sight of Thom and Beth – I'm forsaken beneath a deluge of possessed dancers. Swarms of killer beats drone past, and the colours emanating from the overhead laser-lights turn purple then orange then fuse then rupture then interfuse again before my very eyes. And I'm wondering what time it could possibly be. Whether it's close on two o'clock yet: The Gallery's routine crossover time for the DJs. It's always the same here; two o'clock then four o'clock then six – the beats stay hard and pumping but the style just slightly switches. You hardly ever notice the changeovers; it's all done with pre-eminent subtlety. Some DJs take their entrance with a stonking opener, some like to build up sublimely, but for the untrained observer it all proceeds so seamlessly. It's Tall Paul due up for the next slot.

I love following the sets, just shut my eyes in my somniferous state, wondering what track's due next on the turntables. Wishing I was up there like some Messiah controlling the crowds. It's like being a kid again in a time when my brother was slim and respected, and when he bought all these New Order bootlegs and we'd sit there in our shared bedroom, him lying prostrate on the floor, arms folded serenely behind his head; me in my corner, hunched up, crouched forward, swaying to Hooky's bass, willing the current track out of the stereo, desperate for it to finish, to unearth the next track in their set, then the next, then the next beyond that. I lived some of the great gigs through the bootleggers' recording equipment: that miner's benefit at the Festival Hall with the 'Decades' encore, my brother telling me it had been such a solemn affair, audience wise, until it got to the encores. But to me it all sounded so perfect, me soaking up the tracks there in our bedroom, living the dream.

I remember Ray going to see New Order at the old Town and Country one Saturday, not returning till early next day 'cos the band had come on late and he'd missed the last train home, left twiddling his thumbs on the platform at Kentish Town station till a milk train pulled through. Then him seeing them at the Royal Albert the Monday night, deciding to leave home late, then missing the first four tracks 'cos they'd gone on early that time. I was just too young in those days: my mother not letting me near any of the venues. Ray was lucky: he was twenty. He was my eyes at those gigs, the bootlegs my ears.

This small unblonde thing in a yellow vest, sopping with sweat, asks me if I've 'got any spare Es' and, though I hear her query first time, I still have to ask her, 'Sorry?' and when she repeats the enquiry, I answer 'Sorry,' again, this time apologetically and I shrug my shoulders. She taps my side, as if in consolement, and her hand feels icy, and then she's away, lost through the crowd, head-swimming her way in hyperspace. I'm glued to the spot, making small jerky arm movements like I'm aerobicizing with free weights or something, and then I'm performing more pronounced motions, like some spasticated oarsman, rowing hard but getting nowhere. I can feel the ketamine taking a stranglehold – I'm trying hard to steady my breathing, keeping focused on my X and Y axis, making sure I can determine my left from my right from my up from my down, a Disney cartoonland now unfolding before me. Something by the X-Cabs is unleashed on the crowd and the dance-floor swells tenfold at the familiarity of good hard teutonic trance. This is what we're all here for, the fare we so desire. I'm trying hard to steady my breathing, keeping focused on my X and Y axis, fighting the ataxia, making sure I can determine my left from my right from my up from my down, a Disney cartoonland now unfolding before me. I wish Jo was with me; I do not enjoy the unknown, dancing with strangers. I don't want to be sharing this with outsiders right now. My head jerks involuntarily – or at least I think it does.

I shut my eyes and my feet keep missing beats. It's the ketamine fracturing my senses, undoing cerebral doors to my past and my future. As if seized by some bizarre flashback, my mindscape's enrapturing me to another era, to a parallel feast of bright-lights, narcotics and chugging beatscapes, to a holiday Jo and I took to Goa last January, and we're at this huge rave on Vagator Beach in the small hours of the morning and we're wasted on white doves and this weird acid which came from a huge blotting-paper map of the world which this dealer, some French geezer, said he'd picked up in Amsterdam, and we're sharing an amyl bottle to bring on our rushes, and Jo's dressed in really vivid colours which only serve to accentuate her contours and she has this luminous orange dot on her forehead and a yellow stripe across her nose which combine to make her look like some kind of Krishna follower, and I'm wearing an old white New Order T-shirt which appears fluorescent under the lighting and these black jeans shorts and my Timberland boots which are caked in red dust, and this is our last rave of the holiday, our seventh in three weeks, and my left knee is playing me up, keeps jarring, but otherwise I've never felt leaner or fitter before in my entire life and there's not one ounce of spare flesh on my jaw or my throat or my shoulders or my stomach and we've seen Richard Gere in Tito's bar in Baga and Jo was unable to take her eyes off him (*An Officer and a Gentleman* is, sadly, her all-time favourite film) and we saw George Harrison at Anjuna Market and when I pointed him out to Jo she just said 'George who?' and when I said he was in The Beatles she just asked, 'Which one was he – Ringo?' but I still loved her all the more for it, and we found this small chapel in Nehrul where Jo said she wanted us to marry one day and we tried the water-skiing up at Fort Aguada and I couldn't even get out of the water yet Jo was a real natural, and we spent our last week there hanging out with these two old hommes from Croydon and I wish I'd taken more photos and I just want to remain for ever, here with Jo, with the mad Italians and Israelis with their heads right up in the speakers, and all the hard trance tracks and I really don't want to come back to a luckless reality.

I discover myself dancing to something off Oaken-fold's last Essential Mix on Radio One, this hardbag thing that made the charts recently, dancing, bug-eyed, near that blonde jail-bait again, inching myself ever closer, thinking I want to fuck you hard tonight, sweet-heart, bury my head between your nutcracker thighs. I'm whirling around like a dervish, lost in the epicentre of my own little universe, wailing like a loon, moaning to myself (or is this all in my mindscape?). Some oldish geezer with a hairline like a Rhesus monkey beams up at me, asks me if I'm 'having a good time?' and he looks so supremely happy, like this is the greatest single day of his existence, and then his mate pushes through the crowd behind him, informs me, 'It's his first time, mate!' and I acknowledge his comment with a smile and suddenly nothing seems to make sense. *Why must my memory be so good where you're concerned, Jo? Do you not remember any of what passed between us? Those passions? Our emotions? The stark beauty of the way we once were?*

Then Beth's pinching my side – the ketamine's still controlling, but I'm starting to feel a tiny bit anxious. *I guess I'm just missing you, Jo – you sneak past my defences, interfere with my emotions, send me careering into a neurotic tailspin just when I'm least expecting it.*

We linger at the first bar a short while – Beth back on Hooch, me now on full-sugar Cola, the liquid fizzing past my teeth. Two topless bi-boys, close-cropped hair and tanned torsos, cavort together like glistening reptiles drawn to a slamming trance snake-charmer. A solid blonde in fluffy bra and grey satin shorts, near spray-painted on, dances before us, lurches her arms like trying to guide an oncoming plane in to land. I sense all eyes fondling her semi-naked body, but she's oblivious to this unspoken worship, her own eyes agog, fixed above all our heads, taking her guidance from the optics across the bar, and the invisible plane preparing to crashland through the ceiling.

And I'm thinking about Peter Hook from New Order, and how the last time I saw him was at an ACR gig in the Subterannia, years back, where he was wearing a long beige trenchcoat, and Thom thought he looked like Eric Clapton and he was with this waif: young and sexy, but nowhere near voluptuous enough for my tastes. And how the last time I spoke to Hooky was at this Robs Records party in the SW1 club years back, when ACR and Sub Sub were playing short sets, around the time Factory Records went bust, maybe six months before *Republic* was released and I was E'd up, kept asking him how the new album was going and he kept telling me that he was 'looking after it for me', and I told him that I'd actually had a New Order tattoo done on my right shoulder – which was and still is an arrant lie.

The jail-bait is leant against a pillar before us, her friends mooching around in close attendance, looking lost like they cannot decide upon their next course of action. Dance a little more? Perhaps buy themselves some alcohol? A Hooch, a Bud or a Stella? Maybe do a little charlie, or head off to catch Danny Rampling's set down the Ministry? Maybe make their way upstairs to the Electronica bar, buying some tea or coffee on the way up so as to smooth down the taste of the bittersweet hash they've smuggled in to smoke? I cannot catch the jail-bait's eye. The jail-bait has such burly thighs, they appear to coalesce into one single solid mass. I would maybe like to fuck her hard against the pillar, push my way between her sturdy thighs, maybe fuck her in just her kinky boots, our bodies shifting in time to the heavy backdrop pulsing all around. Only a maybe, though – this thing is not Jo. Three big black geezers in tight ribbed T-shirts and varying shades of off-white jeans, exchange money and banter and sideways glances. The shortest of the three catches my absent gaze and smiles at me. Involuntarily, I return an inane grin and mouth 'Alright, mate?' in his direction. Beth wants to leave; it's only just gone four. I comply; life is so completely indigestible without you, Jo. I head off to give Jay and Thom farewell hugs, but cannot find Lisa to bid my goodbyes to.

Beth and I catch a taxi, some newly beached African piloting a perilous death-trap. I fall asleep in the car, seeking comfort in some unfathomable dreamscape, categorically at odds with all my senses.

I don't register anything further of purport until early next afternoon when Beth jostles me awake and giggles and asks me, 'Damian, have you changed to a new shaving gel?'

'Er, yeah,' I tell her, my mindscape unsettled, my voice discordant. 'Yeah, I think so. Why?'

'Well, I thought you'd just got a new deodorant,' Beth announces and raises her left arm to reveal a greenish glob of gel squelched into her armpit. 'Silly me,' she chirps ingenuously.

I regard her blankly for a split second, a fondness lavishly sonorous within, then take Beth in my arms and make fierce love to her right there in my bed, the ecstasy still wetting my body prolonging the lovemaking for an hour or more, and for that short time everything in the world seems so equably close to interminable peace.

I'm in deepest suburbia, sitting in the Jolly Topers in Round Green with my father and my brother Ray, who is looking fatter than ever, like he's really going to seed. This pub used to be called the Toppers, but one of the 'p's got lost somewhere down the line – in a renovation or something. However, everyone I know still refers to it as the Top-pers, not the Toe-pers. This is Ray's local. Vexingly, my father has called me 'Henry' three times in the past two hours. Henry is my middle name, was my grandfather's Christian name, and my father had wanted me christened likewise. My father is drunk again.

My favourite film today is Russ Meyer's *SuperVixens* – admittedly, my favourite Meyer woman, Uschi Digard, is a total letdown in it (in *SuperVixens* you get to realize that she's actually quite short), but Shari Eubank in the lead role and Christy Hartburg as SuperLorna are just so totally voluptuous, sensuous, perfectly formed, that they more than compensate for Uschi's utter failings. It's just a crying shame you don't actually get to see Christy naked in said film but, whenever I think of her scene, dancing with her breasts straining to burst free of a flimsy red top, think of that naked midriff, the red kinky boots, white hot-pants, her hair tied up in girlie bunches like some twee rave cadet, looking so utterly clubby, I can most readily drift into alchera overtime, can muster up images of some equivalent creature gyrating her body to some nu-trance or hardbag down The Gallery or at Frisky, maybe the Fast Forward bar at Bagley's, some club, any club, I'll be happening by in the not-too-distant future.

'Hey, remember your old English teacher, boys?' my father is asking, his arm hung around the back of my chair. 'You know, that young fella at Stopsley . . . young, good-looking, lived just up the road from us. Went off with that tall girl who was in your year, Ray – oh, what was his name?'

'Er, I don't remember . . . Mr Turner, maybe?' Ray says, unsure.

'Mr Taylor,' I correct him, not looking up.

'That's right . . . that's right, son.' My father pats my right shoulder with his right hand, his left arm still hung behind me, and he leans on me a touch too heavily. 'Mr Taylor, that's right. Went off to London, yeah? With that tall girl in Ray's year, yeah?'

I don't answer him, just sit staring sullenly into my pint.

Ray answers for me. 'Yeah, Dad. Went off to London. That's right.'

'Well,' my father starts again, 'wait till you hear this . . . I'm in the flower shop – the one next-door – and I'm just buying some flowers for my lovely Gillian and . . . guess who should walk in, eh? C'mon . . . guess.' My father leans away from me.

'The Pope?' I offer and look up, staring straight ahead at Ray, who maybe mouths 'Humour him!' at me, then looks to my father and says, cheerily, 'Mr Taylor, right, Dad?'

'Mr Taylor . . . as large . . . as bloody life,' my father says, distracted, and I can sense him studying me, can just picture his face, that look I've seen so many times, that look of disdain he throws so well. I turn my head to face him but he just smiles at me, his steely-grey eyes almost smiling too.

'Yes, now where was I? Ah, yes, Mr Taylor.' My father turns his attention to Ray once more. 'Mr Taylor walks into the flower shop and he says hello to me and I'm thinking, I know this fella, but I can't quite place him and then, of course, I realize it's your old chemistry teacher, Mr Taylor. So, I'm stood next to him in the shop and I start to make polite conversation. I ask him if he's still living up in London and he says yes, and I ask him if he's still with that tall girl, the pretty one, and he says yes and then I ask him what he's doing back in Round Green and he says that he's visiting family.' My father stops to gulp his Guinness. 'Then I ask him if he's still teaching chemistry and he turns to me, and guess what he says? Go on, guess.' He wipes his mouth across the back of his sleeve.

'That he's back teaching at Stopsley?' Ray enquires.

'No. He says, "Sorry, mate, but I think you've mistaken me for someone else."'

A moment's silence, then I snap, 'And?'

Ray shoots me a nervous glance, then looks back to my father who says, seemingly oblivious to my outburst, 'And then I realized it wasn't Mr Taylor . . . It was Paul Young . . . Paul Young the bloody pop-star off the telly.'

'Wow,' Ray says, sounds like a little child.

I mimic him. 'Yeah . . . Wow.'

'Paul . . . bloody . . . Young . . . who'd have thought it, eh?' my father is saying, and I'm silently praying to heaven that Jo will be waiting for me when I finally return home tonight because I've never felt so alone and assailable in my life before.

Paul Young once covered Joy Division's 'Love Will Tear Us Apart'. My brother has seen New Order do 'Love Will Tear Us Apart' at five of its six UK airings to date; at Liverpool, Poole, Glasgow, the Hacienda and Wembley. I only caught the Wembley offering, Ray's attended so many more New Order gigs than me. Ray once took in five concerts in just seven days, in April 89, the early stages of the *Technique* tour, flying to Miami and the Knight Centre where Hooky teased the travelling English with, 'We've come 4,000 miles to get away from you bastards,' then heading on to St Petersburg, brawling with local youths down the front, then to Gainsville, gatecrashing *Animal House* frat parties, before embarking on a marathon road journey, much further afield, through strange Southern states to a gig in an Atlanta fun-park, finally rounding off a colossal week at the Saenger Theatre in the French quarter of New Orleans. I was just sixteen, I couldn't finance such a trip. How I resent this now. Ray travelled over with all the old New Order heads; diehard acid casuals, mostly hailing from the band's heartland in the North-West; the same respected faces I would run into abroad at festivals in Dublin and Germany and Denmark in 93, determined devotees still keeping the faith long after my brother deserted the cause. I've slotted neatly into Ray's wake. I deserve New Order so much more than my brother ever should, I'm the one who still truly cares, the one keeping our most precious memories alive.

*

I'm in an off-licence on Turnpike Lane. I'm going to visit Five and his woman, Rachel. I didn't plan on coming here tonight, but after a quick visit to Thomas Pink's on Jermyn Street I'd caught the Piccadilly Line home and, drifting off to sleep on the tube, I'd failed to register my stop at Finsbury Park so, once at Manor House, I elected to travel on to visit Five. It's a long time since I was last at his flat – with Jo, as I recall, a veritable lifetime ago.

I check out the chill cabinet, opt for a bottle of Evian. I must also buy some Rizlas and some cigarettes: there's a bag of weed stashed in my inside jacket pocket – a small sample, free, from Russell Bishop, the old homme at work. Pucka gear he said, check it out he said, there's plenty more where that came from. I'm sure Five'll be gagging for a good smoke.

Four Asian boys walk in, all small, stunted. They stop to study the proprietor, then me, then dismiss us and silently scan the shelves. One of them is wearing a beige Kangol flat-cap.

I put the Evian down on the counter. 'And ten Silk Cut, please. No, make that twenty. No, sorry, better just stick to ten.' I don't want to get too wasted tonight, as I have an eight o'clock meeting tomorrow – with my project manager, Hubert Dodd. 'And a packet of king-size Rizla papers as well.'

The proprietor, another Asian, casts me a knowing eye, and smiles.

As I turn to leave, the Kangol-cap kid slips a bottle of vodka inside his jacket. I make toward the door, then –

for some indeterminable reason – slowly turn to watch as the proprietor circles the counter, watch him bark something at the boys, something in a language I do not understand.

Kangol snaps back at him, and his friends join the affray. The proprietor motions towards Kangol's jacket, continues towards the four, flailing his arms, demonstrating his point. A punch is thrown, he takes it well, but a second dwarf swings, catches him high on the cheek. The proprietor stumbles to one side, loses his balance, only for an instant, but giving the bantam-weight bastards enough time to launch a full-scale assault on his person. He's knocked to the ground under a hail of indiscriminate blows, the four continuing to aim kicks at his head and his stomach. And, as he attempts to scrunch himself up into a tight ball, I just stand there watching, transfixed, hypnotized by the soap-opera unfolding before me. This is so unreal – like a low-grade B-movie.

Enter, stage-right, via the storeroom, a young elfin woman grasping a tiny baby to her chest. Upon seeing the fracas, said elfin woman begins to wail and shriek and shout, and the baby bursts into tears. I'm rooted to the spot, cannot accept that I'm here, that I actually exist in any of this. One of the four boys spits in the direction of the woman; she turns to look despairingly toward me – not at me, but through me. The boys grab more bottles then desert, leaving the proprietor and this woman sobbing mercilessly in their separate corners. Kangol halts, looks me full in the face and grins, his eyes searching my features for some indication of approval but my façade registers no outward emotion.

He leaves, I follow. Then, for some split analytic, with his little chumps away in the distance and with equable ground put between them and him and me, I swoop Kangol's limited legs from beneath him, dispatching him shattering full-tilt into brutal pavement, his paperweight body bouncing against concrete against bone against concrete, and struggling back to his feet he shoots me an incendiary glance and possibly offers me out, I'm not sure; I don't understand the idiom – but then he's away once more, scrambling up the road, me tracking his form with my requisite nothing smile.

I sense a vacuum. I'm not alarmed or shaken or even ashamed at ducking the bulk of this confrontation. The shop-owners will get over it in time. Their problems are minuscule in direct comparison to mine, mere drams in my emotional ocean. All I want is to mellow out, get stoned with Five. And, most importantly, I just want Jo back.

There's no answer at Five and Rachel's so I sit in their local, the Tollgate, and kill an hour drinking draught Kronenbourg, dissecting the *Evening Standard*. With still no answer from Five and Rachel's, I catch a black cab and travel to visit Matt and Jenny at their flat just off Crouch Hill, to discover that Toolboy's also paid the two a visit and is sitting, cross-legged, on their lounge carpet, wearing this T-shirt which reads WHAT DO YOU

WANT FROM ME? and he's busily skinning up as I arrive, so I persuade him to put my new weed to use, and, after a few generous spliffs, the general consensus attests that this gear really is as good as the Bishop predicted, and Toolboy asks me to score a quarter for him, telling me that he'll weigh me in after his next pay-day, which puzzles me just slightly because I know that Toolboy is loaded and always carries at least two hundred notes on him whenever we're out, but in this instance I comply and decide against pressing him for the money here and now. I inform the three of the off-licence altercation.

'Fucking Pakis,' Toolboy comments.

'Yeah, fucking cheese sarnies,' Matt adds.

'You can talk,' Toolboy says to Matt. 'You always went for a bit of dark at uni.'

'Stop it right now, you two,' Jenny interrupts. 'You don't mean it. Stop being so nasty, the pair of you.'

'Look, darling,' Toolboy condescends. 'I live next door to Hounslow, right. You got it easy up here; there's not so many of 'em about. Let them beat the shit out of each other if they want. Give 'em guns, then they can shoot each other. See if I give a flying fuck.'

Jenny's offended, looks to Matt for sympathy, but Matt's eyes remain glued to the television, so I comfort Jenny with a smile instead. I can't figure out why Toolboy comes out with such racist crap, especially seeing as how Jinxy John's his best friend. I fear Toolboy's been drifting away from our little assembly of late, been squandering too much of his time with work and his old friends out west, not hazarding into town as often as I'd like to see, just taking the easy option, ageing speedily in his local amongst the assembled old duffers and suburbanites. I presume we were correct to see him blackballed from our scam, which is a blight on both our friendships that it came to such an ignoble resolution. I cannot but feel I've maybe let him down somewhere, someway.

We're all sitting in silence and watching *Brookside*, and during the adverts Toolboy offers Jenny first toke on this titanic spliff he's built. 'A pipe of peace,' he advises her.

'Toolboy, you know I don't smoke,' Jenny maintains as several grass seeds sputter 'Tsssch' within the flaring embers of the mutant spliff.

'Well, it's about time you fucking learned,' Toolboy remarks neutrally, and Jenny looks to Matt once again, but Matt is too monopolized by the adverts to notice.

I'm just sitting here, insouciantly stoned, soaking up gliding lo-fi rushes, fantasizing about Jo's elegant hands and her long luxuriant fingernails painted a delirious scarlet. On Matt and Jenny's sideboard they've proudly displayed Matt's copy of our eulogized holiday shot outside Lineker's Bar last year, all the boys looking tanned and happy, lined up before a billboard which reads THANKS FOR YOUR VISIT, SEE YOU SOON.

Later, like five more spliffs later, Toolboy offers me a lift home, but I'm not nearly wasted enough to leave so I decline his offer and Jenny asks me if I've heard from Joanna and I tell her that I spoke to her only yesterday – but I'm lying. I'm still living in the hope that Jo is missing the sound of my voice, that she'll maybe come to her senses and forgive me, that she'll take the initiative to phone sometime soon.

For some unfathomable reason, but most probably because he's stoned, Matt tells me how bad he still feels for hitting Gerry in a row at university almost four years ago, and how he feels that it's ruined their relationship ever since because they were really close before, and he asks me if Gerry ever mentions the incident, and I tell him that he doesn't – and I'm telling the truth. Matt says he tried to talk to Gerry a couple of weeks back to help him confront his hang-ups about his ex, Andrea, but he says that Gerry just shrugged off the whole thing, said that he honestly didn't care one way or the other. I tell Matt that this is just the way Gerry is with everyone, that Matt shouldn't take it personally.

After Jenny retires to revise for some exam, I ask Matt how things are between them and he tells me things are better than ever, that he cannot keep pace with Jenny in bed. I tell Matt that I'm glad for him, and I wonder if I should maybe inform him that Jenny had confided in Jo, telling her she was unhappy in London and wanted to return to the north, and that she'd had a brief affair with someone at work and wasn't sure that Matt was the right man for her any more, but I decide against saying anything, figuring that Jenny may have since changed the way she feels, or that maybe Jo was just lying in the first place, though I seriously doubt it's the latter.

Matt then tells me I'm so-o-o lucky to have found a

girl like Beth but I attempt to cut short this conversation, start talking about Gerry and Andrea again, whittle on about Mike's E scam, try to expand on Gerry and Matt's disagreement ... but Matt is relentless, absolutely unstoppable, and a bone-chilling shroud of despair collapses around me, my heart sinks and vast oceans run dry as Matt liquidates six long auspicious years of unquestionable friendship with, 'Just forget about Joanna, Dame – she's all in the past. You'll probably never see her again, anyway . . .'

I'm lingering with Tyler outside Tower Records, Piccadilly. Jay's still inside, trying to sort a present for his mother's birthday.

'Do you like my new specs?' Tyler is asking me.

'They're okay,' I tell him, though in all honesty his last pair looked maximally better. These make him look stupid, a little too round in the face, but then what do I really care?

'That's good, I was worried they made my face look fat,' Tyler says, doesn't seem sure of himself.

'No, no – they look fine,' I lie to him.

'That's good,' Tyler utters, hesitates, draws breath between his teeth, then drops his bombshell. 'Look, Dame, call me a cunt if you want, but I think I'm gonna drop out of the scam.'

'You're a cunt,' I tell Tyler politely, my eyes following this clubby blonde's legs, endless like Dali's elephants, as she traverses the road, her skirt hitched so high I can very nearly see what she'd had for breakfast.

'Dame,' Tyler pules, 'this ain't a joke, honey-child. I'm serious.'

'Me, too,' I tell him with ineffable sunniness. 'I think you're a cunt, Tyler.'

'Dame,' Tyler whines again.

'Why, then? Is it the money: is that why you want out?'

'No, I can do the overtime to get that. No, it's just—'

'Just what?' I sort of simper.

'It's just . . . oh, you'll probably think I'm just paranoid.'

'And?'

Tyler hands me this wrinkled tea-stained envelope. His disrespect for all cleanliness nauseates me, but I still sense an electric tingle as I welcome this proverbial spanner in the works.

'What's this?' I ask.

'You'd better open it,' Tyler says, runs his fingers through his hair and realigns his ugly glasses once again.

I look at him for a moment too long, like I really can't be bothered to open the envelope, then I retrieve this photocopied composition of Tyler's head pasted onto the body of a kneeling footballer – a picture you might have found in *Shoot* or something. Jo always said I thought more of my friends than I ever did of her. If only she could see me now. She'd be so incomparably proud. On our way out this morning, Thom gave me this photograph of Jo and me which I'd not previously seen before, this one he'd taken maybe a couple of weeks prior to our break-up, after we'd all been out for a bracing post-club trek over Highgate Woods, and I look quite pissed – or is that stoned? – and Jo is wearing this white ski-hat with an Italian flag sewn into it and an Irish Tricolour and the name of her favourite footballer, ENRICO ANNONI, and she looks so fulfilled and we look phenomenally close, but I just felt so unhappy to finally see this picture, yet Thom seemed quite understanding about my grief and I'm not really sure how to judge him nowadays.

'I think someone's trying to stir up trouble,' Tyler is telling me.

'Who?' I ask, then suggest, 'Could it be Benny?'

'Eh? . . . Er, no,' Tyler says, looks confused. 'Benny's the last I'd suspect. Oh, after you of course, Dame. No, well, I originally thought it was one of the others.'

'The . . . others?'

'Yeah, the others,' Tyler says, then confides, 'the honey-children in on the scam.'

'What makes you think that?' I ask him. If I freeze-frame the urban view before me, could capture my proximate vision on canvas, compassing Lillywhite's to the right, straight through Eros, any loafing tourists and rent-boys, then take the Gap as my left-hand border, I still only estimate that four, possibly five, blondes would be captured before me in this single moment, none of whom probably stand little more than five six, maybe seven. Jo has no rivals in Piccadilly today, no one of Meyer proportions.

Tyler still continues, the majority of his nebulous words lost to white noise. 'Well, look at this picture. That's the body of my hero, Trevor Brooking; and that haircut, it's far too short – it's like I had it back in uni.'

I glance at the picture and tut to myself. 'Hmmm, you could be right.'

'I think someone's trying to scare me,' Tyler says. 'Hoping I'll drop out of the scam.'

'Who would do such a thing?' I ask. 'It's all a bit cloak and dagger.'

'Thom,' Tyler says. 'I think he might know something.'

'Er, eh – why Thom?' I ask, perplexed.

'I reckon he's found out about the scam, and he's trying to break it up 'cos he's not included. And now Brooking's gone missing, as well. I dunno where he is.'

'Brooking, eh? When was this?'

'A couple of weeks back. I mean, he's gone missing for ages before, but this time my next-door neighbour – this old bird with bad breath – thinks she might remember seeing Brooking being ushered into a big blue car parked right outside my flat.'

'R-r-really?' I ask, almost panic for a second.

'And Thom's got that company car – that navy BMW.'

'Thom wouldn't do such a thing . . . surely?'

'No, you're probably right,' Tyler sighs. 'I know Thom isn't usually malicious like that but, I mean, you and him had that run-in and, er . . . well, I'm more concerned for Brooking than anything else. I just hope he turns up soon.'

'Yeah. Look, I'm really sorry about Brooking, but maybe you should drop out if you're not entirely sure . . . I'll square everything with the boys. They'll understand.'

'I have been thinking about it, and if you can't trust your mates, Dame, then who can you trust? And this E scam is a pretty serious affair.'

'So-o-o, you gonna drop out, then?'

'Mind you,' Tyler says.

'Mind you . . . what?' I ask, smooth down my tie and wait in anticipation for Tyler's reply.

'Oh, nothing,' Tyler says and purses his lips. 'I'm still in.'

'But . . . eh?' I ask, stand with my mouth agape, shellshocked.

'But nothing, Dame,' Tyler tells me. 'No one's gonna isolate me from my mates.'

'But, Tyler—' I blurt.

'But, nothing,' he says. 'Just talking to you has really put my mind at ease again. Thanks, Dame. You're a good friend to have around.'

'But—' is all I can manage again as Jay wanders out, looking disappointed, says, 'Bollocks, I can't find anything suitable. Either of you two know where I can find a candle shop near here?'

Tyler realigns his stupid specs for the umpteenth time and suggests, 'Oxford Street?'

Jay just screws up his little nose, looks left along Regent's Street, gauging the situation. 'Bollocks,' he says for the second time in thirty seconds, 'I'll send her some cash. Anyone fancy a swift one in the Atlantic?'

'Definitely,' Tyler consents.

'I'll catch you in there,' I tell the pair. 'Nothing's gone right for me today. I'm gonna seek solace down Jermyn Street, buy meself another shirt from Thomas Pink and waste sixty notes on a tie.'

Spend the next ten days away on business. Stop at hotel in Sindlesham, west of London, deepest suburbia, hell on earth. Stop drinking and doing 'the other' for the duration. Work out in the hotel gym each evening. Clock up twenty hours in overtime – eight of which at double-time. Sit up late each night, watching MTV and adult movies on the hotel cable channels. Memorize each soft-porn aired, knowing when to catch the best action on the reruns. Become obsessed by a documentary called *Ibiza Uncovered* – scores of boys and birds out on the ale and the pull, which prods my mindscape back to Tenerife last Easter, our climactic boys' holiday with Mike and Weatherface, Five, Jay, Thom and Gerry and that unholiest of trinities Tyler, Benny and Matt, and reminds me of this big blonde stupid thing I'd met there, Donna. Convinced that she inhabits the Thames Valley area, I curse myself for not having written her phone number into my address book, picturing it on a scrap of paper lying scrunched up in my bottom desk-drawer at home, alongside countless other memorabilia from glories now past.

Batteries on my Walkman run out after one day. Decide against replacing them – listening to too much loud dance music can't be doing my eardrums any good. Second day: phone my brother for an hour. Hotel bills me twenty notes for the privilege – daylight robbery. Only make phone calls from call-boxes from then on. Have this weird dream where I meet Jo in a park (at a festival possibly?) and she's with some geezer and they're lying on a blanket, and she looks somehow different – maybe older? – and this geezer is wiry and has blond curly hair, does not look a threat, and she leans back and says to him, 'It's okay you don't know him,' then to me, 'But I know you, don't I? It's Damian isn't it? You look strange – I wouldn't have recognized you,' and she's, like, totally composed and relaxed and this guy's name is Wayne and I just murmur, 'Oh, so you've broken up with Gavin then?' and I don't know from where I conjured up either of these names.

Third day: read Revelations from the Bible, and this scares me a bit.

Fourth day: take an aerobics class being run at the hotel; for the sole purpose of getting fitter, not for introductions to young things.

Fifth day: joined in gym sauna by this big blonde, possibly as old as thirty, attractive, though certainly not pretty, close-cropped hair complimented by sharp features – my first company in the gym since day one. Strike up conversation – find her to be surprisingly softly spoken, despite her daunting physique. Discuss our workouts in the gymnasium, our best times on the cycling and rowing machines, what we think of the hotel food, of its bar, and of the service in general. Then we pet and she goes down on me. Attempt to coerce her back to my hotel room but she says she wants to stay on, says she's never given head in a sauna before. And who am I to deny her such an opportunity? Sucks me too silently, too slowly for my liking. Scolds me when I slip my hand up and inside the back of her peach towel. Swallows when I cum, thanks me, lingers for a while longer sitting in silence, then tuts, says she'll maybe see me around and departs. Don't even catch her name.

Joined in the sauna the subsequent night by an overweight Irishman emblazoned with crude, home-drawn, tattoos. Equally amiable. Hope that he isn't a homme. Feel uncomfortable due to the heat – not due to him – and don't stick around for long.

Don't visit the sauna again for the rest of my stay. Watch all the soaps. Drink three litres of Evian each day. Phone Thom three or four times to keep abreast of the gossip: Marky Mullen's been down for a conference but didn't have time to see anyone; Toolboy and Jinxy John held a 'paining' competition, burning one another's arms with cigarettes to see who'd hold out the longest – Jinxy won but his arm's swollen up like a balloon; Thom's had no luck on the lady-front but has 'hit the side-netting' a couple of times, and Tyler's found Brooking dead on some wasteground by his flat and, whilst the probable cause of death suggests a car accident where the motorist just panicked and dumped the body, Tyler is convinced that Brooking was purposely murdered, but then ... who in their right mindscape would do such a thing, and who could possibly hold such a grudge against dear sweet tenderfoot Tyler?

See the sauna blonde seated in the hotel restaurant with a balding skinny man. Can't catch her eye, but think she looks fantastic in black tights and high heels. Eat far too much rich food but somehow still lose three pounds in weight. In another dream, Jo marries Thom in this huge plush wedding up in Scotland and at the ceremony I end up in bed with Lisa, making passionate love. I wake up damped by an arctic sweat, my heart racing like I'm exercising. Eat grapefruit each morning.

Last day: proposition the restaurant manageress – this blonde Australian with a weird Welsh name I'd inadvertently forgotten since our initial introduction. Turns me down flat, but thanks me for my interest. Advises me to try the hotel manager as he, allegedly, has a penchant for raffish young men away from home. Steal two towels before checking out, and a kettle and as many sachets of shower gel as I can cram into my toilet bag. Urinate in my room's pot-plants and sever the lead to the TV. And Beth phones me daily – twice daily.

'What would you call a house?' I'm asking Beth. We're on the platform at Putney Station, waiting for our rush-hour train bound for the futility of work and mindless oblivion. Though the overland is a much quicker, more direct service, as a rule I usually prefer to travel to and from Putney by tube – it doesn't seem quite so suburban. It's seven-thirty a.m.; Beth likes to get into her daily rut that much earlier than me. I can't see the attraction meself.

'How do you mean, "What would I call a house"?' Beth asks by way of reply.

'You know . . . like "Southfork" or "Green Acres" or something. If you had to name your flat, what would you call it?'

'I'd name it after somewhere close – like a wood or something.'

'So, what would you call a racing horse if you owned one?'

'I'd give a racing horse a proper name.'

'What – like Peter or Sarah or something?'

'Yes, I think that'd be nice. Harry would be a good name for a horse.'

'So, what would you call a son?'

Beth regards me sceptically. 'A son?'

'Yeah,' I tell her. 'You know, like offspring.'

'I know what a son is,' Beth contemns, screws her eyes up like she's maybe trying to affix my mindscape with ESP. 'I'm just wondering why you're asking me, that's all.'

'Oh,' I balk. 'You didn't think . . .? Not with me?'

Beth considers me neutrally. 'No, I didn't think that, not for one minute. But, since you asked, I like long names, like Benjamin – so you can call them Benjamin as a child and Ben as an adult.' Beth turns her attention away from me for a moment. 'Or Timothy . . .' she muses: 'Timothy for a child, Tim for a man.'

'They sound better the other way round,' I quip. 'What about a daughter then?'

'I like the name Chloë.'

'Oh,' I sigh. 'Jo's sister's called Chloë.'

'Sorry?' Beth asks.

'Nothing,' I tell her.

'Who's Jo, Damian?'

'No one,' I tell her then blench at my unsubtle blasphemy. 'I mean, not no one, certainly not a no one. Jo, short for, erm, Joseph. An old mate from uni. Sound geezer.'

'Oh, right? And you had a thing with his sister?'

'Chloë?' I laugh out loud. 'Beth! She was only eight!' And then it hits me that Chloë still is only eight and that word 'was' looms within me like I've now finally accepted the sentiment that Chloë and Jo and Scotland and indeed my entire quota of a gratified life are now all forfeited to just distant, pilfered memories.

On our delayed train, on the way here last night, this little bespectacled fucker piled into our carriage at Waterloo, when we were already so close to spilling out onto the very platform, and sent everyone careering into one another – Beth accidentally knocking me on the jaw with the top of her head and, as is so typical in these situations, no one said a word; but when we reached Clapham Junction this big blond geezer stepped from the carriage, then turned, head-butted the little fucker straight in the face and called him an 'imbecile', before casually wandering away, leaving the little cunt nursing a bloodied nose and muttering, 'Mindless hooligan,' under his breath, Beth and I beaming wordlessly to one another before Beth whispered, 'Mindless hooligan? I think he's talking to you, sugar,' and giggled.

'So, what would you call a horse, Damian?' Beth is asking me now.

'I dunno,' I answer in all honesty. 'Something to do with New Order, maybe?'

'Oh, and I suppose you're gonna call your son Hooky?'

I think about this. 'Yeah, you know, that's not such a bad idea.'

'Dame-ee-ern,' Beth groans and playfully prods me. 'And – what? – Anna-Nicole for a daughter, I presume?'

'Ooh no,' I have to tell her. 'That throws up all sorts of complex connotations.'

Beth sighs in reply.

Glancing about me, I suddenly realize that the platform's filled up tenfold since our arrival. Suburban commuters clocking in for their daily routine. By rights the congregated businessmen should allow Beth and me leading admittance to any forthcoming train; after all, we were here first in line while they were still safely ensconced, legs under the kitchen table, cornflakes peppered with Mogadon, an attentive little wifey shepherding them on their way, out into the cold, before she lies back to anticipate yet another hard sex and even harder drugs session with the latest in a long line of milkman demigods.

'Damian,' Beth murmurs in removed tones, 'do you think . . . you love me?'

'Er, I dunno,' I falter, nonsensical thoughts careering back and forth like sharks on a feeding frenzy. 'I . . . don't . . . really . . . know, Beth. Why? Do you love me?'

She draws between her teeth. 'Thought I did for about five seconds last night.'

'Oh?' I ask slowly.

'Yeah, during sex . . . when I thought you were about to make me cum.'

'Oh, ha-ha,' I semi-sneer, as Beth just titters to herself unremittingly.

This sloppy fat geezer wanders past, dressed in this crumpled cream suit so badly creased he must surely have calculatedly ironed the lines in himself.

'Hmmm . . . shall I buy you a suit like that, sugar?' Beth jokes, her eyes following this geezer up the platform.

'He's obviously just crashed out at some bird's last night,' I tell her.

'Damian, he's wearing a wedding ring.'

'So, he's playing an away fixture – cheating on the little Mrs at home.'

'Damian!' Beth snaps.

'Whaaaat? Men do it all the time.'

'You don't,' Beth says.

'How would you know?' I ask, a wicked glint in my steel-grey eyes.

'Damian, I know you love me really,' Beth says, as our train stutters into the station.

I'm playing with the Photoshop on my works' PC, admiring that snapshot of our holidays last year, all the boys on a jolly down Playa las Americas, the one where we're all lined up to order outside Lineker's Bar before this billboard which reads, THANKS FOR YOUR VISIT, SEE YOU SOON, and there's me, back left, one arm slung behind Mike's shoulder who in turn leans into Benny. But it's no longer Benny in the shot, just his torso with an out-of-date, slimmer snap of my brother replacing Benny's head, this additional picture much brighter than the rest of the shot, and so it's this I'm trying to tone down, to get the colours to map properly, knit more evenly. Then there's Thom next in line – whose picture I should also perhaps overwrite? – then Weatherface. Then in front it's Five, Jay, Matt, Tyler that was – his face now supplanted by a shot of Toolboy which doesn't look at all out of place in the overall context of the photo, and if I were to print this off and show it to, say, Beth, she might actually believe Toolboy was indeed in Tenerife with us at the time. Gerry, bottom right, completes our fabled line-up. I blow up the area encircling my brother's head in huge pixels across my screen and am just trying to decide on which shade of navy I should use to replace the paler blues around Ray's face, when Warwick Griffin's phone, on the vacant desk next to me, starts to chime with an outside call. And when heads start to raise after the fifth or sixth ring, and people start to give me a look as if to say, 'Are you gonna answer that or what?' I finally decide to reach for the call, answering it with a slothful, 'Good morning. Damian Shaw speaking.'

'Good morning, Mr Shaw. Is that really you?'

'Yes.'

'At this hour?'

'Er, yes.'

'Damian, it's Gregor. It's a bit early for you, isn't it?'

'Gregor, it's nearly ten o'clock,' I tell him.

'Like I said . . . it's a bit early for you, isn't it?'

'Hmmm.' Bizarrely, subconsciously, I actually find myself standing up from my seat – it's an unwritten office rule that every employee must raise himself as a spectacle, as and when one receives any incoming call. On a good day, when we're all in telecommunication, our project resembles a gaggle of scouting Meerkats, ever vigilant for rogue scavengers.

'You'll never win the Latecomer Award at this rate,' Daley tells me. 'Look, can you tell Hubert Dodd that I'm off sick today, mate?'

'Oh, yeah? Hangover from last night?'

'Yeah, something like that. What happened to you, anyway?'

'Had to see my better half. Besides, I didn't fancy a birthday drink with Beryl Edwards that much – not on a Wednesday.'

'Oh, we only stopped for the one at her do – too many managers there. Nah, we all headed off up to Covent Garden after that. You missed a cracking night.'

'Hold on, Gregor,' I exclaim, eyeing my terminal. 'I've just received an e-mail from Russell Bishop with the subject title "About last night".'

'Read it to me,' Gregor says.

'Right, it's addressed to you, me, James—'

'James Comley? The Sperminator wasn't there.'

'Nor was I, but I still got the e-mail . . . You know what the Bishop's memory's like . . . Right: Rod Ellis, Steve Kerr, Ashwin Patel – Ashwin from Credit Risk? Was he there?'

'Ash? Yeah, he was really drunk.'

'I've never known him to drink.'

'Me neither. He's a bit of a handful when he's had a few.'

'Nicholas Spencer-Jones – Allison Coyle wasn't with him, was she?' I ask.

'No, thank God. He's a better laugh when that little cow's not around.'

'Graham Watson, Carl Smith, Dino Denton—'

Gregor interrupts me again. 'Dino? He kept insisting on buying everyone drinks, bought me two quadruple Bloody Marys – the daft sod.'

I start again: 'Bob Wakefield – who's he?'

'Just some mate of Russell's. Not a fag, though, or at least I don't think he is. Didn't say a lot – not that any of us did – just kept grinning away like some crack-brained court jester.'

'And Warren Rennie? Another of the Bishop's chums?'

'Don't know, never heard of him. Maybe it was just someone Russell picked up on the way home?'

'On the way homme,' I joke.

'So, what does Mr Bishop's message say, then?' Daley asks me.

'Just "How did I get home last night?" . . . Well, how did he?'

'Er, I think Ash Patel stuck him in a black cab on our way to the Roadhouse. It was only about eight or so, but you know what the Bishop's like – can't drink a bloody thing. He was virtually comatosed.'

'Anyone . . . pull?' I ask, my voice suddenly remote as I spy Alasdair Marshall making his way up the corridor, waddling along like some oversized Gentoo.

'Maybe,' Daley probably says.

'Yeah . . . like who?' I ask, as Alasdair finally catches sight of me and totters just slightly in his step, the fear plentiful in his contused face. He then swiftly cuts off to the left, straight through the project area across from us, thus bypassing my immediate area, but I'm heedful to follow his head bobbing away behind distant partitioning boards, until he finally looks back once again and I greet his petrified mask with a mis-stated smile and a courteous nod of my head. Alasdair had to learn the hard way that there is *nothing* wrong with Damian Henry Shaw.

'Oi!' Gregor Daley bellows down the phone. 'Maybe you should ask me where I'm phoning from.'

'You're surely not phoning from a thing's house, Mr Daley?'

'We-e-ell . . .' Gregor pauses. 'Nah, sorry to get your hopes up. I fell asleep on the District line, didn't I? Ended up spending the night at my brother's gaff in Dagenham.'

'Stupid homme,' I tell him.

'Yeah, well, I guess I'll probably see you tomorrow, then.'

'Yeah, take care,' I mumble.

Inexplicably, I'm actually disappointed, almost distressed, that I missed out on this evening of frivolities with the Lunchboys.

I e-mail the boys on Russell Bishop's list, carefully omitting the names of Bob Wakefield and Warren Rennie – I've no idea who these two are, or indeed what they are, and the last thing I need is another couple of hommes thinking I'm 'one of the family' – telling them all that Gregor just phoned in to say that he pulled some six-foot blonde on the tube home last night and that he'll be spending the rest of the week with her in deepest Essex, shagging away to his heart's content. I then recheck my in-basket but there's no new mails, just about sixteen unread mails from Benny dating back a month or more, and a couple more from Matt which I should maybe delete, but I just like the temptation of having them there to try my inner resolve.

Warwick Griffin wanders back to his desk and says, before even going to sit down, 'I've just had the weirdest experience, Damian.'

I'm just admiring my personalized mouse-mat, with this postcard of Jayne Mansfield slipped under its clear plastic cover. 'Go on,' I say.

'Well, you know Julian Robertson? He's a bit of an old hippy.' I nod (I've bought grass from Julian before). 'Well, we just had this meeting in one of the meeting areas on the fifth floor, and we turn up there and there's no tables or chairs in the room. So Julian says, "Why not just squat on the floor", and I'm thinking, "Yeah, I'm cool", so we're sitting there, on the floor, and this removal guy comes in, with, you know, overalls on and everything, and I turn to him and say, "Oh, I suppose you've come to take the carpet now as well", and he says, get this, he says, "No, I've come for your walls." And he starts to dismantle the partitioning walls . . . Like, freaky, or what?'

I maybe raise my eyebrows a little.

'You had to be there,' Warwick tells me, turns back towards his desk.

'Hubert,' I call out, as the Sod wanders past.

Hubert Dodd turns to stop in the corridor, expectantly waiting for me. I reluctantly trudge my way towards him and tell him, 'Gregor Daley's just phoned in sick. He won't be coming in today.'

'How did he sound?' Dodd asks.

'Oh, bad – chesty.'

'Shame,' he says, then turns to walk away, but I carry on after him and add, 'Oh, and, Hubert, I appear to have run short of work.'

The Sod stops again and says in this stupid I-think-

I'm-so-o-o-bloody-funny voice, 'Yeessss, Mr Shaw, I've
been wondering just what you've been up to since the
start of the week!'

This is the man who recently gave me a five per cent
pay-rise when everyone else in my peer group received
eight – even Carl Smith. This is a man who wears grey
shoes with a green suit. I smile but don't blush, and it's
as much as I can do to stop myself kicking the arrogant
son-of-a-bitch from here to kingdom come.

Five and I are returning to the flat after playing football
at the home ground of Five's club – me guesting in
defence for their fifth team after Five phoned this afternoon, at one hour's notice, their regular centre-half
having been glassed in the face in some pub brawl in
Edmonton late last night. Being only their fifths I'd had
heavenly visions of me lighting up the park like some
dashing libero, clearing up the dregs at the back and
steeling into midfield to set up goalscoring opportunities
for shadowy strikers but, as is usually the case, I just
enacted the pretence of the classic English central
defender, only making it into the opposition's half when
trotting up to use my height at set-pieces, spending
most of my afternoon getting turned this way and that
by some nippy little black geezer half my height, a third
of my weight and five years my junior, who called me a
'homme' and a 'donkey' for my full sixty-eight minutes
(I was substituted) and who eventually claimed his hat-
trick from the penalty spot after I'd lost my temper,

clinically taking away his legs after he'd gone past me just that once too often.

Today is Thom's birthday – he's twenty-six, a year older than the rest of us because he took a year out, travelling, before he decided to enlist on a degree course. Scotty Morris from Leicester – one of Thom's university flatmates – arrived just before I left for the match.

'So, what time did Mad Dog get here?' Five asks me. We're both armed with chips from my local kebab shop.

'About midday,' I tell him, turn to stare at this big blonde thing waiting in the queue by the Lloyd's cash-point. Two boys are stood directly behind her, and one of them is shouting (to the old lady at the front of the queue? actually at the big blonde thing? or just to his mate?), 'Cash-points don't give money to fucking coke dealers. They just don't do it. They won't give any money out to fucking coke dealers, I tell ya.'

'Were those two pissed when you left them?' Five asks.

'No, they'd only had the one.'

'Er, the one what?'

'The one Kronenbourg,' I admit.

'So, they've had – what? – four hours' solid drinking since then?'

'Drinking roughly one can every half an hour,' I muse.

Five tuts. 'That's eight cans of Kronie. They're gonna be fucked, Dame.'

'This is gonna be a nightmare,' I tell him. 'Oh, yeah, there's something else I forgot to mention.'

'What's that?' Five asks as I turn the key in our front door.

'They were also getting started on a bottle of tequila that Mad Dog bought Thom for his birthday.'

Five sighs, exasperated.

'Alright, boys?' I attempt to say heartily as we pass from the hallway to the lounge, the air thick with the smell of skunk smoke and littered with George Michael's abominable vocals. I switch the stereo to OFF, instantly engendering a more pleasurable milieu.

'These two are fucked,' Gerry returns, slumped in the armchair furthest from the door, pointing to Mad Dog Scotty, vertical, asleep on the rug before the sofa, and Thom frantically ironing something in the corner of the room. Jay's also in attendance – sitting in the armchair closest to me.

'Look, Dame,' Thom beckons, holds something purple up to me. 'Silky boxers. Present from Lisa for my birthday.'

'Why are you ironing them?' Five asks, rather abruptly I think.

'I wanna look smart for the bird I'm gonna shag tonight,' Thom answers, beavering away at his ironing.

'Have you—?' Mad Dog starts to say, waking, pointing up at me from the rug. 'Have you got a hard punch, Damian?'

'Get back to sleep, Scotty,' I tell him, not wishing to get dragged into another of his fighting debates.

I turn to Jay. 'You alright?'

'Yeah, I'm alright, geez,' Jay says, doesn't look up, is too engrossed in watching another of my Russ Meyer videos: an overtly farcical scene where this patrolman gets a blowjob from some black girl in the back of his squad car, and all you can see is this mad seventies afro bobbing up and down on his lap. I turn to leave the room. Gerry, Jay and Five all continue to watch the film, Scotty the Mad Dog has fallen back to sleep, and Thom is still ironing his boxer shorts, seemingly oblivious to our presence. I count maybe ten crushed cans of Kronenbourg on the floor, guessing there may be a further half-a-dozen hidden from view behind the stereo or under the sofa. On the coffee table there's an empty litre bottle of blue-label vodka and a half-empty bottle of tequila.

I bathe and shave and sit naked on my futon listening to this old New Order bootleg CD, whilst watching the *Brookside Omnibus* with the volume turned down. Atop the television there's this huge skull ring, which I personally find quite ugly and distasteful, but which Jo fell in love with in Goa last January, and bought me as a present. She has a matching one, though not quite as cumbersome. It's two months since Jo told me she couldn't love me any more. I turn the CD off, stick on some Paul Oakenfold, some hard house, and stand near-naked in the centre of my room, posing before my mirror, modelling this pair of white Ralph Lauren boxer-shorts – possibly just a little too big for me – that Jo bought me as a present when we were in the States together two years ago.

I snort what little coke I have left in my desk top drawer, give Wagner's 'Ride of the Valkyries' one quick blast on the stereo, mindlessly dance around for a bit, punch the air distractedly maybe two or three times, then slip into this lime-green Fred Perry polo with navy trim and a pair of electric-blue moleskins. Jo always maintained I should wear my moleskins to bed; she loved their velvety touch, sensualistic against her skin.

Thom insists we finish his bottle of birthday tequila before we head out, so I pour, making sure that Five and I get the largest measures. We catch two taxis to Upper Street: Jay, Thom and I – we're all wearing Fred Perry – in the first; with Gerry, Mad Dog and Five following. We're met at the Slug and Lettuce by Benny and Mike. I get in a round at the bar, then we grab a table upstairs. I'm expecting Carl Smith and Nicholas Spencer-Jones from work to show some time tonight, having bumped into Carl cheering on his flatmate against us in the football this afternoon. Mike and Jay buy two further rounds. I buy myself a treble vodka at the bar downstairs, on a trip to the toilet, and neck it quickly as I make my way back up to join the others. Carl Smith arrives, no Nicholas in sight; instead he has Niall Wheeler, also from work, tagging along. Niall is wearing an old-style football shirt which reads SEATTLE SOUNDERS.

I don't get on with Niall, having had a one-night stand with his flatmate – Tasha Doran, Jack Howe's secretary – some three years ago, just weeks before I met Jo. That night with the big blonde – 'Adorable' Doran – scored me a lot of brownie points with the boys on the project. This, I presume, is the reason Niall despises me so; not that he shows it, but I can sense it stagnating within him. Niall and Tasha are close – just friends, though I've heard idle gossip insinuating that Niall wishes to take their friendship that one step further.

I still want to fuck the Blonde from Financial Services but every time I e-mail her, the messages just sit there in my out-basket until I get bored and delete them. I doubt if she's left the company – wouldn't someone have the sense to remove her e-mail id if she did? – so hopefully she's just taking some long-term holiday, or is away on training courses, or is maybe just ill (if she is, I do hope it's nothing too serious – nothing that might affect her sumptuous looks, glorious figure).

'Tasha's meeting some friends here later,' Niall informs me nonchalantly.

'Tasha here?' I ask excitedly, then, calmer, more composed, 'Later? It'll be good to see her.'

'Another pint, Damian?' Mad Dog asks me. He's oblivious to the fact we've already started leaving him and Thom out of rounds.

'Nah,' I tell him.

'Anyone else?' he asks the table. No one accepts his offer.

'God, you lot are such slow drinkers,' Thom guffaws. To my dismay Mad Dog buys chasers to match their pints.

'Bit of advice,' I whisper to Niall, close to his ear, motioning to our dangerous duo. 'Don't fuck with either of those two tonight . . . they're psychopaths.'

Niall frowns, looks confused, possibly shaken.

Gerry tells us he spoke to Marky Mullen this afternoon, that he phoned to say he wasn't able to make it down because he's broken up with his woman – Harriet – again.

'Broken up with the Chariot, again?' Jay asks, bewildered.

'So he said,' Gerry recounts, rubs his buckled nose – a break, he claims, incurred during a ruck in his teens, away at Elland Road.

'Bollocks. Those two sad fuckers are made for one another,' Benny says. 'Who else'd have either of them?'

'Yeah, Marky wouldn't know a proper break-up if it chucked a diamond engagement ring back in his face,' Five says, referring to an incident at university when Marky's woman of the time – one Julie Jefferson – chucked his ring back at him after he'd proposed.

'Oi, that's a bit harsh, geez!' Jay warns, the rest of us all laughing at Five's line.

'Yeah? Didn't you shag Jefferson once, Jay?' Five returns.

Jay scratches his head. 'No, no. I don't think so.'

'Dame did,' Gerry shouts, points at me.

'Just snogged her at a party once,' I tell everyone.

'Marky threatened to kill you over that, didn't he?' Mike asks me.

'Nah, he threatened to kill Julie. He forgave me – told me he still loved me,' I say in this distant voice, like I'm reminiscing or something, which I most certainly am not. 'She had fucking nice lips though.'

Benny giggles. 'And to which lips are you referring, pray tell?'

Carl and Niall sit smiling inanely, both lost in our closet conversation. Thom and Mad Dog announce to the world that they're both off to the toilets. We're all painfully aware that Mad Dog has maybe four or five gs of coke on him.

'Well, they do need a little pick-me-up,' Jay says, attempts to reassure us. No one acknowledges him. I look into my pint, wonder where Toolboy and Jinxy John could have got to, why haven't they showed? Sadly I just couldn't find the time to reach Tyler or Matt – it's been such a busy week. Fools I suffer gladly, but not wankers. Mind you, the Slug and Lettuce is perhaps a befitting representation of this pair. Benny's only here by default – Jay had stupidly e-mailed him late yesterday afternoon and passed on the news about tonight. I countered this, telling Benny my mail to him must have simply vanished, eternally bound to orbit cyberspace; you just can't trust my office connection.

'Anyone for another?' Gerry is asking, is motioning with his glass.

Niall disappears, I chat to Carl and neck two more

pints, then Niall reappears, tells us that Tasha is down-
stairs. I wait maybe half an hour – during which time I
neck another two pints, and Thom and Scotty still fail
to return from the toilets – before I wander off to find
Tasha out by the front door, stood with two things I do
not recognize.

'Hello,' I say, sidling up to her, beaming, my
shoulders held back, standing tall.

'Hello, Damian,' Tasha returns. 'Oh, were you aware
that Niall's here as well?'

'Yeah, he's with us upstairs.'

'Oh, he never told me you were here.'

Yeah, well the little cunt's doubtless worried that I'm
going to fuck you again tonight, I'm thinking to myself.

'Yeah, I'm just here with a few mates,' I say.

'A few? I thought you always travelled with a whole
army in tow?'

'Oh, you know,' I say, shrug my shoulders.

'Damian, this is Claire, and this is Siobhan.' Tasha
motions to her friends. I smile and nod at them both
and ask them what they do and enquire as to how they
know Tasha. Jo always accused me of being too dismis-
sive of her friends. The two things are both short, both
unblonde and with no obvious Meyer features. Both
are dressed head-to-toe in black: Siobhan very pretty,
though I would prefer to fuck Claire; she appears . . .
dirtier. Perhaps I will get to fuck Claire? I will romance
Tasha and fuck Claire behind her back.

'Damian, leave these two alone,' Tasha jokes. 'You've
paid them more than enough attention. How about

me?' I spent over two hours talking to Tasha at last year's works' Christmas party, but she terminated our conversation saying I was only being pleasant so I could get 'back into her knickers' (her words, not mine). Tasha looks fantastic tonight. Her plumped-up cushion lips so eminently complete and provoking, I would maybe like to fuck her mouth.

'So, you want to talk to me, sweetheart?' I half-ask, sigh, roll my eyes.

'Ooh, those eyes of yours, Damian – they can be pretty scary at times,' Tasha says. She has this fabulous chest, so huge and robust, so womanly – her entire body an effervescing altar of voluptuous curves yowling sexuality at me from every square inch. She stands with her hands on her hips, parting her black leather jacket, thrusting her magnificent breasts toward me. 'Two Good Reasons,' Carl Smith calls her. I think one day I would maybe like to marry Tasha as I'd be happy to spend the rest of my life in the company of such a celestial form.

'And how's the Scottish romance?' Tasha is asking, dipping her head in an attempt to make eye contact with me, fully aware I'm staring wide-eyed at her breasts, dazzled like a rabbit caught before full-beam headlamps.

'Broke up,' I say, and look away through the window at the cinema across the road. It's raining outside.

'Yeah, I heard a rumour,' she says, asks, 'for good?'

'Yeah . . . for good,' I lie. 'Me and Jo Kennedy are incommunicado.'

Tasha sighs, says to her friends, 'Spook-ee. That was

Ewan's surname too,' then to me, 'He was an ex-boyfriend, a blond – you're one for blondes, aren't you Damian?'

'Yeah, especially big blondes,' I tell her idiotically.

'I like tall men,' she says, like she didn't hear me.

'Oh?' I manage, sense a faint rush.

'Yeah . . . like six-foot-five tall men,' she gloats.

Thinking, I'd better not introduce her to Gerry then, I sharply change the subject with, 'Why weren't you at my last party?'

'Oh, I dunno, I've no excuse. I'll be at the next one I promise.'

I grin. 'You can be my guest of honour.'

'I'd like that.' Tasha has a long black and white silk scarf tied tight around her throat.

'Unless of course you want to go out before that?' I have to ask. 'Maybe tomorrow?'

Tasha sighs. 'Maybe Monday instead.'

'Maybe Monday after work?'

'Six o'clock, the Doggett's. Just friends, okay?' she states.

'Just friends,' I entreat.

Tasha Doran, the future Mrs Shaw, smiles at me and all I can muster up to say is 'Monday, then.' Who needs Es and amyl when you can experience a natural rush like this?

I make my excuses and head off back to the boys upstairs to find: Jay braying at Gerry, telling him, 'You should get yourself a decent bird'; Benny and Carl Smith complaining, 'Where the fuck have you been, Damian?';

Five telling me that Thom and Mad Dog have, 'Been and gone, both well out of it, have headed off to play in the funfair on Islington Green'; Mike sat smiling, laughing at nothing – everyone appearing well and truly fucked. I sit next to Niall, in the only vacant chair, but don't make any effort to talk to him.

Mike presents us with this long scarlet strip of acid perforated into thirty, maybe forty squares.

'Doesn't look up to much,' Five says.

'Yeah. I like my acid with a pretty motif on it,' someone says.

'Look, lads, this is a private batch from an acquaintance of my brother,' Mike tells us. 'No fancy pictures – just heavy-duty acid for my closest friends.'

'You got any close friends, Mike?' Benny asks, sniggers.

I laugh too – out loud – thinking it hilarious that this gigantic fool, Benny, has the effrontery to ridicule the good name of my close friend Mike.

Mike just pushes his long blond fringe from his eyes. 'What's so funny, Dame?' he asks, half smiles like he's really forcing himself to.

'Oh, nothing. It's not you,' I tell him, continue to cackle, raise my hands and look to Benny who just seems totally confused.

Mike leans closer, whispers audibly, 'Shall I tell you what's funny, Dame?' He pauses, waits for my face to drop. 'What's funny . . . is that Beth is probably getting shagged by some pretty boy down in Putney whilst you're sat here with us.'

'Oh, right, like I care,' I quip, stick my tongue out at him.

But Mike still fumes, persists with, '. . . Or that Joanna is getting fucked in every orifice by a posse of kilt-wearing, bagpipe-players. That is what's funny, Dame-ee-ern.'

A stilted hush descends over our table as I'm thrown headlong over another calamity cliff-face, into a name-less vortex where the festered spirits of Benny and Tyler and Matt and, now, this Mike all reside – their lone purpose to bait and torture me, wrench the dignity from my scarred soul with gruesome wrought-iron mandibles.

Jay and maybe even Benny – funnily enough – make motions, mouth words which I'm oblivious to, in an attempt to placate matters.

I watch Mike's façade crumble, the guilt start to shine through. 'Look, I'm sorry, Dame. That one was well out of order,' he tells me, offers his hand in friendship. 'I don't know what I was thinking.'

'No worries,' I return, and watch myself take this infidel's hand, shaking it as if we might still be friends or something. But, of course, we're friends no longer; all acquaintances are now severed.

'C'mon, geezers. C'mon,' Jay pipes up. 'Here, raise your glasses everyone. C'mon now, let us all propose a toast . . . to friendship.'

No one can decide on a club. Benny wants to head down as far as the SW1, close to his and that Natalie-thing's flat, but no one's prepared to venture such a distance, so we decide on a short-list of two: the Lights, back in Muzzy Hill, or some garage night at the Complex, close by. Niall declines to join us, which pleases me greatly, as it means I can misbehave without recrimination from Tasha. Only Mike – really humming on some acid – is intent on the Complex and, thankfully, in his euphoric state decides to chance it alone, the rest of us opting for a boozy session at the Lights, which will offer an earlier end to the night and a less-frenetic musical backdrop. It also keeps Mike at a good arm's length from me, a sagacious move considering his earlier outburst.

Once in the club, Five gets the first round: five pints of Extra, a bitter for Gerry, and matching tequila slammers. Jay is the first to leave – thrown out for throwing ice-cubes at Benny, the bouncers taking exception to his good-hearted indecorousness. Gerry follows soon after – caught pissing down the side of the cigarette machine, right near the bar, too drunk to even make it to the toilets across the dancefloor.

I am at the bar talking to this thing – Susannah – who is maybe five-foot-six, is twenty-three years old, and is at bar school, is overweight, though only slightly, and has pale blue eyes set perhaps too far apart. She is wearing this little yellow badge, which has scrawled upon it, in red felt-tip pen, the immortal line, 'I told you so.' I think she is ugly, but she has the most wonderfully severe bobbed haircut – blonde, shaved high at the back. She approached me, asking a light for her cigarette, full-strength Marlboro, and lingered until I continued the conversation. I don't know what we are talking about, and I do not care. I wish we'd not let Mad Dog go astray quite so early, as I'm now craving a blast of his coke and its super-amphetamine high.

'You got any drugs on you?' I ask Susannah above the din of another crap chart track. She pretends not to hear me. I want to fuck her so deep in her throat that my cum explodes back through her nose when I ejaculate, my loins still moiling hot for Tasha. The concept of such carnal intimacies sets me wondering what Jo's doing right now.

'So, you fancy a coffee?' I ask her.

She asks, 'Where?'

'My flat,' I say.

'Where's that?' she asks.

'Just up the Broadway – only five minutes away.'

'Can I trust you?' she says coyly, then, as I smile, adds, 'I'll get my coat.' I do not think she should trust me. I am drunk and I'm hoping that I will be able to maintain an erection. Out of sheer laziness, Susannah and I catch a minicab to the flat, just a quarter of a mile, probably less. I let her pay.

Thom, Mad Dog and Jay are all crashed out in the lounge, the lights on low, the television closing in on Al Pacino as he buries his face in a veritable Ben Nevis of cocaine.

I'm in my bedroom, toying with the idea of phoning the Complex, getting them to give Mike a going over, a lordly bastinading, for the thirty or so tabs of acid he's still got on him. Susannah is topless, is knelt before me and is giving me head. I do not like her breasts – they are big but not firm, too podgy. I shut my eyes and picture Tasha's breasts, and sense my erection swell. I start to whisper Tasha's name over and over to myself, quietly, secretly hoping that Susannah will hear me; but she is far too engrossed in giving me the best head she's ever had the pleasure to deliver. She's probably falling in love with me – she sucks on me with such determined enthusiasm.

The doorbell rings and someone wakes and wanders into the hallway to answer it. I hear Benny's and Carl Smith's voices – they're looking for a place to crash, not wanting to travel the distance home to South London. Jay tells someone I've got 'a tart' in my room. I clench my buttocks, try to force myself to cum. Susannah continues to suck on me, grunting, squealing, slurping. I'm enjoying the noises she's making, but all I really want to do is to join the swashy powwow in the lounge and smoke a little blow and listen to some tunes and watch videos, and so I'm willing myself to cum soon, to cum before she pulls away from me, looks longingly up at me and begs me to fuck her slowly, maybe tenderly, on my futon, and so I consider grabbing the back of her head to force myself deeper into her mouth but I fear she may gag on my cum, may vomit into my lap, in my moleskins, over my boots, over the rug that Jo, still so ubiquitous in my life, bought for my room, so instead I pull away and vigorously wank myself into her face, cuming in small spurts into her eyes, over her nose, across her cheeks.

She looks dazed, possibly confused, her right eye appears bloodshot. 'That was . . . different,' is all she says.

This Susannah is a marked five inches shorter than Jo – what in God's name do I think I'm doing? 'There's my mobile by the futon. You can call yourself a cab,' comes my curt reply. I haul up my moleskins and throw on my Fred Perry and, after plucking a bag of weed from my desk drawer, I stop to tell her, 'Better wash your face, sweetheart,' then head for the lounge.

The credits to *Scarface* are rolling across the screen as Susannah leaves. Jay replaces the film with one of Thom's porns.

'Tell me if I'm being out of order here, Dame,' Jay says, 'but what exactly did you do to make her bugger off so quickly?'

I tell Carl, Benny and Jay exactly what I did. Thom and Mad Dog are slumped asleep – Thom snoring heavily, spittle dribbling from the corner of his open mouth. Jay leans across to me and shakes my hand and tells me that I'm a 'complete bastard'. Surprisingly, despite the fact he's little more than a work colleague, I'm delighted to have Carl here. On the television a beautiful young thing is giving head to this heavy Mediterranean guy who I'm sure I've seen in many porn films before. They are spread-eagled on a red picnic blanket set down on a verge with an idyllic view before a crystal clear lake.

I light a joint and tell Carl, 'I've got a date with "Adorable" on Monday.'

'Have you, bollocks,' Carl whirrs, doesn't take his eye off the porn.

'I have, honest.'

'Damian, she's flying to Ireland tomorrow for a week's holiday – Niall told me – to visit her Gran or her cousins or something,' Carl says.

'She isn't,' I blurt.

'She is, mate,' he tells me sincerely, but it's already dawning on me that he's probably right, that perhaps Tasha does not love me, that we will not be wedded one day, and that I will not again be exploring the pleasures her body can offer this coming Monday, and I think that maybe her tits are also just a little on the fat side anyway – not a touch on Jo's imposing pair. On the screen, the hairy Mediterranean is fucking the beautiful young thing backwards – 'Up the arse,' Jay claims, but none of us agree, the shot not being close enough to tell.

Mad Dog looks up from his stupor, giggles. 'Have you got a hard punch, Damian?'

The doorbell rings.

'Looks like that sort's come back for some more, geez,' Jay says and, for an instant, I am hoping he's right, as I'm starting to feel horny again and I want to treat Susannah with more . . . respect this time.

It's Beth at the door. 'Oh . . . I've, er, just been thinking about you,' I tell her.

154

The beautiful young thing is definitely getting fucked up the arse. A close-up shot confirms this.

'You look sad,' Kelly is telling me. 'What's wrong, Damian?'

'I dunno . . . Life maybe?'

It's late and we're sitting in the Falcon by Clapham Junction. Kelly is drinking cider, I'm drinking Perrier, slowly coming down off another E, another sample from Mike – not too good this one, blows a bit hot and cold, not nearly mellowing enough, not one I'd recommend him to invest heavily in. A copy of the *Big Issue* sits between us on the table. Kelly has told me she is leaving for Australia as soon as she can get her act together – which'll probably take her a couple of months or so.

'Why do you have to go?' I manage to ask her.

Without pausing for breath Kelly answers, 'Because of my family. Because . . . because there's someone there who loves me, who really cares.'

I'm flicking through the pages of the *Big Issue*, pretending to concentrate hard on the text, but really I'm just looking out for pictures of any blondes, or even unblondes, I might consider fucking. 'A boyfriend?'

'Sort of.'

'You never said. Do you love him?' I mumble as I reach for my glass, still not looking up.

'No. I don't know. We'll see when I get back home. Now, Damian, are you going to tell me why you look so sad?' This comes as more of a threat than an actual question.

'What will you do if I don't tell you?'

'Don't even think about it!' Kelly warns me.

'Well, there was this girl . . .' I'm still not looking up.

'I might've known,' Kelly sighs. 'What was her name?'

'Joanna.'

'And did you love her, Damian?'

'Yes,' I say, think: I still do.

'Right, and you two have just broken up, yes?'

'Er, yes, just broken up.' I'm now playing with the ice cubes at the bottom of my glass, am momentarily lost deep within their reflecting blue shards.

'How long were you together?' Kelly is probing me.

'Oh, I don't know . . . Erm, a couple of months maybe?'

'That figures . . . I was wondering why you hadn't been in touch for a while.'

How can I tell Kelly that Jo and I were together for two and a half years? That we broke up over two months ago? That Kelly was just another number, an ersatz Jo, another lay to tide me over till the next time I saw Jo? And I'm wondering what Jo's doing at this exact same moment in time.

'My life's a chaotic shambles without Jo,' I suddenly gasp, grab Kelly's forearm, grip it with both hands and look her hard in the face. 'Nothing is going right for me. There's no direction to my life. Even people I once thought of as close friends are starting to desert me.

There just doesn't seem any point in living any more. I have . . . no . . . future.' I am on the verge of tears, battling away from a proximate breakdown. 'Oh, what am I gonna do without her, Kelly?'

After a pause, Kelly smiles nervously and says, 'Oh, Damian, you are such a kidder. You're awful. You know, I nearly believed you there for a minute. As if a woman could ever get one over on Damian Shaw, huh?' She's gently caressing my hands as I loosen my grip on her forearm, the strength sapping from me. 'Now, how's Thom and the gang these days?'

'They're . . . they're . . . But Jo, she—'

'Oh, forget her, Damian. There's plenty more fish in the sea.'

'But—'

'But nothing, Damian. C'mon, she's not worth it.'

I bow my head again and, looking from side to side, mutter, 'Did you . . . ever . . . love me, Kelly?'

'Hey, Damian!' – Kelly puts her hand to my forehead – 'Have you got a temperature or something? What's brought all this on? Question is, did you ever love me?'

I smirk. 'Erm, no. I guess not. Not really.'

'Well, there you are. I liked you a lot, sure. Maybe we'd have even lasted a bit longer than we did – say three months or so – but that's about the level of it. I mean, I had to finish with you when I did. What was it – after a month or something?'

I look up again. 'Only two weeks.'

'Two weeks? Nah, you sure? Oh, well, if you say so. No, I had to finish with you, Damian, because you always seemed far too preoccupied whenever you were with me, like you just weren't really there or something. Your mind always seemed someplace else. You blew hot and cold so frequently that I really didn't know if I was coming or going half the time . . . Now, c'mon, give us a smile, eh, Damian? Please, huh?'

I manage a kind of mangled half-smile-cum-sneer in order to propitiate her.

Later we're stood outside the pub. It's cold and we've both got our hands in our pockets.

Kelly asks me, 'Listen, do you wanna nip back and grab a coffee or something?'

'You know I don't drink coffee,' I say, teasing her.

'A tea then?' she asks suggestively. 'Or a Horlicks?'

'No, I don't think so. It's late. I'd best be getting home.'

'You can stop over,' she semi-sings coyly, bites her bottom lip.

I'm tempted, but say, 'Er, no. Not tonight, eh?'

'Dame-ee-ern,' Kelly starts, reaches toward me, and runs the back of her finger across the stubble on my chin. 'I . . . want . . . you . . . to . . . fuck me.'

I take a deep breath and just say, 'Sorry.'

Kelly is wearing her stack-heeled kinky boots tonight but, even with this fact at the fore of my mindscape, coupled with the notion that she is tall, blonde and beautiful and has a 36D(?) chest, her whole persona still fails to strike a chord within me, doesn't appear to arouse me in any way whatsoever. Besides, I've memories afresh in my mindscape of complete sex with Kelly, stripped bare except for her boots, and it's not like I really love her or anything so there's no burning incentive to repeat this act just yet.

All I really want to do is get home and obliterate Matt's and Mike's visages from that celebrated snap of the boys outside Lineker's Bar in Tenerife last Easter. I think it might actually be quite comical – and indeed quite topical – to introduce the Spice Girls into said picture. Benny could be Ginger Spice, simply because of his distinctive red barnet. Mike could perhaps be Baby, again due solely to hair colour and no other reason. I could then employ Sporty to replace Tyler, and perhaps Scary as a substitute for Matt – Matt who is probably the least scariest person I know. It might then be an idea to finally scrub Thom's face from the shot – Posh Spice would then be a suitable replacement. Actually, this is all probably a most fair comparison, as I do not like the Spice Girls, nor indeed any of the aforementioned five ex-friends. If I were obliged to choose, I'd say my favourite Spice Girl would have to be a six-foot version of Baby Spice, but only with Ginger Spice's baronial breasts transplanted.

'Hey, still thinking about what's-her-name?' Kelly is asking me.

'The Spice Girls?' I hazard out aloud.

'God, you have really lost it,' Kelly says sadly. 'No, I meant that girl you mentioned before.'

'Oh, right – Jo?'

'Yeah, Jo. Well?'

'Maybe.'

'Look, Damian, we don't have to have sex but, well . . . I'm leaving the country soon.'

'You'll leave me your address, though, yeah?'

'Yeah, of course I will. But – hey! – I guess I'm only going home to finish my final year at college. I'll be back here after that, maybe move up to Scotland.'

'Scotland?' I ask, suddenly interested, slightly perplexed.

'Didn't I tell you? I was born there. My parents emigrated when I was six years old. I've still got lots of family there: grandparents, cousins and stuff. You'll have to visit me there. My family are all from this place called Bearsden. It's in—'

'Glasgow,' I tell her, stare off into space, as two tiny blondes and two tallish unblondes skitter past us.

'Oh, wow, do you know it?'

The two unblondes avert my attention for a split nanosecond before I find myself sighing, 'I know Glasgow.'

'Oh, cool, Damian. You'll visit then?'

'Yeah, sure, why not.'

'Look, are you going to come over before I leave? I'm planning a huge going-away party.'

'Yeah, of course I will.'

'Oh, great. Guess I'll see you before I go, then.'

I stand rooted to the spot, as Kelly turns to make her way towards home.

'Kelly!' I call after her.

'Yeah?' she shouts back.

'Give us a growl, eh, sweetheart? Just for old time's sake.'

Kelly smiles, grits her teeth and makes her hands like talons. 'Grrrrrr.'

This morning, I received another postcard from Jo's cousin, Slinky – this time from India. The postcard made absolutely no reference to Jo.

I'm in Beth's flat and it's late and I'm standing in her kitchen, rummaging through her fridge, and I'm naked and I'm drunk (on champagne) and the fridge appears full of nothing but Tupperware, and Beth is in her bedroom and is drunk also and is shouting, telling me not to eat any more pickled onions – but I'm not; I'm picking at a strawberry cheesecake – and then I'm going through the bread bin, and I'm shouting back at Beth, demanding to know why she didn't tell me that she had some meringue nests, asking why she's hidden them away in the bread bin, and then she's next to me and she's naked and I'm chewing on a frankfurter, and Beth tells me I shouldn't eat it because it's not cooked, and I'm telling her, slowly, purposely, that I need . . . my intake . . . of . . . pig . . . meat to survive else I will surely perish, will fly away to a better(?) place, and Beth tells me that it's a turkey frankfurter, so I spit what remains clear from my mouth and I'm thinking about the journey here tonight, about how I was the only one in the tube carriage when this little fat geezer got on at

Gloucester Road and proceeded to smash the train up, started ripping down posters and things, whilst I just sat there watching, not batting an eyelid, and then he alighted at Earls Court where a huge contingent of people got on and, spying the debris, all looked at me cautiously like I was the guilty party, maybe some kind of madman and right now Beth and I are dancing in the lounge, Beth is grooving on the coffee table and I'm shimmying on a rug in the corner, partnering a five-foot Yucca plant, and I'm singing 'Joanna, I Love You' by Kool & The Gang in this shrill vocal style, my voice drowned out by some George Michael crap blasting out from Beth's stereo, and Beth says she should have her camera here, to take a picture of me for Readers' Wives and I tell her she surely means Readers' Boyfriends, and then I'm staring at the ceiling, tracing etched swirls in the Artex, and I'm both exhilarated and yet curiously woeful at the self-same time, and I'm wondering what in God's name I am doing with Beth.

I'm in Matt's local, the Shaftesbury Tavern, down where Shaftesbury Road marauds into Hornsey Rise.

'If I lost Jenny, then . . .' Matt is saying. 'Well, I know I've got really good mates and everything, and I'd probably never go lonely, but they just wouldn't be enough, not without Jenny. Do you know what I mean, Dame?'

I nod and sip at the head on my Kronenbourg.

'I mean, I know I've got good mates, but Jenny, she's so . . . so—'

I guillotine Matt's address with, 'Have you ever seen *The Wizard of Oz*?'

'Er, yes,' he says.

'The way that film starts out in black and white, then suddenly transforms into glorious technicolour?'

'Yes, but—'

'Well, that was my life the day I met Jo,' I tell him.

Matt just looks at me blankly, then tuts. 'That's as maybe, Dame, but as I was trying to tell you before – look, I hate springing this on you but—' He stops to collect his thoughts, but I'm already fully versed on what's coming. 'I think I might have to drop out of the scam – for Jenny's sake if nothing else.'

'Fine,' I tell him, let my eyes wander round the room searching for a more appeasing face to fall on.

'What, that's it? Fine?'

'Yeah, fine,' I repeat, as my eyes fall back on Matt's insalubrious muzzle once again.

'But I thought this deal meant so much to everyone?' Matt moans, seems slightly distressed.

'If you don't want to be a part of it, then so be it,' I tell him.

'Don't you at least want to know why?'

'Alright, then, why?' I sort of snap, as I dunk an index finger into the too-thick froth atop my Kronenbourg and slowly whirl it around, making patterns as I go.

Matt glances round the room furtively, then slips his hand inside his jacket pocket to withdraw a familiar envelope.

'What's this?' I ask him.

'You'd better open it,' he says, takes a measured sip of his drink, his eyes still darting covertly about the place.

'You okay, mate?' I ask him.

'Yes, course,' he tells me.

'Someone not following you, are they?'

'I really don't know, Dame. I really don't know.'

'Oh, right,' I chuckle, and make a concerted effort to appear baffled. I give the envelope a brisk shake, then cautiously retrieve a sheet of A4 paper and unfold it, revealing a crude photocopy of Matt and Gerry: a picture of the two, taken way, way back at university, with their arms hung round one another, Matt holding this huge spliff up to the camera. Someone has scrawled a red line between the pair.

'And what is this supposed to be?'

Matt draws air between his teeth. 'I'm not sure,' he sighs. 'But I think one of the boys is trying to get at me.'

'Tyler?'

'Tyler? No, I was just talking to him yesterday.' Matt stops, shakes his head. 'Tyler is the last one I'd suspect. Oh, after you, of course, Dame. No, I reckon that it might be one of the others.'

'The others?' I whisper surreptitiously and pinch Matt's side, regard this like it's all some great big joke.

'Stop taking the piss, Dame,' he moans.

'Sorry, Matthew sweetheart,' I coo, and blow him an exaggerated kiss.

'This is serious. I think one of the boys is having a pop at me.'

'And, what makes you think that?' I ask him.

Matt continues. 'Well, the photo was from uni – I'd recognize it anywhere. It was at one of our big smoking sessions, so one of the boys must've taken it.'

'Hmmm. I s'pose so,' I nod my head, but pull a face like I'm not taking this seriously.

Matt used to be a big New Order fan, or so he said; claimed to be at some of the same gigs as me when we were in our mid-teens, but he didn't make any attempt at getting the money together to see them in Europe shortly after we graduated, and when they played the Reading Festival that same summer he was touring in the south of France, contending it would be his one last chance of a long holiday before embarking on a career. I should've been more awake to the cracks appearing in our relationship even at that early stage. Matt was the third of them to insult the memory of Jo.

Matt's still waffling on. 'And there was that incident with Gerry – I mentioned it to you recently. You know, when I whacked him that one time. I reckon someone's playing on that, trying to stir up trouble, hoping to drive some kind of wedge between us, to get me to drop out of the scam, thus isolating me from the rest of the guys. And this isn't the only shit I'm getting. Someone orders a pizza to be delivered to my house just about every fucking night. Jenny's already worried, and I don't want to run the risk of her finding out about the scam.'

'Who would do all this?' I eventually ask in a semi-jokey voice, when I'm absolutely sure he's concluded his grave monologue.

'Benny,' Matt says flatly.

'Benny?' I ask after a pause, slightly dumbfounded but intrigued nevertheless. 'Benny? Why Benny?'

'I reckon he's bottled it, Dame. He's got this new woman on the go, so he's worried about the scam and he's got cold feet.'

'Cold feet,' I parrot without thinking, then add for good measure, 'Brrrrrr,' and stamp my feet and chatter my teeth.

'Yeah, cold feet, Dame. Don't take the piss. Benny doesn't want to be seen to be the first one to drop out, so he's trying to put the frighteners on someone else, to make them drop out before him, making things easier for himself.'

'Well, Matt, maybe you *should* drop out, and save yourself all this grief.'

'Yeah, I have been giving it some thought.'

'So-o-o, are you gonna drop out, then?' I ask, still adopting a giddy voice.

'Oh, I dunno. I can't figure out why someone's having a pop at me like this.'

'There's some sick people out there,' I tell him.

'Yeah, don't I know it,' Matt sighs. 'I almost wish it was you who had it in for me.'

'Er, me?' I ask, my voice suddenly sounding hoarse for some reason.

'Yeah, you, Dame,' Matt drawls lazily. 'At least you'd have a more direct approach.'

'Direct . . . approach?' I enquire.

'Yeah, you know. None of this fannying around with thinly veiled threats and stuff. You'd just come straight out with it and give me a good twatting if you thought it necessary.'

'A good twatting?'

'Yeah. I remember the first time I saw you in action. God, I could've only known you a few days then, just when we'd started uni, and our flat went down the dancehall en masse, and those pissed-up townies caught sight of Lisa's breasts and threw lager over her, like some kind of wet T-shirt competition or something.'

'Yeah,' I remember, then add mindlessly, 'Happy times.'

'You went through the first two like they weren't there.'

'No one ever expects a student to smack them, do they?'

'I know, I'd never seen a big bloke move so fast.'

'Er, big bloke?' I ask, my voice tone a touch accusatory.

'Yeah, you know – big, tall, er, well-built.'

'But, Matt, I only weigh twelve stone ten,' I mention darkly.

'No, I didn't mean it like that.'

I follow up with, 'And I only weighed around twelve stone two then.'

'Yeah, sorry, wrong choice of words, Dame. Look, I didn't mean to piss you off, mate.'

'Don't worry. No offence taken,' I tell him in all honesty. Matt's just employed a poor choice in words, and there's little he can do to affront me now anyway. His opinion is of trivial consequence. To Matt I must indeed appear big in every way. I earn a healthy 10K a year more than him, I have always had so much more success sexually and, whereas we're both of a similar weight and height, his bulk is averted southerly towards his stomach, and doesn't distribute quite so evenly across his frame as it does in my physique.

'You sure you're okay?' Matt is asking me.

'Yeah, course,' I tell him, and slap his shoulder the way friends sometimes do.

'Only . . . me and Tyler were talking about you yesterday.'

'Yeah?' I ask.

'Yeah. You sure there's nothing worrying you? Tyler says you've been a little off of late, you sure you don't want to talk about something?'

'Nah, course not,' I say.

'This ain't because of Thom and Jo and—'

'No,' I curtail him.

'Right. Just trying to help, Dame. I didn't want to upset you or anything.'

'Upset me? I thought it was *your* problems we were here to discuss.'

'Yeah, look,' Matt starts in a hushed voice, 'I guess I'm still in on the scam, okay? I just needed someone to talk to.'

'You're still in?'

'Yeah.'

'Still . . . in . . . on . . . the . . . scam?'

'Yeah, course I am. Mates are important, Dame. Jenny's special to me but you lot have been my mates for years now. So what if someone's been bothering me? I'm staying in this for you, Dame. I don't want to let you down.' And with that Matt actually rabbit-punches me playfully on the upper arm, and attempts to give me a big heartfelt hug just as if we're old roister-doister drinking buddies from yesteryear or something.

I sprawl back on the sofa. This lounge, this house, was simply 'home' for the first eighteen years of my senseless existence. Nothing much has changed since my frenetic childhood days. Oh, about five sofas and umpteen television sets may have been and gone in that time, and the wallpaper has transmuted through various greens and blues, a particularly violent shade of orange that only lasted a month or so in the late seventies, through paisley patterns and stripes, and now sits collectedly and eye-pleasingly at an off-white. But the layout of the room has remained constant – the armchair, the fire-place, the television and stereo cabinet all spread out, left to right, on the opposite wall – with another arm-chair (my armchair, my sanctuary as a child) to the right of this sofa, and an aged Yucca plant ('Barbara,' my mother calls it), maybe seven feet high now, to the left. As a boy, I always thought I'd outgrow the Yucca one day. A glass-covered coffee table marked the centre of this lounge for years, but that was broken in a scuffle I had with my father when he returned home roaring drunk on the night of my seventeenth birthday.

My mother is perched parlously on the armchair by the fireplace, my father is slobbing out in my old armchair, a tumbler of whisky clutched in his left hand, the remote control in his right. He's busy flicking between the racing on the BBC and on Channel 4, with occasional sorties into teletext to check the latest sports betting. I don't know why he bothers – he only ever gambles properly when it's my mother's money he's wasting.

I was due at Beth's maybe an hour ago. We're expected at some dinner party a work colleague of hers is throwing tonight. That is of no importance to me, however. This is a far more pressing engagement.

I draw a deep breath. 'So, you're back together, then?' I ask my mother.

My mother just smiles, looks to my father.

'Sure we are, son,' my father slurs, still looks at the television. 'Sure we are.'

I repeat the question to my mother. 'So, you're back together then?'

'Yes, yes. Dad came home again, dear,' my mother tells me, and smiles in my father's direction.

'Yeah. Came home again, didn't I, love?' my father

says, smiles back at my mother – a sickly, fetid smile that wrenches hard my very stomach.

'And what about Cassie?' I ask curtly, turn to glare at my damnable father.

'I'll see she's taken care of,' he says quite calmly, and turns his attention back to the sports betting once again.

'And the unborn child?'

'I'll see he or she's taken care of, too,' my father says, again without raising his voice.

I look back across to my mother but she just sits with her head bowed, doesn't utter a word. The three of us then stew in this stilted orbiting silence for maybe the next quarter of an hour, and this stupid Spice Girls' song just loops mindlessly around inside my skull, bounces back and forth like a tennis ball on Angel Dust, and I'm visualizing this big red-head playing Janet King in Russ Meyer's *Vixen* and she's naked and she's lying back, spread-eagled across a tree trunk, her arms reaching for the sun, and she's whining over and over, in this obnoxious Deep South drawl, 'Don't you think I've got a beautiful body?', and then the oven timer starts to bleep in the kitchen, my mother rises slowly to her feet and tells my father, softly, almost apologetically, 'That'll be our tea ready, Dad,' and my father fails to acknowledge her words.

My mother retires to the kitchen. I sit glaring at my father, then sigh heavily and spit a token gesture of conversation at him. 'You look like you've caught some colour.'

He sighs, too. 'Yeah. Picked it up at London Zoo.

Took your mother up there on Thursday.' I'm taken back to this image of Jo, of a Sunday afternoon last spring, when we floated through the zoo on Es, soaking up the weird and wonderful scents and screech-calls.

I snap back to reality and ask, or rather state, 'Didn't know mother had a soft spot for animals.'

'Yeah. Like I said, it was a hot day on Thursday,' my father replies, avoids any hint of confrontation.

'And the animals? Just how were the animals, father?'

'Asleep.'

'Asleep?'

'Yeah, asleep. Like I said, it was a hot day.'

'What? All of them?'

'Except for the little monkeys.'

'The little monkeys?' I ask without thinking.

'The gibbons.' My father arcs his head towards me. 'They were deliriously happy, son – just like your mother.' He smiles that septic smile again.

Galvanized by his blatant indifference, I find myself grinding my teeth and my eyes dart round the room. Why is my graduation photo no longer above the fireplace? Has he maybe hidden it? There's Ray in high school, and a shot of his wedding day, but there's no graduation photo. I hated the photo, but that's not the point.

Seething, struggling to disguise my anger, I bite into my lower lip, then open my mouth to speak. I pause to look skyward, as if seeking divine inspiration, hold that pose for a second too long, close my mouth again.

Then, just when I'm convinced that my father believes he has me rattled, I burn my iridium eyes into his and rasp through a half-smiling mouth, 'If you ever hurt my mother again I will tear your fucking head off, you miserable drunken bastard.'

My mother appears from nowhere, says, 'Oh, heavens, I've made more than enough for the two of us. Would you care to join us, Damian?'

'Damian was just saying he had to leave,' my father says. 'He's probably got himself a date with some girl . . . isn't that right, son?'

My father and I sit facing one another – him making these ridiculous warm, fatherly faces, me just glaring back, breathing heavily through napalmed nostrils.

'Oh, might you be seeing Elizabeth, dear?' my mother chirps, oblivious to the stench of hostility in the air.

'Beth? Er, yeah,' I answer.

'Look at your mother when she's talking to you, son,' my father is telling me, like he's mustered up all the charm in the world. I laugh in disgust. My father just smiles again.

I stand, skirt round my mother. She suddenly seems so small, so fragile, so weak. 'I'd best be going.'

'You must bring Elizabeth home soon, dear,' my mother tells me.

'Yes, mother,' I mumble.

'Take care, Henry,' my father calls out as I step into the hall. I stop to shake my head in disbelief, then pace back to the edge of the lounge, but my father has turned his attention back to the racing once again and he fails to register my presence.

My mother follows me to the front door and puts her hand to my left arm as I step out onto the pavement. 'Damian, I . . .' she starts to say, but I'm away, across the road and down the other side, not interested in hearing any explanations. I'm convinced that she continues to linger at the door until I disappear from sight and, just yards round the corner, I have to turn back.

But when I look up at the house the front door is closed, there's no sign of my mother, and this polar spasm blankets the length of my spine, so I'm obliged to stand there for maybe five minutes or more, just taking in the peace and serenity of the suburbs, the tranquillity I knew so well as a child, so solacing, just stand there spellbound, humming Wagner's 'Ride of the Valkyries' to myself, before I have to turn away once again and begin to tread the distance to my brother's house.

He'll know Gillian's address. There's questions I want answering.

I'm in the Maynard Arms on Park Road, with Five and Rachel and Thom. Five and I are both wearing cream moleskins, Armani polo shirts, his in beige, mine in navy. Thom – the odd one out – is wearing these orange cords from Teddy Smith, and is swamped by this oversized brown ribbed roll-neck from Hope and Glory. In

Thom's defence however, they're *my* orange cords and *my* brown roll-neck.

Thom is tripping. He's tripping and he's talking bollocks about Chelsea FC and how they're by far the best team in London, and how their manager, Gianluca Vialli, is higher than God, and how their captain, Dennis Wise, should be captain of England, and how Chelsea are going to win the Cup Winners' cup this season, and the league, and the Champions league the season after that, and how he hates Tottenham and West Ham and Millwall and Arsenal and Man United and how . . .

We've all already necked four pints of Export and I'm hoping the alcohol will go some way to quelling the effects of Thom's microdot. The jukebox is in full effect towards the front of the pub, blasting out some hard house anthems, but we're near the back, looking out on their aviary, where the music is quieter, the cooped budgerigars making all the racket, but none of the others seem to mind, and I'm wishing I was up mingling, closer to the bar, because there's a few things in here I think I might like to fuck tonight, though no one I would wish to get involved with, no Meyer-class things.

But Five's with his woman and Thom's going nowhere fast and it's not even nine o'clock and we're looking at sinking a fair few jars yet and I probably wouldn't be able to get it up tonight anyway, and Beth will probably pay me an unannounced visit later so we may as well just veg out here, killing time, at our table in the least inhabited corner of the pub, away from the throng and the interesting people.

I catch the eye of this black geezer sitting at a mixed table – three men, two women – across from us, and he maybe holds my unblinking gaze for a moment too long, and I think that I recognize him from somewhere but I can't be certain.

'Here's a good one, boys. Hey, listen, Thom,' Five says. 'Do you reckon, right . . . Do you reckon you could have Mike Tyson, if you went into the ring with him, armed with a baseball bat?'

'Do you mean Mike Tyson, the boxer? Or little Mickey Tyson, this kid I went to junior school with?' I ask, detached. 'Mickey Tyson who got his fifteen minutes of infamy for baking his pet tortoise in his mum's oven?'

'Mike Tyson the boxer,' Five states.

'No,' I say flatly, look away. 'He'd bite my ear off.'

'Ugh!' Rachel shrieks. 'He really baked his pet tortoise? That's gross, Damian.'

'No fucking way, man. I could never have Tyson. No way, not Tyson, man. No way,' Thom says loudly, giggles.

'Tyson would be too quick,' I say. 'We'd be standing there – me in my corner, him in his corner – psyching each other out. The bell would ring, I'd walk out to meet him, then "Bam!"' – I punch the flattened palm of my left hand with my clenched right fist – 'Tyson would hit me and lay me flat out before I even had a chance to swing the bat back.'

'Yeah, he'd be too quick, too quick, too quick,' Thom repeats.

176

Rachel lours at Thom. Thom just sits and stares at his pint. The black geezer on the opposite table is still looking over, and I think he might want to know, might want to have a pop at me for some reason.

'Your baseball bat would probably just snap in two across Tyson's arm, or his skull, even if you did get to hit him,' Rachel reflects.

I offer, 'Tyson would've knocked me out whilst I was still swinging the bat back – would probably have hit me twenty or thirty times whilst I was still swinging the bat back, if the truth be known . . . He'd surely be that fast.'

'Too quick,' Thom shouts.

'Well, it's just lucky for you boys you're not likely to meet him,' Rachel warns.

'Yeah, I wouldn't step in the ring with him if I was armed with anything less than a sub-machine-gun,' I admit.

'Anti-tank gun,' Thom blurts.

'You reckon?' Five smirks.

'Come on then, Mr Tough-Guy. I suppose you've got it all worked out?'

'Yeah, I've been giving this one a lot of thought, as it happens,' Five says.

'Do tell,' I prompt him.

'Well, what I reckon I'd do – right – is rush at him with the bat ready to swing, you know, off-balancing him like, then suddenly drop to the floor, and' – Five motions the swing of a baseball bat – 'crack him one in the shins, dead hard.'

'Crack . . . him . . . one . . . in . . . the . . . shins?' I repeat slowly.

'Yeah.'

'Crack Mike Tyson in the shins? Is that what you're saying?'

'Yeah.'

'Wow,' I whisper, deadpan.

'Yeah, because then, right, then he'll fall to the floor, he'll crumple up because I'll have, like, shattered his shinbone or something, so he'll be at my mercy, then I can pummel him to within an inch of his life. He won't stand a chance.'

'Whatever happened to Queensberry rules, love?' Rachel asks Five.

'They went out of the window with the baseball bat.'

'Like I said, he'd still be too quick for you,' I say.

'And the bat would just snap across his shins, anyway,' Rachel says.

'Which would probably get him really angry,' I add.

'Yeah,' Thom says, and we all look at him, but he just stares at his pint.

'Yeeaaaah,' Rachel says slowly.

'I'll get another round in,' Five says, and stands up.

The banter continues as the ales start to flow. Conversation soundbites subsume predominantly boy-talk: how we all came together, the women we've all slept with, women we all wish we'd slept with, the fights we've had, the fights we didn't have but perhaps should've had, anecdotes of fabled nights down the Union dancehall and huge smoking sessions and who did what to whom, when and why. Rachel is just a voiceless and slightly irritated bystander throughout.

I start drinking Pernod and Black chasers with my pints, then stop the chasing and pour the shorts straight into my lager. Thom farts and we all laugh. Rachel is wearing a tight white T-shirt with this huge navy Umbro motif across her chest like the England team might wear, but which somehow just helps to accentuate her small pert breasts, arousing me ever so slightly. I'm fully aware, however, that you should never regard mate's girlfriends with such quixotic insights. I've learned that lesson the hard way before.

I spot the black face again. I'd long since forgotten about him. I catch his eye and look at him, straight-faced, make out that I'm unconcerned. He retains eye contact – I don't know why I'm looking at him – and, as I stand to leave our table, pass by on my way toward the toilets, he says, as clear as day, as if his is the only voice in the pub, 'You're not leaving, are you, honey?'

I find myself blushing, and I'm thinking: he's not looking for a fight, he's not some vicious cunt looking for aggro – he's a homme, he's looking for a shag, he wants to . . . *fuck me*.

I urinate quickly in the toilets, wondering what on earth I'm even doing in here now, why I've cornered myself, unsettled that he's going to walk in on me at any moment. I don't bother to wash my hands. I have to walk back past this black homme's table again, there's no avoiding it, and he's sat there leaning towards one of his companions – Greek, squat, similarly clean-shaven, well groomed and immaculately dressed – and I hear his voice again above the din of the pub, and I hear him say, surprisingly gruffly, though still well pronounced, 'Isn't he gorgeous,' and I know that he's looking directly at me, and I don't know where to put my face, so I just stare blankly ahead, gulping inwardly. Bizarrely, I actually feel . . . flattered.

Rachel's at the bar. I interrupt Thom's and Five's inane conversation.

'I've just been pulled,' I say, flustered.

'Oh, yeah? What's she look like?' Thom asks with a touch too much enthusiasm, still tripping out slightly.

'Not a she, a he. The black geezer on the next table.'

'Where?' Five asks, strains his neck.

'Don't look now,' I snap at him, burying my head in my hands.

'Bollocks . . . what did he say?' Five asks, leaning closer.

I recount the homme's comments.

'So, Dame, you gonna do the black guy, or what?' Thom enquires, attempting to sound serious.

'Oi, less of the language, young man,' Five says to Thom. 'I believe the correct terminology in this instance is: are you gonna batter the coon?'

The two fall about laughing. Five's drunk, Thom's still tripping and I've sobered up surprisingly quickly.

'Are you gonna batter the coon?' Thom squeals, then giggles.

I look over to my new-found friend, and the black cunt actually winks back at me.

I turn to Thom and Five and demand, 'Do-I-*look*-gay?'

Thom is still laughing.

'Yeah, you look like a fucking homme, Dame,' Five says to me, points at me, then says to Thom, 'Backs to the wall, eh, Thom?'

Thom continues to laugh out loud, and repeats, 'Backs to the wall,' then laughs again, annoying me. He wanders off towards the toilets, still laughing insanely.

'I'll follow him,' Five says.

'Bollocks, will you – you're not leaving me on my own.'

'Oh, fuck off. I thought I'd give you some quality time alone with your new fella.'

'Shut it, Five – and stay put.'

Five puts his arm round me, and whispers, 'Temper temper, sweetie,' and air-kisses my right cheek.

I do love my friends, but my tolerance levels have limits.

Rachel returns. Thom's gone for more than ten minutes, so I offer to go and look for him, to check that he's alright.

'If the black geezer follows me, then you follow, too – you got that?' I tell Five.

'What, and play gooseberry?'

'Fuck you, Five. Just do it.'

There's no sight of Thom in the toilets, and, as I return to the bar, the homme's there stood in front of me, waiting for me, and he puts his hand up to my chest to stop me and asks me my name. He is wearing bright blue contact lenses – a nice touch.

'Er, Thom,' I lie, then add for good measure, 'Thomas Faulkner.'

'Hi, Thomas Faulkner, I'm Damian,' he says.

I have to smirk. 'Look, er . . . I'll have to talk to you later, um, Damian.' I brush past him, wondering what the hell's happened to the real Mr Faulkner.

Two things sit at our quiet table in the corner, one blonde, one unblonde, neither anything to write home about. I just stand and look at them, confused for an instant, doubtless unnerving them. Then I head outside through the side-door, to find Five rubbing Rachel's back, her doubled-over, being sick against the kerb.

'Thanks for following me,' I say to him.

'I said I didn't want to play gooseberry.'

'Git.'

'Faggot! Besides, Rachel's feeling a bit queasy. So, where's Thom, then?'

'I don't know. He wasn't in the toilets.'

'He didn't come back to the table. He must've headed off home. You got any blow at your place?'

'Yeah, loads.'

'Good. We may as well head back up to your gaff, then. I don't really fancy listening to Rachel throwing up, anyway. Unless, of course, you want to go back in to sit with your new fella?'

We put Rachel on a W7 heading south toward Finsbury Park, then both catch a similar W7 heading in the opposite direction, north up to Muswell Hill where we grab a couple of kebabs – Five a chicken, me a kofte – then head on up to the flat, to find Thom sat in the lounge, smoking this mammoth spliff, sat staring blankly at the TV – the only source of light in the flat – dazed like the little *Poltergeist* girl.

'Where did you get to?' Five and I both ask him.

Thom says nothing, sits hushed, lips pursed.

'Where did you get to?' Five restates.

'Eat your bollocks!' Thom replies irrationally, doesn't look up.

Five and I both look to one another, then return to Thom. 'You what?' we holler.

'Eat . . . your . . . bollocks!' Thom responds again, and puts the TV remote to his lips, attempting to sip from it like it's a pint or something, his latent rationale shot to pieces.

We stick *Apocalypse Now* on the video, with the sound turned down, and Five wants to hear some Rolling Stones, but we're fresh out of Stones so Five makes do with this record I find in Thom's collection – a copy of Bryan Ferry singing 'Sympathy For The Devil'. We smoke some weed and I make a bong out of a plastic cordial bottle and a biro pen, and we smoke some more weed through that, and we stick on some tunes, listen to some Paul Oakenfold on CD and to an old cassette of *Bummed* by the original love-thugs, Happy Mondays, and I turn the volume back up on the TV when Wagner's 'Ride of the Valkyries' is given an airing during the attack of the helicopter gun-ships, and we demolish two bottles of wine Thom had bought for Lisa, and Thom screams 'You fat bastard' at the telly – his only words to make any sense – when Marlon Brando appears and we keep rewinding and replaying the bit where the sacrificial cow gets its head cleaved off, and the woman upstairs phones to tell us to keep the noise down, then Five catches a minicab home and I stick on my Anna Nicole Smith video and Thom falls asleep on the sofa.

I retire to my bedroom but leave the TV on, having turned the lounge lights to full beam, and before I get into bed I masturbate quickly, fantasizing that Jo is knelt before me, my cock pushed deep into her mouth, her bushbaby blue eyes staring up at me, but her face transmutes into the face of that black homme and this upsets my rhythm, so I don't cum. And I crawl up into a tight ball beneath my duvet and think that I really miss Jo, and that I cannot live without her, and I cry myself to sleep and have this really freakish dream where Jo and I . . .

Thom and Lisa have just left for the opening of a new restaurant in Chalk Farm, or was it maybe Gospel Oak? – somewhere on that 'other' fork of the Northern Line – and I'm sat here toking on a sweetening spliff, watching *Brookside*, my inner calm disordered by the immediate presence of the demonic form that constitutes Mike. I resent Mike being here – it was Thom who let him in, invited him across the threshold. And if that stupid thing Lisa had only applied her warpaint that bit quicker, then the pair of them would have been away and I would not have had to answer the fucking door to Mike, and I would not have had to sit and listen to George Michael booming out of Thom's stereo for half the blessed evening. Looking down at my feet, I notice that I'm wearing odd socks – one navy, one black. It was dark and I was hungover when I got up this morning.

'So anyway,' Mike says, sweeps that stupid blond fringe – when will he get it cut? – from his eyes and takes the spliff from me, 'my boss turns to me in this huge staff meeting and goes, "Michael." He goes, "Michael"' – Mike stops to chuckle, then draws quickly on the spliff – 'he goes, "Michael, it's not big and it's not clever"' – Mike chuckles again – 'and I turn to him and say, in front of all these people, "I'm six foot one, I weigh thirteen stone, and I've got a first-class degree in Biochemistry. Therefore it *is* big and it *is* clever."' Mike guffaws, cries, can't control his imbecilic laughter onslaught that follows. I only have ears for a perishing grass-seed as it pops 'Tsssch' in the spliff he's holding. I can barely manage a sardonic grin to humour him. I think that he's certainly speeding – he's too hyper, talking too quickly.

Mike, too, once had a thing for big clubby blondes, real Meyer types. We'd battle it out to see who could pull the tallest, the blondest, whenever we went club-bing together. But, to the best of my broad knowledge, his last five conquests have all been either short or unblonde. He's been failing me miserably for such a time, yet it's only now I've actually begun to sit up and take notice of his glaring infidelity.

Mike suddenly switches his mood with, 'Dame, I'm worried about Weatherface.' He whispers this through the side of his mouth, and his pale eyes scan the room furtively as if seeking out sniping eavesdroppers.

'We're all worried about Weatherface,' I attempt to joke, flick casually through a small pile of CDs at my side – Kraftwerk, Orbital, Oakenfold's *Goa Mix*, New Order, New Order again, Orbital again, New Order yet again.

'He hasn't phoned. Have you heard from him?'

'Not since that night in the Doggett's. I might have had an e-mail, though.'

Mike scowls. 'Everyone's phoned me – even Tyler just to tell me how much he's got saved each time. So, what's happened to Weatherface?'

'I don't know,' I mutter offhandedly.

'Do you think he's bottled it?'

I pause, take the deepest of breaths. Mike has over-stepped a sacrosanct mark here – deeming to near affront a friend of mine. I swill another mouthful of Kronenbourg round my mouth to clear the taste of the spliff, then place the empty can down on the floor. 'Weatherface will come through, don't worry. And he'll have the money.'

'You reckon?'

'He doesn't go out, so it's not like he spends any.'

Mike titters, then asks, 'Do you think he's told Heather?'

I stall for a moment, switch the telly off, then stick

some New Order on the stereo. Would I have told Jo? No question about it. I trusted her implicitly. But Heather's an exception to the rule: she's anti-drugs in a big way, she's anti-everything in a big way. I shrug my shoulders and use the remote to flick channels on the TV, appearing unconcerned, indifferent.

'Weatherface tell Heather?' I sigh. 'Nah, don't be stupid. He'd never tell Heather.' I must keep faith with Weatherface, show committal to his resilience. So many others have rebuked my friendship of late.

'Yeah, well, if you say so, Dame.'

'I do say so,' I tell Mike calmly, and smile.

'Yeah, you're probably right. I trust you, Dame,' Mike says, sounds sincere, then says to himself, almost absentmindedly, 'I wonder if Weatherface's been sending me those letters?'

'Er . . . what letters?' I enquire.

'Oh, one of the boys has been sending me some joke letters.'

I sit up, show interest. 'Really?'

'Yeah. There's these pictures of me from university, with jokey captions calling me "drug-dealing scum" and stuff like that. They're all really funny.'

'Maybe it's Matt who's behind it?' I bluster all of a sudden.

'Matt?' Mike asks.

'Yeah, Matt.'

'Matt?' Mike repeats again. 'Nah. He's the last one I'd suspect.'

allen jarvis

'The last one?' I ask.

'Oh, after you of course, Dame. No, I bet it's that cheeky git Tyler.'

'Hold on, hold on,' I virtually snap. 'Aren't you worried? I mean, "drug-dealing scum". It sounds to me like you might have some trouble brewing.'

'Nah, don't be silly, Dame. It's obviously just a joke,' Mike says, sounds like he really doesn't care, like he's not troubled by any of this. Then, as I sit bemused, he starts to tell me this tale about a thing he picked up last Friday after the pub, the Photographer & Firkin back over Ealing way, this thing I'd have liked – tallish, blonde, clubby-looking, great legs, voluptuous, deprived of braincells but then you can't expect everything – and he gets this thing back to his flat, she's all over him, can't get enough of him, but remarkably, he decides not to sleep with her; he's well E'd up, really calm, decides to wait this time, maybe show her a little respect, just fucking her didn't feel right; then in the morning this thing wakes, wanders out into the corridor naked and Mike panics, prays that his flatmate's not around, but the thing rushes back in, asks, 'Where are we?' and Mike answers, 'Ealing,' then the thing shoots him an accusatory glance, demanding, 'And who . . . are . . . you?' and, before Mike has chance to reply, she slays him with the immortal, 'Ohmygod, it's my husband's birthday – he'll kill me for not making it home last night.'

I scratch the side of my nose, enquire, 'And the moral of the story is?'

'Should've shagged her when she was drunk,' Mike

188

says, with just a hint of regret. We fall about laughing. It's like old times when I regarded Mike as an undoubted friend, sharing such confidences, swapping tales of woe. Now he's just an acquaintance, someone I simply have to deal with in order to get through the day – a business partner at best. The added fact that he let such a blonde escape his clutches serves only to confirm the doubts I already have in him.

'Right, boss, time I was chipping,' Mike declares, picks up his mobile phone and slips it in his jacket pocket.

'Oh, right, er, that was a flying stop,' I say. I hadn't stopped to question Mike's unannounced visit – as I said, we're almost bordering on old times here. Only, those times no longer exist.

'Yeah, I was just passing through. I've been away to visit someone.' Mike seems preoccupied, he jiggles the car keys in his hand, says, 'Oh, well, gotta be chipping,' brushes past me, then adds quietly, 'I've got to give Mum an update on my brother.'

I digest his words for an age before quizzing, 'An update on your brother?'

Mike stops in his tracks. 'Yeah,' he says, almost inaudibly.

'What *about* your brother, Mike?'

Mike pauses, says, 'He's in a bad way.'

I prompt him further with, 'Oh?'

'He's in prison.'

'Oh,' is all I can say again, this time sullenly.

'Yeah. He got a kicking a couple of nights back. Got

caught up in some gang war on his landing. My brother can't fight for toffee – you know that. He's got a fractured skull, a punctured lung, few broken ribs—'

I furrow my brow, look concerned. 'You never said he was inside.'

Mike just laughs, gazes through the window. 'Yeah, well – you know this dealer we're getting the gear from?'

'Yeah.'

'My brother took the rap for him – got caught with close on three hundred Es. My stupid little brother kept his mouth shut, didn't grass anyone up, so they sent him down for three years.'

'Oh.'

'That was five months back.'

'I'm sorry,' I tell him.

'Don't be. He's being kept financially sweet while he's inside . . . as long as he *survives* his stretch inside.' There's this pause where I presume I'm expected to say something to maybe placate matters, but I'm lost for words, so Mike continues with, 'Yeah, the gear's just a favour to me by my brother's "man". I think he feels guilty. That's why he's selling to us cheap, like he owes the family a favour or something. He originally offered me some gear for free, just a few Es, but the ten thousand was my idea. I thought I'd get everyone in on the act, really hit him where it hurts – in his pocket. I mean, he never usually sells to my brother for less than five, maybe five-fifty, but he's had to make an exception in this case.'

There's this parturient pause, the only voice in the

flat being Barney from New Order singing something about it not being my right to be his enemy, then I just blurt, 'I hope your brother's gonna be alright.'

'Cheers, mate,' Mike says, then makes a move for the door again. 'Look, I really don't want this to go any further, okay? I mean, I only told you 'cos I trust you, Dame. You're a good mate, you know that.'

'No worries,' I say in this utterly trustworthy voice, but I'm just thinking that it's the wrong brother lying broken in a prison hospital bed.

After Mike leaves I plant myself on the sofa, pick up the phone, dial the number for Weatherface and, as an answering machine clicks into life and Heather's abhorrent tones inform me 'There's no one home to take your call', I find myself mindlessly scribbling 'drug-dealing scum' across the front cover of a *Voluptuous* magazine on the table before me.

Jo always said I thought more of my friends than I did of her. I think I'm finally proving her wrong.

I'm in the Minories, by Tower Hill. I'm not comfortable here: I'm not nearly drunk enough, have no drugs, and it's too full and too noisy. There's too many other suits who love the sound of their own voices, but I had no other plans for tonight, no pre-arranged drinks with the boys, so here I stand at the bar, listening to Nicholas Spencer-Jones from work telling me how depressed he is at the break-up of him and that Allison Coyle, how he's going to quit England, find work abroad, in America or maybe France or Belgium or anywhere, maybe not even work at all, just travel, shag anything remotely female that moves, dissipate that Coyle thing from his harried soul. He tells me I should do the same now that I've split with Jo, that I should work abroad whilst I'm still young, to expand my horizons beyond the 'restricting' (Spencer-Jones's words) confines of London.

I'm bored by his comments, am becoming increasingly distracted, and so it's a relief when this black thing sidles up to us, asks me, 'Can I introduce you to my mate, please? It's her birthday today – she'd really like to meet you.'

'How old is she?' I ask after a pause, look past her, attempt to ascertain from which gaggle of things she's hailed.

'Twenty-one,' she says.

I look to Nicholas. 'Nice age,' he says reassuringly.

'I'll come over in a minute,' I tell her.

'I'll grab you in five,' she says and asks me my name.

I lie to her. 'Thom – Thomas Faulkner.'

An overwhelming sense of déjà vu – have I maybe had this very same conversation with someone else recently? Or is it that I've actually met this black thing somewhere before?

'Nice name,' the black thing is saying.

'What is?' I snap.

'Thom,' she says.

'No, it's not,' I whisper at her through clenched teeth.

I turn back toward the bar to order another two

bottles of Kronenbourg. I don't watch the black thing return to her friends, knowing full well that Spencer-Jones – the sad homme – will be doing this for me.

'There's five of them, Damian,' Nicholas reports. 'Look like a bunch of secretaries. Three blacks and two white. Actually, I think it's one of the white girls that likes you.'

'And?' I prompt him. 'Description?'

Spencer-Jones sucks on his gums, waits for my brow to furrow at his apparent timewasting in view of my question, then delivers, quite surreptitiously, once our eyes have locked, '*Baywatch . . . Crimewatch*,' and then giggles into his drink.

'*Baywatch Crimewatch*?' I ask in a monotone, and my steely-grey eyes prompt Nicholas further.

'She's got a body from *Baywatch*,' he starts, giggles slightly. 'And a . . . a face from *Crimewatch*.'

'Oh,' I say quite flatly. 'A most humorous analogy.'

'Well, *I* thought it was funny.' Nicholas sulks.

'Is she tall?' I return quickly, then tut.

'Maybe only five-six,' Spencer-Jones moans out, chastened. 'Not really tall enough for you.'

'And her hair?'

'Bleached: her roots are showing.'

'Breasts?'

'Damian, you can't really tell from here.'

'Well, would you fuck her?'

'Listen, I would fuck anything, mate. You're the one with the rigid guidelines on height, hair, et cetera.'

'I'll neck this Kronie first, then think about it,' I tell

193

him, but I'm not really interested in meeting anyone tonight because earlier today, in the office, I found myself staring at Jackie Gray from the project team in our adjacent area and, locking eyes, she smiled and actually raised her hand to wave at me and blushed, like she's hopelessly in love with me or something, and even though her blonde hair is starting to grey slowly and she dresses like someone in their forties (she's only early thirties, I think – far too old for me really) and even though her face is too wide and her lips mouth a permanent grimace, I would still love to fuck Jackie Gray, maybe even see her for a week or two, steal some small special part of her life, because, when I first heard her talking in the lifts, just two weeks ago, I was briefly swept away to this magical arcadia: Jackie Gray's voice, her pronunciations, her very accent were all virtually identical to Jo's – this sensual Scottish lilt that sloshed through me and over me. I think I will e-mail her tomorrow, try and attempt to strike up some kind of rapport, maybe even ask her out for a drink or possibly a meal.

A Japanese tourist in a flat-cap snapped a photograph of me as I careered down the escalator (late again) in Highgate tube station this morning. I caught myself wondering just how many strangers have rogue photos of me amongst their collections. Me, Damian Henry Shaw, caught in the background propped against a bar or maybe ambling slothfully past in some sickly family snapshot? I'm actually contemplating whether or not Jo ever looks through old photos of me? Her father's got a camcorder video of us together at some cousin's wedding out Stirling way. I'm wondering if Jo ever watches out-takes of that, ever reminisces.

Nicholas and I begin to discuss office politics. The customary stuff: who we'd like to fuck in our department, then on our floor, then in the entire company; who we think would be the hardest person in our department, then on our floor, then in the entire company; what vicious little deeds we could commit to exasperate one Hubert Dodd. Then this ugly little blonde thing – really badly made up, wearing a jumper which reads ARMANI JEANS – approaches Nicholas and me, pushes up against my compatriot, tells him that he looks like a man who'd like to buy a woman a stiff drink.

Nicholas throws his arm around me, probably sensing that I'm ready to up and leave him at the mercy of this vamp, and tells her, 'Darling, this is the only person who'll receive anything stiff from this young buck tonight.'

'Fags!' she maybe mouths at us. Or maybe she just pouts. I'm not sure.

'Well, er, when I said I'd fuck *any*thing, I do have some limitations,' Spencer-Jones says, looks almost sheepish in the bar's half-light. 'Damian, look, you've just got to come to America with me. We'd pull over there, no problem.' Nicholas puts his hand to my shoulder, very gingerly. 'I mean, just your accent is enough to guarantee you a blowjob from some big blonde bimbo. Look at me, I got laid three times that month I was out in Chicago last year, and I wasn't even trying.'

'Hmmm,' I reflect, and tap the mouth of my Kronenbourg bottle against my two front teeth. This unblonde thing in a clingy dress and clunking kinky boots brushes past us, and four short words illuminate the forefront of my mindscape: *The . . . boots . . . on . . . that.*

Nicholas lines me up a whisky chaser, and though I do not like whisky I drink it, but quickly clear the taste from my mouth with another gulp of the salvaging Kronie. I try to fix this clubby blonde, just up the bar from us, with the look that Jo so zealously revered – my head tilted slightly forward, my brow furrowed, trying to look serious with my mouth pursed like I'm about to blow a kiss – but this blonde just screws up her face, resembles a shih-tzu chewing on a wasp, and wanders back to her friends, doesn't even grant me the dignity of a backward glance over her shoulder as she retreats. For all she cares, I may as well simply not exist.

Spencer-Jones and I are both obdurately bored and so ridiculously tired, so I'm relieved when he tells me he doesn't fancy sticking around, because he's got an early start tomorrow – a seven-thirty meeting with both the Sod and the Sperminator. We make our excuses to one another, and Nicholas tells me I should sleep on the American idea. I wouldn't have entertained such a namby-pamby suggestion from any Lunchboy just two months ago, but I'm oddly flattered that Nicholas regards my level of friendship so highly. It's just a shame some of the boys – some of my so-called friends – do not revere me with an equivalent degree of compassion.

Once on the street, I fall into a black cab, bark out my directions, then shut my eyes to visualize myself fucking Jo backwards on my futon – me fully dressed, suited, her naked, tossing her mane of long blonde hair back, telling me she wishes I had two cocks so that she could suck on one whilst the other one fucked her hot wet pussy. This month's shot in my Anna Nicole Smith calendar is undoubtedly and, for want of a better word, tremendous – by far and away the best shot I think I have ever witnessed of her ambrosial form.

Again, everything appears in this luxurious tomato red. This time it's not just Anna's lips and nails painted this delirious colour, but she's also wearing a pair of open-toed shoes to match and this scanty negligee thingy, and the shot appears to have been taken from slightly overhead, as if the cameraman was perhaps hanging from the ceiling or maybe Anna was lying prostrate on the floor, though her posture doesn't suggest this, and with one hand Anna appears to be pulling the negligee down towards her knee as if to cover herself up, but with her second hand she seems to be straining to pull the negligee ever higher and, with her mouth slightly agape and almost pursed and with one eyebrow deliciously raised, it's as if she's saying to me, 'C'mon, Dame, *you* decide. Do you want the negligee on . . . or off?'

*

I'm standing alone outside the Covent Garden General Store, counting the blondes and the unblondes that've passed through the ticket barriers during my brief spell waiting here. Sixteen blondes, none of which were over five-eight, and thirty-seven unblondes, only two of whom were tall, though both, alas, willowy and anaemic-looking – really studenty. It's six p.m. My Walkman is knackered and any songs I play on it sound really eerie, all distant and echoey, with the vocals totally adrift, lost in the background – sounds like listening to a gig in an aircraft hangar with bad acoustics – and so I'm playing this New Order compilation tape on it to remind me of gigs from some foregone era, of better times with my brother. I'm waiting for Gerry and Jay and Caroline Kirkland, who's up from Southampton on business, when I spy a familiar face in the throng leaving the station: an Asian, someone I have not seen for a long time, someone—

'Damian,' he says, reaches to shake my hand. 'Is that really you? I can't believe it. How the hell are you? I haven't seen you for – what? – must be three years now?'

'Fine. I'm, um, fine, you know . . . I'm sweet,' I stutter, racking my brainvault, desperate to remember this individual's name. He asks me what I'm doing now, wants to know where I live, tells me that he's been away travelling, has seen the world, got briefly engaged to a fat girl in Australia, got massively sick in India and lost two stone, and he's now back in London at some accountancy practice off Chancery Lane, and living with his parents and five sisters in Leytonstone.

'And how's Lisa these days?' he asks, eyes bright.

'Lisa?' I sort of repeat, like I didn't really hear him correctly.

'Yeah, Lisa,' he says again, but I just avoid his prying gaze, so he continues, 'you know: Lisa, Jay, Matt – anyone? How's all your old gang?'

'Still together,' I tell him proudly, then add sadly, once the flagrancy of what I'm actually saying suddenly smashes home to me, 'Well, er, most of us.'

'Drifted apart from some of 'em, eh?'

'Yeah, something like that,' I find myself utter lugubriously.

'That's just life, mate.'

'Yeah,' I say into the ground. 'Isn't it just.'

Sensing my prostrating loss, my abrupt deprival of spirit, this Asian says he must rush but we should meet up soon; says he obviously has a lot of catching up to do. He leaves me his phone number but I don't have the heart to actually ask him his name, and I'm still stood there brainstorming as Caroline falls upon me, hugging me, telling me I look great. Eyeing her up and down, I tell her that she looks fantastic – which she does – and kid her that she's put on a few pounds – which she most certainly hasn't. Caroline's wearing a navy suit, and I'm thinking that this is maybe the first time I've ever seen her dressed in anything other than jeans.

Five and Marky Mullen both fucked Caroline after a heavy smoking session in Jay's room in our first year at university – Five going first, Marky following only minutes later, Marky claiming he forced a bottle of Jay's deodorant spray up inside her. This is something I am not a party to, something that only Five and Marky share. Caroline does possess a fantastic pair of breasts, near Meyer-esque proportions.

We look one another up and down again.

'So, tell me all the gossip,' she says cheerily. 'How are you and Joanna getting along?'

I pause and sigh, have to enlighten her, 'Erm, look, Caroline . . . there's something you really ought to know about me and Jo . . .'

Much, much later, after God-knows-how-many tequilas slammed in Café Pacifico, after Gerry drunkenly admitted that he was, in fact, still in love with Andrea, or at least in love with the special memories he still holds of Andrea even though they've now been apart some three years and she's now finally having his name surgically removed from her right tit; after Jay nearly started a fight with these three Italians whilst staggering back up Long Acre, a fight which Gerry and I were all too happy to finish off before Caroline dragged us away; after Caroline virtually broke down and disclosed that she'd actually failed her P2 Accountancy exams when she'd already told us she passed them earlier in the year and that she's been walking a tightrope at work ever since, and that Nathan, her boyfriend down in Southampton, wasn't so much a boyfriend any more, that he's now her fiancé and they're living together, but that even this part of her life is nothing more than a laughable farce and she really didn't think they'd see the year out . . . after all this, and more, I'm lying on my back in

Caroline's hotel room in Russell Square, and I'm naked except for a blue check Thomas Pink shirt and a navy and tangerine Romeo Gigli tie which has been pulled halfway down my front, and Caroline is looming above me, also naked, except for her bra and her blouse, and she is slowly rocking back and forth on me, and is fucking me far too . . . gently, her eyes shut tight, murmuring something softly to herself and, though Caroline is proving to be a really good fuck and her cunt is so wet and tight, I may as well simply . . . not . . . be . . . here, my mindscape is wandering someplace else, over distant boundless planes . . . just what is the point in having sex if it's not with Jo, where . . . is . . . the . . . romance?

Half-heartedly, I pull at Caroline's blouse, unbuttoning it as I go, and reach into her bra to paw at her swollen breasts. I attempt to steady myself on my elbows, to unhook Caroline's bra, but I collapse under her weight, and so instead I clumsily push the bra up, back over her breasts, forcing her tits down and out towards me, and I chew and bite at her full nipples, which only results in spurring Caroline on even further, and she blubbers something in her euphoria – Frank Sinatra? Did she just say 'Frank Sinatra'? No – 'Fuck-me-harder,' she said. 'Fuck-me-harder,' so I'm trying to thrust upwards at her, but the position I'm faced with is awkward and uncomfortable, and instead I push Caroline off me, then turn her round on all fours and, standing by the side of the bed, start to fuck her backwards, slowly at first, but gaining momentum with each pummel. I'm still in fear of losing my erection, so

I'm trying to visualize women I long for: Jane Fonda in *Barbarella*, then Jo, Anita Ekberg in *La Dolce Vita*, then this feisty big black thing from my tube carriage this morning, and then I'm visualizing Jayne Mansfield – this striptease I saw Jayne Mansfield play-act in some documentary on her too-short life; this striptease where Jayne had on a long blonde wig, and was wearing this black negligee and this tangerine sleeveless, jacket-thingy and, though you never actually got to see her naked except for her broad bare back, this somehow made the whole scenario so much more tantalizing, more watchable, more . . . and then I'm thinking – just how tall was Jayne Mansfield? How old was she when she died? And I make a mental missive to look up these facts. And then I cum, a feeble purposeless orgasm. Caroline still bucks against me, pointlessly, until I have to inform her, 'I've cum.'

Caroline is a diabetic and I have this ghastly recollection of her, years back, at some university disco, doubled up in convulsions after taking this speed polluted with glucose . . . memories of her coughing up blood, of her near foaming at the mouth, all of us powerless, not knowing what on earth to do or say.

I stand there, before her, an awkward silence loitering emphatically between us, then mumble, 'Er . . . I guess I'd better leave, then?'

'Yeah, s'pose . . . whatever,' comes the reply, but by then I'm already gathering up my clothes, hastily pulling on my suit trousers.

'Damian,' Caroline says as I make for the door.

'Yeah?' I stop to ask.

'Nothing,' she mutters, but I'm still standing here, waiting for . . . what? 'Give my love to Lisa,' she sighs after a while, and laughs.

I take one frangible step toward her. 'Look, Caroline, I, erm . . . are you really sure about this?'

'Yeah, why not? It's okay, Damian. Please don't fret on my behalf.'

I'm overwhelmed by an image from sometime last spring: an image of a drunk squatting down by a bus stop on Muswell Hill, of this self-same drunk toppling back into the road as a W7 pulled in, of the driver slamming on his brakes just in the nick of time, the front wheels squealing to a halt barely inches from the drunkard's face – as Jo and I looked on, both transfixed, thinking the drunk must surely be a goner. I feel a touch nauseous, and I bid a retreat without saying another word to Caroline.

I catch my reflection in a mirror in the hotel bar as I order myself a large vodka and tonic. I appear flushed. I stop to wonder what Jo's doing right now.

'You took your time,' Gerry tells me.

'Hmmm . . . anyone got a cigarette?' I ask.

Jay passes me a Silk Cut and lights it for me.

'Well?' Gerry again.

I drag hard on the cigarette, cough to clear my lungs, then ask, 'So . . . who's next?'

'I am. I am,' Gerry tells me, almost excitedly.

'Well, then . . . what are you waiting for?' I ask him flatly.

When it's just me and Jay and my vodka and tonic sat alone in the hotel bar, Jay confides in me, 'I think I'm just gonna settle for a blowjob, Dame. I'm too tired to do anything that'll require exertion.'

Gerry, Jay and I are all close: we're prepared to share and share alike. This was just too good an opportunity to be missed. I do love my friends, the people that still warrant that accolade. This is just the sort of experience that allies you to friends for eternity, an experience for which these people will always remember you. I swallow half my drink in one, but it tastes really bitter, worse than I've tasted before, so I offer the rest to Jay, but he just shakes his head, turns his nose up and takes a final toke on his cigarette before stubbing it out in the ashtray.

'Look, I'm gonna have to make a move now,' I tell him.

'What?' Jay exclaims as I stand up. 'And leave me here all on my own?'

'Your turn'll come soon. Gerry's not been laid in years – he'll be back before you know it,' I say. Then, as I turn to walk away I put my hands to my head and just utter, 'Amyl.'

'Nitrate?' Jay asks me.

'Amyl – from university – remember?' I gasp as I spin back towards him, my mindscape awash with reappearing memories. 'I met Amyl earlier tonight. I couldn't think of his name, but it's just come to me.' I discover myself snapping my fingers.

' "Amyl" Amir? Yeah, I remember him,' Jay says, then

smiles. 'Are you sure it was him though, Dame? I heard he got sent down for dealing a few years back.'

'He what? Nah, he said he'd been travelling.'

'No way, Amir was a well notorious geezer, Dame, a marked man – always carried a big fuck-off blade wher-ever he went. Who do you think I used to get all the speed off at uni? He's the cunt who cut that stuff up with glucose that sent Caroline into a fit that time.' Jay looks quite lost, his mindscape wandering. 'Mind, I s'pose he could be out of jail by now – what with good behaviour and all that.'

'Well, I never,' I can only murmur, and find myself toying with the notion that I'd quite like to sit down and take the weight off my feet, but instead I disappear into the night and hail a black cab which I take to Beth's flat, in Putney. My favourite Russ Meyer film today is *Mondo Topless*: so banal it makes me laugh, just an hour's footage of go-go girls performing routines in remote outback locations. Choice woman in said film is Babette Bardot. Her face isn't anything special, but she has a good body, looks like she's probably fairly tall, has blonde hair, and does this wonderful trick whereby she keeps exaggeratedly sucking on her thumb whilst she remains dancing.

We've rendezvoused for a pre-club drink in the Slug and Lettuce in Leicester Square, mixing it up west with the tourist crowd, and I'm wearing a new red short-sleeved shirt from D&G, these orange cords, and an old green

Schott MA1 jacket – the jacket borrowed from Thom, so it's obviously a bit tight on the shoulders. Jay's wearing this navy Dolce & Gabbana T-shirt with that stupid D&G IS D&G motif, Toolboy's modelling a pair of red velvet trousers.

Jay presents Toolboy with this opening gambit: 'How's Jinxy John? We've not seen him out for a while.'

To which Toolboy answers, 'Jinxy? Oh, he's okay. I guess . . . To tell the truth I haven't seen much of him myself, lately. Except for football on Sunday mornings, he just spends all his time with this nurse he's met – Camilla. In fact, come to think of it, she even turns up to watch him play footie as well.'

I join their conversation with, 'Yeah, Jinxy? Blimey, I thought he was the fancy-free type? Forever the bachelor boy, eh?'

Toolboy thinks about this, then answers, rather sadly I think, with, 'Used to be, maybe. Not any more though.' He sighs heavily and continues, 'He's even thinking about moving in with Camilla now . . . at her place out by Heathrow. I mean, I think he's even gonna rent out the gaff he's just bought in Osterley, just so he can move to some dump in the sticks with her.' Jay lets out a long whistle as Toolboy relents, 'And that's not all: she's got a four-year-old kid as well.'

The rest of the conversation continues in much the same vain.

Jay: 'Oh, man, that's, like, serious commitment, you know what I'm saying?'

Toolboy: 'I know. Who'd ever have thought it of John, eh?'

Me: 'End of an era, eh, boys?'

Toolboy: 'I just can't believe he's gonna go through with it.'

Jay: 'Well, I guess he probably knows what he's doing.'

Toolboy: 'Yeah, I mean she's nice enough, I guess. But, moving in with a bird? It's just not on at our age.'

Me: 'Yeah, that really is unheard of.'

Jay: 'Well, not unheard of, maybe . . . just look at Five and Matt. Oh, and Weatherface. Mind, definitely not this side of thirty for me, I'm glad to say.'

Toolboy looks forlorn, and I'm looking at Jay, and we're probably both thinking the same thing: that we should say something, anything to try and cheer Toolboy up, to reassure him that life ain't so bad after all, but Jay just shrugs his shoulders and all I can think of to say is: *We-e-ell, look on the bright side, Toolboy. You never know your luck. This Camilla might get hit by a bus tomorrow.* But I don't actually utter this; instead I just get Toolboy a treble whisky, and say, 'Chin up, eh?' But Toolboy still looks decidedly miserable.

We're also with Benny and his woman, Natalie, a lively little thing in tight black leather jeans, who I'm sure Jay really fancies but, though Natalie appears openly flirtatious – i.e. she's too intense: she retains eye contact in all her conversations for far too long, unnerving me just slightly – she hasn't taken her hand away from

Benny's back pocket all evening, and just two weeks ago she announced to Benny that she's pregnant. Stupidly, they're actually planning to have said baby.

One of the very last times I saw Jo, she asked me if I would move to Scotland if, say, she ever became pregnant by accident. I asked if she really was pregnant – or did she at least want to have a baby already – and she answered no, but what if? And I told her straight: no way – she would have to move down to London. I don't think that this was the answer she was necessarily looking for.

It's well past closing time and I'm wondering out loud as to where we'll actually head off next. Jay's suggested the Cross – there's some Renaissance do on – but Toolboy wants us to head back west with him, stop at some meat-market out that way, then all pile round Jinxy's gaff in the morning to give him a lecture on his future. Natalie has said however that she simply has to go to the Ministry because some of her mates might be meeting in there at twelve. At the promise of possible introductions to an uncharted gaggle of women, Jay and I decide to go with the Ministry option, even though Toolboy is slightly nettled by such a selfish choice.

Jay heads outside to bell Five on his mobile; he hadn't fancied an early drink, so said he'd meet up with us later, wherever we went.

I make my way down the spiral staircase, bound for the toilets, then wander out through the swing-doors at the back, careering into this tall thing coming through the other way – this real glamour puss. She's wearing this shimmering pink babydoll – the maximal in cheesy clubby dressing.

'I'm sorry,' I manage, slightly flustered.

Her long blonde hair is drawn across one side of her face, showing only the one eye, which appears to sparkle at me. 'It's okay,' she tells me, smiles, and pushes the drooping lock of hair away from her face. I find myself smiling at her for what seems like eternity, until she puts her hand to my arm and says to me, looking concerned, 'You shouldn't think so much, fella.' She turns to leave and makes her way up the spiral staircase, my eyes shadowing her captivating form as she goes, long legs slung beneath an arousing figure of eight – twenty-four-carat Meyer material.

The lighting is too bright and overbearing in the toilets. I'm toying with the idea of making myself sick in order to maybe sober myself up a touch, but I think better of it and just piss instead. There's a joke freshly scrawled across the cubicle wall, which reads, 'Why do blondes wear hooped earrings? To give them somewhere to hang their ankles,' and this enrages me a bit, simply because Jo was blonde and always wore a pair of hooped earrings. There's also this religious crap about Glasgow Rangers, with some Nazi shit thrown in, and I'm trying to fathom out whether there's some common thread linking this graffiti with the odious blonde jokes (another reads: 'What does a blonde say after making love? Thanks, guys'). Maybe this was all penned by some Scottish nobody who actually knew Jo? I breathe steadily, controlled, and try to dismiss such insane thoughts.

The piped music in the toilets is some George Michael crap and I find myself tutting disgustedly for all to hear.

When I return to the bar, Toolboy asks everyone, 'Right, are we all set?' The Babydoll is nowhere to be seen. We exit.

Favourite New Order song today: 'Love Vigilantes'. I like the title, it just seems rather fitting, hits the right note within, though I'm not actually sure quite what it means.

Once in the Ministry, after a surprisingly short queue of twenty-five minutes, and with the bouncers being unusually convivial, we immediately lose Jay, our resident groove disciple, to the plunging darkness of the abyssal back room, and I'm thinking that he might just be on something slightly more hallucinogenic than E, but I'm not entirely sure, but if he is, then I'm just a touch annoyed that he hasn't offered anything to me, and I'm remembering the last time Jay went 'solo' – when we were in Ibiza, two summers back, some of the boys on a club tour with a couple of the girlfriends in tow – when Jay scored some really bad gear, these purple ohms, and Jo and Lisa had to spend the entire night and half the next day babysitting him, stroking his forehead, whispering softly to him, trying to calm him down to stop him from going unconditionally over that mental edge.

Benny interrupts my train of thought. 'So, what do you reckon to me and Natalie then, Dame?' He looks away, like he's pretending he didn't ask the question or something. I don't know what to say, so just answer him with, 'What?!' like I didn't really hear him the first time – not that I care anyway.

'What did you think of me and Natalie?' he repeats, looks away again, this time towards the old film room.

'Er, yeah, you two look good together.'

He just smiles, seems satisfied with my response.

'You going to get married, then?' I ask him.

'No,' Benny says sharply, adds, 'Well, she wants to, but I guess we're too young.' Benny is my age and, at a guess, I'd say Natalie is older . . . maybe twenty-seven?

'Yeah, but you're not too young to have a kid, are you?' I have to point out.

'But I still want to go out with the boys,' he continues, shouting in my ear to counter the music. 'You know, drink a lot, flirt a bit, still have some fun.'

'So why are you letting her have the child?'

Benny looks at me. 'Why not? I'm happy with her. She's happy with me . . . I think. At least, I seem to make her laugh. Everything's fine for the time being. Why spoil the status quo? I haven't really got a valid reason to finish it, I guess.'

For some strange reason I'm suddenly thinking about Beth. A thing along the bar from us, this thing with mad bad dangerous eyes, wearing a T-shirt which says COCKY SUCKY FUCKY, smiles at me and, though I smile back warmly, I sense a tremor of trepidation rock throughout my body.

Natalie returns from the toilets, looking radiant,

throws her arm round Benny's waist and asks him, 'Alright, lover?' but Benny just stares at me and raises his eyebrows a little and something unsaid – I'm not sure what – passes between us.

I'm talking to Five, who's suddenly popped up from nowhere, who's got on his black Schott MA2 jacket and is E'ing out of his face and we're trying to discuss Benny's predicament, talking about how Five would feel if Rachel were to suddenly announce she'd fallen pregnant, when I spy the Babydoll from the Slug standing in the very . . . same . . . club . . . as me, glorious in her pink frippery. Like some irretrievably untamed spirit, I dump Five and make a direct beeline for her.

'Hi,' is all I find to say.

She half-smiles, 'Er, hi,' and continues to drink her Lucozade through a straw as she half-heartedly wiggles her hips to the music.

'You were in the Slug,' I tell her. 'Leicester Square.'

She looks puzzled. 'Er—'

'I bumped into you . . . The Thinker . . . By the swing-doors, down by the toilets.'

'Oh, right. I remember. That was you?'

Of course that was me, I am thinking. 'Yeah, that was me. Er, I like your hair.'

She's flattered, seems suddenly bright. 'Yes, my friend Lizzie created it for me after work today.'

'Created?' I ask, not really sure if that's exactly what she said – if I heard her quite right.

'Yes, created,' she starts, enthused. 'We're hairdressers.'

Hairdressers? I am thinking.

'From Stepney,' she adds.

From Stepney? I am thinking. Why, for once, can I not be done with it and just meet a plain old model from Chelsea or some professional sort 'in the City'? Maybe I'm in the wrong line of work, hanging out in all the wrong places.

'Look, I'll, um, talk to you later,' I tell her and head back to the boys.

Benny and Natalie leave early. 'For a curry,' Benny explains, but I can't figure out where in God's name they're gonna find a decent Indian at this time of the morning. It's two a.m. Natalie pinches Five's bottom as they depart. I'm sure it meant nothing, but it was on the blind side of Benny, and I think I'm the only one to – unwittingly – catch sight of the act. This is no more than Benny deserves – he's got a shit suburban lifestyle to contend with now. He's little better than my pitiful brother, scourged by an accelerated ageing bordering on progeria. Still, it's good that him and Natalie are having a child together; it takes them both out of society's gene pool. None of Natalie's mates have shown their faces here tonight anyway, and Benny looked stupidly uncool: wasn't wearing anything red or anything by D&G or Schott. Logically, he didn't belong with us.

I drink some bottled water, share a damp, encrusted wrap of speed with Toolboy in the toilets, score two Es for twenty-five quid the pair – a bloody rip-off, but what can you do? – off this twat I recognize as a mate of

Mike's brother who tells me the drugs will 'take me to Heaven tonight' so I score two more pills off him, telling him I'll need them 'to get me back home again'. Toolboy leaves around three to catch the tail-end of some party in Ealing.

The thing with the mad bad dangerous eyes in the COCKY SUCKY FUCKY T-shirt approaches us and, as I draw hard on a Silk Cut, asks me, 'Do you smoke?' With an incredulous look on my face, I answer her, 'Yes,' and she says, 'Good, I like a man who smokes,' then skips past us. Five points out that the thing with the dangerous eyes in the COCKY SUCKY FUCKY T-shirt was wearing a wedding ring. I think I should strive to avoid her as she's unnerving me.

I'm standing upstairs with Jay, who's finally surfaced from the back room, and we're looking down at the bar and all the amassed dancers beneath us, pointing out things we'd quite like to fuck tonight. It's so bright in here, Jay comments that it's almost like dancing in a pub. I have to agree with him. We also both agree that we fucking hate it in here; there's too many tourists and pushy people making for an unsettled atmosphere. The DJ's playing this really cheesy version of 'You're Not Alone', and I'm wishing they'd stick on the turbo-nutter thrust of Oakenfold's reworking instead. Jay's D&G T-shirt is soaked through with perspiration and he's telling me how wonderful I am and what a good friend I've been to him and how he wants me to be a godfather to one of his kids – if and when he has any – and I'm systematically ripping up this condom packet I found in

Thom's jacket pocket and I'm carefully writing down my phone number on each minuscule piece of cardboard then having Jay check that each phone number is legible and is, indeed, my actual home phone number and then I proceed to give my first piece of card out to this unblonde thing who's lingering beside us but she just pockets the number without registering any superficial emotion, like she's doing me a favour or something and so I call her a boreal bitch above my breath, possibly too loudly, much to the annoyance of Jay.

I've been wandering aimlessly around the club for what seems like hours, upstairs then downstairs, then circling the back room in the pitch-dark, then through to the Playstations, then up across the gantry again, when I finally catch up with Five huddled in a corner of the old film room – there doesn't appear to be any flicks showing here any more – and he's talking to these two things, both, apparently, foreign students (there's too many bloody foreigners in here), and I hand the taller of the two things my phone number and she mispronounces my name, 'Damon.'

The thing with the mad bad dangerous eyes in the COCKY SUCKY FUCKY T-shirt corners me outside the toilets and questions me, 'Do you smoke?' This time I reply, 'No,' and she says, 'Good, I like a man who doesn't smoke,' then skips past me once again.

I head off to the back room to look for Jay. Instead I spy the Babydoll, then move in on her. We dance. I'm frugging around her, two-stepping mindlessly to the huge housey beats, my facial expression a blank façade.

The Babydoll swoons back and forth, flirtatiously disco-squiggling, a shimmering rhapsody in pink. She has long luscious nails painted a startling scarlet red: pure perfection. *The . . . nails . . . on . . . that*, my mindscape informs me, like I've a second friend entrapped inside my head, and he's pointing out this thing's plus points in the event that I'd not already espied them for myself. The Babydoll's hair flops across her face and she pushes against me, grinding close to my body, and mesmerizes me through the half-light with that one visible eye. Then, from nowhere, Jay is close. He is thrusting some poppers into my face, which I unthinkingly accept, inflating each nostril with that chemical stench. The Babydoll is waving, wafting away the sorry odour. Jay is thrusting some poppers into my face, smiling, gripped by dementia, wide-eyed and dangerous.

My world is all spinning. I am excruciated by anxiety, my breathing hurried and fitful: what if the Babydoll is truly the one for me? What if I make her pregnant and have to spend the rest of my life stuck with a hairdresser in – God forbid – Stepney? My scalp feels ablaze. I stumble back into two ultra-glam boy-babes, both cloned with bleached crops, swarthy tans, both born on the Planet Camp, one gyrating topless to the music, the other sporting a skin-hugging BOYS 'R' US T-shirt. Fucking hommes, I am thinking.

I can hear my very heart pounding, mushrooming through a myriad of atoms, molecules, embracing the tunes, the bumpy backdrop, pounding faster, louder, to a point where I'm near sure to combust. *You must find*

Five, my mindscape is shrieking. Must ride this unwelcome rush before it rides me. Heart valves opening and closing, the mitral and tricuspid harmonizing with the aortic and pulmonary, their coalitions sounding out a Burundi death rattle from within. *You must find Five*, my mindscape is shrieking. *Sit down, Damian Henry Shaw. Sit down. You must get away* – from this dance-floor, from the Babydoll, the putrid stench of this amyl nitrate. *You're never doing poppers again. Must ride this rush*, my mindscape is shrieking. *Must—*

'Fuck's sake, Dame. You okay, mate?' Jay is asking me. 'Come on, you okay? Looks like you took a bit of a turn there.'

I'm sitting on the central podium, Jay is bent down gripping my arm tightly. The Babydoll stands behind him, looks down on me, seems unimpressed. Life carries on all around us, people oblivious to my plight.

'I'm okay,' I mouth back at him, and struggle to get to my feet.

Jay just smiles, still holds my arm to steady me, waves the amyl bottle before my face, shouting, 'Wanna little something to bring on those Es again, geezer?'

Five looms from nowhere, asks, 'Er, what's up, boys?' then takes me by my other arm and shouts above the music, 'Look, Dame, I need a really big favour, mate. Can I stay at yours tonight? I mean, I've met this bird—'

'Not one of those bloody students?' I blurt.

He guides me off to one of the adjoining corridors. 'No, not a student. Well, yes, a student. But not one of those foreign birds – this English one down in London for the weekend. And, well, she's staying at her mates, and of course I can't bring her back to my place "for the obvious reason" and, well, I was wondering if I could maybe take her to yours. I mean, is Thom at Lisa's for the night, yeah?'

We wander back to the main room and I ask the Babydoll her name, she says Angela, and I ask her if I can maybe see her some time and, to my utter astonishment, she actually says, 'Yes.' I think about giving her my phone number written down on a strip of condom packet but, as luck would have it, there's no need as she hands me over her very own business card. A hairdresser with a fucking business card!

I follow Five and Jay to get some water at the bar, where I'm introduced to Karen, Five's piece for the night. I find her instantly unattractive: she is unblonde, too short, is solid, but has such small tits and is wearing this grotesque T-shirt which screams the line I CAN FLY at me in Day-glo orange lettering. As we turn to leave we pass Angela by the cloakroom, talking to another man – someone far uglier and shorter than me, probably standing at only five-eight or something, but weighing in around the fourteen-stone mark. I choose to ignore the Babydoll.

She catches up with me as we head for the daylight outside. 'You just ignored me.'

'You were talking to someone else,' I say.

'He's just a friend.'

'I didn't know that.'

'You've got no right to ignore me.' Fine words from a fucking hairdresser.

I can't look her in the eye. 'I was, um, jealous. I'm sorry.'

She tuts.

'Like I said, I'm sorry,' I tell her again.

She sighs, looks totally unfazed and alluring, a regular femme fatale. 'Damian, you can phone me tomorrow, okay?'

'Promise?' I ask.

'Promise,' she finishes, exits.

'Thanks,' I find myself whispering, once she's gone. The Taste God has undeniably sprinkled his lucky-dust over Damian Henry Shaw tonight.

Back at the flat – it's now seven a.m. – Jay and I are lounging on the sofa and are having to watch *State of Grace* on video because (1) Jay hasn't seen it, (2) Toolboy was raving on about how good it was at some point last night, and (3) because it was actually a present from Jo for my birthday last year. Five and what's-her-name are crashed out – or maybe even fucking – in Thom's room. Two incense cones sit smouldering on the back of this brass-elephant candlestick holder, gorging the lounge with their sensational scent.

'You're a lucky man, Dame-ee-ern,' Jay is muttering.

'How do you figure that out?' I ask.

'That bird in the pink babydoll . . .' he says. 'She looked filthy.'

My chest swells with pride. 'You reckon?'

'Yeah, course,' Jay tells me. 'You've got rid of Jo, got

yourself another decent bird, yet you're still shagging other women.'

I'm confused for an instant, wondering if I should take offence at these querulous words. I decide to ask, 'Got rid of Jo? . . . Got another decent bird?'

'Yeah, you know – no more long weekends away in Scotland. You just bang your regular woman during the week, and leave the weekends free for nights out with the boys, adding even more birds to your list.' On the screen, Gary Oldman is blowing away three puffy Italiano hoods in a late-night bar. 'Ugh, did you see that, Dame? Did you see that?'

'Is that what you think's important to me? "Adding more . . . birds . . . to my list"?'

'What?' Jay croaks, his attention diverted. 'Eh, oh, yeah. You gonna tell me you'd rather have Joanna back, and to hell with Beth and all the women you're free to meet?'

'Yes, Jay, that's precisely the case,' I say bluntly.

'Fuck me, Gary Oldman looks a mad bastard,' Jay sighs, lost in thought.

'I said that's precisely the case,' I repeat.

Jay turns towards me, looks bemused, then his face starts to crack. 'Nah. You? Stick with one woman? Pull the other one, geez. I know you better than you know yourself.' He sits heehawing to himself dementedly, and I just sit, cackling too, laughing at my own folly, laughing for having squandered so much of my precious life on sullage like this Jay.

'I know you better than you know yourself,' Jay repeats, cries.

I just grin and whisper, 'You don't know me at all, you filthy fucking nigger.'

I'm woken from a slumber by the sound of the telephone ringing. I seek to ignore it but the ringing persists. Images of the caller flash through my mindscape and . . . it might just be Jo? Maybe she's even down in London, trying to reach me from King's Cross or possibly from Highgate tube station or from the phonebooth just along the Broadway? I scamper off my futon, bound for the lounge.

'Hello?' I say into the receiver, shocked at the croak that emanates from my throat.

'Hi. Thomas?'

'No, sorry – it's Damian,' I say, disheartened. It's Lisa.

'Oh, sorry, Damian. You two sound so alike. Is Thomas around?'

Er, no, sorry, Lisa . . . Look, I really do hate to be the one who has to tell you, but Thom was having dinner with this unblonde thing last night – dead fucking classy, you should've seen her, someone we met in Quaglino's last Thursday – and he's not made it home, so one can only assume he's probably giving her one as we speak . . . Bet she's loving every minute of it as well, eh? – I am thinking.

'No, he's popped out to do a fixed-odds coupon on the footie,' I lie instead.

'Tell him I phoned then.'

'Of course I will. He should be back soon,' I tell her, and glance toward the time on the video, which tells me that it's now two o'clock. I've overslept.

'Oh, well, tell him I called, then.' Pause. 'So-o-o, how are you, Damian?'

'Me? I'm fine. Look, I think that was someone at the door. Best be going, Lisa.' I put the phone down abruptly, then stop to pity Lisa for an instant, but quickly propel such a retarded emotion to the back of my mindscape and reread the note Thom left last night: *Dame, dinner with that Mary sort. Don't expect me home. Check out the vid I've left. Lisa taped it for you.* A Mary, eh? I don't think Thom's fucked any Marys before. I know I certainly haven't. One day I will leave one such note hanging around for Lisa to stumble across. It's no more than either her or Thom deserves.

I am sweating heavily, stinking of alcohol, my boxer shorts riding high, causing me extreme discomfort, but I cannot be bothered to shift my position so I remain slumped in the armchair for maybe a further ten minutes, flicking through the football gossip on teletext, attempting to recollect last night's itinerary – nothing special, just a spur-of-the-moment Lunchboys drinking session in the Doggett's: Graham Watson drunkenly vociferating on the break-up of his marriage, Nicholas Spencer-Jones pouring out his heart about that hideous Allison Coyle thing – tales we'd all heard before. There are some things I appear to have in common with the Lunchboys, as I seem to be drinking with them ever more regularly. Such a pity it's lost loved ones that unite us.

On the way home towards the station, Dino Denton told me he thought I was enigmatic, which surprised me because I'd always assumed he thought I was an arrogant fucker. Someone had scrawled the words NIGGERS STINK across some poster on the underground, and this made me a little sad and I had to stand for an age just attempting to digest these two pointless watchwords . . . But then visions of Jay entered my head and compelled me into smiling smuttily. I've discovered that Jayne Mansfield was thirty-four when she died. I have no idea how tall she was. I did ask Beth, but she just looked at me as if I was mad or something.

I coerce Thom's new tape into the video recorder, realign my boxer shorts, then slob back in the armchair to watch. This voice-over, atop a primitive map of Southern England, is warbling on about the weather in London, telling me it's going to be cloudy and rainy today. Cloudy possibly, but it's not rained in London for the best part of a month, so I'm wondering just when this tape was made. The video then coughs up Richard Madeley of *Richard and Judy* fame, sitting spruce in a cosy daytime-TV studio, as he welcomes me back to *This Morning*.

'What . . . the . . . fuck?' I catch myself, sigh.

'On with the show,' Madeley grins. I grin back at him mindlessly, extending my mouth like something from *Hellraiser*, then a full-screen picture of Anne Nicole Smith vanquishes Madeley's palling façade, jettisoning me to a precipitate attention.

Madeley continues, 'We'll be starting off in a second with a live and exclusive interview from Anna Nicole Smith,' then banal adverts for the rest of the show fritter away inestimable air time before Madeley sounds again, 'Her vital statistics were 39–28–39 . . . his were 89 years and 330 million dollars.' Madonna's 'Material Girl' pipes through the television, and I am treated to an absorbing collage of Anna snapshots – the majority of which with deceased husband J. Howard Marshall – and select newspaper cuttings with tawdry headlines ('It Bust Be Love', indeed) and then . . . Anna's there, as . . . large . . . as . . . life itself, her momentous form silhouetted against an acquainted backdrop of the Thames, the embankment side patent in the distance, past moored coffinesque longboats. I always thought Richard and Judy broadcast their banal bile from someplace up north? Liverpool, surely? This interview was filmed at the LWT Centre: the LWT Centre on the South Bank, less than one . . . *quarter* of a mile from my very office. I would surely have been able to smell Anna, she came so surpassingly close. It abruptly strikes me that this is maybe Lisa's or Campbell's or indeed both of them's inhuman stab at a prank, only confessing that Anna was in town when that celebrated moment had since withdrawn, both of them luxuriating in my anguish of knowing that Anna had been so near, yet now so seemingly far.

'Hi,' Anna grins.

'Nice of you to come dressed,' Madeley jokes sadly.

'Thank you,' Anna returns, remains grinning. Anna's hair is clipped up in an elegant, near dainty, far too girly, fashion and she's wearing this long ivory ballgown of a dress, one strap discreetly slipped from her right shoulder, ample expanses of milky flesh in abundant evidence across extended shoulders and prolonged swan neck. The cleavage is kept closely under wraps, however, without so much as a quarter-inch valley on parade; but a miniature black microphone affixed neatly at her front only serves to bring my attention back towards that wondrous point in her form.

Madeley maybe recounts the qualification 'gold-digger' – I'm not sure, I do not care, I'm little concerned with his quota of the ensuing conversation – and Anna begins, 'Well, what most people don't understand' – the word 'understa-yand' suffering most from her throaty Texan drawl – 'is that I knew my husband four years prior to our marriage.'

This isn't necessarily the tack I wanted to hear, listening to an affirmation of love for another man, but I remain enslaved to her bidding as she continues to speak.

'I made him smile,' she says.

'I made him happy,' she says.

'It made me happy to make him happy,' she says.

'It made him happy to make me happy,' she says.

'He was very brilliant,' she says.

'He made me more intelligent,' she says.

allen jarvis

'He . . . he . . .' she stalls for words.

'Enriched you more than just financially?' Madeley offers.

'Right, right,' Anna responds.

I dearly desire to enrich her worldly existence – more than just financially.

Madeley tries to draw Anna on the litigation proceedings surrounding her husband's will, but Anna doesn't want to discuss the ongoings of the situation and she sounds so tremendously sad, so distressed that I catch myself gnawing into my fist out of sympathy for her plight.

Madeley says something about Anna losing weight: he'd heard it was over five stone.

'It was over fifty pounds,' she informs him. 'I don't know what that means in London.'

Madeley asks Anna to stand up to show off her figure, and she does so, gladly, doing a slow spin anticlockwise to reveal a compact box jutting awkwardly from the back of her dress – forming part of the microphone ensemble presumably? I half convince myself that I can make out the ready contours of Anna's heaving nipples forced up against the inside of that dress.

'How many pounds are you now?' Madeley asks her.

'I don't know the scales,' Anna answers, and looks confused.

'What are your statistics now?' Madeley asks her.

'I don't know,' Anna answers again, flounders.

'It's okay. They speak for themselves,' Madeley tells her smugly. 'Is this the slimmest you've ever been.'

Anna pauses, then repeats, 'I would say that this is the slimmest I've ever been.'

Madeley quizzes if Anna intends to lose any more weight, whether she thinks she's in danger of losing her following if she sheds more pounds, and I shift uncomfortably forward in my seat, drawn to her next statement, trepidation ghouls canting to the fore of my mindscape.

'I'm staying parked right here,' Anna replies. 'I'm not gonna disappoint my fans and go any slimmer.'

I shadow-box with the air and shout a rebel-rousing, 'Yeessss,' at the television set.

'You look great,' Madeley tells Anna, then repeats the phrase, casually, for good measure, still holds the professional air of indifference he's maintained all inter-view, and I cannot help but admire Madeley's assured calm: that capacity to appear so cool and controlled in the presence of a goddess. I would be diminished to a quivering wreck with just one flash of Anna's teeth, spangling white doors of enamel, which could be the very reason why Madeley is a semi-successful television presenter and I shall doubtless never be. I'm starting to wonder where Madeley's better half Judy is today, and whether in fact Madeley finagled her absence to award himself carte blanche over this Anna interview?

This Morning then switches to some item on cooking in New Orleans, so I switch the television to standby, then sit staring at the blank screen for a minute or so, recollecting my thoughts. I must thank Campbell and Lisa for such an unmissable delicacy. I think about phoning the Babydoll – Angela – from the Ministry, but decide against this action. Any woman blessed with Jay's seal of approval is not worth the effort. I telephone Steve Kerr from work instead, to see if he fancies a few drinks later, but he says he's got to see his (older) woman – Vanessa – so instead I just run myself a hot bath and soak for a good half hour and sing along to this old Funkadelic album that I've not listened to for many years – since before I met Jo – but can yet somehow still remember the words to all the songs.

Beth and I are slumbering in semiconsciousness. It's late morning, Sunday. The radio is on, and the DJ on some crap pirate dance station makes this comment about getting one together at last year's Notting Hill Carnival.

'Getting one together – nice one,' I think out aloud.

'What?' Beth asks, raising her head, sounding sleepy.

'Getting one together. You know, like building a spliff.'

'Drugs! Is that all you ever think about, Damian?'

'No,' I say then, after a pause, add, 'There's Anna Nicole Smith as well.'

Beth playfully punches my chest and murmurs, 'I was gonna say dirty great blondes with big tits.'

Mock horror on my part. 'Are you calling Anna Nicole Smith a dirty great blonde with big tits?'

'Did I say that?' Beth teases me, scratches at the stubble on my chin.

When the adverts waft in, I lean across Beth's diminutive form to fiddle with the dial on the radio, but I can't find anything even remotely half-decent to listen to, so I realign the dial to the original pirate waveband as another shite jingle is playing for another shite jungle club somewhere.

After an age, Beth says, 'Damian . . .' in a voice which suggests she's going to ask/tell me something of great importance, 'have you got any regrets?'

'What – about us?' I ask.

'No, about life in general.'

'Erm, no,' I lie. 'Not really. None that I can think of, anyway.'

Beth sighs. 'I've only got the one.'

'Oh, yeah? What's that?' I ask semi-excited, thinking I may at last find something of interest in Beth's past life to give her very existence some depth, some clarity, more . . . substance.

'Oh, just this lad I had a fling with on holiday in Majorca years back – when I was only twenty or nineteen, maybe – this thirty-year-old fireman with red hair. I mean, I didn't really like him at the time, but I phoned him up when I got back to England. I was at Poly in Leeds then.'

'And?' I ask in anticipation.

'And he answered the phone and pretended it wasn't him – though it obviously was.'

'And,' I start, despairing. 'That's it?'

'Yeah, it was definitely him. I felt so small, being shunned like that.'

'So, what made you think of him?'

'Nigel? Oh, the Carnival. He was from Notting Hill.'

'Hold on. I thought you had a long-term boyfriend when you were at Polytechnic?' I ask, sensing a new inspiring angle to this sorry affair.

'Yeah – Anthony,' she drones, sounds distant. 'We'd broken up for a short while.'

'What? So you could shag around on holiday?'

'No, so he could, whilst I was away.'

'Oh, so-o-o why did you phone this fireman if you didn't really like him?'

'Don't know . . . to see if I could get him up to Leeds, I s'pose – to get Anthony jealous?'

'And that – Beth – is the only thing that you regret in your life?'

'Yeah.'

'What? That you fucked him? That he had ginger hair? Or that you didn't get him to come up to Leeds?'

'I didn't shag him, Damian. I'm not like that – not on holiday,' Beth snaps at me. 'No, just that I ever associated with him in the first place, I guess.'

I roll away from Beth, onto my left side, where the sheets are cooler and unruffled, my mindscape devoured by carnivorous bacteria, plotting revenge on Benny, Tyler, Matt, Mike and Jay, trying to figure out an absolute game-plan linking these fifth-columnists.

'So, don't you regret anything at all, Damian?' Beth is asking me.

'Erm, no. I haven't any regrets.' I sigh, think just the one – that single fatal encounter which effectively ruined my entire future: the catalyst behind my enforced split with Jo.

'Really?' Beth asks in a tone which suggests she doesn't quite believe me.

'Yeah, really,' I lie and close my eyes to picture myself in a happier place, running my fingers gently through Jo's long blonde hair. The image is bright, overexposed, everything in soft-focus, captured in pale pastels. I wonder what Jo's doing right now?

'Come on, sugar, humour me. There must be something you regret,' Beth asks me, closer now, her arm slung around my waist.

'Yeah, there is maybe just the one thing,' I finally admit.

'And? What's that?'

'Not beating the fuck out of this mangy traveller type who insulted me on an Edinburgh to London Inter-City a couple of months back.'

'Damian,' Beth sighs. 'That . . . is . . . sad.'

'Story of my life, sweetheart,' I mutter under my breath. I cannot bring myself to fully comprehend what it can possibly be that's stopping Beth from ending our relationship. Surely she cannot be happy the way things are at present? I never see her more than twice in any given week, hardly ever at weekends, and even then we rarely have good sex, don't seem to communicate that much. Why . . . doesn't . . . she . . . just . . . finish with me?! I mean, I would enforce the break myself, but I don't want her ending up in a similar position to me –

compounded by remorse, lamenting for a lost love. I have to make Beth feel that any split has been as a direct result of her own stark decisiveness, without any external coercion from me.

I'm sitting upstairs in De Hems in China Town. I'm with Slinky – Jo's cousin on her mother's side. We're not so much as sitting: more lounging really – lounging in one of the sofas by the windows. There are five unblondes gracing the tables nearest us, one of them wearing a T-shirt which reads UNNATURAL BLONDE. I'm drinking Oranjeboom. Slinky's drinking Perrier – she doesn't 'do' alcohol.

'De *Hommes*?' Warwick Griffin asked me as I left work. 'Is that a gay pub?'

'No, it's sort of a Dutch pub really,' I told him.

'What? You mean it's full of . . . dykes?' he joked.

'Aye, and blokes sticking their fingers in them!' Carl Smith added.

The Lunchboys are growing on me, slowly.

I hadn't arranged to meet Slinky here till seven and – as I felt I couldn't face her sober – I attempted to kill an hour or two, perched on a stool in the corner of Soho Soho, drinking Kronenbourg, nervously chain-smoking Marlboro Lights, reading the *Evening Standard* and listening to 'Ride of the Valkyries' over and over on my Walkman. When I'd finally exhausted every avenue of interest from the paper, I sat circling the names of horses at random on the racing page, in an attempt to appear somewhat preoccupied – like I was actually studying their form over course or distance or something. This blonde thing in a brown suit, who I thought I might know from somewhere, lingered by me for a while and I was just thinking up a plausible excuse to strike up a conversation with her ('Oh, you're drinking on your own, as well? I was supposed to be meeting someone here for a drink, but they appear to have stood me up. Waffle waffle. Do you mind if I join you? Et cetera, et cetera . . .') when she was joined by this other thing who I really *did* know – this pretentious little unblonde thing (Jill?) from Five's publishing house who actually air-kissed this blonde which, in turn, made me feel physically sick, quaked my inner being to its very foundations. Sharp exit.

Wasted the rest of the time wandering aimlessly in and out of sex shops, perusing big-breast videos with stupid names like *Thunderboobs*, *Pumpin' Plumpers* and *Boobarella*. Bought some amyl gold-top and meandered lazily down Old Compton Street sucking on this Marlboro Light which I'd first dipped in said bottle of poppers, psyching myself up to this planetary encounter with Slinky.

Slinky used to work alongside Benny at the advertising agency he still works for in Camden Lock, and it was Slinky who introduced me to Jo at a private party in a club in Kensington somewhere – Jo was down visiting for a long weekend. It was a couple of weeks before Jo's nineteenth birthday. I distinctly remember Slinky's words of initiation: 'Damey just luuuurrvs tall women,

Joanna.' I have slept with Slinky twice – the first time only a couple of weeks or so before I met Jo. I refused to actually 'see' Slinky. She's tall (five-nineish?) and always seems to be wearing hooped earrings, and she has a 36D chest and a penchant for anal sex, but she's unblonde, has this really big chin, and insists on wearing these ridiculous horn-rimmed glasses that make her look about forty-eight. The second time I slept with Slinky was a little over six months later, after we'd both been smoking skunk with Thom, Lisa and Jay on Hampstead Heath. Jo only knows about the first time; the second time Slinky gave me the very first love-bite I'd received in well over ten years. I wouldn't like to say where she placed it.

Matt e-mailed me today – I thought it wise to start reading any separatists' mails again, as I don't want to miss out on any gossip – and said he thought I might've popped down for a drink to celebrate Jenny's birthday two days ago, seeing as how he'd mailed me about this last week; said that him and Jenny and Toolboy and Jinxy John had all got 'totally bollocksed on red wine and pink speed' had stayed up all night buzzing fever-ishly, all done sickies yesterday and were all genuinely astounded that I'd actually not shown, seeing as how I'd partaken in parallel frivolities at Jenny's birthday last year. I couldn't be bothered to reply, to explain to that germ, to that Matt, that he was mistaken – that I hadn't savoured such a similar date last year, because I had in fact been in Scotland with Jo.

Slinky is telling me about her recent excursion into

India, Thailand and Singapore and wherever and, though she's genuinely enthused and keeps going off at tangents about this temple and, oh, that village and, oh, this Swedish girl told me blah-blah-blah, and though I strive to remain attentive, appear at least a little interested in what she is telling me, feigning surprise at the appropriate times, lowering and raising my eyebrows as required, murmuring *oh*s and *hmmm*s and *I-know-what-you-mean*s every minute or so, and though I only break eye contact the once – to light a cigarette (not the one drenched in amyl) – I am simply not taking any of this in. The single super-chilled thread of thought bursting to escape my very skull, the sole reason I am actually here, the nagging statement of intent I'm on the verge of shouting from the rooftops is: What . . . about . . . Jo?

'Oh, Damey, I must be boring you,' Slinky finally says.

I just smile and fantasize about ringing her neck.

'Oh, I must be. It's just . . .' Sigh. 'There's such a big world out there waiting for us to explore – so many new experiences to encounter.' She sighs again. 'You must come and see the photos. I'm back at my old place in Stoke Newington.' Slinky takes a deliberated sip of her mineral water. 'So, tell me . . . what's been happening in your life?'

At last an opening. 'Nothing much,' I just grumble, wasting my opportunity.

'Drinking? Eating? Shagging?' she says, smiles.

'Yeah.' It suddenly strikes me that Slinky has no idea

whatsoever that Jo and I have split up, and that this has been a purposeless trip after all. Surely they must have corresponded whilst Slinky was away? Slinky has been back in the country a week – they must have spoken to one another in this time? Or maybe she can't contact Jo? Maybe Jo's travelling somewhere, too? Or maybe . . .

'You seen much of Benny?' Slinky asks.

I nod my head, appeasing her, but grunt under my breath, 'I avoid that scum like the plague.'

'How is he?' she asks.

'Pregnant,' I mutter.

'Pregnant?'

'He's got his woman pregnant.'

'Benny is going to be a . . . father?'

'Yeah, frightening, isn't it?'

'I'll say.' She sighs. 'And how is your love life?'

A starting point – another opportunity not to be squandered – but before I have chance to speak she adds, 'I must say I was really sorry to hear about you and Joanna.'

'Yeah, well . . . these things happen,' I say, appear nonchalant – perhaps too much so? 'But, um, life goes on . . . I'm seeing this new girl now – Beth – great girl, great personality. We get on really well together. She looks like that actress, that Elizabeth Hurley . . . I'm, um, really happy.'

Slinky grins, says 'Great,' but I sense that she doesn't believe a word of it; she sees straight through me.

'Yeah, er, great,' I say again then stop for a pause,

wondering why I mentioned Beth. It's not like she's that special to me, anything worth crowing about.

Still smiling, Slinky looks past me, stares off into space like she's trying to recollect a misplaced image or something. 'Guess what?' she asks.

'What?' I ask, laugh nervously, reach for my glass. *What?* That Jo misses me? That I'm to be forgiven? That she's coming down to London this very weekend?

'I'm engaged,' Slinky tells me, purses her lips, tries to contain a smile.

I sit, open-mouthed, half-smiling like I'm awaiting further information.

'Damey, I'm engaged,' she says again. Her eyes scrutinize my face for a reaction.

I just sit there, still open-mouthed, before finally saying, without any genuine enthusiasm, 'Oh, yeah – great.' I'm thinking: is that . . . it? Slinky, however, appears warmed by this acknowledgement.

'Yep.' She sighs. 'To this Australian surfer I met in Delhi: his name's Bruce. Look.' She pulls the chain round her neck out from her top and presents this small tinny-looking ring hanging on it. 'This is the ring he gave me. Said it was his mother's.'

Again, as if directed by an autocue drifting before my mindscape, I just say, 'Great.'

'Yep.' She tucks the ring back inside her top. 'I'm gonna emigrate – gonna go and live in Australia with him. Mind, he's not going to be back there for another four months or so, but I'm happy to wait.'

I glance at my watch: it's close on nine o'clock. In

nearly two hours of mindless chitchat this is the singularly most important thing that Slinky, who is Jo's cousin
and who is twenty-four years old and who I and Benny
and – allegedly – half of Benny's workmates have all
fucked and who all probably know that Slinky has a
mole four inches below her right armpit the size of
Mount fucking Kilimanjaro, has said: that she is engaged
to some dumb-fuck Aussie surfer who's doubtless
already forgotten her name and who, at this precise
moment in time, is betrothing his undying love to
another wide-eyed traveller on a hillside by some remote
village in Sri Lanka or Laos or some other backwater on
the opposite side of the planet.

'How is . . . Jo?' I find myself uttering. In the eternal
neverland that hangs between this question and Slinky's
deliberated response, my mindscape's eye insists on
replaying me this scene where Jo and I made love in a
wood somewhere (Scotland or England? I'm not sure)
as a brick-red sun set between snaking black trees.

'She's okay,' is all that Slinky tells me.

'Just . . . okay?' I ask her. The sun dies. Darkness
prevails. I lose Jo to the night.

'Yep, you know . . . just okay. Spoke to her on the
phone two days back. I mean, I was shocked to hear
that you two had split, but – hey! – that's life, I guess.
But she sounded okay, seemed really happy with things.'
How on earth can Jo be happy when my life is a limitless
desert without her at my side?

'Er, any men?' I have to ask, immediately wishing I
hadn't.

'Nah, none that she mentioned.' I dissolve in a pool of palatial relief.

'So, er, did she mention me at all?' I ask.

'Only that you two had broken up. She said she hadn't heard from you for a while. Besides, I didn't really give her much of a chance to get a word in edgeways. I mean, I had my whole trip to tell her about.'

You egocentric bitch, I am thinking. The sole reason I have wasted my precious time with you tonight is to get an insight into Jo's life – her loves, her failings, her regrets, her hopes now that we're apart – and all that you doubtless talked to her (talked at her) about was some half-wit surfing Antipodean ape called Bruce who, no doubt, has a beer-keg tattooed on his right forearm and whose sexual technique was developed solely from fucking countless sheep on some uncle's remote outback farm (and from probably fucking half his family on said farm).

'Joanna might be coming down to London soon,' Slinky is saying.

'When?' I ask, suddenly alive, motivation pulsing from deep in my soul.

'Well, maybe not soon. Soonish, though. I'm actually off up to Motherwell this weekend to see my mum and dad – to show them my photos and stuff. I'll probably chat to Joanna then.'

'Soonish,' I repeat, almost awestruck, meteor showers whooshing by.

'Yep, er, she said she actually misses coming down to London.'

'Yeah?'

'Yep, said I'd take her clubbing one weekend. Think she's pissed off with the curfews they've got in Glasgow. Clubbing doesn't seem so much fun up there.' The number of London club venues I've visited with Jo – Nineteen. Bagleys, Café de Paris, Chunnel, Cloud 9, Complex, Cross, EC1, Fridge, Gardening Clubs I and II, Heaven, Ministry, Plastic People, RAW, SW1, Turn-mills, UK, Velvet Underground, The Wag. Club venues Jo and I fucked in – just one. Heaven, in the toilets, at a Megatripolis bash, on a night when Jo was doing acid, I was doing these forget-me-not Es, and neither of us came.

'So, erm, any message for Joanna, Damey?'

'Um, I can't really think of anything,' I mutter. Just tell her that I love her, that I've always loved her, always will love her, that I cannot envisage ever finding another to replace her, that my life effectively ended the day we split, that people still talk to me and drink with me and hug me and fuck me, but for all intents and purposes I am . . . not . . . here. I am no more than an apparition, some defunct spirit condemned to walk this earth for eternity, questing for a past love now lost.

'So, no message then?' Slinky asks, disbelieving.

'Just tell her I'm sorry,' I whisper; 'that I'd do anything to turn back the clock.'

'What?' she asks.

'Just say "hello" for me,' I say, then panic, ask, 'Do you think I've put on weight?'

'Er, no. Why?'

'Oh, no reason. What about my hair? Has it changed since you last saw me?'

'Erm, nope, Damey. You look exactly the same.'

'Good. That's good,' I say.

'Why-y-y?' she playfully asks, interrogates me with her eyes.

'Oh, just – you know – didn't want you to go and tell Jo that I looked any different, that I'd changed at all.' I playfully rap the table with my knuckle.

'No, Damey, you've not changed at all,' she tells me, shakes her head, maybe tuts.

'Sweetheart, you won't mention Beth to Jo, will you?'

'Not if you don't want me to.'

'I don't.'

'Okay, then. I won't mention her.'

'Besides, I made her up. It was all a joke, ha-ha-ha. I'm single. I haven't been with anyone since Jo and I broke up.' By now I'm virtually crying, struggling to hold back the tears.

'Damey, are you okay?' Slinky is asking me.

Slinky's birthday is the seventh of July; the seventh day of the seventh month. The seventh US president was a Democrat named Andrew Jackson. I used to play Sunday league football with this black kid called Andrew Jackson who died of cancer when I was just fourteen. Which is seven times two. Cracks appear in the ground and buildings collapse at a seven on the Richter scale. There are seven Virtues, of which I can only name three (Faith, Hope and Charity). Seven images of Jo that spring to mind: (1) lying naked on a bed in this chintzy guest-house in Brighton, masturbating; (2) crying while watching *Bambi* on pirate video round Matt and Jenny's; (3) retelling this joke in some pub down Balham and the punch-line where she blows beer in the faces of Gerry and Five and Marky Mullen, doing this impersonation of a blow-whale, all three just sitting stunned, po-faced, finally breaking into embarrassed smirks as our entire entourage fell about laughing at their expense; (4) standing in the background of this photograph of me with Rod Ellis from work, taken at one of his summer barbecues, looking longingly on at me like she really truly loved me or something; (5) keeping a healthy production line of spliffs going when I was too fucked to roll at Mike's last party out Ealing way; (6) our first night together, making love back in the flat after the Kensington party, me praying that I'd see her again, some cheesy house compilation burbling away in the background, ill fitting the mood but patently memorable all the same; (7) Jo's wounded visage – memories of me finding her with Lisa and Thom on that fateful day, hell unleashed; that little-girl-lost look, her entire universe razed in a solitary burst . . . the look that torments me to this very day . . . Tokyo, I think, or maybe Mexico City, is the seventh largest city in the world. There are seven Deadly Sins and seven Wonders of the Ancient World. Slinky's birthday is the seventh of July; the seventh day of the seventh month.

'Damey, are you okay?' Slinky is asking me.

*

Lunchtime drinks in the Doggett's with Russell Bishop, Steve Kerr, Carl Smith and Dino Denton from the third floor. This is becoming a regular occurrence, these people now rising as more than just work colleagues, providing an escape route to a sanitized dimension, green fields away from the Jays, the Mikes, the mephitic scum of this world. I've just done a little charlie in the toilets. This unblonde thing in a brown suit and awesomely huge hooped earrings pushes past our table, bound for the ladies, and four weighty words illuminate the forefront of my mindscape: *the . . . earrings . . . on . . . that.*

' – besides, dear boy,' Russell adds, 'I can only assume Dino must always have his sex whilst he's on some very serious acid.'

'Hey! I wouldn't knock it – sex on acid, that is,' I splutter through thick rubbery lips. The coke has sterilized my mouth and throat. I've virtually no sensation there.

'Oh, I know,' Russell says. 'It can be a wonderful experience.'

'Sex?' Carl asks, looks disgusted. 'On acid? Describe it.'

'Well, it's so odd.' Russell puts his hand to lips, appears overtly pensive. 'I remember one particularly fine morning in Battersea Park, after a party in, um, oh-I-forget, and it was around six a.m. just as the sun was coming up and I was with this Australian—'

'Male or female?'

'Don't ask such stupid questions. And we were both

243

out of our heads on acid and we just, you know, got down to it, and the sex was so-o-o different.'

Kerr asks, 'Different? As in?'

Pregnant pause. 'Well, one minute we were over there.' Russell points past me. 'Then we were over here.' He motions behind Dino. 'Oh, we were here, there, everywhere . . . without actually getting *any*where.'

Jo and I had sex on acid once, locked away in her parents' bedroom whilst they were abroad on holiday. I unclearly remember contorted snapshots of the sex that took place – like my mindscape was on some timer-released camera that only opened itself up every thirty seconds or so. I remember how she said the acid made my cock all the bigger and remember how I started panicking because I was so out of it, but Jo calmed me down, told me that she was going to take control of things. But when I looked into her bushbaby eyes I realized that there was absolutely no one home, and this scared me even more.

'The acid made everything seem so much bigger as well,' Russell finishes.

I laugh inwardly.

'Hmmm, must try it sometime,' someone mutters.

I bite hard into my tongue, maybe draw a little blood, yet still feel no pain – the coke still in full effect.

Last night, Matt and Jenny were round, and we were just watching *Brookside* when Matt asked Thom how he'd got on with that Mary thing from Quaglino's the other week. 'JFK-ed her,' Thom told him. Matt cackled and said, 'Nice one, guy.' Jenny tutted and digged Matt in the ribs, and I just sat there laughing along nervously, confused by what Thom had said, sensing some dastardly plot against Jo – her initials are in fact JMK – until I finally summoned up the courage to ask exactly what 'JFK'ed her' meant. Thom has been fairly understanding through all of this, as if he's been trying to make amends. I thought this was maybe an opportunity for him to show his true colours, to enlist in the ranks of the heretics. But there was no Scottish connection inferred – just that John F. Kennedy was alleged to have once said, so Thom claims he's been told, something along the lines of 'You've never really had a woman until you've had her all three ways.' Or was it his brother, or maybe Fidel Castro who said this? Someone way back in the sixties anyway – Thom wasn't entirely sure.

'You must've seen the *Sun* today, Damian. Lovely big picture of Jackie Dixon.'

'What?' I'm asking, lost in thought.

'Jackie Dixon from *Brookside*,' Smith tells me. 'Lovely clubby blonde. Aw, just your type, Damian.'

'But she is only about five . . . feet . . . tall . . . or something,' I tell Carl, and shake my head. 'And has no discernible breasts. Give me Anna Nicole Smith any day.'

And I'm thinking about Jackie Gray from the project team in the adjacent area to ours, smiting her for turning down my eventual offer of a drink, for telling me I was 'far too young to be seen out with'. But I shouldn't let this rile me – I was only after the one thing anyway. And

how would I have been able to soak myself in that
bedazzling Scottish accent if she had insisted on having
my cock shoved down her throat? Favourite New Order
song today: can't bring myself to decide between 'Sun-
rise' and 'Age Of Consent'. Both tracks represent New
Order at their fluid peak, offer Hooky's breakneck bass-
lines coupled with Steve's awesome drumscapes and
Gillian's soaring keyboards, each ensemble rounded off
by Bernard's fractured guitar patterns and signature
little-boy-lost vocal refrains. Both songs really kick.

' – you Northerners, I dunno,' Steve sighs, and
rounds off another conversation to which I am
anaesthetized.

'We-e-ell . . . it's all ferrets down the trousers with
our lot, lad,' Dino says cheerily, and this is the last part
of their super-addled babble that registers with me,
because I'm just sitting here in utter silence for maybe
the next quarter of an hour or so, watching the Bishop
and Denton and Kerr and Smith mouth meaningless
words at one another and at me, but I'm not paying any
attention – and no one seems to care. I'm too preoccupied with other points from this morning's agenda, like:
(1) why did Hubert Dodd have to arrange an eight
o'clock development meeting on the very day they
decide to give an early preview of the very next Anna
Nicole Smith calendar on *The Big Breakfast*? and (2)
why did Benny insist on e-mailing me at both work and
at home just to say that he'd come back from some
family conference at his father's place down near
Gatwick, where there'd been a big get-together to

decide what to do with his aged grandmother, whether they could maybe afford to put her into a home or not? Benny said they should just smother her with a pillow, so his father threw him out on the street. 'Well,' he e-mailed me, 'she was ninety-two, senile, and everyone hated her.' Like, I really care.

I'm standing on the balcony of the Punch & Judy, Covent Garden, with an ex-friend, Jay. Five and Gerry were due here half an hour ago, but they're both late, and have left me all alone with this bastard, wondering what on earth I'm expected to talk to him about. Jay was the fifth to affront the memory of Jo.

'Look, I hate to spring this on you, Dame, but um—' Jay says, rubs the palm of his hand across his freshly shaved head, wiping away moist perspiration. 'I think I might, er . . . might have to drop out of the scam.'

I take a long cool drink from my pint, smack my lips and let my eyes wander, taking in the various things criss-crossing down below. 'Is it because of the money?' I ask.

'No, nothing like that. I can get that on credit. No, it's just—'

'Just what?'

'It's just . . . oh, you'll just think I'm being daft or paranoid or something.'

'And?'

Jay hands me an envelope.

'What's this?' I ask him.

'You'd better open it,' he says, swigs from his bottle of Beck's.

I huff and quickly retrieve this A4 photocopied sheet, yet another poorly produced samizdat showing a cut-out snap of Jay pasted next to a snapshot of Arnold Schwarzenegger. 'And what is this supposed to be?'

Jay seems confused by my lack of concern. 'I'm not sure,' he tells me, 'but I think someone's maybe trying to stir up trouble.'

'Who?' I ask, suggest half-heartedly, 'Mike?'

'Er, Mike who?' Jay asks.

'What do you mean, "Mike who"?'

'Well . . . which Mike?'

'*Mike*-Mike. *Our* Mike.' I take a deep breath, my patience frayed. 'Drug . . . dealing . . . Mike!'

'Oh, right . . . Er, no,' Jay says, shakes his little head. 'Mike's the last person I'd suspect. After you of course, geez. No, I think it's one of the others.'

'The others?' I sigh.

'Yeah, the others,' Jay whispers. 'The other boys in on the scam.'

'What makes you think that?' I ask him.

Jay carries on, 'Well, that photo of me was taken at uni, or at least around that time, 'cos I didn't have the shaved head then.'

'Erm, whatever.' I nod my head, don't really look concerned.

'And this Schwarzenegger thing – I only brought that

up the once, when I was a bit pissed after a Chinese a few months ago.'

'Can't say I remember it,' I lie to him.

'You wouldn't,' Jay returns. 'It's trivial stuff. But, I've been getting loads of shit through the post, like pictures of burning crosses, and that. I reckon some-one's playing on my colour, stirring up trouble for me, hoping to get me to drop out of the scam.'

'And who would do such a thing?' I ask in a comic voice.

'Matt,' Jay says flatly.

'Er, eh? Why Matt?' I ask, bewildered.

'I think he's got cold feet. He doesn't want Jenny to find out about the scam, but he doesn't want to be seen to be the first to drop out, so he's trying to frighten me into making me drop out, making things all the more easy for himself.'

'Well, Jay, maybe you *should* drop out, then you'd avoid all this grief.'

'Or kick the fuck out of Matt?' Jay asides, and I can't tell whether he's being serious or not.

'Hmmm, whatever,' is all I reply. I've fought along-side Jay in the past, just minor skirmishes, nothing of note – purposeless rows with townies down the union dancehall, a tempered bout with these Greeks in some kebab house by Turnpike Lane where one of the fuckers pulled a machete on us – but I've seen enough of him in action to realize his potential as a worthy adversary, yet he's a difficult target to truly appraise, very compact, with no real nose to break or features to aim for, and though Jay may only stand at five eight or something he must weigh in close on the fourteen-stone mark and he exhibits a fearsome physique any self-respecting Rottweiler would be eminently proud of. Indeed, despite our marked difference in height, Jay and I do in fact share the same collar-size: a sixteen and a half, bull-necks all round. Just about the only thing of any worth we perhaps do share.

'Well, I can't deny I haven't thought about dropping out,' Jay is saying. 'I mean, if you can't trust the boys, then who can you trust?'

'Your family?' I offer mindlessly as some big blonde, all cleavage, considerable hair and these big hooped earrings, skirts past us, looks lost, then, just as I sense a welcome fervour ignite deep within me, some big geezer in a T-shirt blurting KENNY taps her on the shoulder, goes, 'Alright, Janice,' in this thick ugly Brummie accent and said blonde goddess wheels round, throws her arms about this geezer and kisses him like she completely loves him with every bone in her body or something.

'Yeah, right,' Jay chokes. 'Like my mother wouldn't shop me straight to the police if she knew I was getting hitched up in some drug deal.'

'So-o-o, you gonna drop out, then?' I ask, raise my eyebrows a notch and smack my lips in slight annoyance, tempted to bury my glass deep into that stupid Brummie's face, casually flap his cheek open like some unstuck envelope.

'Oh, I dunno.' Jay sighs, puts his bottle down on the

ledge and starts to fiddle with these green and red Turk's-head cufflinks, a poor choice, commendable only to people not used to such measured attire, fiddles with his tawdry green-and-red Turk's head cufflinks pinpointed in a broad double cuff, a cuff criss-crossed by near tasteful pink-and-navy check, a cuff . . .

'Jay,' I bluster. 'That's a . . . a . . . Thomas . . . Pink shirt.'

'Yeah,' Jay says. 'Smart, eh?'

'But *I* always wear Thomas Pink shirts.'

'Yeah, I know. That's why I got one.'

'That's why you got one?'

'Yeah, we can even swap from time to time, can't we?'

'We can even swap from time to time?' I ask, revolted, then gaze down to catch sight of Gerry's towering form ambling slowly towards the pub. 'Oh, here comes the big man now. Perhaps he'll let you swap shirts with him, too – that is if he's still talking to you after you've told him you're dropping out of the scam.'

'Oh, yeah, forget what I said before,' Jay tells me. 'I was behaving like an idiot.'

'You were behaving like an idiot?' I ask him glibly.

'Yeah,' Jay says, grins. 'I'm still in.'

'You're . . . still . . . in?' I comment, slightly fretted.

'Yeah, I'm still in, geez,' Jay tells me, picks up his bottle and chinks it against my pint glass.

'Whatever,' I say, then sigh.

'And it's all down to you, Dame,' Jay tells me. 'Just talking to you has really put my mind at ease. Thanks, geez. You're a real pal.'

'I . . . am . . . a . . . real . . . pal,' I repeat slowly, then tut. But as I raise my glass to my lips again the big Brummie stumbles back into me, the weight of the stimulated blonde adhered to him knocking him just slightly off balance.

'Sorry, mate,' the Brummie smiles, his vocal inflexion supremely ugly.

'Fuck you,' I tell him, disrupted.

'I said I was sorry, mate,' he repeats as if this is really going to appease me.

'Fuck you,' I tell him again, my words knife-edged and nasty, then take another long slurp of my pint and align my tie, though I'm not exactly sure why I dramatize this last otiose skit.

'Fucking suit,' this geezer just gruffs, not an insult in itself, but it's at this juncture that I decide to headbutt him. If I'm being honest I'm probably only really galvanized because the blonde with the big hair and the even bigger hooped earrings takes it upon herself to laugh at this last comment. The Brummie's a big geezer but he's at an impeccable butting height, and all I have to do is literally take one pace forwards with just the slightest of springs to my step as if I'm perhaps scaling a small flight of stairs. I can almost walk into his face. However, though clean and spot on target, I get virtually no power behind my offensive and the Brummie just rocks back a bit and stands there wide-eyed, disbelieving, like I've just told him he was born a woman or something.

It's Jay that closes the dispute for me, punching

upwards and purposely right underneath this geezer's jaw, Jay's whole manoeuvre – from setting his stance to connecting magnanimously with his mark – passing as if in slow motion, as if me and the Brummie and that blonde piece and each and every individual garnered here in this establishment tonight could see exactly what was going through Jay's mind and could, at any time, have stepped, almost sauntered, into the affray and raised a peaceable hand to say, 'Now come on, Jay, I don't think you really want to hit him, do you?'

The Brummie pitches, I swear, at least six inches into the air, his eyes dimming into unconsciousness as he commences his short-lived ascension, then he crumbles back into the blonde, his turn to knock her backwards, and sort of just topples, with the very minimum in grace and decorum, back on his fat Black Country arse.

Jay raises his hand to me as if in a high five. I slap his palm weakly and tell him quite deliberately, spitting almost, 'Don't you ever finish a fight for me again.'

'You wankers. You fucking Cockney wankers,' the blonde shrieks up at us, cradling the Brummie oaf in her arms. I look at her and all I can think about is her tits and how I would still really like to fuck them.

'Hey, who rattled her cage?' Gerry asks us, looking quizzical, as he appears as if from nowhere, head and shoulders above the crowd.

I'm nervous, waiting tentatively as the phone rings at the other end.

'Hello, 2604,' comes a voice I don't recognize.

'Er, good afternoon. Could I speak to Tasha Doran, please?' I ask politely, my palms sweated.

'Hold the line please. Can I ask who's—?'

'Hello,' Tasha cuts in, picking up the other extension.

'Hi, Tasha.' Silence – she doesn't recognize my voice. 'It's, um, Damian here.'

'Oh, hi-i-i, Damian. This is an honour. How are you?'

'I'm, er, fine, fine. And yourself?'

'Oh, bored. You know how it is.'

'Sure, sure I do,' I say, shift uncomfortably in my seat.

Pause. 'So-o-o . . .' she says, her voice trailing off.

'Tonight?' I ask, cringe.

'Drinks with you, I guess . . . I'll pop down and grab you at, say, six?'

'Er, okay. Six is just fine,' I blurt, sense a rush of blood to my head.

'See you,' is all she says, and the line goes dead.

I replace the phone in its cradle, wipe my moist palms across my suit trousers, lean back in my chair, place my hands behind my head, grin widely and utter a single word, 'Result.'

Warwick Griffin looks up from his work. I blow him an impudent kiss, then he shakes his head and buries himself in his work once again.

Since our little misunderstanding in the Slug, I've striven to avoid Tasha at all costs, but last week I came up against her in a meeting, taking minutes for her boss,

Jack Howe. I'll admit I was probably rude and standoffish during the course of said meeting so, afterwards, for some inexplicable reason, I e-mailed her and apologized for my ignorance. Much to my surprise, she mailed me back, said, 'Not to worry,' so I leapt in both-feet-first, mailed her again, asked if she fancied a quick 'purely platonic' drink after work. Tasha mailed me back again saying she was busy most of the week, but if I wished to pursue the offer she was free Thursday, and so tonight I am hoping for another shot at those magnificent breasts of hers.

The rest of the afternoon blazes past. People start to drift away around four. By five the office is virtually deserted. By six I'm alone.

'Hi, Damian.'

Tasha looms behind me. I glance up. She looks fantastic: this close-fitting top, tight purple trousers, and stack-heeled boots that only serve to add inches to her height. To round off this effervescent ensemble, she's adorned with a pair of stupendous hooped earrings, one of which is plain for all to see, as one side of her hair is brushed back past her ear. Tasha also has a long black-and-white silk scarf tied tight around her throat.

'Alright, sweetheart,' I say, smile broadly.

'Where is everyone?' Tasha asks.

'Home – where else?' I say, stand up, close my folder.

'What? Your department not on overtime, then?'

'Oh, of course, but who wants to do it? The work's so mind-numbingly dull,' I say, slipping on my jacket, switching off my overhead lamp.

Tasha nods in agreement, peruses the cuttings pinned up above my desk. 'Who's this, Damian?' she asks, pulls away one cutting.

'Oh, that? That's Russ Meyer, an American film director. You heard of him?'

'No, don't fancy him. He's too old for me.'

'It's my idea of a joke, sort of. We're not allowed, like, big-breasted women pinned up on our desks, so instead I've got this picture of a director who makes films that always feature these big Valkyries with really oversized bodies. It's cryptic, don't you think?'

Tasha tuts, pauses. 'Sometimes I worry about you, Damian. Pictures of men, indeed. Are you sure you haven't got homosexual tendencies?'

'Positive. I'm just after someone who's all woman,' I flute.

We leave, make our way along Stamford Street toward Blackfriars Road.

I blow my nose for the third time in ten minutes. I haven't got a cold, or at least I don't believe I have. I should just maybe lay off the coke for a day or two. 'So, where are we off to?' I ask.

'The Anchor,' Tasha answers.

I pace alongside her, my attention diverted by her wondrous hooped earring.

'Have I got something in my hair, Damian?' Tasha asks me.

'Eh? Er, no,' I tell her, change the subject. 'Um, Niall doesn't like me – does he?'

'Nah, he doesn't seem to.'

'I didn't think he did – doesn't make a secret of the fact. Any ideas as to why, though?'

'He's my friend, Damian. Maybe you upset me a couple of years back. He holds a grudge for a long time.'

'And you? Do you hold any grudges?'

'Me? Nah, I just get on with life, put it behind me.'

'So, what did I do to upset you?'

Tasha halts us in our tracks. 'Oh, I really can't begin to imagine,' she says condescendingly, throws an unconvincing glare at me.

'Whatever I did it really wasn't intentional,' I tell her.

'Oh, no? Ever heard of the phrase "pumped and dumped"?'

'Yeah, but—'

'Well, remember Martin Murphy? Now, why did he ask me – at that Alasdair Marshall's party – if it was true that I had big nipples and that I liked talking dirty in bed?'

Kowtowing to her, I say, 'Maybe Niall said something to him?'

Tasha sighs. 'You're incorrigible, Damian.'

'But lovable all the same?' I semi-ask.

Tasha and I seat ourselves upstairs in the Anchor, me settled with a Kronenbourg, her with a gin and Slimline tonic. I'm trying to figure out just why Tasha insists on drinking Slimline. I'm hoping she's not on a diet or something. Last time I was here was with Jo, but that was more than a year or so back, when she met me for a drink after work when she'd taken some time off to come down to London for a long visit. I remember us picking out tunes from the jukebox; some hardbag tracks on compilation albums, with some classic New Order thrown in for good measure.

'Good jukebox in here,' I mutter, slurp at the head on my Kronenbourg.

'Sorry?' Tasha asks.

'Er, nothing.'

'So-o-o, Damian,' Tasha starts. 'Tell me about your Scots babe.'

'Why-y-y?' I ask slowly.

'Just like to hear about good old Damian getting dumped. Another fabulous victory for womankind.'

'She didn't dump me.'

'C'mon now, Damian. That's not how the office grapevine tells it,' Tasha says, sips delicately at her G and T.

'Well, she didn't. It was a . . . a mutual split,' I retort, sneer.

Tasha then switches the subject abruptly, complaining at how badly her appraisal went today and at how worthless the past working year has been. I admit that I feel the same way about my own position. Tasha wants to know if it's the job or the company that's getting me down. I tell her it's the company, then interchange my mindscape and say it's the job, then switch again and say it's probably both, though inside I'm thinking about neither. It's the absence of Jo that's decimating my life, my very sense of being.

'So, your Scots babe – I heard she was tall,' Tasha says, leans closer, sharply changes the subject once again.

'Yeah,' I state, nod, then frown slightly to indicate my annoyance at this line of questioning.

'Hmmm . . . taller than me?'

'Yeah, a good two inches or so.'

'That's tall,' Tasha muses, raising her eyebrows.

'Yeah,' I say. Tasha stands perhaps five-nine as an absolute max, though always appears taller than this visage because she wears such huge shoes. On her plus side, she weighs in at an approximate eleven stone seven with all her curves most definitely projecting in the right places but, due to her subordinate role in the office, and, even despite being as high as a secretary might go before reaching director level, she still takes home something in the region of 14K per annum less than me, again, according to my unchallengeable source in Payroll.

'So-o-o . . . you, um, gonna tell me why you two broke up?' Tasha probes, toying with her empty glass.

'Er, nope. I don't think so,' I say, and swill the remains of my pint around the base of my glass, then finish it off, down in one. I replace the glass on the table, smack my lips, and add, 'A Kronenbourg, please.'

I gaze longingly after Tasha as she heads down the stairs towards the bar. I have only vague blurred recollections of our one night together. My clearest memory is only of waking early with a searing headache – Tasha, already dressed, armed with tea and toast, chivvying me out of bed, cajoling me into getting ready for work. 'Two Good Reasons,' Carl Smith calls her.

Carl is virtually running away with the Latecomer of the Year Award, having invented three mythical doctor's appointments in the last two weeks, enabling him to arrive in the office after midday on each occasion. I would, too, adopt this ruse but I'm convinced that Hubert Dodd would see straight through it.

'Would you have seen me?' I blurt, catching Tasha mid-sentence. I wasn't taking in what she was saying anyway.

She looks aghast, takes a deep breath, and blows out her cheeks.

'I – I really don't know,' she says, looks away from me to my left, then back directly at me, and adds, 'I wasn't presented with the opportunity. You'd set the gossipmongers in perpetual motion before we had chance to discuss it.'

I smile at Tasha reassuringly, but she just stares back at me blankly.

'Like I was saying before I was so rudely inter-rupted . . .' she continues, slowly, her expression fixed. 'Long-distance relationships never work. How long was it you were seeing your Glasgwegian babe?'

'Two and a half years.'

'I don't know how you managed.'

'We worked at it.'

'Well, I saw my Ewan for three years,' Tasha begins. 'Went to India with him and everything, then I started work here and he went on to Australia.' I try to retain eye contact, to appear interested. 'Then, three months into his trip, he decides that he can't live without me, he comes home early, and when I met him at the airport I realized I just didn't fancy him any more. *C'est la vie.*'

I smile wryly, attempt to stifle a small yawn. I wonder what Jo's doing right now? I also wonder if Tasha might take umbrage if I were to ask her to take the long silk scarf currently garnishing her neck and use it to perhaps tie her hair back in such a fashion so as to let her stupendous hooped earrings dangle freely and publicly. Mind, I'll probably get the chance to tie her hair back myself later tonight, unless, of course, Tasha has in fact denigrated into some squalid S&M freak and the scarf is now merely in place as a precursor to some debased quasi-strangulation rite.

'I wasn't a bitch about it, though,' Tasha is saying. 'Ewan and I are still good friends to this day. He's working in Toronto now. Good place for a holiday, eh?'

I do not think Beth slept well last night. She was badgering me for sex, but I just wasn't interested. I told her I was too tired, that I had to have an early night because I'd a long day ahead of me today. She didn't seem to understand what I was attempting to say.

'So-o-o, do anything interesting last night?' I ask Tasha.

'Went to the theatre, actually,' she answers. 'With a friend. Well, it should have been two friends, but Fiona – the daft cow – stayed home to nurse Gary.' Tasha puts her empty glass down rather heavy-handedly. I've barely touched my second pint. 'She missed a good play . . . Why do people have to live together, Damian?'

'Well, erm, you live with Niall,' I offer.

'It's not the same – you know what I mean,' she snaps, remains looking away.

'Yeah, but you're living with Niall . . . It's just, well, you're not sharing the same bedroom.'

'Or bonking,' Tasha says.

'Or sharing the same bedroom,' I repeat.

'Yeah, I guess so. I just can't imagine living with someone I'm actually bonking, though.'

'Yeah,' I sigh.

'Doing anything this weekend?' I ask after a pause, attempt to get things bubbling.

'Off to the Hanover Grand tomorrow,' she says briskly, straightens up and adds, 'You clubbing?'

'Boys' night out with some of the boys from the project – you know, Steve Kerr, Dino, Carl, the usual lot. Probably be legless by nine and end up in a meat-market somewhere, throwing up over one another.' I've been doing this a lot recently – actually enjoying the Lunchboys' company.

Tasha appears unimpressed. 'You're friends with Jamie Comley, aren't you?'

I nod.

'He's a big clubber, isn't he?' Tasha asks.

I shrug my shoulders, but she continues to ask, 'Does he go to Love Muscle? Does he go to DTPM?'

I shrug my shoulders, look detached.

'And Russell Bishop – he's big on the club scene. I've seen him around Soho a few times. Actually, you know a lot of fags, Damian. I do worry about you. But Russell – does he go to Sherbet? Is he, like, really big on the club scene? He seems to know just about *every*body. Does he go to G.A.Y.? My ex-boyfriend, Stefan, now he was a really big clubber – drop-dead gorgeous. All bisexuals always fancied him and they always fancied me . . . even if they didn't know we were actually together as a couple.' She senses my lack of interest. 'We had some wonderful threesomes that way.'

I dismiss this comment, barely raise an eyebrow. Tasha is a regular Meyer woman: a doppelgänger for Rena Horten in *Mudhoney*, this statuesque German beauty, except in the film Rena was cast as a mute, quite the extreme opposite of our loquacious self-loving Tasha.

'What about Richard Moore, Damian? He's gay, isn't he? Is *he* a big clubber? Does he go to WayOut or Warriors or Kitty Lips or Trade? Oh, you do know he's gay, don't you? . . . Only, he sent Niall a love letter . . . Of course, Niall took it really badly and threatened to kill Richard if he ever so much as looked at him again, but then Niall's kinda funny that way. Of course, I could never be like that to an admirer . . . I'm far too much of a cool chick to ever be that nasty to someone just because they want to fuck me . . . And before you say it, Damian, or even think it – Yes! Lots of people really do want to fuck me. Well, silly me, of course, you should already know that – you've been after me for years, haven't you? Mind, we did have quite a good night together didn't we, but I guess I've moved on from there now. I'm no longer the same innocent little girlie you took advantage of – how many years has it been? Three? Maybe four? Seems like a lifetime ago . . . Mind, you used to go clubbing quite a bit with that Scottish babe didn't you, Damian? I mean, I heard she really did have the clubby look, didn't she? Long blonde hair, lovely long legs, baby blue eyes. Anyway, blah blah blah blah blah . . . I was in Soho just last week, this new gay bar opened in Wardour Street – God, the men there were so-o-o bitchy, just so horrible to women, you would not believe it . . . And on Saturday I'm planning to go to . . . And I was talking to some actor out of *This Life* in this bar on Frith Street last Tuesday. Of course, I can't really tell you what I was doing on Frith Street last Tuesday, or where I was going. You'd only set the gossips off again, you naughty boy . . . I've been to blah blah blah . . . And I've even met, and I've done and – Oh, goddamn it, Damian – I am just so-o-o fucking pretentious . . . Every-body loves me . . . I am one dumb fucking stuck-up pretentious bitch . . . I am just so—'

'Another G and T?' I ask brusquely, terminating her sermon.

'No, better not,' Tasha says. 'I'm expected in Notting Hill in less than an hour.'

Shell-shocked by this admission, I just mumble, 'Eh?'

'Damian.' Tasha half-sighs. 'Remember? You said, "Just a quick, purely platonic drink."'

'Oh, right. Never mind, then.'

We leave. I'm forlorn. We part at Southwark Bridge.

'See you tomorrow,' I call as I turn to walk away from her, back along the river-front, back along the same route I'd trod so expectantly only one hour earlier, back past the Flounders, across Blackfriars Road, down Stamford Street toward Waterloo, desolate in the driving rain, Wagner's 'Ride of the Valkyries' kicking loud in my headphones, cursing Jo for ever leaving me, for putting me through further heartache with even more women. I am downhearted, confused, crestfallen, dejected, embittered for having let Tasha escape so lightly. I catch sight of this big message daubed in huge white lettering across a wall in the bull-ring – HI PAUL, REMEMBER ME? JUDY FROM BATTERSEA? GET IN TOUCH SOON – and this sets me wondering . . . could I maybe do something like this for Jo? Plaster some big message on a billboard or a street corner or a chip-shop wall somewhere near her parents' house? Maybe I could hire one of those corporate airships with a banner trailing underneath in the slipstream, displaying, JOANNA KENNEDY, I AM SO VERY SORRY, LOVE, DAME – make some huge gesture to grab her attention?

Once home, I discard the remnants of my kebab (which a good vet could probably get back on its feet) by the side of the sofa, rescue the phone from its cradle, and dial Beth's number.

'Hello?'

'Alright?'

'Where are you?' Beth asks.

'Toronto . . . Canada.'

'No? . . . I thought you said you were going to be drinking with your workmates?'

'Nah, only a quick one for someone's birthday . . . You fancy coming over?'

'What? Now?'

'Yeah.'

'Could do, I suppose.'

'See you later then, sweetheart,' I thrum, then switch on the stereo and stick on some really old tunes from my high-school days: some electro – Hashim, Man Parrish, Egyptian Lover, Africa Bambaataa.

Saturday morning. We're in Scratchwood Services, just out of London – me, Matt, Five and Thom – on our way to a game of golf at Five's father's club out by Birmingham somewhere. It's earlyish, only eight a.m. Somehow I've managed to blow nearly nine pounds on the price of a fried breakfast, but I don't care about the expense. I'm too hungry to be concerned about such trivialities. There's two blondes on the table next to us, both expressly ugly, one wearing a jumper with the wording SI FIRMIR O GRIDO.

'You see,' Five continues, through a mouthful of food, 'we're not really mates, none of us. Not like proper mates, not really.'

'You not eating, Matt?' Thom indolently interrupts Five's sermon, slowly turning a page of his paper as he does so.

'Traditional English at home,' Matt answers and rubs his belly.

'Hey, I was talking,' Five moans, looks slightly cross.

'Traditional English?' I ask Matt. 'Sausage? Bacon? Egg?'

'Nah,' Matt says. 'Chicken tikka masalla, lamb dupiaza, mushroom pilau, Bombay aloo.'

'For breakfast?' I ask.

'Yeah, had a curry last night. Microwaved the remains for breakfast.'

'Got Jenny to rustle it up for you, did you?' Thom asks, turning another page of his paper.

'No, she was still out when I left. She went down Turnmills with some of her workmates last night. Obviously decided to stick it out till the end, or went back to someone's flat for a smoke.'

I think about the bloke from Jenny's office that Jenny had told Jo she'd been shagging, and it's as much as I can do to stop myself from actually raising this point to the table. And I'm wondering what it'd be like to, say, actually fuck Jenny. I mean, I've never really thought about such an action before; mate's partners are usually out of bounds, but this might prove the perfect opportunity to totally fuck Matt off, put his nose categorically out of joint.

'Look, as I was saying before,' Five speaks out, attempts to impose himself on the flow of the conversation once again, 'we're not really mates, none of us. Not like proper mates, not really.'

'Who was DJ-ing at Turnmills last night?' I ask Matt, ignore Five, chew on some fried bread.

'I dunno,' he says, offers, 'Brandon Block maybe?'

'Hey!' Five clamours.

'Yes, yes, we know,' Thom conforms. 'We're not really mates, none of us. Not like proper mates, not really.'

'Bollocks,' Matt sighs.

'Oh, I dunno,' I say. 'I quite agree with Five's point.'

'Why?' Matt asks.

'Well, for starters, you're a wanker, Matt, and Jenny's probably getting shafted by someone from her work as we speak, and will be eloping back to the north with him within the coming year.'

'Er, ha-ha,' Matt chuckles, though doesn't seem quite sure of himself.

'It's true,' I tell him quite candidly. 'And, as far as Five's point goes, we really are not mates, none of us, not proper mates.'

''Course we are,' Matt says, attempts a half chuckle again, and I allow myself an inward laugh at this rent-a-freak's gullible comment.

'No, we're not,' Five carries on, motioning with his hands as if to accentuate his point. 'Thanks for your input, Dame. You see, we're not proper mates 'cos all we ever do is take the piss . . . especially behind one another's backs.'

'You lot been talking about me again?' I ask, incising into another sausage, my fourth of five. 'Cheers, boys.'

'No, but you know what I mean,' Five says. 'We're

not nice to one another. You wait and see. Marky Mullen is gonna meet up with us today—'

'Marky Mullen?' I ask, surprised, wondering if I'd heard him quite right.

'Yeah, Marky Mullen,' Five returns. 'Marky Mullen is gonna meet up with us today, and I bet the first thing anyone says to him is "Marky, you're a cunt".'

'Marky's coming, yeah?' I have to ask again.

'Got his number out of your address book,' Thom tells me, doesn't look up from his paper. 'I phoned him up last night. Told him we'd be up in his neck of the woods today. So, it looks like the Kitten Killer is actually gonna make the effort to meet up with us this time.'

After a pause, Matt asks Thom, 'The what?'

Thom looks up. 'The Kitten Killer.' Pause. 'You lot not heard that story?'

'Er, no,' Matt answers. Five and I both shake our heads in unison.

'Oh,' Thom says, 'this is a good one.' Thom pulls himself closer to the table, unfolds his legs. 'I thought everyone knew this? Maybe not, eh? Anyhow, it must have been in our third year at uni and I was with Lisa and we were getting stoned in that bird's flat, the one Gerry's still hung up about – whatshername?'

'Andrea,' I tell him.

'Yeah, Andrea, that's it,' Thom says. 'Anyhow, Marky was there, and was, like, really morose and Gerry's trying to get out of him what's wrong, and he tells us this story about how him and his dad drowned these kittens when he was younger, because their cat had a big litter and they didn't know what to do with any of them. It was the anniversary and, like, every year he commemorates the date when he drowned them. Sad, huh?'

No one says a thing, then Matt finally manages, 'So, er, do you think he'll really show this time?'

'Said he couldn't really wriggle out of this one – what with us being so close by to where he lives,' Thom says, laughs. Marky never shows on any dates we arrange with him. I've not seen him since my birthday last year.

'Look, I was *try*ing to make a point before I was interrupted,' Five says, slamming his cutlery down hard as if to gain our attention. ' "You're a cunt" – I bet that's the first thing anyone says to Marky.'

'Or "Killed any kittens lately?" ' Thom.

'Yeah, but Five . . . Marky *is* a cunt.' Me.

'Yeah.' Matt this time. 'He *is*, Five.'

'He won't show anyway. Never does,' Thom again.

'Yeah, maybe. Maybe you're right,' Five says. 'But why can't we be nice to one another, like proper mates, just for once, eh? I mean, we've got to stick together for the sake of the Es.'

'What Es?' Thom asks, looks confused.

Five's quick to react. 'Oh, sorry – it's early. I mean, people like us have to stick together for when we're doing Es – you know, in clubs and that. Look out for one another . . . make sure no one loses it.'

Matt defies even his own stupidity, and actually aids Five with, 'Yeah, but the main point of what you were saying was why can't we be nice to one another, like proper mates? Right, Five?'

'Because we're all cunts, that's why,' Thom answers, doesn't appear troubled by Five's slip of the tongue.

'Look,' I add, 'we always stick up for one another when pushed, right?' Though I'm secretly thinking I'd now probably go as far as to actually pay someone else just to give Matt a good kicking. Why did Five have to invite such vermin along today?

'Bollocks,' Thom interjects. 'If I so much as saw anyone caning any of you lot, I'd fucking join in on their side.'

'Thom,' I say.

Thom looks up. 'Yeah?'

'You are a complete cunt,' I tell him, and smile. I like Thom's attitude. He smiles too, and makes a play at cuffing me with the back of his right hand.

I'm spending my Sunday lunchtime power-drinking with Gerry in the Green Man. I'm on Kronenbourg, he's on some crap bitter, me on my fourth pint, him on his fifth – all in little over an hour – and we're watching these three big black geezers, one wearing a seventies Arsenal top, one with a T-shirt which says TART TART, all three playing killer on the pool table. We didn't make it back from the golf till gone ten last night, to find a note from Gerry telling us he was 'supping in the Fantail and Firkin', so we all trotted merrily down, to find him almost stupefied, lurking upstairs in the pub, and afterwards we naturally ended up in The Lights, where Thom wasted some two hours chatting up this Swedish au pair only for her to blow him out, and I kept getting hassled by this ugly little thing with a gold front tooth who insisted on calling me Ralph (I was wearing an old Ralph Lauren polo shirt) and, in turn, I approached the only tall thing in the place and said dumbly, 'You're tall,' to which she retorted, 'Fuck right off,' and I just stood there bemused, looking a right homme, until her mate came over to me and apologized, said, 'You shouldn't have mentioned her height. She's really sensitive about it,' which is an eternal shame because it was the only thing I found even remotely attractive about her. Oh, and Gerry actually took some young thing's phone number – to everyone's utter astonishment.

'What shall I do tomorrow, Dame?' Gerry is asking me.

'How do you mean?' I ask back.

'With Debbie – that bird from The Lights, last night.'

'Um . . . fuck her?'

'No, what should I do with her first?'

'Oh, you mean foreplay?'

'Nah . . . come on, Dame. Where should I take her?'

'To a pub. Get her pissed.'

'You reckon that's wise? I can be a right cunt when I'm pissed.'

'Gerry,' I say. 'You're a right cunt when you're not.'

He nods his head in agreement. 'Hmmm . . . true.'

I head for the toilet, where, whilst I'm standing there pissing against a urinal, some big-nosed geek asks me if I want to buy some hash. 'Sorry, mate, I'm strictly a grass smoker,' I tell him. 'Rock burns too many holes in your clothes,' and as I pass on by, back through to the bar, he maybe calls me a faggot, I'm not sure, and I can't be bothered to challenge him to the contrary. I find myself wondering what Jo's doing right now.

'Got any more cash?' I ask Gerry.

'Nah, sorry, I'm skint,' he concedes, slaps his pocket as if to justify his lack of funds.

'No worries. Fancy a curry?' I'm asking as we head through the front entrance, and out onto the main road, where the sun half-blinds me momentarily.

'Like I said, no cash, Dame. I'm still putting it aside for those fucking Es.'

'Fuck it,' I tell him. 'My treat. Credit – that's the secret. I'll phone somewhere up. I know a curry house that'll deliver ales as well.' I remove my Access card from my pocket and wiggle it in Gerry's face. We cross the road, pass Ritchie's and the Swiss Village, then cross again at the zebra crossing opposite the B2 store and make our way along the Broadway towards the flat. I suddenly feel so petite and inconsequential, almost childlike, with Gerry's sky-high figure pacing alongside me.

Gerry never got to fuck Caroline Kirkland in her hotel room that night. After I left, Jay sat there for an age, waiting for Gerry to return, until an hour or so later Caroline finally wandered down to the bar to see where everyone had got to. We figure Gerry must've had second thoughts, legged it through a fire-exit or something. I've never asked Jay whether he got his blowjob or not. If he did, I don't think I'd wish to associate with Caroline Kirkland ever again: don't want to affiliate with the Jezebel who'd take that infested Neanderthal deep down the back of her throat.

Once home, I dial out for a curry. Gerry's after a meat madras; I want a chicken vindaloo, which will probably prove too hot for me, but I'm not that hungry anyway, so I don't really care. To this order I add one portion of mushroom pilau, one portion of Bombay potato and one portion of sag panir – all for sharing – plus six cans of Kronenbourg, six cans of bitter, and two bottles of house wine – one red, one white. The cunt on the other end of the line keeps wrongly rereading my card number back to me and I sense myself slowly losing patience with him. I then phone Beth, ask her to come over and bring more wine.

By the time Beth arrives Gerry and I are now smoking ourselves stupid and are watching my Anna Nicole Smith video with the sound turned down and we're singing along in stupid shrill voices to this George Michael CD which I've pilfered from Thom's collection. We've caned most of the ale, and polished off the bottle of red, and my vindaloo sits, largely untouched, on the coffee table, unfit for further human consumption. Gerry phones that Debbie thing to arrange a date. They agree to meet outside Charing Cross at eight tomorrow.

'Take Debbie to a pub and get her drunk,' Beth says to Gerry. 'That always works for me.'

I belch and nod in agreement, take another long, cerebrated toke on a spliff.

Jay phones – God knows why. He sounds as high as

a kite to me, though he claims he's not. I switch the phone to conference, so that Gerry and I can both rant at him.

'Uh, what? Gerry's there as well?' the black fucker's voice squeaks through the phone.

'Yeah, alright, Jay?' Gerry shouts.

'Oh, er . . . alright, Gerry? What are you two up to?'

'We're pissed,' Gerry shouts.

'Fucking pissed,' I elaborate, not knowing why I'm even talking to this cunt.

'Uh. Oh, yeah. You two sound it.'

'*I'm* here, Jay. I'm sober,' Beth says.

'What are those two like?' Jay asks.

'A mess,' Beth tells him.

'Oh, uh, I'm not pissed you know,' Jay whines.

'You sound pissed!' I shout.

'No, he doesn't,' I hear Beth say, then tut.

'Dame, it's only Sunday bloody afternoon,' Jay says.

'Yeah, and we're wasting valuable drinking time talking to you, you miserable bastard!' Gerry shouts.

'Yeah,' I agree, stumbling forward onto my knees.

'You okay?' Beth asks me.

All I can tell her is, 'I am fucking pissed.'

'Hey, Jay, I've got a shag lined up for tomorrow!' Gerry shouts.

Beth tuts.

'Yeah? You? What's she like?' Jay asks.

'A dog,' I say and giggle, but Gerry glares at me so I apologize and then laugh.

'She's alright. She's okay!' Gerry shouts, remains glaring at me.

I'm lying on the carpet stroking Beth's calf, looking up at Gerry. The phone is by my head.

'A shag's a shag,' I think Jay says.

'Yeah. Debbie-doggy style,' I yelp.

'Damian!' Beth snaps.

'No, no, honestly, Jay . . . honestly. Listen, right, listen . . . Gerry's got himself lined up a right top-notch thing here, this Debbie . . . This Debbie, this Deb-or-ah . . . she's quality, a mighty fine thing. Only, what? Twenty, Gerry? And with lovely big tits . . . Mighty fine piece of fluff.'

'Twenty-one, Dame,' Gerry says, not looking at me, suddenly sounding sober.

'What?' I have to ask.

'She is twenty-one, Dame.'

'Oh . . . oh, yeah, right . . . makes . . . makes all the difference.' And then I'm drooling into the mouthpiece, 'She's twenty-one, Jay. Forget what I said. Forget what I said. She's twenty-one, *twen-tee-wun* . . . Got it?'

'Got it,' Jays says. 'The same age as Joanna, right?'

I'm abruptly sober, drop-kicked into reality at the mere mention of her sacred name, but then Gerry says, I think, 'Yeah, but Deborah's one hundred times better than Joanna,' or some such phrase, and I can register the contempt in his face, can perceive his immortal desire to denigrate our friendship here and now in this very room, to sully the good name of Jo before Beth, and I'm looking to the ceiling but my vision is somehow

blurred, all spinning around me, and there's an enemy
in the phone with his accomplice to the left of me, and
Beth's to the right, then, no, this foe, Gerry, is to my
right, and Beth's to my left, no right, no left, then I've
the massiveness of the world on my chest and I sense
myself vomiting across the carpet, ale and curry oozing
out in a pungent pool before me and then I'm doubled
up on my futon, my head in Beth's lap, and then I pass
out.

'Good weekend, babes?' Russell Bishop asks me, as we
lounge in these huge congenial chairs in the company
coffee bar.

'Er, no, not really. Did nothing – just played a bit of
golf,' I have to admit.

'No lovely girlies?' he enquires.

'No, none. More's the pity.'

'Not like you,' he simpers. 'I thought you had lots of
lovelies you could call on?'

I just smile. This morning I received an invite to
Kelly's going-away party. She's leaving the country in a
couple of weeks. This news somehow saddens me
slightly, and this, plus the fact that it's now over three
months since Jo told me she couldn't love me any more,
and the fact that Marky Mullen never showed again on
Saturday, and that Tasha Doran still hasn't responded
to an e-mail I sent on Friday, saying 'Thanks for last
night, must do it again', and that now even that lanky
cunt Gerry has found himself a woman that he might

just get to fuck tonight, all add up to weigh heftily on my shoulders, play havoc with my present mindscape, and I actually found myself e-mailing all the Lunchboys this morning with a message which read 'Roll on the weekend' – even though it is only Monday today.

'Ended up in a threesome Saturday night,' Russell is saying, the way some might say, 'Visited my gran on Sunday.'

'Just the three?' I ask. I am not fazed by his comment – it's no more than I've come to expect from the Bishop, his tales of full-on Bacchanalian orgies. Aside from us, there are twelve bodies in the coffee bar this lunchtime: ten geezers and two unblondes, both of whom are short. One of the geezers, this smallish bloke that Dino Denton knows, actually has a hallowed hooped earring in place and this bewilders me no end, and I subconsciously find myself leaning forward from my seat to see if he's indeed also wearing a pair of Jo-style kinky boots, stacked heels with long leather lashing his calves.

'The group stuff's always on the first Saturday of the month,' Russell mentions matter-of-factly.

'So, what sexes were they?' I ask, careful to appear nonchalant, realign myself in my seat, happy in the gnosis that the geezer with the hooped earring is wearing nothing more depraved than a pair of black DM shoes.

'Oh, a man and a woman,' he says, places his coffee cup firmly in its saucer. 'Mike and Miriam. Wonderful couple. You'd like them.'

'How old?'

'Mim, she's early thirties I believe, or at least has the body of someone of that age. But Mike – oh, he's my age I'm afraid: mid-forties, poor thing. Though, of course, he's not quite as versatile as me in the sack.'

I catch the glint in Bishop's eyes as he delivers this last line, though he refrains from sounding too boastful or pompous.

There's little I can say in response.

'Actually, there was a reason I wanted to see you down here, away from prying eyes,' the Bishop mentions to me. 'It's about your extracurricular activities.'

'Oh,' I ask, alarmed for a second, all manner of sexual deviancy amok through my mindscape. 'You, er, know I'm not like, like that, Russell.'

The Bishop just looks at me blankly, then says. 'Well, I can always wish, Mr Shaw. No, it wasn't your sexual practices to which I was referring. It's your refuelling technique which might be causing some consternation with them upstairs.'

'Refuelling technique?' I ask, sense my lip curl in mock-Elvis fashion.

'Yes,' the Bishop just tells me, looks away, as if I'm already fully versed on such a subject.

'Er, meaning?' I ask him.

'Drugs,' the Bishop tells me.

'Drugs?'

'Yes . . . drugs.'

I think about this for a moment then respond, 'Oh, right, you want me to get hold of some for you?'

But the Bishop just shoots me a look of abject horror

and answers, very precisely, 'Fuck off. I have my own specialist suppliers, thank you very much.'

'Oh, right, so what's this drug stuff, then?'

Russell leans closer, looks so surreptitious. 'Hubert's heard a whisper that some of the younger lads on the project are dabbling in drugs.'

'Me?' I ask.

'Well, no, funnily enough.' The Bishop chuckles. 'He didn't think you were the type: said you were always too well turned out. No, actually Carl's his principal candidate.'

'Carl?' I laugh. 'But Carl's probably never touched drugs in his life.'

'He always comes in late.'

'What?' I have to ask.

'Exactly,' Russell answers. 'It's stupid, I know, but Hubert thinks Carl's a druggy simply because he comes in late every morning.'

'Well,' I say in all seriousness, 'I hope you informed the Sod that Carl's doing it for the prestige of the Latecomer Award.'

'Did I, fuck?' The Bishop coughs. 'But you've had your warning, okay?'

'Yeah, thanks. Hey, you see that tall thing, over there?' I say to the Bishop, point out some unblonde approaching one of the vending machines, not very attractive, with rather unkempt hair, but possessing a fantastic pair of Meyer breasts.

'What of her?' he asks, scrutinizing her lofty heights

as she turns to walk back through the coffee bar, past us and towards reception.

'Fucked her on some external course last year.' I'm lying, never actually having even seen this thing before today, but singling her out, assuming that Russell will believe I've taken a shine to her due to her giraffe-like stature and robust chest.

'Nice legs,' Russell says and asks, 'she any good betwixt the sheets, dear boy?'

'Er, can't remember,' I stutter, slightly alarmed. 'I think so . . . I was seriously coked up at the time.'

The Bishop smiles, and I sense that he's proud of me all the same.

'Do you take sugar, Damian, dear? I'm so sorry, but I can never remember if you take sugar or not,' my mother says as she pours the tea.

'No, er, no sugar,' I tell her then look to my brother. His face just voices a look of concern. 'I don't take sugar because I'm sweet enough as it is.' I then attempt a half-laugh but this somehow seems totally inappropriate.

We make our way through to the dining room and seat ourselves at the meal table – me, my mother and my brother. I cast a side glance into the lounge. A new glass-covered coffee table proudly marks the centre of the room.

'Your father bought it,' my mother mentions, as if reading my thoughts. 'He said it wouldn't get damaged now that there's . . . now that there's . . .' My mother's voice falters, she chokes a little and I sense a macabre fear of her crying, a vision I've only confronted once before, after she'd unintentionally drowned Brady, our pet Persian, in the washing machine when I was maybe ten or so, and the runt next-door laughed at such news so I carved the back of his hand open with this blade I'd unscrewed from a pencil sharpener. And so now I'm turning to face my mother, redoubtable thoughts stacked high in my head like traffic above Gatwick, half expecting to see acid tears swelling in her absolute eyes, but my mother simply purses her lips, stares straight ahead, and retains her ennobled composure. Such dignity, such grace. I slurp my tea.

'So, what now, Mum?' my brother asks.

'Nothing's changed, son,' my mother answers brightly, sounds false.

'But—' I start to say.

'But nothing, dear,' my mother tells me, puts her hand to my left wrist. 'Now, tell your mother how you and Elizabeth are getting along these days.'

I look to my brother once again, but he just raises his eyebrows. 'Oh, we're doing fine,' I manage, even though we're not, and I cannot understand why Beth possibly wants to continue to go out with me, or what she imagines I see in her.

'That's good, dear. That's good,' my mother says, pats my wrist, turns her attention back to the glass-covered coffee table once again. 'That's good.'

My brother shifts the conversation. 'I, erm, may have some news to cheer everyone up.'

'Really?' my mother asks, wide-eyed.

'Er, yeah . . . maybe.' My brother looks sheepish, almost comically so. 'Sharon and me . . . Well, we think that Sharon may be, um, may be pregnant.'

'Oh, congratulations, son.' My mother stands and throws her tiny frame around my brother's bulbous neck and kisses him hard on his right cheek.

'Nice one,' I tell Ray, but he just looks flushed with embarrassment. As well he should – this is the final nail in the coffin of what little life he had left to spare. He now has virtually the entire ensemble of manacles: the career job, the pension, the semi-detached, the mortgage, the wife and, very soon, the child. 'Commitments' spelt with a capital C. Only another 1.4 children to complete the set. 'Nice one,' I say again to my sad, corpulent brother. He just shrugs his shoulders in an infantile fashion.

I've started up a new competition with Carl Smith from work, whereby we e-mail women from the office directory at random, sending them the eternal line: *You are like a rose growing in the compost heap of this company. I love you, do you love me?* Any replies we then get, we forward on to one another. I've actually received four replies from a possible twenty, all along the lines of *I think you must have the wrong person.* Smith actually received one reply accusing him of sexual harassment, but he coolly responded, apologizing, claiming that someone must have hacked his id – an age-old excuse guaranteed to get you out of trouble. I did actually mail one of my messages to the Blonde from Financial Services, Pamela Ward – from my own id this time, not Connor Ferguson's – but it's just hung there in my out-basket for close on two days, so I'm finally coming to the conclusion that she really has left the company.

After gently forcing my mother to withdraw, coaxing her back into her seat, my brother tells us, 'Well, I mean, it's not official yet, the pregnancy – Sharon's seeing Doctor Hornett on Monday – but she is late with her period, and she's been ill every morning this week, and it's not like we haven't been trying or anything . . .'

'I wonder if it will be a boy or a girl?' my mother exclaims. 'What do you think, Damian?' But, before I'm given a chance to answer, she adds, 'Oh, I must read your tea-leaves, Ray. That should give us some clue.'

'You made the tea from tea-bags,' I say, half-laugh.

'What was that?' my mother asks innocently, turning her attention from Ray to me for a split second, then back to Ray again.

Ray repeats my line. 'You made the tea from tea-bags, Mum.'

'Oh, yes, of course. What must I have been thinking?' My mother puts her hand to her mouth and starts to giggle, as if she hadn't a care in the world – the memories of my father tucked safely towards the back of her brainvault for the time being. It feels like a decade since I last saw my mother giggle.

My brother sighs, smiles at me and says, 'You're gonna have to start getting used to being called Uncle Damian.'

'Wow,' I say, deadpan, 'I . . . cannot . . . wait.'

'Oh, my big strong boys,' my mother says proudly, looking to the both of us. 'This calls for a celebration. We should be drinking something a little more suitable.' My mother winks. 'Now, I hid a little half-bottle of Scotch from your father just last week. I think it's in the spare room.' She taps the side of her nose, winks again and rises to her feet. 'And I don't think your father managed to find it before he disappeared again.'

I wait for my mother to get clear of earshot, then I ask Ray, 'Just how did he tell her this time?'

'Not now,' he tells me. 'What did New Order encore with at the Hammersmith Palais in December 1985?'

'What?'

'What did New Order encore with—?'

'I heard the question. How did father tell mother this time?'

'Answer my question first,' Ray advises me.

I sigh. 'They encored with "Confusion" followed by "Ceremony", and it was *November* 1985, not December.'

'Quite right,' my brother says. 'And I was there, wasn't I?'

'Yes,' I inform him through clenched teeth. 'It was a Sunday. You missed the last train home again.'

'Did I?' he asks.

'Yes,' I fume.

'I took you along to your first New Order gig at Hemel on the Friday before that, didn't I?'

'Yeah,' I concede, suddenly sensing a small burst of compassion for my brother – for the way we once were.

'And what did they encore with there?'

'Ray!' I smart.

'Okay, okay,' my brother sighs. 'Dad just left her a note. She read it to me yesterday.'

'What did it say?'

'I dunno. Something about how sorry he was, that she'd not be able to find him, that he'd be in touch when he was settled.'

'Fucking bastard,' I mutter to myself, sip my tea, start counting my brother's chins and the ugly ripples of fat round his swinish throat.

'Do you think we should get in touch with Gillian?' Ray asks.

I tap my finger against the side of my cup. 'Gillian? Whatever for?'

'In case he's gone there . . . because of the kids,' Ray says with misplaced virtue.

I turn to stare at the glass-covered coffee table. 'They . . . weren't . . . his . . . kids.'

'Whaddayamean, they weren't his kids?'

'Just what I said. They weren't his kids.'

My brother looks mystified, just bleats, 'But—'

'But what?!' I interject.

'But Gillian is pregnant. She got pregnant when she was with dad.'

'It's Paul Barclay's kid.'

'Barclay . . .? You mean "Batty" Barclay from school? Who told you that?'

'Gillian did,' I tell him.

I catch Ray's eyes misting over. 'Oh, right. Erm, when was this?'

'I went round to see her when father moved back here. Your Sharon gave me Gillian's address.'

'But . . . "Batty" Barclay?'

'He was there. He'd moved in. After Gillian had done the decent thing and thrown father into the gutter where he belongs.'

Ray now looks entirely at sea. 'But the kids?'

'She said she'd have a DNA test if she had to. Father knew the score though.' I let out a prolonged sigh. 'He's not quite as stupid as I'd like to think.'

'But little Cassie?' my brother laments. 'Our little stepsister?'

'Ex-stepsister, I'm afraid. Sired by some barman she met in Clacton, apparently. Besides, it's obvious that Cassie wasn't a bona-fide Shaw – she was far too sweet from the off.' I look Ray hard in the face. 'You should be happy for the little thing. At least she'll grow up safe in the knowledge that she's not contaminated by father's rogue genes.'

'Christ,' my brother murmurs, just stares at the table between us.

'Now, now,' I tell him, waggle my finger, 'I wouldn't let mother hear you taking the Lord's name in vain.'

'Hold on,' Ray says. 'Paul Barclay is only twenty-four.'

Baffled by his logic, I let slip, 'Yeessss . . . the same age as Gillian.'

'Oh, yeah,' Ray admits.

I continue in this sarcastic voice, doing a shit Michael Caine impression. 'And he's got a job. And he doesn't drink to excess every night of the fucking week. And he's not a complete . . . fucking . . . no-mark.'

Ray sighs. 'Poor father. I don't know, some people, eh?' He sighs again. 'Oh, well, I guess I must be the only Shaw to have been lucky in love.'

It's an eternity before I say, quite soberly, 'Run that by me again, brother dearest.'

Ray continues on his merry path. 'Oh, you know – Mum and Dad, Dad and Gillian, you and Joanna. I seem to be the only Shaw to actually maintain any relationship of worth.'

'Me . . . and . . . Joanna?' I ask, quite deliberately.

'Yeah, you and Joanna.' Ray appears oblivious to his own provincial insanity. 'I mean, I know that you've had loads of girlfriends, but I got the feeling that Joanna was very special to you, that you really liked her. It's just a shame that it couldn't work out.'

'Couldn't . . . work . . . out?'

'All that distance between the two of you.'

'Couldn't . . . work . . . out?' I repeat.

'Yeah, I always thought you were just treading water with Joanna really. I mean, now that you've split up, you should really concentrate your efforts on finding yourself a nice woman in London. Well, you've got this Beth for starters. Who knows, maybe you might find happiness like me? Maybe one day you could be a father too, instead of just frittering your life away on all those casual relationships . . .'

I sit, open-mouthed with incredulity, as my sad suburban brother with his sorry, unsatisfying life continues to dig his own grave ever deeper and deeper, like so many of my supposed friends in recent times.

'What did New Order encore with at the Roskilde Festival in 1993?' I quiz him bitingly.

'Bruv, you know I couldn't afford to go to any of those gigs,' Ray rejoinders.

'I'd only just graduated,' I tell him, snarling a bit. 'I went even though I was skint.'

'Well . . . Sharon was on the scene by then,' Ray concedes.

'It was "Fine Time",' I tell him, snort a signal of derision. 'What did New Order close their set with at London Central Poly in 1985?'

'Oh, I remember this one . . . They played "Atmosphere" there.'

'But what did they close their set with?'

'Erm.'

'You . . . were . . . there, Ray.'

'Yes, I know, Damian,' my brother acknowledges, puts a finger to his temple. 'Now, hold on. Let me see.'

' "Age Of Consent". Alright, what did they open with at the Woolwich Coronet in 1987?'

'Woolwich?'

'We were there together.'

'Yeah, of course. I remember.'

' "Ceremony",' I tell him, caustically.

'Right, yes,' Ray says. 'Ah, it's coming back to me now. They opened with "Ceremony", then played "Shellshock".'

'It was "Paradise" not "Shellshock". They played "Paradise" second, "Shellshock" third.'

'Yeah, sorry, wrong gig.' My brother squirms.

'You . . . know . . . nothing,' I'm hissing at him, as our mother plonks a half-bottle of Scotch on the table between us. She exclaims brightly, 'There we are. I just knew I had it hidden away somewhere.'

The weather's not too bad, so we're having a Lunchboys confab in the garden of the Rose & Crown – barbecued burgers and ice-cold lagers all round. It's mufti day today, but since jeans and T-shirts of any description (including the classic polo) are outlawed, I'm still garbed in my standard office apparel. The rest, however, are bedecked in their smart cotton shirts from Marks and Sparks, inelegant sweaters and the very worst line in chinos and corduroy, and at first glance they resemble a stag-party of Northern oiks all headed for the local Ritzy nightspot, or possibly an off-duty unit of British soldiers. Indeed, in an unofficial army style, one of them's sure to holler 'Kings' at any point now and they'll pile in en masse, driven by brigaded loyalties, to kick the living shit out of me. There are absolutely no things in the pub garden this lunchtime; it's too much of an old man's drinking establishment. Even the sun fails to bring them out.

'Nice night last night, Jamie-babes?' the Bishop is asking the Sperminator.

Gregor Daley decides to interrupt the pair. 'Anything you'd like to tell us? Or is this something only the Family should know about?'

'Oh, only up Stepney Pride,' James Comley says.

'Any good?' Russell Bishop asks him.

'Meet anyone nice, ducky?' Carl Smith asks in this oh-so-camp voice, ribbing the pair.

'Well, it was weird' – James says, puts his pint down on the table – 'because the pub football team were drinking there, yet it's also amateur gay strip night on Thursdays.'

'Pub . . . football . . . team?' I half-ask. 'You sure this isn't just another of your sordid fantasies, James?'

'That's the thing,' he replies. 'It was so-o-o strange. There was, like, this fifty-year-old bloke wandering around naked, with his dick in his hand, and everyone was just trying to ignore him. It was so embarrassing.'

'Bit like a normal Friday night in the Doggett's,' Carl says, aims his comment directly at me. I emit a nervous laugh. For some strange reason I'm thinking about Pamela Ward, the Blonde from Financial Services. Is this a sign? Has she finally returned to the office? I must e-mail her this afternoon to find out.

'Take anyone home with you?' Russell asks James.

'Nah, there was no one I really liked,' James admits, reaches to pick up his pint again.

Russell sighs. 'Well, I've got to say, if it's a straight choice between the Stepney Pride and Attitude, then I'm afraid I'll always plump for Attitude.'

'You would – it's darker in there,' James quips.

Russell almost chokes as he takes a gulp of his drink.

'Where's Attitude?' Carl asks.

Russell coughs. 'That's where I bumped into you last Saturday, dear boy.'

'Aw, ha ha. No, fuck up, Bishop, where is it? So I know where to avoid,' Carl says.

'Chelsea, dear boy. Chelsea,' Russell answers.

'Ah, so you prefer a West End Girl to an East End Boy, eh, Russell,' Gregor offers.

Russell appears thoughtful. 'No, I quite like a bit of East End rough now and again, but I'm afraid that Pride men are strictly second-class. Well' – cough – 'not so much second-class – dear me, wrong word – more second-division, I think you'd say.'

'Why do gay pubs always resemble, like, gangster pubs in old movies?' I wonder out loud. 'I mean, they've all got blacked-out windows and they look really dodgy from the outside.'

'Aye, and you get shafted in both!' Carl jokes.

I laugh. I'm enjoying parleying with the Lunchboys.

Russell just smiles. 'I'll have to ask my friends about that one – Sam and Shelley. They own a rather dubious drinking den down in Streatham.'

'Why, Russell,' James asks, pauses dramatically, 'have all your friends got androgynous names? I mean, Sam and Shelley, they could be men *or* women.'

'They're probably both,' Carl winks, 'at the same time!'

We're interrupted by Ashwin Patel from Credit Risk, as he joins us from the bar, flailing a piece of paper in his hand. 'Hey, lads, have any of you seen this yet?'

'What is it?' Gregor asks.

'Here, Damian, you read it first.' Ash thrusts the paper towards me. 'You work for the Sod.'

'Er, like Gregor said, what is it?' I have to ask.

'It's a memo from Hubert Dodd that's gone out to all departments.'

Puzzled, I ask, 'Yeah . . . and?'

'Fourth line down,' Ash tells me.

'Yes?' I ask again, study the type.

'Check the spelling of head-count,' he tells me.

I laugh aloud as it dawns on me that Hubert has omitted the letter 'o' from the word.

I'm walking up Long Acre with Gerry by my side, him soaring above me, and I'm thinking about this big pneumatic blonde in a red dress I recently saw play a secretary or something in an episode of *The Persuaders* that Beth had on video, and she stood broad inches above Tony Curtis so I assumed she was ideal, a good six-footer, but it's just dawned on me that I have no idea exactly how tall Curtis was or is, so I don't really have any cloudless indication of scale. Beth actually sat up in bed and cried last night when I refused sex with her. I didn't really know how to react, where to put my face. I just knew I couldn't hold her close – though I actually wanted to, for some peculiar reason – through fear of encouraging her, of giving her the totally wrong impression. Beth . . . is . . . simply . . . not . . . getting the message. I wonder how Slinky's getting on up in Scotland? I am wondering what she's been saying to Jo about me.

I'm whistling 'Ride of the Valkyries' to myself but Gerry is gasping for breath. His lengthy legs are faltering as he attempts to keep up with my breakneck pace. 'I hate to spring this on you, Dame, but I, um . . .' He pauses for a moment, seems diverted by his reflection in a shop window, and flags a couple of paces behind me. 'But I think I might have to drop out of the scam,' he calls after me.

I slow for him to catch up, then tut loudly for him to hear, and pull a disgusted face.

'Is it because of the money?'

'No, nothing like that. No, it's just—'

'Just what?' I snap.

'There's no need to be like that,' Gerry yelps.

'Well, it's all the same with you lot,' I scorn. 'You're all bloody drama queens.'

'Er, with what lot?' Gerry asks me.

'Oh, nothing,' I tell him. 'Forget what I said. Why are you dropping out, then?'

'Well . . . oh, you'll think I'm being stupid or something.'

'Yeah, most probably,' I sneer. 'And?'

Gerry hands me this envelope.

'And what . . . is . . . this?' I ask him, tersely.

'You'd best open it,' he says, keeps pace alongside me.

I rip open the blessed envelope to reveal that same bloody picture of Matt and Gerry – again a crude red line scrawled between the two. 'What's this supposed to be, then?'

'I'm not sure,' Gerry says, 'but I think someone's trying to stir up trouble for me.'

'Yeah, and who might that be?' I ask, then suggest furtively, 'Jay possibly?'

'Er, Jay?' Gerry seems bewildered. 'No, Jay is the last person I'd suspect – after you, of course, Dame. No, I think it's one of the others.'

'Yeah, what others are those, then?' I ask dispassionately, as we stop by the General Store. There's no sign of Five. He should really be here by now.

This black geezer stood near us turns to his mate and hollers at him, for all to hear, 'Oi, ain't your wedding ring on the wrong finger?'

'Yeah, the others,' Gerry tells me, then whispers, 'the other boys in on the scam.'

'Hmmm, and what makes you think that, pray tell?' I ask him in a tone suggesting I really don't care and that I'm possibly mocking him a touch.

The black geezer's mate returns. 'Yeah, well, I'm on the pull tonight, aren't I?'

Gerry's the only one of the boys who actually prefers bitter to lager – I didn't really register this treachery until just recently, never really espied it as a problem before. I can't believe I actually regarded such a sad fucker as a friend, that we ever socialized together, that I ever stood in line at a bar and debased myself ordering bitter on this Gerry's behalf.

Gerry's still shooting his mouth off. 'Well, this photo was definitely taken at uni – I'm sure of that much at least – at one of our big drinking sessions.'

'Smoking sessions,' I snap.

'What?'

'Smoking sessions,' I mumble, inaudible for Gerry to make sense of.

'And there was that incident with Matt – he smacked me once, remember? Someone's playing on that, trying to stir things up. I think they're hoping to drive a wedge between me and Matt, to get me to welsh out on the deal. And this letter's just the tip of the iceberg, Dame. I've been getting taxis turning up at all hours, as well.'

I mock him with, 'And who on earth might be waging this campaign?'

'Mike,' Gerry says, flatly.

'Why Mike?' I shoot him a glance which suggests he's stupid or something.

'Oh, c'mon, we all know he's stepped out of his depth, don't we? I mean, it's his brother who should be leading this. Mike's realized that he's made a mistake, and he wants to collapse the whole deal.'

'And he's trying to get you to drop out first – thus making things easier for himself, right?'

'Yeah,' Gerry says, then screws up his eyes, unsure of something.

'God, your logic's so warped,' I mention.

'Sorry?' Gerry asks.

I pause, purse my lips. 'Gerry,' I start condescendingly, then pause for effect again. 'Gerry . . . maybe you *should* drop out of the deal.'

'I have been giving it some thought,' Gerry returns, sounds sincere.

'That's good,' I tell him, place a reassuring hand on his shoulder. 'That's good, Gerry.'

'Yeah, I've been mulling it over for a while now.'

'But!' I sound, sharply.

'But what?' Gerry asks.

'But you're not going to drop out, are you, Gerry?'

'Eh, Dame?'

'You're not going to drop out, Gerry, because . . .' I circle him slowly, my hands clasped behind my back. 'Because, just talking to me has really put your mind at ease . . . hasn't it?'

'Well,' Gerry sighs. 'Now that you mention it . . . Oh, it's probably not Mike anyway. Yeah, I s'pose I'm still in.'

'That is just so-o-o bloody typical,' I say quite deliberately.

'Sorry, Dame?' Gerry asks me.

'Nothing. Just talking to myself as per usual,' I'm telling him, as I spy Five sauntering out of the tube station.

We're slumped in front of the television – me, Five and Thom – watching *Brookside* on video again, drinking Kronenbourg again, sating on hippy-trippy spliffs again. Thom's got his head buried in the latest edition of *Fiesta*, which Five brought round as a gift for our delectation. Five's fresh back from a brief excursion to Tenerife with Rachel, and he's delivered some powerful, zeitgeist-defining news.

'It's gone?' I just ask Five incredulously. 'And . . . nowhere . . . to . . . be . . . seen?'

'Nah, it's a shame,' Five returns, doesn't seem that bothered though, takes the spliff from me and draws a measured toke. 'We wanted to get a picture of me and Rachel underneath it, to match that other one I've got of us lot on me sideboard.' Five then chuckles to himself, a fit of drug-induced giggles. 'I was also gonna get Rachel to take a picture of just me standing under-neath it, then I was going to send a copy to all the boys with a caption like "Tenerife reunion – where were you lot?"'

'Nice one,' Thom smirks, still studies his magazine, and I'm not sure whether his bromidic observation was in response to Five's comment or perhaps aimed at some naked lovely currently ornamenting his lap.

'Hold on,' I sort of snap, trying to steady myself. 'The THANKS FOR YOUR VISIT, SEE YOU SOON sign has gone from Lineker's Bar. Didn't you even think to ask where it had gone, or why had it been removed?'

'Dame,' Five sighs, still doesn't seem bothered. 'Me and Rachel only went down to Las Americas for one day. We only had the one drink in Lineker's. I was more concerned about getting down to Wimbledon Sports to get a load of Lacoste gear.'

'Lacoste . . . gear?' I ask.

'Yeah, you can get shirts for fifty-odd quid down there.'

'I know you can get shirts for fifty-odd quid down there,' I smart at Five. 'Don't you remember, we all bought Lacoste shirts for fifty-odd quid down there last year?'

'Yeah, 'course,' Five says.

'When we were all hol-id-ay-ing together,' I remind him.

'Yeah, and a brilliant holiday it was, too,' Thom mentions, still doesn't look up. 'But you've got to learn to move on, Dame.'

'Yeah, you've got to learn to move on, Dame,' Five repeats.

'Why?' I ask them abruptly.

'Er . . . progress?' Five offers.

'Fuck progress,' I mention offhand, then stamp my feet like I'm cold and go 'Brrrrr,' as if to accentuate this skittish charade, and then I'm thinking about Beth but this vision is swiftly relegated by a searing full-blown image of Jo dolled up in her kinky boots, a black Lycra top and tiger-print skirt, and then I'm looking to both Five and Thom, but both of them just looked bored, uninterested in me or in what I have to say, or indeed think – Five's even started to whistle to himself distract-edly; Thom just blows softly on the end of the spliff to keep the embers alight – and so, instead, I just take one great gulp of Kronenbourg and again snort, 'Fuck pro-gress,' this time under my breath.

'Dame, I think you've been taking too many drugs,' Five sighs: a comment which Thom immediately counters by raising the volume on *Brookside*, but there's really no need for such an action as I'm not about to persist with this pointless debate on the whereabouts of any Lineker's sign, as it's obviously of such trivial and unconsidered importance to my two immediate room companions and long-term friends. Besides, I like my memories just the way they were, forever preserved in formaldehyde.

'Oh, yeah, Dame,' Thom asides once the adverts float in. 'Did you see I rescued your shirts for you?'

'My what?' I ask, turn to face him for an instant.

'That bag of jumble you left out for Lisa to take down Oxfam,' Thom tells me, still studies his magazine.

'What of it?'

'You'd stuck all your Thomas Pink shirts in there by mistake.'

'Yeah, I know,' I say flatly.

'But, Dame, you always wear Thomas fucking Pink to work,' Five tells me.

'I've switched to Hilditch and Key,' I mention matter-of-factly. 'I prefer the cut.'

'Blimey, I'll take your Thomas Pinks off you,' Five voices.

I look Five full in the face and tell him, quite purposely, 'You can't. Jay wears Thomas Pink now,' but I can see in his blank expression, in the way that he regards me so artlessly, that he doesn't quite seem to grasp the basal quintessence of what I am trying to tell him, so it's a smallish relief when Thom interrupts our dialogue, holds a picture from *Fiesta* up towards us – this big blonde thing with a commodious figure – and says, 'Just your type, Dame. All woman.' The model's ruffled hair tumbles across her broad bare shoulders, and she fixes me with the dirtiest of grins.

'All . . . woman,' I repeat.

'What?!' Five says, asks me, 'You fancy that, Dame?'

'Of course,' I tell him.

'Fucking hell, I fancy women I can get me arms around,' he says. 'You'd have to be King-bloody-Kong to get your arms round that thing. Mind, you always did like big fat birds, didn't you, Dame?'

Slightly bemused, I ignore Five's snipe: just attempt to read the spiel on the side of a Kronenbourg can set down before me.

Thom runs his finger along the outline of the model: Hannah's body. 'Buxom,' he mouths silently to us.

'Buxotic,' I add, in a mezzo forte voice.

'She is a sumo-fucking-wrestler,' Five retorts. 'You two just haven't got a clue, have you? You with your

Lisa, Thom. And Dame with Joanna. I mean, take
Beth—'

'I wish you would,' I mutter.

'Take Beth . . .' Five starts again. 'Give me a nice elfin
sort with a sleek waist any day of the week, rather than
some big blonde thing like Joanna was . . . I reckon
you've had a right result there, Dame.'

'You . . . what?' I ask after a pause, astounded by
Five's inane admission.

Thom holds the picture higher, reasons, 'Come on,
Five, you'd be happy to have a bird like this round for
dinner, knowing you're gonna get your hands on her
lovely lungs later.'

Five replies with, 'Lads, I'd be happier getting my
hands on that knowing I'm going to have a good . . .
fucking . . . dinner . . . later.'

Thom and I both laugh: Thom at Five's impish
comment, me initially at the thought of my Photoshop
and how funny it might appear – strange even – to the
untrained observer, that all my betrayers' faces are presently masked out by this beaming shot of Hooky from
New Order and – funny, from my own perspective –
how I'm now going to have to obliterate Five's features
too, and then I'm chuckling at this overwhelming mental image of Five laying dead somewhere, his recreant
body pulped and broken. Then Thom frees Hannah
from the pages of *Fiesta* and pins her on our notice-
board, alongside the takeaway menus, postcards, phone
numbers and bills, and the obligatory pictures of Anna
Nicole Smith and New Order pinned there by me. I lick

along the gummed edge of a liquorice Rizla paper, start to build another spliff for our enjoyment and whisper, almost audibly, 'That makes you number seven, Five. You can't even keep in line with your name, you loathsome imbecile.'

I am in the back of a black cab heading up the Archway Road, sat with Lauren, this American thing, a twenty-one-year-old I met some two hours ago at Renaissance, where she was alone and I was with Thom and Lisa. I've had three riddlers; she's done just the one playboy. Lauren is still E-ing; I'm now sensing only slight tingles of euphoria. Thom is staying at Lisa's for the rest of the weekend. Lauren is tallish with a big chest, but is plain, is unblonde and is dressed badly – like a student. Not at all clubby.

'I've never been to North London before. It's so . . . dark,' Lauren says to me.

I giggle. 'That's because it's five in the morning.'

'Yeah, but I've never been to North London. I've been through it on the way back from my aunt's in Liverpool, but I've never been to it . . . Do you know what I'm saying?'

'Yeah, I think so,' I reply. 'Liverpool's a fabulous place. My brother once saw New Order close a gig with "Love Will Tear Us Apart" up there.'

'I didn't like it,' she tells me flatly, staring out of the window.

'What? You were at the gig, too?' I ask her.

'No, not New Order. Liverpool, you dumbwit.'

'Yeah, course, Liverpool. Silly me,' I repeat to her. The taxi turns right, into Muswell Hill Road. I sit transfixed, staring mesmerized into Highgate woods, imagining that I'm seeing eerie spooks and ghouls flitting amongst the trees, unable to look away.

'Gorgeous flat,' Lauren says as I lead her through our front door. 'You own it?'

'Yes,' I lie to her. 'Well, co-own it with a flatmate.' A smaller lie.

'Male or female?' she asks.

'The flat?'

'Your flatmate, silly,' she says, and stops to laugh at nothing in particular.

'Male.'

'You two involved?' she asks, kisses me. 'Sexually?' She is chewing gum.

'What?' I decry.

'Lighten up,' she tells me.

'No, it's just, well . . . Thom's not blond.'

'Not blond?' she asks me, breathes a sideways sigh. 'So? Neither am I. God, you English are so kooky.'

'Yeah, kooky,' I giggle and shrug my shoulders.

'So, this is the Thom I met earlier, yeah?'

'There's only one Thom,' I am saying.

'Well, he seems to have done alright for himself. That Lisa's one helluva girl.'

'Yeah, she's okay,' I concede.

'Big bloody breasts,' Lauren guffaws, and holds her

hands out like she's clasping two invisible beachballs before her. 'Man, I thought I had big boobies, but that girl is stacked.'

'Yeah,' I just repeat, 'stacked.'

'So, Damian,' Lauren says, looks me straight in the eye, stops patrolling our lounge. 'You never had sex with a guy before?'

'Er, nope,' I say and giggle, then ask, without due consideration of what I am thinking, 'Have you?'

Lauren smirks to herself, shakes her head in pity, and ignores my inane comment. 'Can I have some water?' she asks me.

I make for the kitchen, retrieve a bottle of Evian from the fridge and stop to pour two tall glasses of water.

I return to find Lauren sitting cross-legged by Thom's stereo sifting through his record collection. 'You like the Velvet Underground, then?' she asks me.

'Uh, yeah,' I reply, genuinely surprised that Thom owns any of their records and ultimately gladdened that Lauren hasn't picked one of his George Michael albums for perusal instead.

'I just love guys in black,' Lauren tells me. I'm wearing all black: this old v-neck sweater by John Smedley, and these black moleskin jeans.

'And I love guys with long hair,' she adds in a dispirited voice.

This disheartens me just slightly, but I'm not so sure I want to fuck her anyway. I mean I do want to, but maybe just not tonight. I don't intuit any immediate chemistry between us: no flash-bang volcanic spark. I am not really sure as to why I've brought her home; probably just down to a warped sense of masculine duty?

Lauren slips a Velvet Underground album onto Thom's stereo, and crosses the room to join me on the sofa. She sits beside me, playing with her hair, one leg tucked up high underneath her.

'You know,' she sighs, 'I do occasionally go for guys with short hair.' And with that she kisses me, gently at first, a tender touch, but becomes more forceful with each gyration of her lips. I'm embarrassed, possibly as a by-product of the Es – Lauren appears so immensely turned on, yet I simply feel like laughing aloud. The lights are on full-beam and, whilst I would dearly like to reach for the dimmer to temper them, I don't really want to break this Lauren's momentum just yet.

With her hand inside my top, Lauren scratches at my chest, rakes across my stomach and attempts to force her way into my moleskins. Jo always maintained I should wear my moleskins to bed: she loved their velvety touch, sensualistic against her skin. My belt is bound tight and Lauren struggles, one-handed, to undo it. I help her unclasp the buckle. I'm wondering what Jo's doing right now. Lauren breaks our kiss and, turning her attention to my moleskins, deftly releases each button on my fly and reaches into my boxer shorts to slowly unshackle my erection. She masturbates me quite deliberately. I shut my eyes, murmur quietly, and run my fingers through her hair, across the nape of her neck, caressing the soft flesh there, and she pushes back against my hand, revelling in my touch, pulls faster and harder on my swollen cock and sighs, breathes heavily, and so I exert a little pressure on the back of her head and an alien voice from deep inside me gruffly whispers, 'Take my cock in your mouth.'

Lauren looks into my face, releases the leg from underneath herself, and slowly goes down on me whilst still masturbating me furiously. My moleskins are still high around my thighs. I am sinking into the sofa, ever deeper, being swallowed up by it, being swallowed up by this Lauren thing to the right of me, giving me excellent head.

'Use your mouth only,' I command. She releases her hand and her head bobs slowly up, then down, taking me further into her mouth and I stare up at the ceiling and stroke her back, play with her hair again. The Velvet Underground's black charivari resonates unsubtly in the background, Lou Reed singing something about some woman licking up her big man, that she's busy sucking on his ding-dong. New Order sporadically covered this track at concerts.

Lauren raises herself from the sofa, slips to the floor before me and releases one leg from my moleskins, enabling her to kneel between my thighs, and, with her hands clasped behind her head, fixes me with these deep dark irresistible eyes. She lingers for a moment too long, confusing me slightly, then, without breaking eye contact, tucks her hair behind her right ear – the way Jo always used to – and slowly and deliberately takes me in her mouth again, takes me in one long movement, and

I feel her teeth chafe the shaft of my cock. Oral sex is such a tremendous spectator sport; the delights of participation coupled with the added thrills of voyeur, taking a passenger seat to watch the correspondent weave her magic. Lauren steadily repeats her head-bobbing motion maybe seven, eight times, maintaining eye contact, not appearing to blink. I gulp, Lauren's fringe flops in her face.

She pulls away from me, flicks her hair back and seduces me with, 'Bed?'

'Bed,' I repeat to her.

We undress quickly in the bedroom – Thom's bedroom. Mine in too much of a state to use. I power on Thom's portable telly to illuminate the room, leaving the volume turned down. Displayed above Thom's headboard there's a copy of that shot taken in Tenerife last Easter: all the boys – some friends, some foes – lined up like a football team, before a billboard which reads THANKS FOR YOUR VISIT, SEE YOU SOON.

Lauren is lying spread-eagled on Thom's bed, his juvenile Chelsea bedspread, the early-morning news casting winking shadows across her naked form. I flit back to my own bedroom to snort a quick line of revivifying coke, then stop to do a second, then a third, then retrieve a packet of condoms and, on my overdue return, find a moaning Lauren turned on her side, her face buried deep in Thom's pillow, masturbating. I clumsily roll on a rubber, join her on the bed and carefully force myself into her from behind – her cunt wet and welcoming – then start to fuck her slowly, our bodies superjacent, as she continues to rub at herself vigorously.

'Ooh, where've you been?' she manages – or at least that's what it sounds like. Her frenetic masturbating upsets my own rhythm, and so I persuade her onto her back and fuck her from the front, attempting to kiss her but she turns her head away and bites into my shoulder – possibly too hard, maybe breaking the skin a little there. So, instead I delight in gorging myself on her huge bullet nipples, mounds of Meyer magic. Lauren's eyes are shut tight, her teeth are gritted, and what little noise escapes her mouth comes in small shrieks and gasps.

I am fucking Lauren standing against the wall by Thom's wardrobe – the wardrobe with the ceiling-to-floor mirror. I am watching myself fucking Lauren against the wall in the ceiling-to-floor mirror. Lauren scratches at my shoulders, I bite at her neck. I visualize myself in another lifetime, fucking Jo like this before Thom's mirror – Jo naked except for her kinky boots and those sacred hooped earrings. Lauren is only the third American I have fucked – the other two being Celine Walker and an Erica, this real Meyer type, both conquests at university. To this day I've never dared come clean with the boys about Celine, she was such an embarrassment – peppered her vocabulary with stupid words like snuggle, squodgy and honeykins. In my experience, all Americans give fantastic head.

Lauren has turned, faces the wall, and I am now fucking her backwards, both of us still standing. I wet an index finger and attempt to insert it into her anus but her sphincter tightens, she recoils and moans something under her breath, so I decide against furthering this action. I will fuck her in the arse on a later date. I keep Lauren pinned to the wall, pumping ever harder and faster against her, pulling on her hair, making small bites at her back, feel the baubles of sweat erupting across my torso in bubonic fashion. I am studying my contorted features in the ceiling-to-floor mirror, fantasizing about introducing Lauren to Jo on some away-weekend to Scotland, as I climax inside her.

I awake to find Lauren dressing. Thom's alarm clock informs me it's eight-thirty a.m., we've had little more than three hours' sleep.

'Are you leaving?' I blurt, muddled.

'Yeah, I have to,' she says, doesn't look at me.

'Why?'

'I just have to.'

Lauren has a Donald Duck tattoo on her right ankle. 'You were talking in your sleep,' she enlightens me.

'Nothing too embarrassing, I hope?'

'Well, you kept asking, "Don't you think I've got a beautiful body?" Very quaint.'

'Sorry,' I apologize. 'It's a quote from an old Russ Meyer movie.'

'Ah, the guy who did the big-boobie movies?'

'Yeah, him.'

'So, you're a big boobie man, I take it?'

'Guess so,' I admit.

'Figures. Guys are so shallow – even the English ones.'

'Yeah,' I sort of concede, though immediately wish I hadn't. 'So, well . . . will I see you again?' I ask.

Lauren stops pulling on her jeans, pauses, then says, 'No, I really don't think so,' in a tone which implies she cannot believe I have asked such a strikingly dumb question.

'Oh,' is all I can think of to say.

Fully dressed, Lauren sits by me on the bed. She appears fresh for one with so little sleep. 'I had a nice night,' she sighs. 'But – as I believe I told you – I really do prefer my men with long hair.' Lauren then plants a soused kiss on my forehead. This is simply some higher power's way of telling me I should really stick to blondes.

Lauren leaves. I wait for the sound of the front door opening, then closing. I collect my things and wander out into the corridor, bleary-eyed, and make my way through to my own room. I gather my thoughts for a moment then bring up the Photoshop on my PC, selecting what I consider to be the worst (if there can be such a thing) shot of Jo within my collection – this one of her wearing flat shoes and trite dungarees, crossing some bridge in the Scottish outback, looking worn out, unmade-up, windswept, and giving me a snarling look as if to say, 'Are you gonna hurry up and take this picture or what?' – and so I quickly masturbate over this image for just twenty seconds, maybe less, yet am satisfied to discover that Jo can still cultivate a huge erection within me, no matter how comical or erratic the scenario. And so, instead, I switch to my noted Lineker's Bar shot, the boys all grouped together on holiday in Tenerife, and, where I've inserted pictures of Hooky to mask the idolaters, I then replace each of these with varied bitmaps of Donald Duck. It then strikes me that I have actually slept with a fourth American – twice! – this Tamsin, some second cousin of Five's. And that this Tamsin did not give good head and this minor recollection traumatizes me quite exactingly, that I should forget such an obvious fact and it's worrying too as my memory was always so proficient and defined.

I decide to take a half-tab of acid before I retire to bed, so as to dull the feral night's pain, and in my new-found catatonic state I have these absolutely mental serialized leitmotivs in which Jo, and then my brother, and then Hubert Dodd . . .

I answer the phone with an exhausted 'Hello' after the ninth, maybe tenth, ring – the first three rings of which I'd spent snorting a thick line of speckled powder consisting one quarter-gram of coke and these two crushed Es which had neat little windmill symbols on them – and I'm greeted by a momentary wall of silence until someone lets out a faint, 'Grrrrrr.'

I sigh, roll my eyes. 'Kelly?'

'Damian,' she whines, 'where are you?'

'Er . . . in Muswell Hill?' I sort of ask, the words

coming out dry, my throat suddenly parched waterless as the coke takes its stranglehold.

'Damian, I'm leaving the country in twelve – no, make that eleven – hours. Why aren't you here with me? Everyone else is.'

'Sorry,' is all I can muster to say. Kelly's farewell had, in truth, completely slipped my mind.

She tuts, then sighs. 'It's only ten o'clock now. Please shoot out and grab a taxi. You could be down here in less than an hour. We're going to be up all night.'

As much as I would wish to see Kelly one last time – maybe even go so far as to fuck her, giggle inwardly at her false French mumblings – it's been an exhausting week (thanks chiefly to a series of early-morning meetings arranged by Hubert Dodd and some late drinking sessions fronted by the Lunchboys) and all I want to do is to sit in and endlessly replay fractured scenes from Russ Meyer's *Cherry, Harry and Raquel*, scenes containing temporal flashes of Uschi Digard as the Soul Girl, scenes where she showers herself behind an opaque glass door, only her full breasts really visible, where she's sunning herself aboard a yacht, another where she's running naked through the desert brush or bouncing on a bed, chewing on a celery stick, relaxing in a swimming pool.

And I've been especially looking forward to two scenes in particular (I have thought of little else all day) where she's dressed in no more than a pair of thigh-length black boots: one where she slowly rocks back and forth on her knees, sucking her thumb, taking it deep in her throat like she's giving great head; and my favourite – possibly her longest snippet in the film at four maybe five seconds – where she's caught side-on, the camera to her left, and she's squatting on her haunches, leaning back, her mouth gasping for air, her eyes closed tight, her fine body swaying steadily, like she's being fucked hard by the invisible man or something.

I have no idea just how tall Uschi is (sadly, she looks tiny in *SuperVixens*), but she possesses, quite possibly, the most perfect, most womanly body I've ever laid eyes on, easily the most perfect of the Meyer women, with even bigger, more solid, breasts than Jo's, and though I've no idea as to exactly how old Uschi was when she made *Cherry* (I'll guess early twenties), I am wondering – if I were to be forced into making a straight choice between bedding either Jo or Uschi tonight, would the fact that Jo is blonde and twenty-one, and is five foot eleven, really represent enough information to enable me to favour her ahead of Uschi, an unblonde who's admirable body is abundantly evident in *Cherry* (I wish I had some type of editing kit so I could splice all her shots into one steady stream) but whose precise statistics are an absolute enigma to me?

'Helloooooo . . . Damian!' Kelly is calling, snapping my attention back to reality – a reality where I now only date short, small-breasted, plain women. 'Dame-ee-ern . . . Are you there?'

'Yeah,' I say.

'You sound ill,' Kelly tells me.

I cough involuntarily, my mouth now so desiccated

that this action really hurts. 'Yeah.' Gasp. 'Think I'm maybe' – croak – 'maybe coming down with something. I don't feel too good.'

Kelly sighs, phrases this question like it's a statement: 'You're not coming to see me, are you?' And though I'm genuinely excited at the prospect of fucking Kelly whilst the images of Uschi Digard continue to vividly punctuate my mindscape, or of at least holding close a body whose dimensions map closely to the contours of Jo's celestial form, I have to answer her with a terminal, 'No,' and it's a while before she replies with, 'I didn't really think you would.'

'I'm sorry,' I maybe say – or do I just think this?

'I hurt you, Damian,' Kelly tells me. 'That's why you're not coming down.'

I smile inwardly and, without sounding too sarcastic, reply, 'Yes . . . Yes, you did hurt me, Kelly.'

'That rubbish, when I met you last time, about some girl named, um, whatever her name was – she was just a metaphor, wasn't she? A metaphor for how you felt about me.'

I don't answer, merely strangle a laugh.

Kelly continues. 'It's me that made you sad, isn't it?'

'You're . . . so . . . right,' I tell her, sound sullen – to my own genuine disbelief.

'Well, look, Damian,' she says a touch condescendingly. 'I sent you a postcard this morning because I didn't really think you'd show. It's got my address on it, and my mother's phone number, so you've no excuses not to get in touch now.'

'Hmmm . . . Guess I'll be in touch, then,' I half-croak, half-sigh – the croaking categorically down to my chemical intake.

'Do you want me to leave Nina's number? I know how you really wished you'd got to fuck her.'

I think about this for a minute then half-growl and joke, 'Sweetheart, I did not want . . . to . . . fuck . . . Nina. She's too short, and she's un . . . unblonde!'

Kelly giggles. 'I'll miss you, Damian,' she says like she really means it.

'Yeah, I'll miss you too, Kelly.'

Kelly spouts some more nonsense – which I unwittingly reciprocate, the life-affirming coke propelling me along – bids me one last 'Grrrrrr', and then she's gone. I am suddenly overwhelmed by this great sense of loss, as if having just discarded another piece in the disjointed jigsaw puzzle that is fast becoming my ever-futile existence. I decide against watching the Meyer video, because – with my present cerebral slant – I am finding it increasingly difficult to actually distinguish between the mental images I have for both Jo and Uschi, my imagination playing tricks on me, swapping Jo's lips onto Uschi's face, then Uschi's breasts onto Jo's body then Jo's hair onto Uschi's head . . . until I'm faced with two twin sisters, indistinguishable from one another, neither as visually stimulating as their original versions.

I then sit and wait patiently for the snorted ecstasy to take a brutal hold on my senses, and it's probably no more than half an hour or so before my perception starts to warp then there's this mad black unhinged ten min-utes – worse than the scariest peyote trip – where my mind fragments and I'm crazed and racing around the flat, my brain in freefall, sensorium overloaded, and my return image in the bathroom mirror looks flushed and unlike me, but I know it's not me that's staring back but a whole collage of misted unearthly faces, and then my hands shrink and wither before my very eyes, then sprout coarse hairs like *An American Werewolf in London*, and so I'm endeavouring to purify my mindscape by setting the timer recorder for *Brookside* on the video, but it's a struggle to undertake even this most simplest of acts, so I resolve to just lie back on the sofa and ride out the cerebral onslaught, and it's probably a good hour later before I can sense that I'm now only E-ing gleefully good and hard and that the initial mental aberrations are finally passed, and then it's probably another five hours or more after this before I feel I've returned to a boring normal.

I do, however, make one momentous decision during this drugged spell: for tonight, and tonight only, I would have had sex with Uschi (circa 'Cherry') in preference to Jo but only on the proviso that Uschi was younger than me and stood at least five foot four in her thigh-length boots (short I know, but an absolute min-imum) and, of course, that I could be reunited with Jo immediately after my twenty-four sinned hours of Digard passion.

*

'I'm worried about Nicky-babes,' Russell Bishop mutters.

'Nicholas Spencer-Jones? Why?' I ask, not looking up, carefully cutting into my chicken-en-croûte. I don't want to make eye-contact with anyone, am a touch paranoid that my pupils appear too dilated. I've done seven, maybe eight, lines of coke during the course of this morning, in just three hours and twenty minutes. Office etiquette gone completely to fuck.

'Well, he sent me this bizarre e-mail this morning,' Bishop says.

'Wasn't after a quick shag, was he?' Dino Denton half-asks.

There's only the three of us at lunch today.

'No, it's strange,' Russell is saying, 'but young Nicholas keeps asking me for drugs.'

'Nicholas?' I ask. 'You sure you're not imagining it?'

'No. He honestly keeps asking me for drugs. Do you remember those little speed-balls I had earlier this year?' – Dino and I both nod in unison – 'Well, this morning he's asked if he can buy thirty of those from me.'

'Thirty?' Dino exclaims. 'Thirty speed-balls?'

'Yes, thirty. I mean, I really don't want to get a reputation as a dealer or anything – you know how word can get around here. I don't mind doing little favours for my friends once in a while. But thirty – really?!'

'You sure he didn't mean thirty quid's worth, Bish?' I have to ask.

'No. Well, that's what I thought at first,' Russell

muses, studies a turquoise ring on his right hand, holding it up to the light. 'I mean, thirty's the sort of number I'd imagine *you* squander of an average weekend, Mr Shaw.'

'Cheeky fuck,' I tell him.

'On the contrary, dear boy,' the Bishop starts. 'I'd be more than happy to supply you with such quantities if you'd only let me take full advantage of you afterwards.'

'Russell,' Denton sounds, 'we were talking about Nicholas's new-found addiction.'

'So we were,' Russell says. 'But you still have to allow me my dreams.'

'Spencer-Jones has been on a slippery slope since he split with Allison Coyle,' I mention, as Russell presents his ring to the light once again. I'm trying to fathom what he can find so bewitching – or is it perhaps just me imagining Russell's overt attentiveness. Have the drugs fucked my perception to such an immeasurable punctum that Russell is simply considering his ring for scant nanoseconds, but my sensors are registering the gesture as taking full lifetimes or more?

'You'd be doing Nicholas a favour if you refused to give him anything,' Dino says.

'Yeessss,' the Bishop burrs, now scratches at his ring like he's trying to scrape the sheen from it.

'Just give Spencer-Jones aspirin,' I tell him. 'It's all psychosomatic with Nicholas anyway.' However, with this latest revelation about Spencer-Jones, I think I may just have unearthed another kindred spirit upon whom to offload a few of the Es. (I decided many moons ago that I'll have to approach Russell when I finally take hold of the stock – he's sure to gobble some up.)

'Do either of you two fancy a bevy in the Stamford tonight?' Dino asks us. 'I'm gonna send out an e-mail to all Lunchboys this afternoon, just to see if anyone fancies hooking in there after work tonight. You never know your luck – might even be some tasty birds from IPC Magazines in there.'

'I'm afraid I can't tonight, dear boy,' Russell says, looking past me, over my left shoulder. I turn to try and ascertain just who he's looking at. 'I'm taking my young friend Morgan out.'

I turn to face Russell, and ask, 'Take him out? What? With, like, one punch?'

Dino sniggers, says to me, 'No. With chloroform.'

'From behind,' I add, laughing.

Bishop motions past me. 'Is that the blonde you used to e-mail, Damian, dear boy? You know that Pamela thingy from Financial Services?'

'Pamela Ward? I doubt it. I haven't seen her around for ages – think she must have left the company,' I say and casually turn in my seat, trying to contain my excitement, to catch sight of this big . . . disgusting . . . peroxide thing shuffling past, trussed up like an auroch poured into a lucent lemon suit.

'That is not her,' I state, a touch annoyed. '*She*' – I'm pointing now – '*she* has got a massive arse. I would not touch that with yours, Russell.'

'Thought you liked big arses?' Dino jokes, but tries to sound serious.

'No. That arse' – I still find myself pointing, am probably even shouting by now, but I simply don't care – 'that arse is unusually big. That arse is unsightly. Japanese fishermen will come running through here in a minute and harpoon that fucking arse.'

Dino laughs.

'Oh, I don't know,' Russell says. 'I think it might be something nice to bounce up and down on, actually.'

'Yeah, built for comfort,' Dino muses.

I finish his sentence for him: ' – not for speed.'

Steve Kerr and 'family man' Richard Moore appear from nowhere, join us at our table. 'Sorry we're late, amigos,' Moore gasps. 'The Sod called a twelve o'clock meeting for everyone working under Graham Watson. Doesn't that retard know some of us actually like to eat lunch most days?'

This morning, Gregor Daley e-mailed me to say that Tasha Doran, Jack Howe's secretary, is now actually dating Niall Wheeler, her pitiable flatmate. I couldn't think of anything tangible to say by way of response.

Thom and I are sitting, facing one another across the room: him on the sofa, naked except for a bath-towel wrapped tight around his waist, his translucent skin on full show; me in the armchair, fully dressed, slouching. He is smoking a Marlboro Light, and is nervously fingering the cigarette packet. I am calm, strangely subdued, somehow melancholy. The stereo encircles us with snug electronic melodies courtesy of Kraftwerk.

'I – I don't know what to say,' Thom maybe whispers, still stares at the floor.

'There's not a lot you can say,' I tell him casually.

'Look, Dame, I—'

'Shut up,' I hiss at him.

'Dame, I – I can explain—' His voice falters – he's probably hoping I'll cut him off, halt him mid-sentence.

An uncomfortable silence descends as Kraftwerk chant something about home computers.

'Go on, then – ex-plain,' I tell him.

Humbled, he admits, 'I can't.'

'I thought not,' I exclaim brightly.

I rise to my feet and pace over towards the window and, without turning back, ask aloud, 'So-o-o, how long has this been going on?'

'This was the first time, Dame,' he replies. 'Nothing else happened, really—'

'Liar,' I rasp.

'Okay, okay. I'm sorry, Dame. Once before – one afternoon last week.'

'Here or her place?'

'Dame, please—'

'Here or her place?' I repeat, turn to face Thom. 'A simple question, surely? A one-word answer will suffice.'

'Here. *Here*, Dame.'

'On my futon perhaps?' I ask genially, take a step forwards. 'Thought you'd really go to town, did you?'

'No, honestly.'

'No?' Another calculated step forwards. 'No?'

'No.'

'Or on the sofa, then?' Sitting down beside Thom, I playfully bounce up and down on the sofa. 'Take her on the sofa, did you? Have a good laugh at me, did you – when I came home and sat in the very spot where you'd just been with my woman? Keeping my seat warm for me, were you?' I realize my voice has reached an unnerving crescendo.

I arrived home early from work – I had a bit too much to drink with Steve Kerr in the Doggett's at lunchtime, and made some half-arsed excuse about a migraine coming on in the office – to find Thom with Beth, both half-naked in our hallway, acting out some amusing charade, fucking like animals possessed. Beth made a desperate lunge for her blouse to cover her nakedness: an act which served to make me laugh. I mean, it's not as if I'd not seen it all before. And so, as if guided by auto-pilot, I carefully skirted their rueful forms, pleasantly bidding them a 'Good afternoon', then made my way through to my room where I remained until I heard the front-door click shut minutes later. I can at least credit Beth for having the foresight to leave, to avoid any further unnecessary confrontation.

I had a quick listen to this Essential Mix I'd taped over the weekend (Weatherface e-mailed to say Paul Oakenfold had done this week's mix) only to discover that Oakenfold had ridiculously taken drum and fucking bass to heart this time around, but even this small episode still failed to aggravate me, so – cool and imperturbable – I then made myself a light lunch, and eventually turned my attention to Thom, who just sat silently in the lounge, fretting and chewing on his fingernails. I'd have rather evaded a scene, but I guess it's only expected to raise some commotion under these circumstances. After all, Thom knows that only too well from previous experience. This is a pay-back time, of sorts.

'Give me one good reason why I shouldn't put your head through that wall,' I tell Thom, point past him.

'I can't,' he bleats pitifully, then adds, 'I'm so sorry.'

I say nothing.

'I'm really, really sorry,' he repeats.

'So, she came on to you, did she? My Beth? Came on to you, did she?' I'm asking. I possibly sound a touch hysterical; wholly unintentionally.

'No . . . no, nothing like that.'

'No?'

'No.'

'Oh, so you thought you'd just try it on with my girlfriend, did you?' I am shouting, beating out the three syllables of 'my-girl-friend' across my chest with a clenched fist like some demented Sioux brave.

Thom literally quakes where he sits. 'God, does it really matter, Dame? It just happened,' he cries.

'It matters to me,' I snarl, though this whole incident has, in truth, failed to rile me by a single degree.

'You two weren't getting along. God, she said you hadn't had sex for nearly a month.'

'Beth said that?'

'Yes, well she just wanted to talk.'

'Talk? That's a new word for it,' I quip, then – bored with playing such puerile mindscape games – my mask drops and I smile. I blow Thom an overstated kiss and say, still smiling, in this appallingly contrived Scots accent, 'Och well, you're forgiven then, sweetheart.'

Thom appears bemused, bewildered even.

'You're . . . forgiven,' I tell him.

Thom says nothing.

'Fancy a cuppa?' I ask him jovially.

Thom persists with his vow of silence, as Kraftwerk's teutonic tones trill something about radioactivity.

'I'll take that as a yes then,' I say and skip past him toward the kitchen.

Thom is lingering in the doorway as I squeeze out a tea-bag over his yellow and blue Chelsea Football mug. In this wayward distant voice, he says, 'Dame . . . there's something else I've really got to tell you.'

'What? Two secrets in one day?' I ask heartily.

'I'm trying to be serious,' Thom says.

'It's okay, I already know that Oakenfold did a drum and bass set on this week's Essential Mix.'

'It's not about Oakenfold, Dame,' Thom says, seems almost spiritless. 'Though, of course, that is a tragedy in it's own right.'

'So, what then?' I ask. The sell-by date on a bottle of HP sauce set down before me reads December next year, and I cannot help but wonder how a bottle of such sauce could possibly not get used up by then? I then stop to wonder if Jo and I will be reunited by such a date: will God furnish a panacea to cure my woes, or will I still be embraced by black unremitting sorrow?

'Dame, Lisa is moving in,' Thom is saying, these words hitting me hard like cold sledgehammer blows to the face. I'm swamped with visions of landslides destroying everything in their perilous wake – houses, people, children swept aside in a tidal crush. I see Jo running headlong towards me across some ravaged battlefront shrilling, 'Danger, danger,' at the top of her voice.

'When?' I think I ask.

'Next week. Friday.'

Jo collapses and combusts – lies dead, black and charred. I have to blink in order to focus my eyes once again. 'And you want me out . . . straight away, I suppose?'

'Not straight away,' Thom says reassuringly, his hand to my right shoulder. 'Only once you've found yourself somewhere decent to live.'

Hit by a runaway train of thought, I have to ask Thom, 'Is this revenge? You know, for what happened earlier in the year?'

'God no, Dame. No.'

'But, Beth? And now Lisa—'

'No, Dame, you can't think like that. This was totally unplanned.'

'What *I* did was totally unplanned,' I tell him.

Thom sighs. 'Yeah, I know. I realize that. Look, I'm sorry, I—'

'It's okay,' I say. 'It's all in the past now. It doesn't matter.'

'Thanks, Dame.' He sounds sincere.

'Why, then, Thom?' I ask quite blithely. 'Why is Lisa moving in? My company not enough for you any more?'

He sighs. 'It just seemed like a good idea at the time.'

'What will your mother say?' I ask quietly. 'You two living out of wedlock and all?'

'Lisa and I are buying the flat off my mother,' Thom says quite morosely. 'It's all been decided. We've got the mortgage sorted and everything.'

'Oh,' is all I can manage. I can't help but think Jo's to blame in all this somewhere, though deep down I know this is obviously just a net result of my own wrongdoings.

'You can visit,' Thom maybe jokes.

'Tremendous,' I say, then pace past him, back to the lounge, but Thom still insists on following me.

'So, when were you going to tell me?' I ask, flick on the television, bring Kraftwerk to a stirring halt.

'I've been meaning to for ages. I've just been waiting for the right moment,' Thom says.

'Oh, and this is the right moment?' I laugh.

'Maybe not,' he mumbles.

'Oh, right. I get it. You thought you'd let me catch you fucking my woman, then that way I might actually move out without you having to throw me out,' I say calmly.

'I'm not throwing you out,' Thom moans.

'It feels like that,' I sulk.

'I'm *not*. It's—' Thom's expression switches mid-sentence as a neural depth-charge detonates deep behind his features, mobilizing new thought balloons to the surface. 'Dame, you won't tell Lisa about any of this?' he asks in total sobriety. 'I mean, about me and Beth and what happened here today?'

I smirk and half-ask, 'What's the point? Thom, just how many women have you slept with behind Lisa's back since you've been together?'

'Um, I don't know,' he says.

'C'mon, of course you know. I know you know,' I tell him.

'Oh, I don't know . . . forty . . . maybe?'

'Yeah, and in how many years?'

'Coming up to five nearly,' he admits.

'And how many extracurricular lovers this year alone?'

'Three.'

'So, why should I bother mentioning Beth? She's just the tip of the iceberg.'

'No, four.' He corrects himself. 'Well, three, really. I was actually seeing that Katie bird last year, but we had another little rendezvous in January – just a one-off after work one night.'

'Do you really think you can maintain a monogamous relationship?' I ask.

'I don't know. Guess there's always the back of my car, or the sofa in your new gaff,' he quips.

I shoot him a glance.

'Joke,' he says.

'Suppose I could've always moved in with Beth for a while,' I mention, almost absentmindedly.

'There's still time, Dame.'

'Nah.'

'She *does* love you.'

I find myself admitting, 'Nah. That relationship had long passed its sell-by date. I just didn't have the bottle to end it myself.'

'She might not take the place of Joanna, but she's a lovely kid, you know.'

'What?' I ask.

'I said . . . she might not take the place of Joanna, but—'

I put my hand up, halt Thom bluntly in his tracks, his blissful euphony of words. 'That's all I wanted to hear,' I whisper, then smile. I do so like Thom: he knows me, he truly understands me, my sentient hungers and desires. I could do with more allies like him in the scam; I've now only Weatherface left to sincerely believe in.

'Look . . . I'm going to get dressed now,' Thom tells me after a while.

'And?' I ask him.

'And . . . I thought I'd just tell you, that's all. I'm, um, not running away or anything.'

As Thom traipses towards his room, I shout after him, 'Oh, the reason I was home early, Thom, old chum, was because I'd just been to the doctor's.'

Thom stops and turns slowly toward me.

'Yeah . . . about my crabs,' I tell him

'What?' Thom asks, after a brief pause.

'I'm just hoping I didn't pass anything on to Beth. You never can tell what you might've passed on to someone these days.'

Thom stands rooted to the spot, then takes one step towards me.

'Joke,' I tell him and turn back towards the TV.

I'm standing by the huge bay windows, staring out at three small boys lingering on the pavement, waiting patiently for a car to pass before they can return to their game of football in the road. One of them's dressed in this bright orange top which reads JUNIOR HATTER. I'm off sick again today – well, after leaving the office so early two days back, I thought it best I drag out my 'illness' so as to notch up some points for the Latecomer Award, though I'll have to be sure to get a doctor's note for food poisoning or some such rubbish so as to allay the Sod's lowlife druggy suspicions.

'Remember when we used to play footie in the road?' I ask my brother, attempt to keep the conversation flowing.

'Outside Mum and Dad's?' Ray asks in reply.

'Outside Mum's,' I correct him.

'Yeah, I remember,' he says.

'There was just a bit too much of a slope outside our place though, wasn't there? Whoever played uphill always had to have a two-goal advantage before we got started.' I'm still staring out of the window as one of the small boys skies his shot into Ray's neighbour's front garden, where the ball is immediately pounced upon by a heavyset pit bull tethered by a chain to a rusty metal spike jutting from the ground. The small boy looks forlorn as his friends gesture towards the garden and its menacing occupant.

'I always used to prefer playing round the corner . . . outside Mark Hampden's house,' Ray says. 'The road was flat there. No one had an unfair advantage. Do you ever hear from any of that lot? You know, Mark Hampden, Andy Lausanne, Martin Argyle . . . all that crew?'

I spit a terse, 'No,' back at him and reach up, grip the curtain rail to steady myself. Mother told me to visit Ray, help him through this, but I didn't expect this line in dialogue.

'What? You've not seen them since the incident when you—?'

'No, I've not seen any of them for years.'

'You overstepped the mark there,' my brother tells me in a grave voice.

'Yeah, well, they deserved it. I was just protecting my interests.'

'You know your problem?' Ray asks me.

'You?' I say quite flatly.

'No, you know what your problem is, don't you, Damian?'

'What?' I huff. I thought it was his fucking problems I was here to discuss.

'You're just too bloody sensitive,' Ray tells me.

'Yeah, whatever.'

'And too bloody-minded. You should learn to compromise more.'

'Whatever,' I sigh again.

'Oh, well,' my brother utters. 'Suppose you've always got all your uni friends now.'

I bite my lower lip, whisper, 'Yeah. And the Lunchboys.' I turn to face my brother and park myself on the ledge of the bay window, to take the weight off my feet. Ray does look terrible, all puffy and washed out. He hasn't shaved in days. This is probably the very first time I've seen him with anything remotely classed as stubble. The facial hair hangs like black shadows round his throat, underlining his flab, serving up zero favours in any svelte stakes. 'What did New Order open with at Wembley in 1987?' I ask him: an easy question to take his mind off things.

'Can't remember,' Ray answers deliberately.

'They covered some George Michael track,' I lie to him, expect him to take the bait, but he doesn't spot the ruse.

'Really?' he asks, sounds uninterested.

'No,' I tell him.

'Can't say I care, anyway,' he moans.

'So-o-o,' I start, adopt a different tack. 'What's happening with your job?'

'They've been quite good as it happens,' Ray says, his eyes a little brighter. 'They're not expecting me back till a week Monday. Officially they've got me on extended sick-leave.'

'You too, eh?' I sigh, bereft of anything else to say. 'Must run in the family.'

'Uncle Noel's moved in with Mum,' my brother mentions, matter-of-factly. 'She'll have a devil of a time if she ever wants rid of him.'

I sigh. 'He's already gone.'

'No, no, I don't think so. I was up there yesterday and he looked very settled.'

'Trust me, Ray – mother's well shot of Noel,' I tell him, clenching and unclenching my right fist, sensing a slight twinge there, but convinced that nothing's broken. 'I helped him move some stuff out just this morning.'

'Oh,well. Hey, did you know that Mum's heard from Dad?' Ray asks, almost excitedly.

'No. Where is he?' I ask, straighten up.

'There was a letter, postmarked Antrim or somewhere. Mum thinks he's probably hitched up with another fancy woman.'

'How's mother shaping up?' I ask, then stop to let my mindscape frame the devastation I'm going to inflict on Shaw Senior when I next get hold of him. I catch myself grinning inanely. Luckily, Ray fails to notice this. From his perspective, this is neither the time nor the place for such uplifting thoughts.

Ray just stares at his polished wooden floor. 'Oh,' he sighs, 'you know Mum. She's as strong as an ox. Suppose she's had to be, to cope over all these years.'

'And, er . . .' I pause for words. 'What . . . what about

you?' I'm finally moved to ask, though I'm not quite sure why I should. All this is no more than the outcome Ray should expect from embracing such a futile exist-ence. This is simply the way the cookie crumbles for unfortunates of his standing.

'I . . . I'm not so good,' Ray sort of sobs.

'Have you, um, heard from Sharon?' I ask.

'Yeah, er . . . Ha, it's funny. Well, maybe not funny, but she was just here before you arrived, only an hour or so back.'

'Here? Why?' I ask in anticipation, thinking that Sharon has shown real class in this whole sorry situation: kicking a man when he's at his lowest ebb.

'She said she wanted to see how I was,' Ray says, sniffles a bit.

'And?' This isn't the information I wanted.

'And she said I looked like shit.'

'Well, you do,' I tell him flatly.

'Thanks, bruv,' Ray says, starts to smile for some bizarre reason, then wipes his nose across the back of his hand.

'Well, I *am* your brother. What are brothers for if they can't tell you that you look like shit?'

Ray fails to register the overtly slanderous edge to my voice. He just smiles as if I've actually said something which might placate him. I should've told him he looked like shit many times before – as a rule, he generally does – then he might've got the message and bucked his ideas up, maybe even lost a little of the bulge, invested in some chic Kenzo or Henri Lloyd. I'm starting to wonder what my brother might be like on E – whether or not he'd be a good person to actually go out with once in a while, to treat as if he were a . . . friend or something. On Monday I'm meeting Pamela Ward – the Blonde who used to work in Financial Services – for a drink. I got talking to her in the Stamford last Friday, which is, like, weird because we'd only been talking about her at work that very lunchtime, and though she undoubtedly is stupid, virtually imbecilic, a total dumb blonde in every sense of the word, we did get on rather well. There was the unmistakable aroma of sexual tension in the air and I think I might just be in there, think there's an opening for a good fuck – if I play my cards right.

She now works for some company in Holborn, and was down visiting her old workmates for the evening and, strange as it may seem, she asked me if I knew a Connor Ferguson (I had mentioned that I worked on the fourth floor but I assumed she was too stupid to put two and two together) and I told her, 'Yeah, he's a really sound geezer,' to which she replied, 'Oh, I thought he sounded like a total prick.' Obviously, this annoyed me slightly, but on Monday I intend to show her what a 'total prick' (excuse such a blatant double entendre) really does look like.

'It's just . . .' Ray starts to say then chokes. 'It's just . . . I thought everything was going so well. You know, with the baby and everything.'

'There *was* no baby,' I have to tell him glibly. On second thoughts, my brother would prove a complete failure as a friend. I doubt he's been to a club since his teenage years. He probably thinks glitterballs, slow dances and the fucking 'Birdie Song' are still all the rage. He would just show me up, embarrass me. Then, again, Turnmills is supposed to have a glitterball down there now, slicing its legendary lasers throughout the entirety of the club. But, then again, Ray would never make it through the door: they'd take exception to him turning up in a shit shirt, polyester tie and freshly brushed brogues.

'I know there wasn't a baby,' Ray snaps at me with real venom and since (1) he's my big brother and (2) this is probably the most difficult thing he has had to deal with in his entire non-eventful life and since (3) I am positive that he wouldn't dare bark back at me under any other circumstances, I decide it best to let this little outburst go unchecked. My brother begins to sob to himself mercilessly.

Sharon did, in truth, believe she was pregnant, but she was unsure whether the child had been fathered by my brother or by some Claude geezer from her office – it was possibly the stress of the affair that made her period so late. Sharon left my brother six days ago. She's now living with Claude. It's quite pitiful really; this Claude was probably the first geezer who's given Sharon so much as a second look in her entire time with Ray, and she was more than eager to jump ship at the first sniff of something fresh and new. Suburban life at its nethermost ebb.

I take my place on the sofa next to Ray and put my

arm across his huge rounded shoulders as he continues to cry.

'Why did it have to happen?' Ray asks aloud.

'I don't know,' I tell him, yet I cannot help but think none of this would've happened if Ray hadn't aired his foolish insight on Jo and me. This is simply his just deserts. This is no less than God's wish.

'Oh, Damian, I do still love her,' Ray wails and crumples against my side. This is a ludicrous scenario. How can my very own flesh and blood be so weak, so insipid? How can Ray be so distraught at his loss when women such as Jo walk the earth? Can he truly believe that his own break-up might in some way compare with the personal travesty I have had to endure these past months? And I'm just sitting here, my brother by my side, bellowing out his grief; just sitting here taking in this huge overblown wedding photo of Sharon and Ray set on the wall high above their fireplace; just sitting here losing myself ever deeper into that photograph, whispering to myself Ray's eternal epitaph, 'I guess I must be the only Shaw to have been lucky in love'; just sitting here happy as a sand-boy, grinning insanely like some tortured Cheshire Cat.

No one insults my memory of Jo.

Five flops down in the chair beside me. We're just up from the Cross, waiting for Thom, who's queuing for teas from the catering van. Thom and I are both wearing Moschino long-sleeved T-shirts. Five's wearing one of

my old Thomas Pinks, this blue-and-yellow check number – he's the odd-one-out, as is only to be expected.
To compound my displeasure, he's wearing the thing in
a casual stylee, hanging outside his jeans with the top
three buttons undone, and his choice of cufflinks is
eminently diabolical: just another set of five-pound-a-
pair Turk's heads.

'Fucking hell,' Five sighs as another pair of knee-
length stilletoed boots troops past his line of vision.
'The . . . legs . . . on . . . that.'

'All the way up to her armpits,' I cough. 'Shame she
isn't wearing any hooped earrings, though.'

'Oh, shit,' Five says. 'Here comes another battalion
of boot boys.'

A novice with a helicopter view of our scenario might
assume we'd just been air-dropped into the centre of
some massed neo-Nazi rally, the clubbed-out bodies
milling around us bedecked in a fine array of Ben
Sherman and Fred Perry apparel, combat regalia and
bludgeoning close-cropped haircuts. There is, however,
this fetish night on at the Bunker Bar, and the added
inclusion of a few over-the-top leather men, bondage
women and these gothic pantomime dames dressed in
little more than basques, suspenders and high heels just
serves to lend an air of comic surrealism to the entire
S&M spectacle.

'Look, I hate to spring this on you, Dame, but,
um—' Five starts.

'You're thinking of dropping out of the scam,' I tell
him flatly.

'Er, eh? . . . Er, yeah.'

'Is it the money?' I ask in monotone.

'Er, no. It's j-just—'

I stare at the winking stars painted high in the night sky. 'It's just that you've been receiving some very poor-quality photocopies in the post, right? And you're a little concerned about their origin – about what they might possibly mean?'

'Yeah, er, something like that.'

'So, are you in or out?'

'Erm.'

'In . . . or . . . out? Simple enough question, surely?'

'Er, i-in. But—'

'I thought you might be. Just talking to me has put your mind at ease, right?'

'Erm.'

I tut. 'Typical.'

Five's the only one of the boys who cannot roll a decent spliff: always has to cheat, use a fucking *rolling* machine in order to get one together. I mean, what an inadequate retard bereft of all basic social graces. Why on earth did I wait until now before deciding to finally offload him? We obviously had nothing in common straight from day one.

'Dame, how do you know about the photocopies?' Five burps. 'About the pictures of me when I was really fat? Remember, when we were back at uni, before I lost all that weight . . .? How did you find out about all this hassle?'

'I have heard it all before,' I tell him bluntly, still

stare at the sky. 'You're not the first one who cannot take a hint.'

'Sorry?'

I turn to face him. 'You're not the first one who . . . cannot . . . take . . . a . . . hint.' I emphasize another *tut*. 'God, don't any of you lot ever . . . fucking . . . listen . . . to me?'

'Do you know who sent me the pictures?' Five asks me, sounds like he's almost serious and wants some genuine answers.

'Maybe it was Gerry?' I suggest.

'Gerry? Nah, he's the last one I'd suspect. Oh, after you of course, Dame. No, I thought it might just be Jay, but – oh, that's nonsense. C'mon, tell me who did it.'

'It was Gerry,' I say without conviction.

'No, it can't have been?'

'Okay, it was Mike.'

'No, really.'

'It was Matt, then.'

'No, it can't have been.'

'Well, what do you want me to fucking say?' I sort of bawl at Five, without any real certitude evident in my words, then stand and pace slowly away from him, side-stepping a skinhead couple as I do so, one of them wearing this tight black top which bellows DOMINATRIX in reflecting silver lettering.

'I just want you to tell me the truth,' Five calls after me.

I about turn on one foot and step back towards him.

Towering above him, my arms now clasped behind my back, I sigh, 'I did it.'

'What? Oh, ha-ha. No, really, Dame, who was it?' Five asks.

'It . . . was . . . me,' I say sternly.

'No, be serious for one minute, Dame. I mean, I can see the funny side of it now, but won't you just tell me who it was, so I can send 'em a picture back or something – you know, by way of revenge.'

I tell Five again, 'It was me. Me. Me. Me. Me. Me-e-e.'

'Mr Shaw,' Five says, sounds like a bloody school-teacher, 'who-o-o are you covering up for?'

'Just forget it,' I tell him. 'I am wasting my fucking breath.'

'Damian, what is this black-and-white rubbish?' she asks.

I sigh. 'It's called *Lorna*. It's an old Russ Meyer movie.'

'Oh, Damian, you're incorrigible. You always were a tit man,' she says, chuckles.

I roll my eyes and attempt to cut short the conversation with a wearied, 'Yeah,' but she insists on asking me, 'Is it okay if we have *Brookside* on now? I'm sure you must have watched this film a thousand times before.'

Without uttering a single word I press the STOP button on the video remote, and switch channels. *Brookside* has already started, but the silly mare doesn't shut up – still persists. 'Do you remember the old days, Damian? Back in our first year at uni? When we were only eighteen or so?'

'Yeah,' I reply sullenly, but as age-old memories unshackle themselves from the oubliettes in my mind-scape, I sense a small smile breaking loose on my face.

'What a flat we had, eh? All freshers together. There was you and me and Toolboy and Matt—'

'And Tyler and Gerry, Marky Mullen and Jay,' I interject, overwhelmed by a tomb of nostalgia.

'Yeah, and what about everyone's favourite drug-dealing Canadian?'

'Maurice?'

'Yes, Maurice,' she says, sounds distant but happy. 'God, do you remember that weed he used to smoke all the time?'

'Blue-Boulder-Grass,' I think out loud.

She repeats these words slowly and deliberately like they hold some special meaning for her. 'Blue . . . Boulder . . . Grass.'

'That was really heavy gear,' I tell her.

'Yeah, really trippy,' she adds.

I swivel in the armchair to face her – sprawled across the sofa – and ask, 'Remember that night we went out driving in the Escort with him, and we took the wrong turning on Boundary Road and ended up down by the docks in Wivenhoe?'

'Oh, yeah.' She sits up. 'Was that the night with the kittens?'

'Oh, what? I'd forgotten about the kittens. Have you heard that story about Marky Mullen and the kittens?'

'Yeah, but remember *that* night? Maurice was driving, and his weed was so trippy that it was like we were all in a huge arcade game or something.'

'Oh, but remember the kittens, eh?'

'I never told anyone about that. Did you?' she asks in hushed tones, even though there's no one else in the flat.

'No,' I confide. 'Promised Maurice I wouldn't.'

'Me too,' she whispers.

I start re-telling the tale. 'Driving over that poor kitten dazzled by our headlights—'

Her turn. 'Yeah. Then having to drive back to check if it was alive or not—'

I'm staring off into space, reminiscing. 'And finding that kitten writhing around on the bank by the roadside—'

'Ugh, don't remind me. And Maurice having to stamp on its skull to put it out of its misery.'

'Hoorrrrible,' I say slowly.

'Yeah, but not as bad as when we got back to campus and found that other kitten – the original one – splattered across Maurice's bumper.'

I close the fable. 'Maurice had just stamped a perfectly healthy kitten to death!'

We both burst into hysterics, our eyes streaming. Between laughter, she manages to tell me, 'I got a letter from Maurice, all the way from Quebec. He's got a kid now!'

'Maurice? Oh, that's too much: the thought of him bringing a child into this world!'

'Yeah, frightening . . . Hey, remember how we'd all get stoned in his bedroom?'

'What? When Five was really fat?' I recount. 'And he wouldn't smoke in case he got a bad case of the munchies?'

'Yeah, when Five would just do loads of speed instead!'

It all comes flooding back. 'You, me and Jay and Toolboy would all stare at that huge Pink Floyd poster Maurice had pinned up on his ceiling – the one of *The Wall* – and we'd be there for hours trying to imagine what shapes we could see in it.'

'You said you could see loads of crucifixes—'

'And Toolboy had this story about how he could see the Russians and Americans chasing each other round the world.'

'It was only a poster. I could never see a damned thing,' she admits.

'Oh, but remember that time Jinxy John came up to visit Toolboy and brought that acid onto campus, and you and me spent about two days just lying on our backs on the rug in my room, listening to "Ride of the Valkyries" and Beltram's "Energy Flash" over and over and over again?'

'"Energy Flash",' she recounts, 'what a tune that was.'

'Yeah,' I agree. 'I haven't heard it for years.'

'Hey, remember your nineteenth birthday, when we

344

had that lager fight in your bedroom, spraying each other with cans, and we ruined all those New Order posters on your wall.'

'Or what about Jay's birthday, when we nearly drowned the poor fucker in the university fountain?'

'Well, what about the time when you were fucking me up against that tree by the lake next to Wivenhoe Conference Centre and—'

'Stop it!' I snap.

'What?' she asks, puzzled. 'What's wrong, Damian?'

'Sorry, I just – I don't want to hear about it, that's all.'

She teases me. 'What? You don't want to hear about us fuck-ing . . .? Damian doesn't want to hear about the good . . . ol' . . . days?'

'That's just what they are, Lisa,' I snarl. 'The good old days.'

'Damian, don't be so bloody uptight. What's your problem? I mean, it was you that put an end to it.' Lisa folds her arms across her body and pulls a stupid sulky face.

'Look, I'm, er, sorry, sweetheart,' I mumble.

'For God's sake, Damian,' she huffs. 'We were together for the whole of the first year at uni. There's no reason to be so narky about it. You're always off with me nowadays.'

I really don't want to hear this. 'Look, I said I'm sorry. Now just drop it.' We were close once, I guess. Lisa wanted to get engaged, but I thought we were too young, that there were so many more experiences to explore, sexual or otherwise. She ended up with Thom. The rest, as they say, is history. I find myself wondering what Jo's doing right now.

Lisa is studying me, like she's trying to fathom out what I'm thinking. She finally says, sounds really serious, 'What about us now, Damian?'

I sigh heavily. 'There is no *us*, Lisa.' However, I don't really say this with any conviction.

'So-o-o, what was last time about, then?' she is asking me.

I have to lie. 'I was drunk, Lisa.'

'Damian, you were maybe a little high on coke. You most certainly were not drunk. Why must you always be so evasive with me? Do you really expect me to believe that you don't care just a little bit.'

'I – I can't explain myself,' I'm telling her, studying her long red nails, my eyes nervously flitting up to those mighty heaving breasts, then down once more to her elegant hands.

'Damian, why do you do this to me? I thought that was gonna be it, back at the start of the year.'

'I'm sorry,' is all I can manage.

'You're sorry? Huh! Take a good look at my life, Damian. I've been virtually shunned by the boys since we split up. You've accepted Thom into your little clique, but I'm always left out.'

I try to appear dumbfounded. 'Well – you're a girl.'

Lisa just continues, 'Oh, don't give me that, Damian. And I know what Thom gets up to behind my back.

He's nearly as bad as you. Neither one of you is prepared to grow up. You think more of your friends than you ever could of your partners.'

I'm almost proud of her, am in awe at this show of strength, am yearning to tell her so. But I'm wondering if she maybe knows about Thom and Beth, the truth behind why Beth and I really broke up. 'But, Lisa, you've just got a mortgage with him. Surely that shows his commitment to you?'

'The mortgage – huh! Shows how little you know, Damian, dearest. The mortgage is in my name, and my name alone. Thom's mother's virtually broke: she needed the money to sort her own place out. I got this flat at a knockdown price to save her poor son getting thrown out onto the street. As far as you and Thom are concerned, this place is mine, and you two are no more than sitting tenants.'

'If you feel like this, er, why do you put up with him?'

Lisa smiles. 'Oh, I don't know. Thom's good to me. He treats me well, when I see him. I s'pose I might even love him in my own strange way. Question is, Damian, why do *you* put up with him?'

'Maybe I love him too?' Stupid answer.

'Damian,' she moans, 'after all he did to you?'

'Guess, I'd have done the same in his position,' I mutter under my breath.

'Damian, you would've torn his throat out – not done what he did.'

'I wouldn't,' I tell her. 'I've mellowed.'

'Damian, Thom told Joanna that you and I were having an affair! How can you ever forgive him?'

I can't find anything of any worth to answer back with, just mumble, 'Well, it's not like he was really lying or anything.'

Lisa huffs. 'Damian, at least Thom and I had the chance to try and work through this. But you and Joanna? You live too far apart. This was bound to play on her mind. You two didn't stand a hope in hell.'

'It's just one of those things,' I whisper.

'Damian, Thom caught you and I fucking in this flat less than six months ago, and he told your girlfriend when she was next down. God, Damian, he ridiculed her. I mean, I know he was drunk and upset, but that's really no excuse. The poor girl! Joanna couldn't possibly forgive you after the dressing-down Thom gave her, so why should you forgive him? I mean, I doubt that I could even look her straight in the eye now. I dread to think what she must think of me.'

'But, Thom's a mate – I guess.'

Lisa tuts. 'Some mate.'

'Jo trusted me, you know,' I mention to Lisa. 'She couldn't believe I'd cheated on her.'

'God, you're nearly as bad as Thom. C'mon, Damian, how many women did you actually sleep with in the time you were seeing Joanna, huh?'

'Um, I don't know,' I say.

'C'mon, of course you know. I know you know!'

'Oh, about ten or so . . . maybe?'

'Hmmm?'

'Okay, eighteen then. I slept with eighteen other women.'

'Yeah, and in how many years?'

'Er, two and a half,' I admit.

'And, er, how many extracurricular lovers was it this year alone?'

'Two.'

'God, I don't know . . . men! Aargh!' Lisa bares her teeth, pulls at her hair.

'No, three.' I correct myself. 'Well, two really. I shouldn't include you, I guess, as I'd already fucked you before.'

The phone rings. Lisa and I just sit facing one another – her glaring, me expressionless. After the fifth ring I make as if to answer the call, but Lisa slaps her hand down tight on the receiver and says to me, 'Saved by the bell, eh, Damian?' But when she realizes that I really do wish to pick up the phone, she relaxes her grip.

'Hello?' I ask.

'Hi, Damey, it's me. It's Slinky.'

'Slinky? Oh, hi. How are you?'

'Oh, Joanna's cousin now, is it?' Lisa says spitefully.

'Look, Damey, I thought you should really know. It's Joanna. It looks like she's going to be—' Slinky is possibly saying, but I'm lost someplace else, in a nameless void, caught between the grim actuality passing for my existence and the things which I inwardly yearn for, and I'm staring down, mesmerized, thunderstruck at the sight of the unblonde Lisa's ample cleavage and she's smiling up at me and I'm aching wholeheartedly for her luscious curves as she slowly begins to release the buttons on my fly.

Carl Smith's rolled into the office late again, to find an inflatable penguin sitting upright on his desk. It's the Bishop's idea of a joke, saying he'd probably get more work out of the penguin than he would out of Carl. How I wish someone would leave such a penguin adorning my desk; it's still inevitable that Carl is going to walk off with the Latecomer Award, with such open displays of recognition. He brought even further attention to his late entrance today, wandering up the corridor singing Wham's 'Wake Me Up Before You Go Go' to one and all at the very top of his voice. Does this boy have no shame? I'm quite looking forward to that point at which Hubert Dodd's resolve finally breaks and he falls upon Smith, pulling at Carl's sleeve to check for any tell-tale druggy trammel marks, or maybe forces some publicly witnessed urine test so as to reinforce his (misguided) narcotics theories.

We're now all sat around Carl's desk, admiring his new shorn haircut.

'Bit severe, isn't it, Carl?' Gregor Daley comments.

'Aye, I just fancied a change laddies, just fancied a change,' Carl tells us, motions with his palms, flat to the ground, as if trying to play down the spectacle.

'What number's that, then?' I ask him.

'It's a two across the top, with a one around the back and sides,' he answers, strokes his hand effortlessly across his temple.

'Oh, do let me have a feel, Carl-baby,' Russell Bishop says camply.

'They smoothed it out quite nicely,' I muse. 'You can't see any step from the one to the two.'

The phone's ringing over by my desk. I'm wondering if this is maybe the Blonde calling to arrange another date – she actually had the effrontery to cancel on me last Monday. Warwick Griffin answers and the tension pent up inside me slowly subsides when I realize the call, alas, is actually for him.

Graham Watson recounts, 'I had a skinhead once – when I was young, only twelve or so, in the early seventies. Mind you, everyone round our way had a skinhead when I was a youngster.'

'Yeah, I had a skinhead when I was a kid, as well,' I tell everyone. 'Early eighties, though, the second coming of the skinhead – two-tone, loafers, the moonstomp, et cetera.'

'I had a skinhead on Saturday,' the Sperminator tells us, then sighs. 'He said his name was Justin.'

'Ugh, James!' we all chorus in mock disgust.

'Trouble afoot,' Beryl Edwards, Comley's manager, crows as she passes by. 'There's always trouble afoot when tall men congregate together. Haven't you lot got work to do?'

'Aw, we can dispense with such pleasantries today,'

Carl complains. 'Hubert phoned up. He's not coming into the office.'

'Oh, what's up with him?' I ask.

'His boiler blew up,' Carl enlightens us, and we're all stood here, playing telepathic tennis with the self-same facetious perception, until it's Comley who actually has the front to finally say it: 'What? He had a row with his Mrs?' And we all laugh, out of a false sense of team loyalty, but Edwards still stands there, looks provoked, and makes a thumbing motion towards us, like she's unwittingly trying to hitch a lift, and so we each in turn trudge back toward our separate desks and our daily chores and Russell turns to me and says, 'I'll try not to imagine you with a skinhead. I have enough trouble keeping my hands off you as it is, Dame.'

'What did you call me?' I snap back instantaneously.

'Sorry, babes?' Russell asks.

I repeat my question, relishing this express moment, more composed this time.

'Dame,' Russell repeats, throws me a quizzical look. 'Isn't that what all your little chums call you?'

'I don't seem to have many little chums any more,' I murmur sadly.

'Sorry?' Russell prompts.

'Yeah, yes it is,' I tell him and smile. 'It's what all my little chums call me.'

We have reached a milestone, a landmark development in my three years seven months with the company. This is the first time anyone in my office has ever considered to entitle me 'Dame'. I do love the Lunchboys. Skinheads aside, I believe I'm accruing a vast expanse of common ground alongside them.

I pile into the Spice of Life to find my adversaries already grouped – Benny, Tyler, Matt, Mike, Jay, Gerry and Five – *not* the magnificent seven.

Gerry welcomes me with, 'Dame-ee-ern.'

'Greetings, honey-child,' Tyler says.

Four of the boys are dressed in brightly coloured Ben Sherman shirts, the other three wear work suits. I digress from their communal spirit: I am wearing an Armani jumper.

'Alright boys,' I say, try and look gladdened to see them. 'Er, where's Weatherface?'

'He's nipped out to the cashpoint,' Jay tells me, and points toward one of the side doors.

'And he's got some news,' Five adds.

'What sort of news?' I ask.

No one says a thing. Benny just blows a bubble with his gum.

It slowly dawns on me. 'Oh, no, not that?'

'Oh, yes, that,' Mike admits.

'Weatherface is . . . getting . . . married?' I half ask, half tell them, inwardly praying for one of them to break into a smirk, to spoil the surprise and tell me that Weatherface has in fact . . . broken . . . up with Heather. But I'm just hit by this wall of silence which Matt finally punctures with, 'We didn't tell you that, okay? He wants it to be a surprise.'

I drop my shoulders. 'So, who's gonna be best man?' I ask, look Mike square in the eye.

'You are,' Mike tells me flatly, grins.

'What?' I ask, mystified, my heart skipping a beat. 'Are you sure?'

'Well, he's actually asked me to be the best man—' Mike admits. I breathe a small sigh of allayment. 'But, with the profit I'm gonna make from the Es, I was thinking about taking a long holiday abroad and—'

'You are not getting out of this one,' I bark at him, point and snap my fingers. Mike rocks his head back and laughs. 'When is this wedding anyway?' I ask.

'Next July,' Tyler tells me.

'Seriously, though, Dame,' Mike says. 'I'm planning a jaunt around Australia and the Far East, and – you never know – I might just find myself a nice little job—'

'What as – a sheep-farmer or a Thai rent-boy?'

Mike chortles. 'And I might not be back for the wedding.'

I smile blankly at Mike, then sigh and ask the table, 'Oh, well, what's everyone drinking?'

'It's alright,' Benny tells me. 'It's my round. What you having, Dame?'

'Perrier,' I tell him.

'Eh?' Benny looks disappointed.

'A Perrier, please. I've got a big day ahead tomorrow.'

'Dame, we've all got a big day ahead tomorrow,' Mike says, and adds, 'the biggest.'

Tomorrow, we finally take delivery of the Es.

'Oh, yeah, sorry. I was, er, thinking about something else,' I tell everyone.

'Something else?' Tyler quips, looks at me over the top of his glasses. 'What "something else" could possibly be more important than our little scam?'

'There are other things in life except drugs, Tyler,' I wisecrack back.

'Yeah, there's Kronenbourg 1664,' Jay interjects.

'*Brookside*,' Matt adds.

'Brentford FC,' Mike mentions, 'actually winning the occasional home game.'

But it's Tyler still wishing to hold court. 'Dame, I haven't had a fucking day off since your bloody birthday. I have been slaving away every weekend just to be able to foot my share of this.'

I just stick my tongue out at him.

'Look, guys, can we forget about the scam?' Matt moans. 'Everyone knows the score: meet at Mike's around six p.m., with your four grand in cash, then just sit back and wait for Mike's "man" to deliver the sweeties. Now, before Dame so rudely interrupted us, I was trying to tell you all a story.'

'Oh, forgive me for breathing,' I sneer at Matt, who mirrors my earlier gesture by sticking out his tongue in response.

'Right,' Matt says, 'there's this guy that my workmate Simon knows—'

'Is this fat Simon from Northern Ireland – the mad Rangers fan?'

'Er, yeah.'

'The Simon who told that story about this party where paramilitary boys steamed in to knee-cap some bloke, but the bloke was shaking so much that they put four bullets through the floor into the flat down-stairs before they finally got one into his knee – that Simon?'

'Er, yeah.'

'The Simon who thought that story was a funny story?'

'Yes! That bloody Simon,' Matt barks. 'Now, that Simon's mate was at a party—'

'Not another knee-capping?'

'No! Not another knee-capping. This party was in Fulham . . . England. It was a private do, a family occasion, for this bird's birthday, and they'd arranged a surprise party, so they're all hiding in her lounge waiting for her to come home. But, when she finally does arrive home, she just nips straight upstairs without even venturing into the lounge—'

'Wow, what a story.'

'Yeah, so the family are just sitting there in the dark wondering what on earth to do next, when this bird comes to the top of the stairs and calls down for her Alsatian, Petra—'

'I shagged a Petra once,' someone says.

'Was she a dog?'

'Nah, but I have shagged a fair few dogs in my time.'

'Look, can I just finish my story, per-lease?' Matt fumes. 'So anyway, this cousin calls for her dog, the dog bounds up the stairs, and after ten minutes they still haven't come down, so—'

'So, the family nip upstairs to surprise her in her bedroom,' Tyler says, scratches his temple.

'Er, yeah. And—'

'And they find her writhing on her bed, with the Alsatian licking dog-food off her twat,' Tyler finishes glibly.

'Er, yeah,' Matt admits, sounds disconsolate – his story ruined. 'But I heard it was cheese-spread the dog was licking.'

'Ugh, that's gross,' Benny gurgles.

I sigh and come clean. 'I've heard that one, too – from one of the Lunchboys at work. Only, the woman had kittens lapping at her in his version.'

Weatherface looms from nowhere. 'Alright, Dame?' he asks.

I rise and shake his hand heartily. He's wearing an Armani polo shirt. We two, at least, are in mutual alignment. 'Good to see you. How are things?'

'Well, I've got some news that might interest you,' Weatherface tells me, looks chuffed with himself.

'Oh, yeah? And what news is this?' I have to ask, aware that all eyes are studying my reaction.

Weatherface rubs his hands. 'I'm getting married.'

I break into a smile, feign surprise, and ask, 'No, really?'

'Yeah, straight up.'

'Why-y-y?' I ask, try to look happy for the poor sod, then add before Weatherface's brow has chance to furrow, 'Why, er, have you decided to do it now?'

allen jarvis

'We'd have done it sooner, but, well, we can afford it now.'

'Yeah?'

'Yeah, course . . . with all the profit we're gonna make from these Es.'

'Oh, right. Congratulations, then,' I purr and shake his hand again.

'Well, Heather's had a rough week. She got done for drink-driving on Monday and failed a breathalyser test, so I asked her to marry me to try and cheer her up.'

Gerry speaks up. 'Failed a breathalyser test? She should've tried that trick with a new penny.'

'Er, what trick?' Weatherface asks.

'Well, if you're stopped in a motor when you've had a few, you should suck on a new penny – someone once told me the copper in it can actually screw up a breathalyser.'

'New pennies aren't made of copper . . . are they?' Jays says, looks puzzled.

'Er, I dunno actually,' Gerry answers, just shrugs his shoulders.

Five places his hands behind his head. 'Nah, Gerry, I think you've got it all wrong, mate. To pass a breath-alyser test, you don't have to suck on copper. You have to . . . suck . . . *off* . . . a copper!'

We all fall about laughing.

'So, c'mon then, guys. C'mon, what's everyone gonna do with their money?' Matt is asking our motley bunch.

'Get pissed,' Jay says.

358

'Buy some more drugs,' Benny gushes.

'Stop doing overtime,' Tyler announces. 'And buy a new cat.'

'Well, as you all know, I'm getting married,' Weatherface tells us, most sheepishly.

Mike pouts his lips, calls Weatherface a homme.

'Well, what are *you* gonna do that's so worthwhile?' Weatherface retorts.

'I've already said: I'm gonna emigrate to the other side of the world to avoid your fucking wedding,' Mike tells him.

Weatherface pulls a hurt face.

'Only joking,' Mike says. Weatherface smiles, then Five butts in, joking, 'Nah, maybe not the other side of the world, eh, Mike? You might just go to the States instead.'

'What about you, Dame – what are you gonna do with your money?' Benny asks me.

'I haven't really thought about it,' I tell him in all honesty.

'I know,' Tyler offers. 'You're gonna go out and get yourself a clubby blonde, ain't ya, honey-child?'

'A six-foot clubby blonde,' Gerry adds.

I roll my eyes. 'Maybe.'

'Six-foot clubby blonde? Now would that be male or female, Mr Shaw?' Mike asks me.

'Oh, it's gotta be all woman for Dame,' Jay says.

Weatherface jumps in with, 'Yeah, an Anna Nicole Smith double to replace Joanna.'

Something stirs inside – a light twinkles at the end of

a long tunnel. 'No one can ever replace Jo,' I whisper, sound really distant.

'What? Not even Anna Nicole herself – in the flesh?' Weatherface splutters, sits up and tries to look cocky.

'No, not . . . even . . . Anna . . . Nicole . . . herself,' I tell him, burn my steely-grey eyes deep into his skull.

'Yeah, r-right, Dame,' Weatherface mumbles, shakes his head, tries not to look scared yet suddenly takes on the air of a condemned man being marched to the gas chamber.

'I'm gonna take Rachel to a nice hotel in the country,' Five tells us, looks smug, so the boys deride him and call him a homme. But I'm just sitting here, glaring at Weatherface, sensing the terror rippling through his jellyfish spine, presuming that it's a fake Armani he's wearing, as we've now nothing in common – all ties have been severed. And I can see that I've reached a crossroads. Weatherface's defection has transformed this night into a most resplendent juncture, and by tomorrow I shall reign tall, recrowned king of my destiny. The trials and afflictions of late will be resolved, all wrongs will be righted. And I'm sitting here, smiling, thinking about New Order and my brother and Anna Nicole Smith and the absent Thom and all the things which make me happy, make my new life worth starting to live.

'What are you thinking about, geez?' Jay is asking me.

'Yeah, snap out of it, guy,' Matt says. 'Are you in a trance or something, Dame?'

I smile and tell everyone, 'I'm just thinking about the important things in life.'

Mike draws on a cigarette and blows a smoke ring. 'And these things are?'

'Friendship . . . and . . . trust.'

There's this stilted silence then Five says, 'I'll drink to that,' and raises his pint to me.

The other boys follow suit.

'Erm, forgive my intrusion but . . . have you dropped any Es tonight, Dame?' Benny asks me, looks comically serious. Everyone laughs, and I have to chuckle too. These boys, this raggle-taggle pack, were once dear friends, but they're now nothing more than frivolous nonentities in my nightmarish past. Tomorrow sees a brand new horizon. It's high time I started clearing the dead wood from my life.

I'm off sick, though any days I swindle now will do little to perforate Carl Smith's virtually unassailable lead in the office Latecomer Awards, and I'm sitting here listening to Paul Oakenfold banging out some hard trance on CD, and I'm dallying with my Photoshop on the PC. I double-click this picture I've been working on: a snapshot of a make-believe holiday from yesteryear. There's me, Thom, and all the Lunchboys down Tenerife way, Playa las Americas, and we're lined up to order outside Lineker's Bar, stood before this huge billboard which reads, THANKS FOR YOUR VISIT, SEE YOU SOON, and there I am, back left, wearing Jo's dad's navy Lacoste, a pair of Oakley's on me forehead, one arm slung behind Carl Smith's shoulder, who in turn leans into the Bishop and Thom and Nicholas Spencer-Jones, then there's Steve Kerr, Gregor Daley, Graham Watson, the Sperminator and Ashwin Patel squatting before us, each of us tanned, festive, archetypally male, MDMA and testosterone fuelled. I study this fabricated memory for a moment too long then quit out of the image, the holiday I should've had already safely committed to hard-disk. These are the people that now merit my express friendship, those who've still yet to let me down.

I collect my coat from the hallway – this heavy black leather jacket that Jo and I clubbed together to get me as a present two Christmases back – and stop to study Lisa's fake brown fur hanging there. I catch myself reaching out and touching it, for perhaps a moment too long, rubbing my fingers into its palatial hide like it maybe holds great significance for me, but it doesn't, and so instead I turn my attention to the Anna Nicole Smith calendar adorning the back of our kitchen door.

This month's shot introduces Anna from the knees up, or maybe it's her thighs; it's actually quite difficult to tell, because she's enwrapped in a lengthy white stole which hangs in such a fashion as to obscure the full profile of her delectable form. I carefully lift the calendar from its hook and wish Anna a tender goodbye, then flick the calendar shut to reveal, on its flip-side, this raw, more animal snap of her, about turned and bent over a staircase, and she's wearing these huge gold shoes and a pair of red knickers which leave little to the imagination, vast expanses of rump flesh and thigh and calf in liberal evidence, and just looking at this picture suddenly makes me feel very small and somehow insecure but at the self-same time I am so utterly in awe of Anna's über-feminine sway, as if this snap's been photographed from the stand-point of an innocent: someone taking in such potent sexual vigour for their very first time.

I draw a deep, intentional breath, then sadly, regret-tably, have to jettison this calendar into the wilderness of the kitchen bin. I've no real use for such pictures now; everything must be seen to be cleansed. However, I do take an age to actually lower the bin-lid once the calendar is truly forsaken, and I feel curiously morbid throughout this whole drawn-out manoeuvre. I then step into the lounge to gather my thoughts. There's a George Michael CD cover discarded by the side of the sofa, next to a crushed can of Kronenbourg. A bootleg video of Russ Meyer's *SuperVixens* sits atop the television set, and one of Lisa's ample bras hangs menacingly from the end of the ironing board.

I jangle my keys anxiously and ruminate over my next move. To calm myself, I give New Order's 'Dreams Never End' one quick airing on the stereo and mime along to the lyrics and play bass in a below-the-knee style, believing I'm Peter Hook for just three brief minutes. I then snort two lines of resurrecting cocaine, listen to two renditions of 'Ride of the Valkyries', then finally head off to catch the daylight and my proximate future.

It's shivery yet fresh in Muswell Hill today, and

there's a long queue already convened by the bus stop. There are six things in line at the bus stop: five blonde and one unblonde, a most welcome ratio. One of the things is wearing these enormous stack-heeled kinky boots, and another flaunts huge hooped earrings. I can readily make out that two of them are painted with luxurious tomato-red nails, unqualified excellence. The bus seems to take eternity to arrive, though it's probably just me clock-watching that makes the time seem so much longer, and I'm wishing I'd brought my Walkman with me to allow Wagner to administer his synthetic lift. I am checking my reflection in the front windows of a video store neighbouring the bus stop. My hair is freshly cut, closely cropped all over; everything has to be seen to be faultless. Jo always said she preferred me with short hair.

When a 134 finally arrives, I await my turn patiently in line, withholding any mad urges to bolt to the front, then seat myself on the top level of the bus, four seats from the back and to the left, a vantage point from which I can pigeonhole each and every thing joining the bus. We make three further stops along Muswell Hill Road, during which our numbers increment by four unblondes, all short, and just the one blonde, also short. The blonde is wearing hooped earrings; only her and a single unblonde venture up to the top tier.

It's now 17.10, and in a little under one hour from now – acting on an anonymous tip-off – the authorities will swoop on a West London address to apprehend felons in connection with the buying and selling of a controlled drug. If the timing's right, said miscreants should hopefully be caught red-handed. I alight at the stop for Highgate tube. Virtually everyone alights at the stop for Highgate tube.

I'm nervously fingering this huge skull ring, which I personally find quite unsightly and distasteful, but which Jo fell in love with in Goa last January and bought me as a present. She has a matching one, though not quite as cumbersome. I've just missed a Morden via Charing Cross train – it was pulling away as I arrived on the platform – and now have to wait two mins for a Kennington via Bank number. I can catch either tube today: it's not important to me where the northern line forks, I will be alighting before this point.

I momentarily put my hand to the mobile phone clipped to my belt, tap it twice, three times, as if to reassure myself of something, then return my hand to the safety of my jacket pocket. My palms are sweating and my stomach is wrenched into a tight, constricting knot. I'm possibly a little light-headed – a predicament I can put down to any one of three scenarios: either (a) I'm subconsciously overcome by the enormity of the situation I am to encounter, (b) it's simply a knock-on effect of the class-A narcotics I've been consuming, or (c) I'm perhaps not entirely gratified by shopping the boys in such a craven manner. Personally, I favour the first option.

When the tube finally arrives I step into an empty carriage – a totally unfamiliar event for me – due to the irregularity of human traffic heading into London at this time of day. I am wearing this heavy black leather jacket that Jo and I clubbed together to get me as a present two Christmases back, and underneath this jacket I am wearing the navy Lacoste polo shirt that I borrowed from Jo's father quite some time ago. Added to these, I'm dressed in some new moleskins (black) and my regulation pair of Timberlands. Jo always maintained I should wear my moleskins to bed; she loved their velvety touch, sensualistic against her skin. This pair are fresh from the retailers, untarnished by any washing machine, so should prove utterly orgasmic when rubbed against bare-naked flesh.

Benny, Tyler, Matt, Mike, Jay, Gerry, Five and Weatherface have absolutely no knowledge of the impending whirlwind being sent to crush their precious scam, to wreck their very lives. I almost wish I could be there to witness their sad unfortunate faces. Any fallout in my direction is of little consequence. Jo always said I thought more of my friends than I did of her; I believe I have finally proved her wrong.

This black geezer joins my carriage at Archway, and something about him reminds me of Jay. Jay who so rebuked my total friendship, like many others in recent months. Jay who will pay the price, like all my original friends, with his impending incarceration and resulting public defamation. This black geezer alights at our very next stop, Tufnell Park, where I'm then joined by an okay blonde with a kid in a pram, and two underage girls both bedecked in miniature yet mature kinky boots. Each of these passengers alights at Camden Town where

I'm then joined by too many commuters to categorize, so I just shut my eyes, think favourable thoughts, mostly about Jo, and will the train on towards my climactic destination.

The boxer shorts I'm wearing are a pair of white Ralph Laurens that Jo bought me as a present when we were in the States together two years ago. They're possibly too big, but they hang long and cool on the thighs, like a pair of baggy jockey shorts, and I think they look very sensuous on me when I'm wearing nothing else.

I disembark at Euston station.

I bypass the EXIT SUBURBAN PLATFORMS 8–11 and head for the MAIN-LINE STATION instead, navigating the world's squeakiest escalator en route, whose noise serves to make my very blood creep and heightens my apprehension levels that one extra fragment. I'm checking the ARRIVALS board and am slightly disturbed, though not too much so, to find my plans a little out of kilter, so to relax I buy a *Daily Record* in order to get me further ingrained in the general ambience of the afternoon. My socks today are an aseptic green in colour but they were made by Pringle, the Scottish manufacturers, so are certainly appropriate for the moment. I then take the first seat to become available, right to the back of the hall, and attempt to read my paper, the back pages of which are predominated by stories on either Glasgow's Celtic or Rangers, whilst the first half is controlled by destitute yarns relating semi-alleged news, stories which wouldn't warrant the smallest of column inches in the most parochial of local papers contrived in any English backwater.

Scattergun jolts from the station announcer disturb my panoramic dreamscape, inform me of the imminent arrival of the delayed Glasgow train at platform thirteen. This – as they say – is finally it: my destiny realized. An elderly couple struggle before me, bound for the platform, but I can do little more than stand, dither, then sit backwards to hug my plastic seat, and to wait. It then strikes me that I really ought to start helping Thom out with the flat-hunting. Why am I even thinking about this now? I commit such an inane thought to the back of my mindscape and pace towards the platform, walking slowly, then swiftly, then slowly again, my steps totally deranged.

The train is drawing sluggishly, almost painfully, into the station, and I'm confronted by an agonizing lull – probably only seconds or so, if truth be told – before there's even the slightest hint of activity down on the causeway. Hesitantly I check my nails, my hands, my cuticles, the skull ring, check everything – but everything's fine, hunky-dory, serenely brilliant. As panicked as I shall ever be, I hastily force a mint-sweet past my chattering teeth, an attempt to invigorate my breath, then crunch it into little pieces and swallow too quickly, almost compelling myself to cough. Sheer . . . unmitigated . . . panic submerges me. Should I really be wearing this Lacoste? It's her father's, after all – he's doubtless been cursing her for letting me borrow it, and making her life an interminable misery. Might she take my wearing it as some kind of insult. Perhaps I should've had a T-shirt printed up with the phrase 'I'M SORRY' emblazoned across my chest in huge Day-glo lettering; at least that way I would've put her at ease and broken the ice, maybe even made her laugh by blatantly stating my intentions from the outset.

And then she's there, head and shoulders above the rest, walking like she's limping, struggling with a cumbrous travel-bag and – as if in slow motion – Jo makes her way up through the station, my eyes tracking her as she proceeds, turns this way, then that, stops and looks lost. She drops her bag to her side, checks her watch, and puts her hands to her hips, parting her black leather jacket as she does so. I'm just rooted to the spot, literally glued to the wall behind me – unable to react, unable to approach her. If Jo fails to notice me now she might well be away through the station, absorbed into the lifeblood of London, before I've even thought to invoke the exacted logic obligatory to galvanize myself. Jo has possibly lost weight, her chest not as robust as it appears in my mindscape, and her hair is maybe three or four inches too short. And then she catches sight of me. My heart is freezing hard in the confines of my chest and iced water courses through my veins. Everything is wilting into soft-focus except only for Joanna Marie Kennedy standing maybe twenty feet before Damian Henry Shaw, the initial surprise on her face slowly yielding to – what I assume must be – an ironic grin. I'm trying to fix Jo with the look she so revered – my head tilted slightly forward, my brow furrowed, trying to look serious, and my mouth pursed like I'm about to blow her a kiss – but it's probably looking all wrong. It's likely that I'm frightening her instead, and I'm wondering to myself what Beth's doing right now?

But Jo just throws her head back and laughs to herself, doubtless realizing that this is all a set-up, that Slinky never had any intention of meeting her here today. Then she opens her arms to me and cries out, 'Aw, c'mon here, Damian,' but her voice sounds coarse and unsightly – too Scottish by far – and she's wearing scarcely any make-up and her nails are unvarnished, maybe slightly bitten, and she doesn't look that clubby, looks almost studenty, and she's not wearing her huge kinky boots or her huge hooped earrings, and it appears that she might just . . . have . . . got . . . shorter. And I'm toiling desperately to make my way towards her, but my legs weigh heavily beneath me like sacks of molten lead, and I'm not entirely sure as to whether it's me that's closing the gap between us or if it's actually Jo that's striding towards me or whether this is all just some fanciful illusion I've unwittingly contrived and I'm slowly reaching for my phone, am dialling Mike's mobile number, panicked that it might now be too late to forewarn the boys and, as the sweat rolls caustically into my eyes, all I can hear is the phone line tringing chirpily in my one ear and Jo's unbending tones in my other, interrogating me: 'Damian, are you alright . . .? Damian?'

NICK EARLS

Bachelor Kisses

Pan Books £5.99

'Wonderfully fresh . . . wonderfully funny'
Daily Telegraph

Jon, Rick and Jen share takeaway food rituals, sporadic cocktail nights and the quest for love. Rick seems destined to long, lonely nights beneath his Porky Pig duvet. For Jen, while the nights may be long, they are rarely lonely. Jon, a medical graduate with grand plans for the hormone of darkness, is getting lucky in a way he never expected – more women than he knows how to handle.

Bachelor Kisses is the mess Jon makes of his life when it stops making sense, a chaotic comedy of misjudgement, misinformation and misguided intimacy from the author of *Zigzag Street*.

A PAN PAPERBACK ORIGINAL